THE PO... KHAN

The Khan pushed him over onto his stomach, and David sprawled helplessly.

"She's mine, David Quarrels. You may sleep alongside her and think she's yours, but it's nothing more than borrowed time. She'll never be able to forget what she had with me. She's mine, and I'll claim her again, and when I do, she will come willingly, just as she did last time."

The Khan sat down beside him. "She may try to forget, but every time you touch her, she'll be longing for more than you can give. Let me tell you about the many ways I pleased Sindon. . . ."

THE KHAN'S PERSUASION

Cynthia Felice

ACE BOOKS, NEW YORK

This book is an Ace original edition,
and has never been previously published.

THE KHAN'S PERSUASION

An Ace Book / published by arrangement with
the author

PRINTING HISTORY
Ace edition / January 1991

ISBN: 0-441-42527-5

Ace Books are published by The Berkley Publishing Group,
200 Madison Avenue, New York, New York 10016.
The name "ACE" and the "A" logo
are trademarks belonging to Charter Communications, Inc.

PRINTED IN THE UNITED STATES OF AMERICA

10 9 8 7 6 5 4 3 2 1

PART I.

1.

RUKMANI KHAN AND his vassal lords were eating for normal conditions at the Summer Palace. Each man was surrounded with bowls the size of human skulls filled with the abundance of free foraging. The number of bowls was ritual, determined by the man's persuasive skill. There were seventeen before Rukmani Khan. He was expected to eat the contents of every bowl to the last morsel so he could persuade seventeen magtrees to release their fruit to the unskilled, who would wait below. Natarjan had eleven bowls, Kangra had ten, and the nine other vassal lords had seven or fewer. Behind the lords and to the side of the polished stone table, several attendants waited quietly but alertly, ready to offer more food should any of the lords desire.

"I went to see the abo whose field was burned by the shuttle," Kangra said between handfuls of dewberry. Kangra was the only vassal of sufficient rank, aside from Natarjan and the Khan himself, allowed to break the silence of a meal. Kangra did so regularly, always finding matters of reasonable significance to bring to the Khan's attention before getting to whatever he really wanted to talk about. Such conversations slowed obligatory feedings, but made them more palatable, too. "Her tears were well justified; the field is destroyed."

"Did you see these new traders?" the lords began to ask, finally free to speak as well.

"Why did they bring down two shuttles instead of one?"

"I hear the women are young and beautiful."

Rukmani Khan picked up his seventh bowl of food. It was packed with redroots, which he didn't like. He began eating dutifully, listening equally dutifully to his vassals. He won-

dered if Kangra had supplied young Hazan with the information about the women, and wondered, too, if they were what
this conversation was really about. "Couldn't you repair the
damaged plants?"

"No," Kangra said. "They'd been crisped right through. I'd
have to eat the rest of the abos' harvest to find enough strength
to fix that mess. I went to talk to the traders about restitution.
They don't communicate very well through those talking boxes
of theirs, but I gathered they'd figured out what they'd done to
the abo's field and had paid her."

"She hadn't mentioned being compensated when she interrupted our breakfast yesterday," Rukmani Khan said, annoyed.
The aborigines were wily as well as surly, and much given to
cheating the Khan's Persuaders whenever possible. But the
little band who apparently had been visiting the glacier valley
for generations used their crude spears only on game, so
Rukmani Khan and his vassals tolerated them, and even
persuaded magtrees to drop their nuts for abos to gather. After
a few years the abos expected to share in the magnuts, and
expected protection from traders and wild abos alike, which the
priest told the vassal lords was their duty to provide. In
Rukmani Khan's opinion it was his vassal lords who often
needed protection from the abos, and surely from priests. "Did
she think you wouldn't find out?"

But Kangra was shaking his head. "Those stupid beads
again. Abos aren't interested in their flawed crystal. They can
find those anywhere."

Rukmani Khan shook his head, too. Even wild abos from the
deep forest knew the difference between a persuaded crystal
and a natural one. It seemed, however, the traders from the
stars did not. They came every few months in their shuttles,
landing wherever they found the abo camp, usually down
valley. Their goods never interested Rukmani Khan or his
vassals, but the aborigines always got excited. They, after all,
had to face the winter without the benefit of stone walls
persuaded to give off warmth. "If this abo's crop suffered real
damage and they offered only flawed crystal as compensation,
her tears were real."

"Yes. I think I made the traders understand what they'd
offered was not enough. I suggested a bolt of cloth. Traders
always have interesting cloth. Perhaps the abos will like the

cloth when they realize they don't have to weave it. It would be nice to get them out of those smelly tanned hides they wear."

"The New People are not traders," Natarjan said suddenly. The priest was the eldest among the vassal lords remaining in the Summer Palace. The other old men had gone with the last caravan to make the return journey to the Winter Palace at a leisurely pace. But Natarjan had seen a shooting star, which was an omen when it wasn't the flame of a trader shuttle. He'd stayed behind to find out which, and was very disappointed when he did.

Rukmani Khan looked at the priest expectantly.

"The night before last while I was praying in the courtyard, I was interrupted by a messenger from the New People."

"I saw her," Hazan said, his eyes glittering. "She was not attired like a huntress from a safari shuttle would have been, nor even like a trader. She wore the same blue garb the others from these shuttles wear. She looked . . . innocent enough, so I let her pass."

"This identical garb is puzzling," Rukmani Khan said. "Who but priests or warriors would want to dress alike?"

"This messenger was neither," the old priest said, shaking his head. "She was dressed like the others, but as with all of them, there was no trace of military bearing."

"She wouldn't have passed me if she had been military," Hazan said a bit sharply. Then he added with a smile, "She moved like an ordinary woman—extraordinarily!"

Natarjan frowned at Hazan. "I could not understand her words. But I understood her behavior. It was a visit of respect. She knelt and averted her eyes. She did not hide her hands in submission, but kept them plainly in sight. She even brought gifts."

"Respect!" Kangra said, suddenly looking irritated, no doubt because he'd lost control of the conversation to the priest. Its true intent must have been women, which Kangra would have introduced gracefully had Natarjan not interrupted.

Rukmani Khan's interest was genuine now. "What gifts?" he asked. He'd have to satisfy the priest before Kangra could get back to the women.

Natarjan snapped his fingers. The carved door to the breakfast chamber opened and two sons and one daughter of the vassal lords entered, eyes glittering. The young people were dressed in fine cloth wrapped loosely about their loins or loins and torso, according to their sex. They carried vessels of their own persuasion, and in the vessels were the New People's gifts, which they placed before the vassal lords for inspection: Flawed crystal beads in Hari's almost perfect quartz crystal bowl, a little flint-and-metal flamemaker in Moti's hot-clay platter, a markmaker on Sundari's tablet of perfectly inscribed stone. The two boys kept their eyes averted, as was proper when in the Khan's presence. The girl, Sundari, kept her eyes on Kangra, which Kangra pretended not to notice.

"There's nothing we need," Rukmani Khan said, glancing over the gifts very quickly.

"Nothing even a child can't do," Natarjan said pointedly.

"I understood the comparison," Rukmani Khan said dryly.

The old priest folded his hands in his lap. He had finished eating and liked to make a point of his discipline in not savoring the flavor or texture of food but eating only for sustenance. "The messenger did not speak; she merely presented her gifts, then left. But yesterday, Kangra rode Jabari into their camp. If I understand what he was telling Hazan last night, these New People intend to stay." He gestured to the servants, and an acolyte quickly placed another bowl of food before him. It was filled with redroots.

"Some stay longer than others," Rukmani Khan commented.

"No. These people intend to stay forever." The priest looked at Kangra through rheumy eyes. "Is that not what you reported last night?"

Kangra nodded. "It took me a while to understand; you know how badly they speak. But finally I realized they meant to live here. Something to do with the magtrees on the lateral moraine."

"And I suppose they expect us to persuade the trees to release their nuts?"

Rukmani Khan looked at Kangra, who shrugged.

"They didn't ask; I didn't offer," he said.

"They can't do it without our help," the Khan said with a scoff. Then he paused thoughtfully. "But if they do know a way, we could learn a lot."

"You might also lose your soul in that quest," Natarjan cautioned ominously. "They bring nothing of value."

"They sent gifts," Kangra said softly, and the priest nodded. Clearly the old man was still troubled.

"Kangra, did you observe any weapons in their camp?"

"I saw nothing I recognized as a weapon, not even a hunting stick like the safari people used."

Those had frightened all the vassal lords. How had the hunters caused the pellet to be thrown from the stick with enough force to smash the skull of a waterfowl? The person who did it couldn't have persuaded the fowl to come out of the water, let alone kill it properly. But it was definitely dead. It was about that time that Natarjan began speaking less about the vassal lords' responsibility to the abos and more about taking care that the abos not lose all their foraging habits. The Khan suspected that Natarjan would much have preferred staying all year in the Winter Palace but was too proud to be the only man to do so. For all his insistence on reform to the ways of the Winter Palace, even Natarjan could not bring himself to give up all the teachings of the Summer Palace.

"The gifts were sad," Rukmani Khan said. "Still, it was a civil enough gesture. If they compensate the abo properly, I'll let them stay. We will proceed with caution from there, but we will proceed. Let me know if they come through with that bolt of cloth."

"As you wish," Natarjan said. He snapped his fingers again and the young people left, but not before Sundari gave Kangra a shy smile. Everyone pretended not to see.

"What of their women?" Rukmani Khan asked.

The priest shrugged. "I didn't notice."

Kangra smiled. "They're young, nicely groomed, despite, as Natarjan mentioned, being dressed alike. But I will admit, I hardly noticed their clothes at all after a summer of looking only at abo women."

Abo women and the young Sundari, Rukmani Khan thought. But the girl was almost of her own mind and entitled to do as she pleased, even if it was with Kangra, who was twice her age. It bothered the Khan that she'd made advances to Kangra rather than to him. He was certain is was not because Kangra was more attractive than himself, but that the girl was afraid of what Gulnar might do if she found out when they returned to the Winter Palace. Whatever the reason, it left him only the abo women, for none of the other girls of the clan were as bold as

Sundari. He never could abide the smell of an abo woman long enough to do anything but reconsider his fantasies of sexual contact.

"I could," Kangra was saying, "pursue this matter of the abo's compensation with the New People. If it turns out satisfactorily, I could summon them in your name at the dinner hour and we would have an opportunity to get to know them a little better."

"If they're worth knowing," said one vassal lord.

"They're worth knowing," Hazan assured the first.

"You'll excuse me, milord, if I choose to leave with the children this evening, and return to the Winter Palace?" said Natarjan.

Rukmani Khan nodded amicably, though they both knew Natarjan's absence was mandatory. If anything came of this night, the priest wouldn't want to be around to see it and then have to deal with public sin as an aftermath. It would be humiliating to all concerned, for the penance would last until they reached the Winter Palace, and the women would all know, too. Then the *real* penance would begin.

2.

DAVID QUARRELS WATCHED Theo Tucker lean back in the only padded chair in the hold of Shuttle Two. David and the other managers sat on makeshift stools on either side of the plastic table. The white-haired CEO grinned at his managers, showing large white teeth.

"Now let me get this straight," Theo said. "You want me to decide if you should accept a simple invitation to dinner?"

"Not just me," David said. "He invited all of us. Everyone is included. He made that very clear."

"Anything would be better than eating from the mess," Ivan Mendal said, wiping his brow with the back of his hand. It was hot inside the shuttle.

"It's such a civil gesture," Chloe Brass put in, "and an opportunity we can't afford to miss. And of course it's company policy to get along with the community."

"That policy refers to communities on civilized worlds," David pointed out. He had made time to check *all* the company's policies since last night. He wanted to be certain he understood the risks he was taking, especially the personal ones. "The community is as much a part of this planet as the flora and fauna. That puts it in my jurisdiction. We're not going."

Theo leaned forward and glared at David. "We're not going when I say we're not."

"This isn't a bunch of aborigines we can scare off with a little black powder in the fireplace," David said stubbornly.

"I know that, but it's beginning to look like they're interlopers. If that's the case, we'd be within our rights to scare them off by any means." Theo drummed the arm of his chair

9

with his fingers. "What have you learned about where they come from?"

David shook his head. "Nothing," he said. "The smattering of Indo-European isn't enough to be conclusive."

"What does it take to prove they're interlopers?"

"The language is one of the most important indicators," David said. "We'd have to document their language to demonstrate an Indo-European base of some specific percentage."

"What percent?" Theo asked.

David shrugged. "I don't know—something greater than fifty. A dozen words won't do."

"You don't know?" Theo said, his displeasure as evident in his tone as in the frown on his face.

"You hired me for my experience with sub-primitives and Stone Age natives, not suspected interlopers."

"I hired an experienced change engineer for an off-planet venture because I know it takes an experienced engineer to be versatile enough to stay on-plan under conditions that—by definition of off-planet venture—are unknown. I also put aboard the *Pelican* one of the best databases available. Are you trying to tell me that database doesn't state what percent of a language has to be Indo-European-based to know these people are interlopers?"

David felt a flush of embarrassment creeping up his neck. "It's probably there," he said softly. "I just haven't had the time to look it up. The new plan you and Ivan worked out calls for forty or fifty laborers. I've given our investigation of the Indigenous-aborigines the highest priority so we can have those laborers when we need them. A language study of the other people will take a good six months, whatever the percentage is. The way the new plan reads, we need to start felling trees in six weeks."

Theo nodded, looking slightly mollified. "I have a report from the concessionaire that change engineering hasn't provided a list of local flora for food processing."

"It's true," David admitted reluctantly. "It's next on my priority list, but we're off schedule because of the unexpected work of dealing with this Khan's people; I don't think we'll get to the local flora for another week."

"Have you updated your support plan in the database so the

concessionaire and every other manager will know what to expect?"

"No, sir. I'll do that right away."

Theo looked around the table and David guessed he was not the only manager who would be updating support plans right after this meeting.

"For right now," David said, "based on what little data I do have on these other people, I'm recommending no-contact. We just don't know enough to be certain it's safe to mingle with them."

"You said six months for a language study," Theo said. "Is that how long you want to delay contact?"

"I'd reevaluate, depending on what we learned—but, yes, it could be that long."

"I don't agree," Chloe said, wiping her upper lip with a handkerchief. "You admit to being behind in your work, yet accepting this invitation can put a hundred observers at your disposal. We've seen no hints of hostility, no weapons. Frankly, I think they're just another tribe of aborigines, a minor variation the planetary reports didn't cover."

"The racial-type difference alone would make that assumption too flimsy to satisfy the Council of Worlds," David said.

"That's your opinion," Theo replied sharply. "The Council couldn't fault us for making that assumption, at least not for a while."

"Did you see the steps leading into the rock island they call the Khan's Summer Palace? And the irrigation canals in the magtree forest?"

"I don't pay you to tell me about things I can see with my own eyes. Of course I saw them."

"Did you see my report on how they got built?"

Theo shuffled through the sheaf of reports on the table before him. "Damn things have a life of their own," he muttered, "and they breed."

While Ivan Mendal, Chloe, and the other managers chuckled, David leaned over the table, glanced down the identifiers in the upper right corner of the reports, pulled his out and handed it to the CEO.

Theo took it and read silently for a few minutes, flipping pages so quickly David doubted he was really reading. He glanced up at David. "You interviewed the aborigines, asked them who built the steps," he said. Then he read some of the replies: " 'They built themselves.' Another guy said, 'It is the work of giants.' And 'They must have been persuaded to stand here.' " He looked back at David again, bewildered. "What's this supposed to mean?"

"The conclusion is on the next page, sir."

Theo flipped to the back of the report, and read aloud: " 'The true builders remain unknown. The abos don't know, nor are they even able to describe the techniques or tools used. The structures, however, are architectural wonders, and the company would do well to preserve them in their present form.' " Theo looked up. "I resent the implication that I need to be reminded to keep ruins intact."

"They aren't ruins," said David. "Yet."

"Yet?" Theo raised his brows. "Give you people a pipeline to Council and you use it like a club. I'm not going to have you change-engineers running around telling me where I can fell magtrees. If this Summer Palace's front lawn has the best trees, those are the ones I take."

"The north lateral moraine has the best," said Ivan Mendal eagerly. Again he wiped his brow. He was sweating profusely. "But those are the ones with the irrigation canals. South lateral moraine's growth is pretty stunted."

"Those irrigation canals do bring up the question of rights to the trees," Chloe said uneasily.

"Buy the rights," Theo said briskly. "Even Council would consider that prudent while we're in an investigation mode."

"I'd like the opportunity to try," she said. "Like over dinner." She glared at David.

"It's too soon," David objected, shaking his head. "We just don't know enough. Even the procedures recommend waiting until after at least three meetings. We've barely had two, if you count that fellow Kangra riding into our camp yesterday on that sticktail beast."

"Yes, I'd count it," Theo said, leaning forward in his chair. "And the visit from this Kangra again this morning, when you brought the abos that bolt of cloth. I understand Chloe and Brown even had time to go all the way to the abo village to join you, and from all reports—only Chloe's and Brown's reports—" he said pointedly, "the fellow was civil and obviously well thought of by the abos."

"Yes, he was," David agreed. "My report, which I was nearly ready to file when I had to leave to come to this meeting, will confirm that. But it's still only two contacts."

"And your tech—what's her name? Sindon Liang. Yes, Sindon's visit to them. I'd count that, too. And the way I count, that makes three."

"My tech's visit," David said dully. Then he shook his head and reached for the sheaf of reports still in front of Theo. He hoped he wouldn't find the one from Sindon he hadn't read. But he did.

Theo smiled. "You read them about as quickly as you file them, do you?"

"I guess so," David said, staring unhappily at Sindon's report. Busy as he'd been examining the irrigation systems they'd found, it wouldn't have happened if he hadn't felt compelled to reread every policy in *Pelican*'s memory. Nor would it have happened if Sindon hadn't gone off on her own to do unauthorized work. Or, he reminded himself—trying to restrain his anger and to be fair to Sindon—if he'd read Sindon's report when she asked him to. He scanned the executive summary. She'd gone to the rock island the night he couldn't find her. He finished reading, then looked up at Theo. "Still, it's not much contact, even counting Sindon's visit. She wasn't even carrying a translator or a lingochine, it says here. They used body language, and that's subject to cultural interpretation."

Theo took the report back from David. " 'He remained on his knees, too . . .' " he read, " 'smiled frequently, as if to reassure me . . . palms open and up, a gesture I returned . . .' " Theo looked at David. "Those gestures are universally human; the interpretation varies little. But what about your report?" he asked, exchanging papers. "Is there anything in yours to suggest the locals are anything but what Survey's reports and the trade records indicate? That they're friendly and docile?"

David hesitated. "The abos are pretty much as the reports say. But these other people are not even mentioned."

"So you tell me. I don't happen to agree," Theo said. "I think the reports could have been better, but after fifty years of safari and trade landings, I think if this Khan's people were much different from the abos, they'd have been noticed and mentioned. Since they weren't mentioned, they probably aren't particularly remarkable." He looked around the table, and David followed his gaze. His managers were nodding.

"Um, David," security chief Brown Roberts said quietly. "I did check the original trade and safari reports, like I said I would. They don't mention any people but abos. Leastways, they don't differentiate."

David slumped back and shook his head. "I could file a protest with the Council of Worlds," he said.

Theo Tucker didn't even flinch. "I think a bit more discussion is needed," he said. "After all, I can understand how you feel being taken by surprise. We've all had some surprises to deal with. But I'd like to remind everyone here that the corporate offices expect a successful venture here on Cestry Prime. They've poured a lot of capital into our rigging. If we can't make it pay back on time, they're going to take a very long, hard look at the whole project. They may decide we just weren't the right people to do the job and replace a lot of us. Or they may decide it couldn't be done or that this wasn't the time to do it and recall us all, if we're lucky, or fire us if we're not." He looked around the table; he had everyone's complete attention. "The thing to do is not to give them any reason for a moment's hesitation when they look at our year-end report. Give them a proper profit, and our report gets ten minutes and the budget gets approved."

"Is that the goal?" David asked. "To get next year's budget approved?"

"Quarrels, we're here year to year until we establish a steady profit margin. We're not some research and development project or even a high-tech experimental group pushing the technology for them so they'd be willing to tolerate a drain on the till from us. Those magtrees may be special, but they fall down with ordinary techniques. There's a good niche in the market that Mahania's sales weenies can fill with magwood; it's hardwood, it's not too heavy, and it has the unique quality of blending with plastic, glass, and metal architecture that no other wood has. But it's not like they can't use something else if we can't get it out of here cheaply enough, or fill orders on time."

David nodded.

"Now, for the record, tell me if there's anything in the

Planetary Reports or anything you've seen yourself to suggest that these people are hostile."

"But the structures. It's fairly obvious they were built after the last reports the Council of Worlds used to construct those survey reports."

"Answer my question!"

David sighed. "There's no evidence we'd come to harm."

"Thank you."

"But don't you think it's strange the abos have no idea of how these structures were built? And today even Kangra's answers seemed deliberately evasive," David persisted.

"It was the translators," Chloe said. "I think there's a language barrier that needs to be corrected quickly. My translator hasn't been uploaded with new data since we landed."

Theo Tucker didn't react to Chloe's remark, and David wondered why. Had he chosen not to comment because he knew David's and Sindon's schedule was too tight to squeeze in low priority work? Or was he saving the information to use in some yet unknown way? David shook his head. It had to be for the first reason; the man confronted everything immediately.

"Quarrels?" Chloe said.

"It's not just the language," David said.

"Isn't it? When I asked Kangra about kilns, he didn't seem to know what I was talking about." She turned to Theo. "I showed Kangra shards of clay we found around the canals. He said he did not bake them."

"That's not what he said," David said tiredly. "He said he'd *persuaded* them to look glazed. That word, *persuaded*, keeps coming up."

"I'm sure it will be cleared up soon," Chloe said smoothly. "The linguistics device is still learning. There's bound to be some inaccuracy for a while. It will get better."

"Yes, but . . ."

"Look," Theo said, leaning forward to spread his palms on the table. He had big hands; his shoulders were tensed. David was certain he knew what kind of image he was projecting. "This Khan's people are humans, and humans are Chloe's responsibility. We're just going to have a meal with them, use the opportunity to feel them out a bit and gather your badly needed data on the language—not desecrate the walls of the palace. That okay with you, Quarrels?"

"It's not what I'd recommend," he said, still being stubborn.

"You haven't provided any data that indicates we wouldn't be well treated by them. And if we need to buy those trees, from your own report we have to conclude they're the sellers. We've got to do it before we start felling." He glanced at Ivan. "Six weeks?"

"Four or five, if I get the laborers."

Theo's brows shot up appreciatively. Finally he looked back at David, once again drumming his fingers on the arm of his chair. "There aren't many of these people, are there?"

"Brown has counted fifteen at various times."

"I may have counted some twice," Brown commented. "We identified them by clothes, and those can change."

"We outnumber them twenty to one already. We're going to dine with the Khan. Now that that's settled, what do you recommend we take as gifts?" He turned from David to look at Chloe, who immediately furrowed her brow, thinking.

"Well, they didn't seem impressed with the beads and styluses," she said finally. "But Lord Kangra seemed impressed with the cloth we gave the abos. We have plenty more."

"That was for the abos," David said. "Take wine."

"Cloth it is," Theo said. "The wine's for us, and precious little till the next supply ship."

David shrugged.

"Who's going?"

"Everyone was invited," Chloe said. "It would be a good break, and going would cut down the number of complaints about the bunks and food."

"Oh, no. No, no, no," said Brown Roberts, shaking his head. "Now it may be as you say, T.T., and they may be a gentle people, but it could also be a ruse to get us away from the shuttles so they can pick over our equipment while we're eating. The trade reports mention theft and pilfering."

David wondered when Brown would figure out that Theo didn't like being called T.T. He wondered, too, at Theo's restraint in not objecting. No doubt he considered the security chief too useful to dress down before his fellow managers, and too large a man to call out on his own.

"That was the abos," Theo told Brown. "You could button up these shuttles tighter than a strongbox; they'd never get in."

"Maybe yes, and then again, maybe no. I figure it's better not to take chances."

Theo nodded. "It's your choice, Brown."

"Yessir, mine," he said, smiling proudly.

Theo just shrugged and grinned broadly, watching Brown's smile fade as he realized his decision would not be popular with his security crew. They'd have to stay behind on duty while everyone else dined in the strange palace. That done, Theo glanced at his notes. "Nothing else on the agenda, so let's get out of this hot-box."

The managers pushed back their stools and started to rise. Someone popped the hatch, and fresh air rushed in.

David stayed at the table and reached into the stack of reports Theo had left behind. He pulled Sindon's and reread the executive summary, then started on the body of the report for the first time. Even the details didn't provide much information. They described a brief encounter between Sindon and an old man in the grove of stunted trees at the base of the rock island. She hadn't even gotten to see the magnificent steps up close, let alone examine them or ask questions about them. But at least now he knew how she had lost her lighter. She had given it to the old man as a gift. Feeling frustrated, he threw the report back on the pile, then got up and went to the hatch.

The day had been the hottest yet on Cestry Prime. The glacier valley was hazy with airborne dust, the shuttle camp gritty. Even Shuttle Two's ramp, which had been in place only a few hours, was coated with blue grit. The breeze was barely perceptible, but it felt refreshing compared to being inside. David paused a moment on the top of the ramp to look around for Sindon.

There was a line in front of the shower-dome, and a crew was hosing down Shuttle One. The concessioners in their white coveralls were clustered around the mess-dome, no doubt revising the menu from meal to snack, or maybe they were being instructed to pilfer samples at the Khan's tonight. David knew he'd given them no help and he probably wouldn't until after he learned the abo words for hiring labor. He turned to look at the neat row of managers' domes, and saw Theo Tucker talking to Sindon. She was holding her long red hair up off her neck, trying to tie it back with a strip of cloth. He watched Theo step around to tie a knot for her, surely brushing her neck with his fingers. David shoved his hands in his pockets and started down the ramp.

Theo was gone by the time David crossed the camp, but Sindon was waiting for him.

"What did Theo want?" he asked her. He kept walking toward his own office and Sindon fell in stride beside him.

"He said he liked my report," she said.

"He sure did," David said, shaking his head. The damn report. He'd felt like a fool being surprised with it, and though he knew that was his own fault, he couldn't help being angry that Sindon had put it together without consulting him. Even worse, he felt frightened when he thought of the risk she'd taken to gather the data. "What else did Theo want?"

She gave him a puzzled frown, no doubt sensing his irritation.

"We talked for a while," she said. "He hasn't been in camp long, wanted to know where Ivan's office was."

"That's all?" David asked.

"Yes, that's all," she replied. "Why? Did you think he was asking about us? And maybe that I was telling him?"

Her expression told him she was joking, and his must have told her he wasn't. But she misunderstood the reason.

"Don't worry so much," she said. "I'd never give Theo a reason to think we are lovers. At least, I won't until I make engineering grade. Then it won't matter because I won't be working for you. I'll be working with you. There aren't any policies prohibiting coworkers being lovers, just bosses and their subordinates."

"That isn't what I meant," David said, even more irritated. "Then—what?"

"Didn't Theo give you a report on the meeting?"

Sindon shrugged uncomfortably. "I know we're going to the Khan's Summer Palace to eat. He said he wanted me to carry my lingochine tonight and stay with him as interpreter. He doesn't know how to operate one."

"Why didn't he ask me first?" David said, irritated.

"I assumed he did," Sindon replied.

David shook his head. "What did you tell him?"

"I said yes, of course. What else could I say? He's the CEO."

"Yeah."

They walked silently for a moment, blue dust puffing under their boots.

"David, I'm sorry about the report," Sindon said at last. "I asked you to read it, and when you didn't I got angry. I mean, I lost a lot of sleep getting it done. Then I tried to tell you about it, but you wouldn't listen." She shrugged. "If you'd just read it."

"I probably would have if I'd known you'd gone to the rock island on your own. That was a damn foolish thing to do."

"It didn't seem foolish at the time," she said hotly, "and Theo Tucker didn't seem to think it was foolish. 'Nice report,' is what he said."

"He would think so. He used it to force this dinner with the Khan. We needed at least three contacts, and with your little night visit he had them." He shook his head. "Sindon, this isn't going to work."

"Now wait a minute, David," she said. "Are you blaming me because he ordered us to go tonight and you didn't want to? Do you really think my report made the difference in what our CEO decided?"

They were at David's office now, and he opened the door to let her in. Inside, she sat down on a stool, hands clasped over her knees, looking dejected.

"Do you?" she asked again. "Do you think I sabotaged you with that report?"

David groaned. "All right," he said. "He's the CEO, and if he wanted us to go, he would have found a way, report or none. He's just not going to let caution get in his way."

"And why should he?" Sindon asked. "This is the fourth day. Neither the abos nor the other people have done damage or caused harm to equipment or people. They haven't interfered with our work. Historically, the Planetary Reports show fifty years of intermittent contact, both trade shuttles and safari landings, and they never interfered with them either. What more do you want?"

"Time," David said. "Just enough to fill in the gaps to be certain we're not overlooking anything. Like, what the hell does all this *persuasion* talk mean? And it doesn't help to have my only tech in complete disagreement. If I had six months to dog those people, I could give Theo what he wants, too: a fully documented language. Unless I miss my guess, it's going to show an awfully high percentage Indo-European base."

"I was trying to fill in the gaps with that report," she said. "I was trying to help *you*."

"You might have gotten hurt," David said. "It was damn foolish to go there in the dark, no lingochine, and no one even knowing where you were."

"I didn't plan to go there," she said. "I went for a walk by the lake. I didn't realize how far I'd gone until I met the old man. I was more surprised than he was."

David sat in the hammock next to Sindon's stool. He took her hands in his and looked into her gray-green eyes. "Sindon, this isn't going to work," he said again. "If you were an ordinary tech with some experience, we'd have sat down to discuss what was good and what was not so good about your handling of even a chance encounter with these other people. Together we would have decided what should go in this report and even if there was to be a report. In the end, you might not have agreed with me, but you would have understood my reasons, and I would have reasonable assurance that in like circumstances, you'd do better next time. And if you didn't, you'd know I'd have just cause for being angry, or even wanting you out of my group. But I can't talk about what you do without a huge emotional load coming out with it. And your work, the very things you choose to do, like going for a walk around the lake to the rock island, are calculated to please me, not rational choices a tech would make." He could see her eyes narrowing with anger, and she tried to pull her hands away. David held on. "I know you don't want to hear this. You worked so hard for this tech promotion. You were working on it before you ever met me, so I'm pretty sure doing a good job of it now that you've got it is very important to you. But you said yourself you made the report because you were trying to fill in the gaps for *me*. Any other tech wouldn't have known enough about my worries to try, and wouldn't have been tempted to overstep even if they did."

Head bent, Sindon finally nodded. "It's not working, is it?"

"No," he said, sadly. "It's not. It's not good for me, and it's worse for you."

"So what are you going to do?" she asked. "Transfer me to Ivan's group and ask for a more experienced person?"

David shook his head. He wondered if he'd seriously consider such a change if he weren't worried about Theo Tucker's attraction to Sindon. He wondered, too, if it was wise not to let Sindon know he was angry with Theo, not just for preemptively assigning change-engineering's resources tonight without going through proper chain of command but because he was jealous of the time Theo would get to spend with Sindon.

"If you're not going to transfer me, what *are* we going to do?" Sindon asked.

David shrugged, then kissed her fingertips. "We're going to keep working on it. I'm going to behave like your boss, and you're going to be a good tech."

"What about us?" she said, her voice trembling, her eyes filling with tears.

David lowered their hands until they were resting on Sindon's knees, then he let go and sat up in the hammock. "I think you know the answer to that," he said, unable to meet her eyes.

She started to cry, and he had to steel himself from reflexively taking her into his arms. She looked at him, shaking her head, then stood up and turned her back to him. When she turned around again, her eyes were red, but she'd regained her composure. "Well, this isn't very tech-like behavior," she said with false animation. "But I can assure you it won't happen again."

David nodded unhappily. "Just let me say one last thing . . ."

"If it's not business," she said, "I don't think you should."

"It's not, and I shouldn't, but I'm going to anyway. I'm doing this because I think if we went on the way we were, it would ruin your career. You can be a good technician, and some day, a fine engineer. But the way we were going along, it never would have happened. I . . . care . . . too much about you not to help you."

Sindon shook her head, then lifted her chin. "If it eases your conscience to think that, I doubt I can say anything to change your mind. But maybe, some night when you're lying here alone, you might think through whose career you were really concerned about, and who didn't consult anyone before deciding what to do about it."

David nodded. "I'm the boss," he said. "I'm supposed to make the hard decisions."

"I hope they pay you well for this one," she said.

"Don't"—she slammed the door—"be so sarcastic," he said. He leaned back in the hammock. "Don't build walls between us like this. Don't make it so hard."

Oh, Jesus, why wouldn't she see that the personal betrayal would have been letting them go on?

3.

DEEP INSIDE THE Khan's Summer Palace, servants carried bowls of food to the guests, scurrying over the ice that bridged the islands in the pool. Unseen were other servants balancing platters piled high with more food, running relays between the ice cellars and the great hall. With such a small staff of servants left, Rukmani Khan had been concerned that there were too many guests. They couldn't even call on the children to help; just a few hours ago the three had left with Natarjan on the last caravan. Dancers in sparkling costumes moved among the singing fountains, keeping the guests entertained until they were satiated, and that had happened quickly. At last, the servants had returned to a more normal pace, exchanging heaping bowls of food for ones that the guests had not yet emptied, replenishing vessels of honeyed wine before they were half-consumed.

The vassal lords had distributed themselves among the guests, most of them sitting on the larger islands, grinning like fools because they couldn't converse very well through the talking boxes the guests had brought, but knowing it was Rukmani Khan's wish to convey well-disposed spirit. If these New People could convince the abos to give up their animal-skin clothes and replace them with cloth that was less offensive to olfactory sensibilities, they would not have to contend with the awful fumes from the abos' tanning. Perhaps these New People would succeed where the Khan's people had failed. And of course there was this talk Kangra had reported of the New People's intent to harvest magnuts. If they could, it would be good to know how. It took the Khan and his vassal lords weeks of eating to persuade the trees to loose enough bounty to satisfy both the abos' needs and their own. And last was a natural curiosity to be satisfied regarding the New People themselves, especially the women. They looked nothing like abos, and except for the bright eyes and varicolored-hair, enough like themselves so that even the priest left them alone together without threats of doing penance for bestiality. Natarjan had merely turned his head on the lesser sin by leaving with the caravan.

Rukmani Khan saw Kangra rise from his cushions on the island opposite, where he'd been seated with ten of their guests. His departure seemed to arouse the curiosity of one man, a curly-haired fellow, but Kangra paused to talk with him a moment, and whatever he said through the large talking box seemed to satisfy the man. He sat back, his hand smoothing one of the cushions, apparently delighting in its texture. Earlier Rukmani Khan had seen this same man on his hands and knees, examining the mosaic floor.

Kangra stepped onto the bridge to Rukmani Khan's own island, the central one in the vast pool of the great hall. Stopping midway to adjust the voice in the fountain, he put his hand on the reed and cocked an ear to listen until he was satisfied with the new flow of water. Rukmani Khan had not noticed its being out of tune; likely no one except Kangra would have noticed. Kangra was possessive of the singing fountains, for it was he who had persuaded the fountains to orchestration only weeks ago, and he seemed unable to resist seeking even more perfect accord. Finally pleased with the improved sound, Kangra took his hand out of the water, the droplets clinging to his fingertips persuaded to vaporize during a reflexive clench. The curly-haired guest, who had been watching, frowned and rubbed his eyes when he saw the puff of vapor.

"These people have no knowledge of the arts of persuasion," Rukmani Khan commented as Kangra sat down next to him.

"None," Kangra said. "They're eating everything raw from the bowls. They don't seem to know the difference."

Rukmani Khan was surprised. It hadn't occurred to him to have the food cooked; that was done only for young children and lovers. He shook his head with regret. "I don't think it will hurt them, but I can barely tolerate redroots persuaded to be soft and warm, let alone eat them uncooked." He glanced down at the bowls before him. One was filled with redroots. He took some still cool from the bowl between his practiced fingers and popped them, warm, into his mouth. He offered the bowl to Kangra, who helped himself generously. Kangra did not dislike redroots as much as Rukmani Khan.

"You were right to feed them here in the great hall," Kangra said. "They have an appreciation for their surroundings."

"Especially the singing fountains?" Rukmani Khan asked, noticing Kangra's proud smile.

"To be sure, they are admiring the fountains properly. But they've also commented on the stonework and admired the mosaics."

Now Rukmani Khan smiled. He was especially talented in persuading stone to cling or cleave, and with such a gift he too often performed heavy labor preparing new greencaverns for Gulnar's gardens in the Winter Palace. But here, in the Summer Palace, he strived for—and achieved, he believed— an esthetic quality that pleased him. He could not do anything like this in Gulnar's Winter Palace where her need for self-reliance took precedence over something so indulgent as art. During the long winters of splitting sandstone into bricks the children could carry down to the river, then pulverizing the bricks into pebbles and sand the river could carry away, he had planned how to cleave the bedrock of the Summer Palace to form networks of deep and shallow pools for wading, swimming, and some just to look at. He had left islands for nights like this, where hundreds of people might gather, and tonight he had made bridges of sparkling ice. The lines of the great hall were bold and clean, the colors and textures pleasing. It was a triumph, but it was a singularly empty one. When he had started the work, he had believed it would please Gulnar one day. He knew now it would not. Though he could see a visual feasting in the eyes of these strangers, he knew Gulnar would never share their awe.

"I think," Rukmani Khan said, "I'm beginning to like these people."

"They're a bit peculiar," Kangra said. "Have you looked closely at the ones with dark eyes? They're brown, not purple. And I don't believe I've seen a crooked tooth in any of their smiles, and that makes me wonder if there isn't at least one Persuader among them."

Rukmani Khan shook his head. He didn't understand how they made their shuttles fly either, but there was no denying they did manage to do it. "They obviously have ways of compensating for their limitations, but I don't believe it's persuasion. If you look closely at their clothing, you can tell it's just woven thread. The quality and quantity are admirable, but the technique is a very simple one."

"The fiber of the thread isn't plant fiber, and those belts and boots aren't leather, either."

"I would have liked to learn more about them," Rukmani Khan said. "It's a pity we're leaving so early in the morning."

"Don't remind me. I fear the morning will come too soon; Hazan was right," Kangra said, helping himself to more redroots. "The women are beautiful, and making their acquaintance could take most of the night." Kangra's eyes sparkled as he looked at the women among the guests, as if he could already see what the night might bring.

Rukmani Khan nodded in agreement. Some of them were very beautiful, but even more important, they were unknown. He thought that had something to do with their appeal; even Gulnar, his wife, was once considered beautiful, but he did not desire her anymore. These women, even wearing identical garments that covered them from neck to toe, held more appeal for him. Especially the one with the long red hair. She was sitting with a white-haired man on a pile of brocaded cushions only a short distance away. Almost half the guests had unusually light eyes, but hers were startlingly light. She looked almost unreal to him, more like a spirit-lover might look. She wore blue, like most of them. The few who were dressed in white garments were sitting on another island, and though he had wondered about their being attired differently, his gaze continued to return to the red-haired woman.

"Her name is Sindon," Kangra said.

Rukmani Khan turned to Kangra, who was smiling broadly.

"I saw you looking at her, so I inquired from that man over there," he said, gesturing across the water to the island he'd just left. The curly-haired man sat slightly apart from the other guests, separated by the space Kangra had left vacant. He carried one of the large talking boxes.

"The curly-haired man is the one who goes to the abos every day," Rukmani Khan commented.

"The very same. I paid a price in asking the favor of her name," Kangra said. He picked a morsel of fish from the bowl before Rukmani Khan.

"And now I owe you something?"

"Nothing, milord. I'll pay what he asked gladly," Kangra said.

Rukmani Khan chuckled. Obviously the man had not asked much. He looked over at him, and frowned. The man had pushed aside the cushion Kangra had been sitting on and was now doubled over so that his elbows were practically on the floor. "What is he doing?"

Kangra peered and shrugged. "He keeps looking at the shells you inlaid there."

Rukmani Khan smiled, quite pleased, for acquiring the shells had been a feat in itself, but persuading them to meld with the bedrock had been even more challenging. This stranger had no understanding of the effort, yet he was intrigued. The Khan found himself wanting to talk to the man, but to suggest that to Kangra while watching the man admiring his work would have been unseemly. "Have you identified their leader yet?" he asked, hoping it might be the curly-haired man.

"The white-haired man with Sindon. He isn't named yet, but all of them are deferring to him."

"Even Sindon," Rukmani Khan said, at last turning away from the curly-haired man to look at the beautiful red-haired woman again. She kept stealing glances at Rukmani Khan, which he thought was encouraging, and while she did not seem annoyed by the white-haired man's attentions, she was not in a state of joy. He imagined he could bring her to that, if she would let him. He couldn't help wondering what kind of love people could share when not even one of the pair could persuade. He knew the abos managed to survive and procreate without persuasion, but it was a mystery to Rukmani Khan how that could be. For all the priest's ranting, he could not believe abos were animals.

"Before you go to her," Kangra said, "you should know that another of their women asks to be named to you."

"Which one?" he asked. One so bold as to ask to be named

to him might provide even better companionship later in the evening. A receptive partner, he knew from painful experience, was far more satisfying than any other kind; he knew his persuasive ability was great enough for a mutually satisfying pairing if only she were willing. Not many were willing to pair with even the greatest Persuader like Rukmani Khan, at least not in the Winter Palace, where Gulnar might hear of it.

Kangra pointed out a dark-haired woman who sat stiff-spined near the curly-haired man. She was no longer very young, but would have been pretty if it weren't for the unpleasant set of her mouth.

Rukmani Khan shuddered. "Do not name me to her. Such a stern mouth reminds me of Gulnar."

"As you wish, but that gives me a problem to solve. If I understood her correctly, she's their leader's spokesperson, and claims to have business to conduct. I'd deal with it myself, but I'm already committed to the man who named Sindon."

Rukmani Khan looked at Kangra strangely for a moment; he was not usually attracted to men, especially not when so many women were at hand.

Kangra, catching his look, laughed and shook his head. "He may not be *the* leader among them, but he is one of the leaders. More important, I'm beginning to converse fairly well with him through that box of his. Our time is short; I'll take the opportunity to learn what I can. And besides, once I've done him the favor he asked of me, I can ask him one. And that will be to name me to a beautiful woman."

"Which one?" Rukmani Khan asked.

"I don't know yet. But I'll choose before the evening is done."

"And of course you expect to be free to pursue her when the moment arrives," the Khan said.

"Only if it suits you, milord," Kangra said—correctly but, Rukmani Khan suspected, untruthfully.

"Hazan," Rukmani Khan called out, resignedly. Though the great hall was filled with the singing of the fountains and the guests' conversation, Hazan was attuned to the sound of the Khan's voice. In a moment he appeared at Rukmani Khan's side. "Hazan, that dark-haired woman over there claims to be spokesperson for these people's leader. See to whatever business she finds so pressing."

"Of course," Hazan said. He looked wistfully over his shoulder at three young women on an island off to the side. The look, Rukmani Khan knew, was not calculated to extract his sympathy but theirs. Hazan was very young to be a vassal lord, but his powers of persuasion were equal to those of much older men and still growing. He had never failed Rukmani Khan, who trusted Hazan implicitly to do his duty.

"Perhaps you'll be able to return to your new friends when the Khan's work is done," Kangra said, not kindly.

"Yes, milord," Hazan said, then flushed. "I mean, not unless the Khan's work is done."

"See to it," Kangra said, getting to his feet. Kangra disliked young Hazan, less because of his age, Rukmani Khan knew, than because of his popularity among the young women. Rukmani Khan thought the younger man very wise not to have encouraged Sundari to seek him out, not even when she had been the only girl remaining in the Summer Palace. If provoked, Kangra had enough rank to make the young lord's life miserable.

But Hazan didn't leave immediately. He paused long enough to watch Kangra walk over the bridge of ice and rejoin the tall curly-haired man. "You haven't mingled with the New People yet, have you, milord?" Hazan asked the Khan.

Rukmani shook his head. "But I was about to."

"I could name you to my new friends," he said cautiously.

Rukmani Khan turned to look over at the three women in white. They were young, all pleasant-looking, and eagerly awaiting Hazan's return. He touched his forehead and met the eyes of each. They did not touch their foreheads in return, but they did smile. "I have other plans," Rukmani Khan said to Hazan, and Hazan's face fell. "What's this? I hope that's not disappointment in your face. Are you trying to curry favor with me by procuring women? I have no need. . . ."

"Oh, no, milord," Hazan said quickly. He tucked his hands beneath his knees and bowed his head to show complete humility. "I didn't wish to speak in front of Kangra, and I apologize for my lack of control. But you misinterpret my reasons."

Still in abject posture, Hazan waited for Rukmani Khan to give him leave, either to be on his way or to explain further, whichever the Khan chose. Rukmani Khan glanced at Sindon.

She was smiling at the white-haired man, and he was smiling at her. Rukmani Khan sighed and turned back to Hazan. "Explain yourself."

"Thank you, milord." He lifted his head but left his hands under his knees. It was a calculated gesture—if not sure to please Rukmani Khan for the surrender it implied, then at least to please him with an impression of being in control of himself. It was certain to be noticed with approval by the other vassal lords who, like Kangra, couldn't forgive Hazan his age, though not for Kangra's reasons. They simply judged him too impulsive and lacking in judgment to be in the Khan's confidence. "I should have approached you as I used to when I was a child. As it was, I tried to ask your wisdom like a lord, then reacted like a child when you did not understand. Please believe me when I tell you my wish to share these women, if they be willing, was from the heart."

"Be done with it, Hazan. I won't sit on my hands for my vassals and all the guests to see that I'm sorry I jumped to conclusions. Next thing I know they'll all be asking you why, and . . ."

"I'd never tell them, milord," Hazan said, cutting him off quickly. "I'll risk speaking frankly right now. Some pity you, and maybe they would procure for you out of pity. I would not do that."

Rukmani Khan frowned. Did he mean Kangra? Had the young lord been so attuned to his master's voice that he'd heard every word they'd spoken about Sindon?

"I know this is neither the time nor place to speak of such matters," Hazan said, "and I would not if you were not concerned about what your vassals were thinking at this moment. You do not need to sit on your hands for me here or ever." He smiled slightly. "Not that you would have need," he added. "Not here, or ever."

"I'm glad that's perfectly clear," Rukmani Khan said, almost willing to return the smile. There was always the matter of personal honor, even in a simple conversation between two people. There were vassals who delighted in tarnishing the Khan when they thought they could got away with it. He admired Hazan's restraint. It was another indication of his loyalty.

"Now, milord, let me explain the real reason for my disappointment."

Rukmani Khan had almost forgotten there was one.

"I think the three women I was with are slaves."

"What?"

Hazan nodded. "They have only one of those little talking boxes; it doesn't have many words. But if I understood correctly, they're slaves."

"If you believe that to be true, why didn't you say something immediately?"

"Because Kangra was here," he said, obviously pained to admit it. "Generally when I speak, he finds fault with me. I preferred to wait for a more open-minded audience. You, alone."

Rukmani Khan had to nod with understanding. Kangra would have dismissed Hazan's opinion.

"I was hoping you'd come to meet them, and perhaps confirm what I've learned. *That's* what I was leading up to. I didn't want to sound as if . . ."

"As if you were jumping to conclusions or being impulsive?" Which was, of course, exactly what Rukmani Khan himself had done. If he couldn't be perfect, he didn't really expect Hazan or anyone else to be without fault. But somehow it was expected of all of them to appear to be perfect.

Hazan was nodding.

"What about the rest of them?" the Khan asked, surveying the room. "Are they slaves, too?" His eyes rested on Sindon with the long red hair. She had wrapped a silky strand around her fingers and was playing with it. He would love to free her to come to his bed, and to feel her hair on his chest. But Sindon did not look like a slave to him.

"Only these three," Hazan said. "I asked why they were attired differently. As I listened to their answers, I came to understand they are the chattel of all the others."

Rukmani Khan tore his gaze from Sindon to look at the three women. They sat where Hazan had left them, talking quietly to one another. They were well-fed, their skin unblemished. "Well treated, if they are slaves," he commented.

"That's not the point," Hazan retorted indignantly. "They have no choice in what they do."

"And what do they do?"

"They provide food, labor, and sex to everyone else."

"So do servants," Rukmani Khan commented.

"Servants can refuse to give sex, and even look for another employer if they wish to. These women cannot aspire to whatever it is the others do."

The Khan sighed and nodded. He looked around the hall at the New People. They didn't look like slaves, but then, they didn't look much like anything recognizable. Kangra caught his eye. He and the curly-haired man had walked over to Sindon. The man said something to her and she started to get up, but the white-haired man put his hand on her knee. She sat back in the cushions, and Kangra and the curly-haired man walked on. Sindon stared after them for a moment, clearly disappointed. Was it because she didn't enjoy the white-haired man's company? Or that she would have preferred to be with the curly-haired man? He hoped the former. Rukmani Khan stood up, then realized Hazan was still waiting expectantly. "What is it?"

"Honor, sire, requires me, you, all of us, to free the slaves."

Rukmani groaned. "Not now, you young fool. Can't you see there are twenty of them to every one of us? And especially since we're not even certain."

"It ought to be verified, one way or the other," Hazan said stubbornly.

"All right. But *I'll* see to it," Rukmani Khan said. "You are authorized to conduct whatever business that mean-mouthed woman over there thinks she has with me, but leave this slavery question to me. And you are expressly forbidden from championing those girls unless or until I give you leave to do so!"

"Yes, milord." Hazan left quickly to talk to the dark-haired woman.

Rukmani Khan started over to Sindon. She was watching him, her smile growing as he approached. The white-haired man saw him, too, and seemed pleased, as well. He stretched out his hand to Rukmani Khan.

"You're the Khan, and I'm the leader," he said to Rukmani Khan, at least those were the words that came from the talking box on Sindon's back. "Nice . . ." The rest of the words were unintelligible babble.

The man's hand was still outstretched. Rukmani Khan

extended his own hand, and the white-haired man clasped his fingers, then let go.

"The music . . . dancers . . . Nice."

Rukmani Khan waited patiently for the man to name himself, then began to wonder if he'd recognize the gesture if he did. Half the words that issued from the box were simply incomprehensible. Then too, he wasn't certain the man understood that he should name himself before the Khan did. He had no intention of breaking custom for a visitor, though, so after a polite interval during which he didn't detect a naming, he turned to Sindon.

"You have already been named to me, Sindon," he said. "I am Rukmani Khan."

"I am pleased," she said, "to be named to you." Her voice was melodic. He wondered if that had anything to do with the sudden, corresponding clarity of the words from the talking box.

"I want to know you in every way this evening," he said to her.

She looked startled, but it was the man who answered, or tried to.

"Want . . . learn . . . Common profit." He turned and grinned at Sindon, patting her knee at the same time, as if to comfort her about something. Then he turned back to Rukmani Khan, staring at him expectantly.

Rukmani Khan shook his head. He wouldn't speak to a man who hadn't named himself. But it was difficult to invoke that protocol when he wasn't willing to invoke the rest, which required him to call his servants to have the man taken out of his presence.

Sindon was smiling pleasantly again, more words streaming from the talking box. Some of them were about her wanting to know him, too, but she didn't look like she really understood what she was saying. The man kept speaking to him, also, and was obviously growing puzzled at not being answered. Again Rukmani Khan shook his head. "The only way to save more embarrassment is for me to leave," he said, and he stood up. "Goodbye, Sindon."

Looking both bewildered and disappointed, she reached out to take his hand, much in the same fashion the white-haired man had done only moments ago. Her touch, however, was more intimate.

"Wanted to talk . . ." the man said, along with another stream of words Rukmani Khan couldn't understand. How did Kangra and Hazan manage to converse with these people at all? The talking boxes were worse than he'd imagined.

When the man realized Rukmani Khan still was not going to speak to him, he shrugged and stretched his hand out again. Touching before naming was not in violation of protocol, so Rukmani Khan returned the gesture. This time, however, he did not give the man a chance to squeeze his hand. Rukmani Khan squeezed first, hard. That seemed to please the man.

Bewildered, Rukmani turned away from Sindon and walked past a band of dancers. He stopped and pretended to be looking around the hall for someone.

"How did it go?"

He was startled to find Kangra beside him. Rukmani Khan didn't answer. From the edge of his vision, he saw Sindon glance over at him; the white-haired man was drinking his wine, head tilted back. Quickly he gestured to her, saw a look of understanding come into her eyes. Well, maybe it was understanding. He'd know in a minute.

"Is everything all right?" Kangra asked, perturbed because Rukmani Khan hadn't answered him.

"No," he said finally looking at Kangra. "Do you see those women dressed in the white garments?"

"Yes," he said, taking only a quick glance.

"I have reason to believe they're slaves," Rukmani Khan said. "I want you to find out for certain."

"If they are," Kangra said, his voice very low, "it may be better not to know."

Rukmani Khan shook his head gravely. "I'm not *that* tolerant," he said.

"I will see to it," Kangra said.

Without another glance in Sindon's direction, Rukmani Khan left the great hall. She would follow or not, and he'd deal with it either way.

4.

FROM THE SHADOW of a pillar Rukmani Khan watched Sindon emerge from the great hall. She looked around and, seeing no one, she peered down the corridors. At last she started walking toward the deepest one. Rukmani Khan stepped out from the shadow into a cone of white light.

"You summoned me, milord?" she asked. The light shone red-gold on her hair, her skin so fair it seemed nearly translucent. Her strange pale eyes were bold and beautiful.

Nodding, Rukmani Khan leaned against the pillar. "I did," he said. "Was your leader offended that I would not speak to him?"

"What?" she said. "I do not understand you."

"Offended? Hurt? Angry?"

"You have not angered me," she said, looking as if she wished to reassure him.

"Not you," he said. "The . . . Never mind." It was useless. How would he ever make her understand he wanted to sleep with her? It was bad enough to wait for the talking box to relay the words, but it was worse to realize it wasn't doing so accurately. Frustrated, he shook his head.

"No?" she said, curiously. She touched her head, shook it, and said, "No," again, very hopefully. At least, the word *she* said had a hopeful note, even though the talking box did not reproduce the same inflection.

Then the talking box spoke without either of them having said something to interpret. "Not," it said. "No food. No wine. Not."

"No food?" Rukmani Khan repeated, wondering for the first

35

time if the talking box had a life of its own. "There's no food here," he said, shaking his head.

Suddenly he realized Sindon was shaking her own head again, her eyebrows raised quizzically. She put her hands on her temples while still shaking her head, and said, "No." She shrugged questioningly, her hands open. "No?"

At last he understood. She, or maybe the talking box, was looking for verification of the meaning of the word, perhaps even of the shaking of his head. He smiled and nodded, then abruptly changed to shaking his head again. "No," he said. "You've got it right. No food, no wine, not food, not wine. Just you and me in an empty hall."

"Thank you," said Sindon and the box. She smiled at him with relief. "We know many words. We don't know many words." She shrugged apologetically. "I say words to you, the talking box says words it knows to you."

"The talking box is some kind of translator that isn't a real person," he said. "I don't know how that can be, but it seems to be so."

"The translator knows many words," she agreed.

"Does it know how beautiful you are?" he asked her.

She looked surprised. "This palace is beautiful," she said, gesturing with a sweep of her hand to the hall with its colorful mosaic floors and polished walls. Then she gestured toward him, and added, "and the garments you're wearing are very beautiful."

"And Sindon is beautiful," he said.

She smiled, pleased. "The Khan is beautiful, too."

"No," he said, finally beginning to like the translator, even if it wasn't human. "The Khan knows he is not beautiful."

"That's . . ." Babble again. She seemed to sense it. "I don't have the words. Give me words," she said, stepping closer to him. "Say more words to me."

"Sex," he said, but she shrugged at whatever the translator said. "Lie together naked and touch each other's person, just because it's beautiful."

"Beautiful," she said, brightening. "I understand *beautiful*. The palace is beautiful. We must say words about the palace so the translator can . . ." She shrugged and looked apologetic again. "It doesn't have the word. It sees that the palace is beautiful. It hears you say the palace is beautiful, and then it gives the word to me, and I say the word to you."

"Obviously it understands all the wrong words," Rukmani Khan said, taking her hand in his. She was puzzled but did not resist. "Fingers," he said, touching hers. "Hand, wrist, fore-arm, elbow."

Sindon nodded eagerly. "Yes, now you understand. I need the words. Give me more."

"Shoulder," he said putting his fingers there. "Breast."

She stepped back in surprise.

Rukmani Khan had no doubt from her reaction that touching her there had not been acceptable. "I'm sorry," he said sincerely. "You need the word, don't you?"

She frowned and nodded, her light eyes fixed on him. After a moment, she stepped back, touched her breast and said through the translator, "Breast." Then she touched her stomach.

Rukmani Khan said the word, and watched in amusement as she touched her hips, bypassed her pelvis to touch her knees. He continued to supply the words.

"Give more words," she said eagerly when she'd touched every part of her body except the ones he wanted to touch.

Rukmani Khan put his hands firmly on her shoulders. "Hold," he said. Then he leaned over and touched his lips to hers. "Kiss." He let go of her. She stared at him. "If we're ever going to get anywhere tonight, I think you need those words."

"What?" she said.

"I want to hold you, Sindon. I want to kiss you, and . . ."

"No," she said, looking around uncomfortably.

"Not here," he said, laughing. "I have a wonderful private chamber we can use for that purpose."

"No, not here," she said firmly. "No, not there. No, not . . ." Her meaning was plain enough, but though he sensed she was distressed, she didn't look angry.

"I think there's hope," he said to her with a sly wink. He took her hand so that he could lead her to the stairs. She pulled back suspiciously. "Come along," he persisted gently. "No kissing," he said. "At least, not now. I could persuade you to feel differently, but you'd probably be angry after."

"Persuade?" she said, eagerly. "Persuade?"

Rukmani Khan shook his head. "I'd have to show you, and

it's too soon. Let's go up the stairs so we can go outside. I'll give you more words, and you can supply a few, too."

"Words?" Sindon said, hopefully.

"Stairs," he said, practically pulling her up the first few. "We're climbing stairs. Sindon and Rukmani Khan are climbing stairs to go outside. Rukmani Khan is holding Sindon's hand so she won't fall while climbing the stairs. Not that he thinks she's clumsy, but it's a good excuse to hold her hand."

He talked until they reached the top of the stairs. By the time he led her through the still-rough passageway to the outer balcony, he could feel her quickened pulse. He had not deliberately done that to her, but was pleased to find her so excitable. "Now, you suspicious woman. What do you have to say? Is this where you expected to be? Or did you believe, maybe even hope, I was taking you to my sleeping chamber?"

"Stairs," she said through the translator. She walked all the way out onto the balcony. "These stairs lead to the water." She was pointing down the fine stairs he had persuaded from the natural rock. A breeze blew her hair across her cheek, and she brushed it back. She was still pointing, looking at him expectantly.

"Not merely water," he said. "That's a lake. And above us is the sky, and there are stars in the sky. And pay attention while I point out the rest of the world to you. That's a meadow out there, and behind it are mountains. . . ."

She listened eagerly, sometimes talking to the translator, sometimes stopping him to make him repeat something. She was as excited as a child on a picnic. "This is beautiful," she said to him after a while.

"I think you probably mean *wonderful*," he said. "But I won't agree even to that until your translator has enough words for you to understand what I want from you."

"Probably?" she asked.

He shook his head. "What do you get out of this?" he asked. "What words are *you* looking for, if not sex?"

"Sex?"

Irritated, he made a crude gesture. She frowned, but from the way she looked at him, he was beginning to think she understood. "Sindon, sex is a good way for a man and woman to get to know each other. They relax, they take pleasure from each other."

She was still frowning thoughtfully, and there was starlight enough for him to see her eyes were troubled. "The abos say you people persuade them to have good . . ." She said something softly to the translator and it said, ". . . *sex.*" "The translator offers a word I know not. Abo word, your word, same word. Show me *sex*," she said looking at him questioningly now.

"If only I could believe you meant that," he said, chuckling. "I'd love to. But it's just another word you think you're asking me for."

"A man and a woman kiss," Sindon said, looking very sincere but not at all romantic. "A man and a woman hold together, and a man and a woman . . ." She made the crude gesture to him, straight-faced, and said, "Sex?"

Startled, Rukmani Khan nodded. "Yes, *sex* is the word."

"But persuaded sex to be good. What are the abos trying to say when they say *persuaded*?"

"They're saying someone among my vassal lords is courting disaster again," Rukmani Khan told her, fully realizing she probably wouldn't understand the words. He shook his head. "I can't speak for the abo men, but the abo women like to have sex with my men. We can persuade them to ecstasy, which their own men can't." He frowned. That wasn't entirely true. An abo man and woman together could achieve ecstasy without persuasion, but he gathered it almost never happened.

"Persuade?" she said, cautiously.

"Shall I show you, Sindon?"

"No sex," she said, drawing back in alarm.

"All right," he said. "No sex. Just let me touch you."

"Touch where?" she asked suspiciously.

"Your breasts," he said. "Just let me place my fingers on your breasts."

"Yes," she said. "But nowhere else."

"Nowhere else," he assured her. She bit her lip, then took a half step toward him. He started to reach for her, and she flinched. "Don't be nervous," he said. "It certainly isn't going to hurt." She stepped closer, bracing herself, and he touched her breast. He could sense the heartbeats in the blood flow around her mammary glands, and before he could persuade some of the flow into her nipple, he felt it become erect. It was a simple matter from there to persuade a few uterine contractions. Her eyes grew wide. He took his hand away.

"I . . ." She was holding her stomach, trembling. "Not you!"

"You think not?" he said. He touched her breast again, and she gasped. He made the contractions stronger this time, and she slapped his hand away. "Did I hurt you?" he asked. He was certain he had not, but she seemed confused about what had happened. Then he realized she probably didn't understand the word *hurt*. So he said very gently, "Did it feel beautiful?"

She frowned. Rukmani Khan shook his head. Though he had experience with women who were not skilled in the art of persuasion themselves, he did not know how to proceed with one who did not know about the art. He probably could press on with her—her excited blood flow practically assured a good outcome. But he also sensed she might not be entirely grateful, even if her body was. He waited, watching her watch him.

"I can't . . . persuade you like that," she said finally.

"Don't be so certain," he said. "For you to have said that, you must understand the beauty of sharing, and that can be enough. You do not have the art to persuade. But those without the art do not control or block either. Just feeling that the whole length of my body would be . . ." He stopped. He could tell she did not understand half of what he had said. He shrugged. "It would be beautiful for me to have sex with you."

She stared at him, but he couldn't tell if it was in disbelief, fear, or amazement.

"Can I touch you again?" he asked. When she didn't answer, he lifted his hand and gestured toward her.

"I understood," she said. She drew back, staring at his hand.

Obviously she was uncertain. He put his hands behind his back. "It's no fun if you can't get past being afraid," he said. "I would not enjoy feeling that every time your heart pounded."

She seemed puzzled now; no doubt he'd used more words she didn't understand.

"You persuade . . . stairs?" she asked. "Not stairs, more stairs?" She held up her hands. "Hands persuade?"

"Well, the hands help, but it's what goes on in your head that makes the work get done. Stairs are hard work," he said. "I mean, persuading the stone to cleave in just the right places is one thing, but then you have to carry away what isn't steps. And when that's finished, you want them to look nice, so you go back and persuade them to be smooth or to shine."

Sindon nodded hesitantly. "What else . . . persuade?" she asked suspiciously.

But he didn't have time to explain, for he heard footsteps on the stairs. "Someone is coming," he told her.

"Up the stairs," she said, looking away from him. He saw her breathing deeply, deliberately.

"My Khan?" he heard Kangra ask. Kangra was not alone. With him were Hazan and the three white-clad women.

"Milord, let me explain," Hazan said breathlessly.

"Shut up!" Kangra said angrily.

Meanwhile the women spotted Sindon and started talking to her. They were breathless, as was Hazan. Sindon did something to silence the translator.

"I did as you asked, milord, and you were right. These women are slaves," Kangra said.

With a glance to silence Hazan, Rukmani Khan raised his eyebrows. He had not expected it to be true. "Are you certain?"

"As certain as I can be speaking through these damnable talking boxes. From all I can learn, they are mere chattels. I asked if they would leave if I gave them the chance to go to the Winter Palace. And they all said yes."

"You're sure?"

Kangra sighed and shook his head. "How sure can I be, talking through a box?"

Rukmani Khan understood his dismay. He turned back to the women. "Sindon," he said quietly.

Though she was babbling with the women, she was already attuned to his voice. She turned to look at him, reaching behind her to touch the translator. "Yes, milord?"

"Sindon, do you understand what's going on here?"

Sindon frowned. "I understand what these women say to me. I do not understand your question," she said.

"Are these women slaves?"

She looked puzzled and shook her head.

"Do these women want to be here? Do they have any choice?"

Again she shook her head. "These women say they can go

with this man Kangra"—she pointed to Kangra—"to a place this man, Hazan, said many words about. A palace, not this palace."

"Yes, the Winter Palace," Hazan said, finally unable to contain himself any longer. "We will take them with us, won't we?" He hesitated. "I said nothing, milord. Kangra came to this conclusion independently."

"Yes, but you're awfully eager," Rukmani Khan said.

"He doesn't want you to know about the trees before you decide about the women," Kangra said.

"No, no," Hazan said. "That's not true. I did not trust him to tell you with proper perspective, that's all."

"You disobeyed a ranking lord by following me here," Kangra said.

"And you may punish me," Hazan said. "But I would do it again in like circumstances."

"Insolent whelp," Kangra said, lifting his hand to strike Hazan. The younger man stood his ground, and Kangra lowered his hand. "Tell him about the trees," Kangra said more calmly. "Tell him now, before he decides about the women."

"They mean to cut them down," Hazan said simply.

"We can spare some if they have need," Rukmani Khan said.

Hazan shook his head. "All of them, milord."

Rukmani Khan was dumbstruck for a moment. "What could they possibly build with that many trees?"

Hazan shrugged.

"He must have misunderstood," Kangra said. "And he would bother you with such stupid notions as cutting down a forest when you have this issue of slavery to deal with."

Hazan looked at Rukmani Khan, his dark eyes untroubled. He had the good grace not to flaunt knowing about the slavery issue before Kangra, not to mention that it was Kangra who insisted Hazan tell Rukmani Khan about the trees before dealing with the slavery issue.

"Whatever we decide about the trees, that will not affect what we do for these women," the Khan said quietly. Kangra nodded knowingly, and Hazan smiled slightly. He turned back to Sindon. "We will take the women with us, if that is their wish. We do not abide slavery."

Sindon was frowning. "I do not understand all the words. Let me say again, and you say again. These women want to go to the place Hazan told them about. It is the same place he's going to. This place is a good place, No . . . hurt? . . . for these women. It is a good place, a beautiful place."

"Yes," Rukmani Khan said. "It's the Winter Palace, a place they will not be hurt."

Still frowning, Sindon turned and talked to the women. They spoke excitedly. At last, she turned back. She seemed unhappy. "They want to go," she said. "I don't have the words to tell you why. It's not beautiful words I don't have."

"We're obliged," Hazan said quietly. "We cannot in good honor refuse them."

Rukmani Khan nodded and turned back to Sindon. "Would you like to come, too?"

"Say again?" she said, looking puzzled.

"Would you come with us to the Winter Palace?"

"Me?" she said. "Go . . ." She gestured helplessly, then said, "This other place?"

"Yes."

In truth he expected her to refuse out of hand, but she frowned thoughtfully. "You'd give me words?" she asked, suddenly looking almost as eager as the other women. "You'd give me many words?"

"I'd probably give you more than that if you allow me half an opportunity. But yes, we'll start with words. I will give you words."

"No sex," she said flatly, and the three women laughed. Sindon turned to hush them. "No sex," she repeated. "Just words."

"Sindon, if you say yes, there will be sex. But until you do, no sex," he said, then added, "Just words."

"I will go with you," she said, her bright eyes glittering. She was breathing short gasping breaths. Rukmani Khan could tell she had reservations that frightened her. But she had the impulse and courage that made her say yes.

"Milord," Hazan said warily, "I don't think she's a slave. Her leaving should be announced. But I shouldn't think that would be wise if we plan to take them." He gestured to the other three. "That is, not unless you plan to take issue with these people about slaves and not just free them."

"Hazan, you're a fool," Kangra said. "They outnumber us twenty to one. With numbers like that, it would be stupid to take issue with them publicly. Honor will be served by spiriting these women away."

"Three of them, but not Sindon," Hazan said stubbornly.

"Do you think it's better to send her back in there to explain that we're going to free their slaves?" Kangra asked him.

Hazan thought for a moment. "We can take her with us, then let her go once we reach the mists of the canyonlands."

"And if she chooses to stay with us?" Rukmani Khan asked.

Hazan stared at him in amazement. He swallowed hard, then shrugged. "I guess if we get that far safely, she wouldn't present any special jeopardy."

Kangra looked at Sindon, who along with the three other women was staring at them, apparently trying to puzzle out their conversation, but without success. Then Kangra stepped away, gesturing for Rukmani Khan to follow him into the shadows. "I speak to you now as one friend would speak to another," Kangra said softly. "She's very beautiful, but in so short a time how can you know she'll be worth the trouble she may cause?"

Rukmani Khan looked at Sindon, a fair-skinned beautiful woman whose mouth didn't look mean even when she frowned. "Of course you're not speaking of Sindon. You're speaking of Gulnar."

"I mean," Kangra said conspiratorially, "that if you're going to go through hell, you ought to be certain this woman is worth the price. I heard what she said, and if there's not even to be sex, what good is she to you?"

The Khan watched Sindon pluck a white blossom from a potted plant and lift her arms to tuck it in her hair. It had been for her a nervous gesture, he was sure, something to do with still-trembling fingers. But for Rukmani Khan it was one of the most singularly feminine acts he had ever seen.

"She gives me hope, Kangra, and that is enough."

"But . . ."

"I said, Kangra, it is enough." He looked back at his vassal lord.

Kangra shook his head, but he said nothing.

"Can I trust you to arrange it?" Rukmani Khan asked him.

Kangra nodded. "Go back to your guests. I'll take the

women away right now. And I suggest that you and the rest of
our people leave at the first opportunity. I'll have the remaining
servants stampede the grassbears in the meadow when our
guests are walking back to their camp. If we're lucky, they
won't be certain the slaves are missing until morning. That's
when they'll take to the air, and if we aren't in the canyonlands
by then, we're going to be in trouble."

"We'll follow quickly," Rukmani Khan said. "Leave the
swiftest beasts for us."

"My own Jabari for you, milord," Kangra said.

Rukmani Khan put his hand on Kangra's shoulder to let him
know he was pleased to hear him offer Jabari. "Be careful," he
said to Kangra.

"I have the easy part, milord. You're the one who must go
back inside to face them as if nothing were happening."

"I can manage that," he said.

"And Hazan's fears about the trees? An accusation like that
could vex our guests."

"You don't believe it, do you, Kangra?"

Kangra shook his head. "No one can want or need that many
trees. Tell them they can take what they need to build," he
said. "The more generous we are tonight, the less likely they
are to suspect us of freeing their slaves."

"They're more likely to view it as theft of the slaves,"
Rukmani Khan said.

"Their numbers leave us little choice," Kangra said. "That
is, unless you want to wait and try to raise a band of champions
at the Winter Palace."

Rukmani Khan shook his head. "Go now, Kangra," he said.
"But let me talk to Sindon a moment."

Kangra nodded and went back to where Hazan waited with
the women. He motioned for Sindon to go to Rukmani Khan.
She was not happy, not eager like the others.

"Have you changed your mind?"

"I don't understand you," she said.

"Do you want to go to the Winter Palace? Learn more
words?"

Sindon looked out across the lake to the lights in the shuttle
camp, and sighed. "I want to learn more words," she said. "I
want . . ." She shook her head. "I don't have the words."

"You will have them," he said. "And when you do, maybe

then you can explain to me how you can be so frightened that
you're trembling, yet look so eager to proceed. I'm not sure I
would go with you if you offered to take me away in your
shuttle."

"These women should not go," Sindon said. "These women
are not . . . beautiful."

"They're slaves," he said. "And slavery is not beautiful."

"Their words are not beautiful," she said.

"You give me hope, Sindon, but when you defend slavery,
you make me tremble."

Sindon shrugged and shook her head.

"Go now," he said, pointing to Kangra.

"To the Winter Palace?" she said, pointing also at Kangra.

Rukmani Khan nodded. He looked into her eyes. He saw a
fire there that would have seared him if not blurred by tears.
Then she turned and went to Kangra.

5.

DAVID WAS ALONE, staring at a wall inlaid with turquoise, glittery pyrite and colored seashell, to fashion a mural of what appeared to be a pastoral scene of the vassal lords walking among a clique of grassbears sleeping in a golden meadow. The mural had disturbed him when Kangra had showed it to him during the tour of the palace, because it belied what David knew of grassbears. The canny beasts were too alert to be caught napping and too cautious to remain supine when approached. Now, without Kangra to hurry him, he looked again, lighting the dimmer reaches with light from a portable scanner, recording the scene at the same time.

David couldn't recall having seen a sleeping grassbear. He supposed they did sleep, and it wasn't difficult to imagine them with bodies curled and feet tucked as the mural depicted. But the purple-eyed men standing among them, not causing a single grassbear to lift its head or come to its feet, was too odd to accept. What David knew about grassbears was confined to the Planetary Reports and his own observations—precious little, but enough as long as they kept their distance from him. They might be given to fugue states, or it might be some natural fodder that caused them to fall into drugged stupors. Or they might be dead. It was the last thought that had begged closer examination of the mural.

The grassbears weren't sprawled as if they'd fallen. The vassal lords carried nothing that resembled weapons, though David recalled seeing several murals of abo hunting scenes with the abos' crude magtree-branch spears represented with painstaking accuracy. If these grassbears were dead, they had died in their sleep. He had asked Kangra what the scene depicted, but the lingochine had not been able to interpret the reply. Restructuring the question had resulted in the lingochine's interpreting Kangra as saying something about persuasion.

David kept examining the scene for something that might be a weapon, or some telltale sign of damage on the carcasses. Then he saw what he had not noticed earlier. In a shadowy corner of the mural, one vassal lord was peeling the hide from a grassbear. There was no evidence of a knife to indicate how the bloody deed was being accomplished, yet unmistakably the skin was separating from the corpse. There was little doubt left in David's mind now; the vassal lords had killed the grassbears.

Not killed, David reminded himself. They had *persuaded* the grassbears to be that way, Kangra had said. But even with the lingochine learning more than fifty new words an hour, he had not been able to determine exactly what persuaded meant. That was the trouble with lingochines. They learned nouns readily, but acquisition of verbs was slow and imprecise at best. A bit more action tonight would have helped, something more than eat, dance, run, and walk.

"Quarrels!"

David whirled around to find Theo Tucker striding from the great hall.

"Is Sindon with you?"

"No," David said. "I thought she was with you."

Theo shook his head. "I thought she went out to relieve herself, but she hasn't come back. Where's the toilet?" he asked. "I could do with a piss myself."

"Sindon?" David said, instantly forgetting the mosaic. Or maybe it was the freshness of the mosaic's puzzling imagery that made him feel uneasy. Theo, however, did not look alarmed, just annoyed.

"Yeah, Sindon. Where the hell is she? We could use another lingochine back at the party," Theo said. "Those translators aren't worth shit."

"They'll be better after tonight," David said, folding the scanner. "Sindon and I will upload their memories from the lingochines."

"Should have been done before tonight," Theo said.

"It's the abos' language barrier I'm trying to remove."

"Always a *but* with you, isn't there, Quarrels? Even when

you agree, there's always something." Theo shook his head. "Am I going to get a *but* tomorrow in your report on this place?"

"I have a good survey now. The rock island above ground level is merely the tip of a batholith of igneous rock. The chambers up there are rough-outs. The truc palace is down here, and I've got scans of a lot of their artwork. I'll use the computers to try to identify correlations between costumes and events, and whatever else we can learn about customs by analyzing the visual representations."

"Like this one?" Theo said, running his fingers over the mosaic of a grassbear.

"Yes."

Theo flattened his palm against the mosaic, and looked at David in surprise. "It's warm," he said.

David nodded. "So are the floors."

"Any evidence of a heating plant somewhere?"

"No."

"Then it must be natural, maybe radiated heat from the sunlight, or perhaps from hot springs?"

"I doubt it."

"And the bridges in that fountain room are made of ice. Why doesn't it melt where it touches the warm rock?"

"Because the rock isn't hot where it touches the ice. The rock is cold."

Theo shoved his hands in his pockets. "Where's the toilet?"

David gestured down the corridor. "This way to the facilities," he said, leading the way.

"Either you or Sindon should be in there with the lingochinc," Theo said, gesturing with his thumb back to the great hall.

"I'll try to find Sindon," David said. He felt a peculiar dread at the thought of searching her out. He didn't like to think about facing her again while she was so hurt and angry. He couldn't fool himself into thinking he had stopped loving her; he probably never would. And he knew he loved her despite knowing at least some of her faults, the most troublesome of which was her being so unforgiving.

David stopped by the toilet alcove, and gestured for Theo to step through. There were narrow troughs of swiftly running water. "You straddle it," David said. He had had an opportunity to follow Kangra's example earlier in the evening.

"No privacy?" Theo asked, glancing around. The alcove was open to the corridor.

David shook his head.

"Primitive," Theo commented, straddling the closest trough.

David stepped over so as to cut down the angle from the corridor, but there were no passers by.

"Maybe we should check with Brown to see if Sindon went back to the camp," Theo said. "I mean, if you don't know where she is either. . . ."

Sindon was probably off on another self-imposed task, perhaps duplicating David's work. He knew she was hurt and angry enough not to want to talk with him tonight, not even to coordinate work. He felt like hell himself. He'd made one feeble effort to take her away from Theo earlier, and with her endless capacity for jumping to conclusions, he could imagine that Sindon might have taken it upon herself to tour the palace on her own since she didn't get to do it with David and Kangra. It would have been easy to miss her in the labyrinth of corridors and chambers. But he nodded and said, "All right," to Theo. They started walking back to the stairs that led up and to the outside.

David followed Theo up stairs that were light-colored coarse-grained rock peppered with dark and light crystals that caught the light from magnesium torches. Their footsteps echoed as they climbed.

At the top of the stairs where they had line-of-sight to the shuttles in the meadow, Theo reached around to the back of his belt and pulled off his comm-unit. Holding the unit up to his mouth, he said, "Brown?"

"That you, T.T?" Brown's voice said through the comm-unit.

Theo's eyes rolled. "Yes, it's Theo," he said, turning to look out over the lake toward the well-lighted shuttle camp. "Listen, has Sindon Liang checked in for the evening yet?"

"Just a sec," Brown said. Then, "No. She's not back yet. Is there a problem?"

Theo frowned and held the comm-unit away from his mouth. "She's been gone for hours," he said to David. "What do you think?"

David couldn't help feeling a twinge of alarm, but he shook his head. "Let's check inside again," he said. "Maybe the others have seen her."

Theo brought the comm-unit back up to his mouth. "No problem," he said to Brown. "We'll check with you later."

He put the unit back on his belt and started for the stairs. David followed.

"We think we've made a deal on the magtrees," Theo told him as they reached the bottom of the stairs. "But I don't trust the translators. I think we should reconfirm through a lingochine."

"For a minute there I thought you were really worried about Sindon," David said, unable to hide a touch of sarcasm in his voice.

Theo stopped in mid-stride, his face suddenly angry. "I am worried about her, hotshot. You're telling me not to be, and you're the man I pay to know. Now which is it?"

"Sindon can take care of herself," David said, surprised by Theo's vehemence.

"Yes, but this is not your ordinary evening; we're dealing with a lot of unknowns."

David nodded. "I think I've pointed that out a few times already."

"Listen, Quarrels, I'm not playing games here, so cut out the crap. Does Sindon just disappear sometimes? Is this normal behavior for her? Just *yes* or *no*."

"Yes," David said.

Theo looked more resigned than relieved. "Okay. We'll go back and check the magtree deal," he said. He walked, eyes downcast, shaking his head with disapproval. David couldn't help wondering if it was for himself or for Sindon.

"We're not getting everything, are we?" Theo said after yet another attempt to confirm the magtree deal through the lingochine.

"Time is missing," David said. "Maybe quantities, too."

They were sitting with Chloe Brass, Ivan Mendal, and a young man named Hazan. David had met Hazan briefly earlier in the evening, and found him as likable as Kangra. Both men were very intelligent, and both were tolerant and astute in dealing with the language barriers. Hazan seemed the more adept of the two.

"I already confirmed quantities," Chloe said coldly to David. "We can take all the magtrees we want."

Theo heard Chloe and nodded curtly, but his eyes were on Hazan. "How long?" the CEO asked Hazan. "We'd like terms for twenty-five years."

Hazan seemed puzzled. "The forest reaches almost to the mountaintop," he said.

David looked at Theo. "*Long* has already been used in another context, for distance measurement. He doesn't understand it for time duration."

"Twenty-five summers," Theo said to Hazan.

"Twenty-five?" Hazan repeated. He spread one hand five times. "Twenty-five summers, you take trees?"

"Very good, sir," Chloe said, pleased that Hazan finally understood.

"Twenty-five years," Theo said. "We work when the snow falls, too. Summer and winter. Years."

The young emissary smiled and shook his head. "Ten years," he said. "Seeds grow take ten years. Ten years, ten summers, ten winters, same, same."

"We'll plant more seeds," Theo said.

"Plant seeds south slope?" Hazan asked. "Make big magtrees?"

"Careful, sir," Ivan Mendal cautioned. "We'd have to irrigate on the south lateral moraine to get them to grow like they have on the north."

"Cestry Prime doesn't lack for water," Theo replied. He swirled the honeyed wine in his goblet, watching it thoughtfully. Then he said to Hazan, "Twenty years and we'll make the trees on the south lateral moraine grow just as big as the ones on the north."

"Fifteen," Hazan said flatly. "Fifteen, no more."

"Okay," Theo said. "I'm easy to get along with. We'll talk again in fifteen years." He lifted his goblet to salute Hazan, then drank deeply.

Hazan laughed and tipped his own goblet back to drink, emptying the clear crystal vessel to the last rosy drop. It had been obvious to David earlier in the evening that toasting or saluting with wine was not a custom with their hosts, but they came to comprehend it quickly.

Theo Tucker leaned over the cushions toward David. "Have you seen her yet?"

David didn't have to ask who he meant, and he shook his head.

"Me neither." Theo sat up. "Ivan, Chloe, have you seen Sindon Liang around? You know, the red-haired tech?"

When they shook their heads, Theo turned around to look at the Khan, who was sitting alone on the island next to him. "We were with him just before she left."

"Maybe we should ask him if he saw her," David said.

"The bastard wouldn't talk to me," Theo said. He turned to look at David. "You getting worried, too?"

"A little," he admitted. It was already well past midnight, and the crowd in the great hall had thinned considerably. No one would be excused from work in the morning for lack of sleep. Not that the prospect of being sleepy for a day would have deterred Sindon, and he knew that unpredictability was a singularly predictable trait of Sindon's. She might be engrossed somewhere in the palace, even these long hours, even as David would have been if Theo had not interrupted. Or she might have been thoroughly miffed at being stuck with Theo Tucker for the evening, which—if she had had a hint from him that there was something other than a professional need for her presence—would have angered her into giving even the CEO a tongue-lashing, or if her better judgment had prevailed, she might have dealt with the problem simply by leaving. Or, David thought morosely, she might have been unable to cope with the work at hand while feeling so miserable over their breakup. Maybe she was sitting down at the lake, crying. Who knew for certain what Sindon might do?

"I'm going over to talk to the Khan," Theo announced, getting to his feet.

"Don't bother, unless you can get Hazan to introduce you," David said. Theo looked at him quizzically. "The high-ranking ones won't speak without a proper introduction first. That's why this kid, here, has been so popular all night. Apparently he's too insignificant to lose face if he talks to people without an introduction. But he can give them."

Theo shoved his hands in his pockets. "Ask him," he said. He was restless.

David leaned over to touch Hazan's sleeve, and the young man turned. "Will you introduce Theo to Rukmani Khan?"

Hazan seemed hesitant.

"Look, there was a woman sitting with him earlier. We're getting worried about her."

"Worried?" Hazan repeated, gesturing helplessly.

"Yeah, that's a tough one," David said. "Woman," he said. "Her hair was red like your shirt." He touched Hazan's sleeve again. "Woman here, woman not here."

"Sindon?" Hazan asked.

David glanced up at Theo, who frowned at hearing Hazan utter Sindon's name.

"Yeah, Sindon," Theo said. "Introduce me to the Khan so I can ask where Sindon is."

Hazan glanced around the hall, his eyes lingering a moment on the Khan. Then he got up. "Come with me," he said. "I will name you to my Khan."

"Hey, Theo, you need us?" Ivan asked.

"Come," Hazan said, smiling broadly. "Come, come." He stepped over to the bridge. "Come with me."

"Just David," Theo said finally. "The lingochine," he added, no doubt to make clear to David and everyone that it was not David he wanted at his side.

The Khan was staring at them, his face grave, his purple eyes piercing. His face was framed with dense curls that were still mostly dark but beginning to gray. He did not seem pleased to have Hazan bring Theo and David to him. Hazan knelt and lowered his head, eyes downcast and posture still until Rukmani Khan said a single word to him. Then Hazan whispered something to the Khan. The lingochine didn't catch the words, but the Khan turned his gaze resignedly to Theo and David.

"My Khan, this is David Quarrels and Theo Tucker," Hazan said. "My Khan's name is Rukmani."

"I am pleased to be named to you at last," Rukmani Khan said, extending his hand toward Theo.

"No more than I," Theo said, shaking his hand. And quietly to David, he said, "Are we supposed to kneel, too?"

"I wouldn't, sir, unless you want to make a practice of it from now on."

"Hell, no. I just want to know where Sindon is."

"Sindon?" Rukmani Khan said, looking up at them with a frown. He spoke rapidly and quietly to Hazan, who answered equally quickly. David turned up the receiver, but even the words he caught made no sense.

"It's obvious he knows who we mean," David said quietly. He glanced at Theo worriedly.

"Easy," the CEO said. "He knew her name even earlier. Let's ask where she is."

"What have you done with Sindon?" David asked.

"Sindon is not here," Rukmani Khan said. His face was very still as he gestured expansively to indicate the entire hall.

"We know that," David said irritably. "Where is she?"

The Khan looked questioningly from David to Hazan, who shrugged.

"Tell me where she is," David repeated. "Where is Sindon?"

Rukmani Khan leaned over to whisper something to Hazan, who nodded.

"Sindon," Hazan said. "We take you to Sindon. Yes?" He smiled and showed open hands, palms up. "Sindon . . ." He shook his head. "Don't have word, Sindon is."

"Yes, take us to Sindon," Theo said, his smile too broad to be genuine. "I was beginning to get very worried until that opened-palm gesture."

David was still worried. Hazan hadn't even tried for the word he claimed the lingochine didn't have.

The Khan had gotten to his feet and started walking across the bridge. Hazan indicated they should follow, and he walked after them.

The Khan led them past the privy to a narrow staircase David hadn't seen earlier. It was rough-cut in the gray- and black-speckled igneous rock, leading up, and lighted only part of the way. The Khan started up the stairs. When David hesitated, Hazan brushed past him to stay close on the Khan's heels. David and Theo followed.

At the top was a wooden door, which the Khan pushed open and stepped through. He disappeared in the darkness, Hazan with him. The smell of dung assaulted David and Theo, and they could not see.

"I don't like this," the CEO said, hanging back at the doorway. Before David could answer, a bright light came on, blinding them. "Where are we?" Theo said, grimacing in the light.

"I think it's a stable," David said, shielding his eyes with his hands.

"Then where are the animals? And where the hell is Sindon?"

David heard the door close, and with a start, realized the Khan was standing next to him.

There was a squeak behind them. Theo and David turned in time to see Hazan's hand dart out at a small flying creature. Hazan caught it, and the creature squealed pathetically in his hand.

"More light," Hazan said, and he said more words, which the lingochine couldn't translate. The young vassal lord's ready smile was gone.

The Khan reached up and touched a globe hanging from a beam. The globe started to glow.

"That's a magnesium flare in there," Theo said to David, squinting at the globe. "How the hell did he do that without burning his hand?"

"I don't think that's what we're supposed to be watching," David answered, gesturing uneasily at Hazan.

The younger man's face was a picture of concentration, his dark eyes narrow and fixed on the little creature he held. He opened his hand slowly until they could see a tiny gray-furred, winged creature struggling for freedom. Hazan had gripped its feet between his fingers. The wings stretched impressively for half a meter, flapping for balance as Hazan extended his arm full length. Then, while the creature struggled and Theo and David looked on, Hazan took the index finger of his other hand and carefully, gently, touched the animal's head. Instantly the creature collapsed in his hand.

Hazan looked at the two men, his face stern. Then he tossed the limp creature to David.

David caught it with a gasp. It was still warm, but completely lifeless.

"It's dead?" Theo said in a low, not quite steady voice.

"And we're standing here with a guy who can do that with one finger?"

David let the dead thing fall. "Where's Sindon?" he asked, panic and dread flooding him. He remembered starting to step toward Hazan, realized the Khan was no longer standing by the light. Then he didn't remember anything at all.

"David! David!"

Someone was calling his name and rudely shaking him. His body felt as if it were on fire. He tried to open his eyes and failed.

Water on his face. Too cold. He put an arm up to stop the flow.

"Come on, David. Wake up!"

He opened his eyes and tried to get his arms to steady his torso. Someone pulled him up; it was Brown Roberts. David blinked. He was outdoors, the sun already high in the sky. He could see Shuttle Two off to the left, but already he could tell he wasn't in camp.

"What happened?" David asked, his head reeling with pain.

"You tell me," Brown said.

"Sindon!" David cried out, trying to get to his feet. "Where's Sindon?"

"Shuttle One is on its way to her. We've got a fix on her and the others," Brown said, letting go of David. "How did you get here?"

David felt something stiff and furry under his hand. He gripped it and brought his hand up. It was the creature Hazan had killed. Angrily he cast it away. Then he looked around. They were in a little dell surrounded by scrubby-looking magtrees. Theo was only meters away, holding his head, staring at David. He seemed in pain. David's head still hurt, too, but not at all as if from a blow.

Theo got to his feet, looking unsteady. His face was ashen, his eyes red. He looked every bit as confused as David felt.

"Where's the tech?" Theo asked Brown. "Sindon. Where is she?"

"We have a reading on her locater-bracelet, T.T. Shuttle One is homing in, just like we did on you two." Brown handed a canteen to the CEO. "You gonna tell me what happened?"

Theo looked at David and shook his head. He drank from the

canteen and offered it to David. "I don't know what happened. Did you see anything?"

"No." David drank deeply. He must have been lying in the sun for hours. He was parched, and his skin felt sunburned. "The Khan must have been behind us."

"I never saw him move, did you?"

David stood up. "That little show Hazan put on held my attention pretty well."

Theo took the canteen back and drank some more. "They must have planned it. They knocked us out, and took us out here and dumped us. But why?"

"Sindon?" David suggested. He was frightened for her. "They knew we were looking for her."

"Sindon and three other women," Brown said. "Three of the concessioners. Didn't know they were missing until breakfast."

"Breakfast!" Theo barked at him. "What the hell took you until breakfast? You didn't follow up that call I made until breakfast?"

"In spite of your saying there was no problem, I did plan to follow up," Brown replied evenly. "But something stirred up the grassbears not long after you called. We had all we could do to rescue our people caught out in the meadow and get them into the perimeter. It wasn't until morning that we were certain there weren't more still hiding down by the lake."

"I don't like this," David said. "Why would the grassbears suddenly start roaming around at night? Why last night?"

"Deliberate confusion," Theo said, "during which Sindon's disappearance, and probably ours, too, wouldn't be noticed." He looked at Brown. "You said you had a fix on Sindon's locater-bracelet."

Brown nodded. "She's with the concession women, about ten klicks east, and they're not moving. But not to worry. You weren't moving either when we followed your signals in. I don't understand what's going on, but finding you two unharmed gives me some confidence in hoping they're all right, too."

"We were attacked," Theo said flatly. "The Khan and his man knocked us out. I don't know how, but they did. Who knows what they've done to those women, and who knows if they left them alone like they did us. Shuttle One may need help." He was already turning to go to the other shuttle.

Brown stared after the CEO for a second. "I've never seen him look so angry," he said.

"You weren't there," David said, starting to follow Theo to Shuttle Two. The three other security guards fell in behind them. "Did you bring any weapons?" David said over his shoulder to Brown.

"Just our sidearms," Brown told him, having to run a few steps to catch up to David and Theo. "You know the regs."

"We saw deadly force last night," David said to Theo. "If you need the proof, the body's still back there."

"I noticed that," Theo replied, still walking briskly. "A demonstration, wouldn't you say?"

"That's what I figured," David agreed. Panic engulfed him. It could only have been a deliberate reminder of their capacity to kill. But kill who? Sindon and these other women? Or David and Theo, if they continued to search for them?

"What are you talking about?" Brown wanted to know.

Theo stopped. "Go get it, Quarrels." His head jerked a command. "I just hope you didn't break any bones in the damn thing when you threw it. I wouldn't want anyone filing a protest when I order Brown to break out his arsenal."

"Not from me," David said sharply. There were a lot of things he could say to the CEO, but oddly, he had no desire to embarrass him in any way. He was, in fact, vaguely pleased that—at long last—the man was confronting the current problem without equivocation. He couldn't tell if it was just good business practice to express his concerns over missing personnel, or if it was because it was Sindon who was involved. Either way, David was grateful to be on the same side.

David retraced his steps until he found the dead animal. When he picked it up, he examined it closely for signs of a wound. There were none. He went back to the shuttle; the others were waiting for him, all looking grim.

"They found the signal from the bracelets right in the center of a lake," Theo said. He was leaning over Theresa Laurence, who'd given over the pilot's seat to Brown.

"Jesus!" David said. His knees were trembling now.

"Wait now, David," Brown said. "They've put two divers in

the water, and they're lifting the shuttle now to see if they can see . . . anything from above."

"Oh, God, no," David begged aloud. "Please don't let her be dead."

"Wouldn't they float?" Shuttle One's pilot asked through the comm-unit.

"Not if they're weighted down," Brown answered, his voice as mild as ever. But when he looked at David, there was something terrible in Brown's eyes.

"We have a good fix on the locater signals," co-pilot in Shuttle One announced. "We're hovering right over the divers—they came up for air. No signal, and they're diving again. Our turbulence is stirring up the surface too much to see anything below."

"Go high," Theresa said into her comm.

"Gotta stay close enough to . . . they just broke the surface again! One of them is holding—"

David held his breath and squeezed back tears.

"—it's the bracelets! They found the bracelets. Looks like someone just tied the hardware together and tossed them in the lake. No bodies. Just bracelets," Shuttle One's pilot said. "I don't think they're in there."

"Keep checking," Brown ordered.

David took a few deep breaths. Theo met his eyes for an instant. There was something approximating sympathy in the CEO's expression. Bitterly David wondered if it was his most practiced professional mien, reserved for rare moments when human understanding was supposed to be more important than the work. Or was it inspired by genuine gratitude that he'd not had time enough to become more involved himself and thus be the man devastated with fear for his lover's well-being?

Theo turned to the security chief. "We assume they're alive," he said to Brown as matter-of-factly as if he were stating a hypothesis gleaned form real data. His tone indicated that everyone was to treat it as if it were. "Now what?"

"We start searching, too," Brown said.

"We start now," Theo announced decisively. "We comb this area like it's never been combed. Shuttle One, as well." And when Brown frowned, he said more quietly, "If they're in that lake, it's all over for them anyhow. If they're not, two shuttles can cover the terrain around here more quickly than one."

David tried not to choke up as he listened to Theo's reasoning. He had to think every bit as clearly as the CEO. "Wait," he said. "Not here. At least, not only here." Everyone turned to look at him. Brown offered him a handkerchief, and David realized his face must be tear-stained. "Look," he said, wiping his cheeks with the back of his hand. He still had the dead animal in his hand. But even realizing it, he didn't let go. Holding it was somehow a reaffirmation of his resolve, a reminder of what he was dealing with. "If they're smart enough to know to get the bracelets off of them, they'd also be smart enough to use them to mislead us. We know they have another palace somewhere. It's not around here. We have to look for the Winter Palace."

The security chief nodded thoughtfully. "Where, then?"

"West, I think. In the canyonlands. That's what the abos say."

Brown looked questioningly at Theo, who shrugged. "He knows what the stakes are, and I think he has the best information. Let's go west."

Brown reached for the microphone and started to tell Shuttle One the plan.

"Brown, are we east of the shuttle camp?" Theo asked.

"Yes, T.T. About twenty klicks."

"Then we have to pass the camp to get to the search area," he said, frowning thoughtfully. "I think we ought to stop long enough for your people to arm themselves."

Brown looked at the dead creature in David's hand. "I could kill something like that one-handed," he said. "And I think you could, too."

"Not like Hazan did," Theo said. He shuddered visibly, his face almost purple with rage. "Not like that."

6.

WHEN RUKMANI KHAN and the rest of the vassal lords reached the canyon of the secret pool in the late afternoon, the pack animals and mounts were exhausted. Even Jabari, Kangra's fabled bannertail, heaved for breath between Rukmani Khan's knees. He was pleased to see a hasty camp already installed, indicating Kangra had arrived safely before them with Sindon and the three other women.

"Where is Sindon?" Rukmani Khan asked when Kangra presented himself.

Kangra gestured to the shadows at the far side of the secret pool. In the gathering darkness, the Khan could just make out the forms of four women lying on a pile of furs. "I persuaded them to rest," Kangra said.

Rukmani Khan slid down from Jabari's back. "We'll have to awaken them soon to make it to Dark Canyon before dawn," the Khan said, pausing to touch Jabari's snout before pulling the reins over the bannertail's head. The animal was sweating and breathing heavily.

"We should take time to tend the animals," Kangra said, running his hand lovingly down Jabari's sleek flanks. Tired as he was, Jabari rubbed his furry face against Kangra's shoulder.

"We've asked a lot, but we'll have to ask more. I've had Hazan backtracking; we're being pursued. If they knew where to look, they could have us in minutes. We'll be safer in the Dark Canyon where it's too narrow for their craft. At least, I think it's too narrow. It's difficult to know precisely what their capabilities are."

Kangra nodded and frowned. "They have ears that hear what we cannot," he said, his frown deepening in puzzlement.

"They might have already found us, if it hadn't been for your Sindon-woman. I didn't believe her at first."

"Believe what?"

"She said those bracelets they wear sing loudly enough for the shuttles to hear them. Yet the bracelets were completely silent to my ears. But she insisted on leaving them behind. I had a rider go back to find them and hide them elsewhere." Kangra shrugged sheepishly. "I didn't trust her. I thought perhaps she was leaving them as a marker for searchers to find, and I didn't tell her what I had ordered done. Then, just as we were about to step onto the trail down into the canyonlands, I chanced to look back and saw their shuttle rise. It flew east. The rider said he'd flung the bracelets in a lake to the east."

Rukmani Khan frowned, too. "And we deposited two men who came looking for Sindon well to the east of their camp, as well. It didn't seem to fool them for long. They came west in a circling pattern, searching for the slaves, I must presume." His eyes were drawn back to the sleeping women.

"Let me cool Jabari down for you," Kangra suggested, reaching for the reins.

Rukmani Khan touched Kangra's shoulder. His old friend preferred to deal with his prize bannertail personally, even to the boring task of walking the beast until he stopped heaving for breath. But the Khan was remiss in not offering to assume the task himself. "Thank you," he said. "Hope has done something to my sense of priorities."

Kangra laughed and led Jabari away.

Sindon and the other women were sleeping soundly. She was on the outer edge of the robes, and Rukmani Khan sat down beside her, hand on her head.

Gently, he disrupted the sleep patterns. She stirred and opened her eyes. "I should let you sleep," he said to her, "but I was worried about you. I keep thinking you'll change your mind."

She rubbed her eyes and looked at him in puzzlement.

"Well, you're not a slave and you don't want to have sex with me. I fear whatever it was that made you come will seem less compelling once you've had a chance to think it over."

She shook her head and reached for the translator. "What?" she asked, and it translated her query.

"Nothing," he replied, leaning back against a rock. "You

know, that translator is learning a lot, but I'm not convinced it really benefits us. You don't really learn our language when you talk through it."

Her answer was lost to the more compelling sound of paws scraping over rock as Hazan rode into the canyon. He reined up his bannertail; then, spying Jabari in sentinel stance with Kangra still holding the reins, he urged the beast on. Jabari dropped from the tripod stance to all fours when Hazan's bannertail whistled. Kangra greeted Hazan and the two talked a moment, then together they came to Rukmani Khan.

"We'd better move on now, milord," Hazan said breathlessly. "One of the shuttles is down in the canyons. If they follow the right trail . . ."

The animals were too tired to go on for long in their present condition, but the Khan could see Hazan already running his hands over his mount's legs, easing the acids out of the muscles. It was a false freshness, hastily achieved, but there was no help for it.

"Hazan, did you see any sign of Natarjan's caravan? Do we know if they're ahead of us?"

"No sign, milord. But Natarjan would use the eastern trail, for it's less demanding on the beasts. We should find him at the Dark Canyon, or signs that they passed before us."

"Groundfog might keep them from seeing us," Hazan ventured. "The currents are perfect."

"I'll send two men back to the river to start the mists," Kangra said, not even hesitating at the younger man's suggestion.

"All right, then," Rukmani Khan declared. "Let's prepare to move out." With that he turned his back on Hazan and Kangra. "Sindon," he said urgently. "Wake those women."

"What?" she asked.

Instead of trying to explain, he leaned over and shook the first woman. When he saw Sindon following his example with the other two, he turned to help his vassal lords with the animals.

7.

DAVID REMEMBERED FROM the imagery he had looked at while still on board *Pelican* that there were many levels of canyons in Xanthippe's Chasm. He had no idea how far down they'd come, for Theresa had simply nosed the craft through rock-littered hollows wherever the readouts said the stubby wings would clear. There was mist growing in the shallows, the swirling haze like cerecloth hanging from stunted trees, blanketing the stringy turf. Dark shadows were settling in gulches and niches, and the witchery of darkness made them feel as if the canyon walls were closing in on the shuttle.

"What I wouldn't do for just one groundcraft lifter," Brown said, sucking in his breath as Theresa edged the craft forward yet another few meters. The cold-jets were straining to keep the craft aloft by brute force, aerodynamics being nearly unnoticeable at such slow speeds.

"You and me both," Theresa said. She was trying to see the images being projected onto the screens and to make sense of the data being correlated on the readouts. The viewplates were almost useless in the mist and growing darkness. "This is it, you guys," she said finally. "We either pull up and out now, or I put her down the first opportunity I get and we stay here until morning. This bird wasn't made for this kind of work."

"Down," David said without hesitation.

"We'd be too easy a target in something this big, and there's no way to hide the ship," Brown argued. "Take it up."

"No, goddammit," David insisted. "We can search on foot during the night." He knew he sounded agitated, but the thought of discontinuing the search was more than he could

65

bear. They'd been searching since before noon, and neither shuttle's searches had turned up anything since the bracelets.

"Up," Brown directed, ignoring him.

Theresa started to pull the throttle back.

"Can you land on the top of this canyon wall?" Theo asked her. "It's a plateau."

Theresa shrugged. "Maybe." The shuttle started gaining altitude.

"Brown's right," Theo said. "We don't want to be down in these canyons all night, where they know their way around and we don't. But maybe we'll see or hear something from above." He shrank back in the seat, his chin in his hand. "Besides," he added, more for David than anyone else, "I don't want to go back without them either."

When she got the cumbersome shuttle above the mists, Theresa turned on her landing lights. There was a table of rock a few hundred meters above the canyon floor, one end of which was flat and green, like a tiny park. She angled the shuttle toward it, leveled, and took some readings from the instruments on the panel. "Does this look good?" she asked. "I don't think we'll get a second chance the way that mist is rising."

Everyone craned his neck to see through the viewplate. To the right of the shuttle and far above were cliffs and overhanging ledges. On the other side were more cliffs, the rocks broken and ragged.

"It looks about as good as any," Brown said.

David could tell the security chief was unhappy with the CEO's decision to stay.

The pilot eased the craft down; they could feel it touch ground unevenly, and when she backed off the throttle they came to rest at an angle.

David popped the hatch, jumped out, and walked briskly to the canyon rim. The soil was thin and easily dislodged by his feet, the vegetation sparse and brittle. The mists were thick and swirling below but he could tell it was too steep to climb, up or down. Agitated, he paced. Theo walked up behind him, hands in his pockets.

"We can set up infrared scanners and at least be watching these two canyons," Theo said. He seemed reluctant to be settling for so little, but resigned.

David looked at him. They'd said little to each other all day.

It was very peculiar to have gone from being at constant odds to some semblance of understanding through such a bizarre incident. Knowing Theo Tucker as well as he did, he didn't expect any kind of apology or even an expression of regret over his decision to accept the Khan's invitation. The CEO always said not to tell him you were sorry. Just show him. It seemed to David that Theo couldn't have set a better example under these circumstances. His doing so provoked as much gall as admiration.

"Come on," Theo said. "I'll help you carry the gear."

The mists continued rising, and by the time they had the scanners set up, a swirling whiteness had enveloped them. With the dampness came cold, but they could see the screens well enough. David was shivering.

"I'll take the first shift," Brown told him. "You go back to the shuttle and get warmed up."

"No," David said. "I don't need to be warm to watch a screen."

Brown Roberts seemed about to object, but Theo shook his head. "Let him have it his way," he said. Brown shrugged and walked back toward the shuttle. The CEO waited until Brown was gone, then said: "Displaying your personal involvement isn't . . ."

"I think you're *personally* responsible," David said through clenched teeth. He looked up at Theo.

The CEO looked disappointed. "I was beginning to think we'd overcome some of our differences today," he said.

"So you wanted to warn me about appearing too personally involved?" David said, incredulous. "Which one of us ordered her companionship for the evening without bothering to go through chain of command?"

Theo shook his head. "Forget it. Trying to talk to you is like trying to talk to the goddam canyon wall," he said, and turned to walk away.

For a moment, David watched him, the CEO's big shoulders bunched against the cold. Theo was going to give him some kind of warning, but about what? David could guess that his own intensity had already been noted by Theresa, Brown, and the security guards, but he couldn't imagine anyone faulting him for it. Besides, he couldn't stop it if he tried. He wondered if Theo Tucker had ever experienced anything like what he was feeling. Angrily, he turned back to the screen.

David sat shivering. The mists grew thicker and colder with each passing moment, but he didn't move. He sat staring at the gray, unmoving shapes of rock on the screen, praying to see Sindon there. Damn! After what he said to her last night, what would she say when she saw him next? David would want to hold her tightly—and pray as he might that the trauma of being kidnapped would make her feel likewise, he was also trying to prepare himself for one of her steely looks. That would be better than not seeing her at all or imagining why they'd kidnapped the women. The images he conjured up were not pleasant ones.

Later, when he had taken his eyes away from the screen just long enough to drink some hot broth Theresa had brought him, he heard her say, "What's that?"

He turned back to the screen so quickly, the scalding liquid spilled over his hand and he dropped the mug. He could see steady movement among the rocks on the floor of the canyon, people leading sticktails. One of the beasts stopped and stood on its hind legs, leaning heavily on its stiff tail while sniffing the air. Then it dropped back to all fours, and resumed walking.

"Get Brown," he hissed. "It's them."

There were ten animals and perhaps twelve people in view by the time Brown and Theo arrived. The security chief studied the screen, then glanced at his watch. "They're moving slowly, but if we let them get past us, they'll be long gone, much deeper into the canyons by morning. It would be dumb luck to find them again." He straightened. "But I don't know how we'd get down there to stop them now. We don't have the right equipment to try climbing down, and for sure Theresa can't take the shuttle down there." He was sorely disappointed.

"Do you have what you need to destroy all the animals?" Theo asked. "The right weapons? Sharpshooters?"

"Yes, but that would just alert them to our being here," Brown said. "They could still move pretty quickly on foot, even without the animals."

Theo nodded somberly and looked back at the screen. "Can you tell which of the people are ours?"

Staring at the screen, Brown shook his head.

"The men from the women, then?" Theo asked.

"Maybe. Why?"

"Shoot the men. Our people are all women."

For a moment Brown stared at Theo, his mouth agape, as if he didn't believe what he'd heard. But the deadly seriousness in Theo's eyes must have told him he'd heard correctly, and he looked as if he was seriously considering the suggestion.

"God, if we made a mistake . . ." David started to say.

"I'm asking the man if he can do it without making a mistake," Theo said, crossing his arms over his chest. "We've got an opportunity here we might never get again. Can we do something with it? Or are we going to let them walk on by with our people? We don't know where they're going or if we'll ever see them again if we don't act now."

"They could have killed us last night, but they didn't," David said hesitantly.

"No, but they sure wanted us to know they were capable of killing us, that it would have been easy to do. That's pretty hostile behavior. Or do you want to wait for more evidence, Quarrels? Maybe long enough for our people to disappear forever in those canyons?"

David bit his lip. "No," he said. The canyons were a hopeless maze, and they were not equipped to search them thoroughly. Now he looked at Brown, wondering if what Theo had proposed could be done.

Brown looked from David to Theo Tucker, and must have seen something in their faces. He turned to the scope without flinching. "The first one's a man," he said. "This one, and this one, too," he said, fingering the images on the infrared scope. He stood up and wiped his palms on his coveralls. "We'd have to count on our people running and hiding until morning. Risky."

"We've got a loudspeaker," David suggested, thinking quickly of how to minimize the danger to the women, "and we can tell them what the hell to do. Our people are the only ones who'll understand. The Khan's people don't understand the language."

Theo nodded. "Anyone have any better ideas?" he asked. And when no one spoke, he said, "Get the weapons and the loudspeakers."

Brown's people brought rifles and scopes from the shuttle,

and worked in three teams of two. They selected stances, carefully moving loose rocks from beneath their feet by picking them up and placing them elsewhere. The only sounds were the soft snicks of barrels snapping onto stock, scopes clicking into fittings. Someone put a microphone in David's hand. He flipped the rocker and heard the amplifier hum. Then the sharpshooters were ready, Brown among them. They whispered among themselves for a moment.

"There are twelve people walking," Brown said softly to Theo, who was standing directly behind him. "We can positively sex only three."

"As men? Or women?" Theo asked, his voice also low.

"Men," Brown replied.

"That's what we need," Theo said.

Brown breathed deeply, then nodded.

"Okay, here's the plan," Theo said. "David calls on the loudspeaker; Sindon, at least, may recognize his voice. Tell them . . . What the hell are we firing, anyhow, Brown?"

"Ballistic rifles," Brown said tersely. "They'll hear it."

"Okay. David, tell them to drop. After they hear the first volley of shots, you give them a five-count to run and hide. Brown, you take out those three men first, then all the animals. Our people must stay still after that five-count. If we see anyone moving, we shoot some more." Theo took another look at the scope. "Are your people ready, Brown?"

"We're ready," Brown said.

"Okay, Quarrels. You're on."

David started to raise the microphone, then hesitated. He was vaguely aware that he was sweating despite the cold. One last time he weighed the risk of making an error, of Sindon being shot, against losing her forever to the uncertain depths of the canyons. He looked again at the three figures in the scope and asked himself if he would be willing to fire the weapon himself if he possessed sufficient skill to know the bullet would reach the mark. They were men, he decided, and at last he raised the microphone to his lips.

"Sindon," he called, and his voice boomed through the canyon. "Sindon Liang and the women of Mahania Corporation, listen carefully. Drop where you are. Drop to the ground." Already he could see the people and animals in the column pulling up, no doubt startled by his voice. "Drop now."

"Fire!" Theo ordered, and David braced himself.

The firing was swift, the sounds of Brown's and his sharpshooters' rifles ripping through David. The three figures Brown had identified as men went down.

"Mahania people, run for the canyon walls. Drop on the count of five. One . . . Two . . . Three . . . Four . . . Five." Then the animals started falling as Brown and his people continued to fire. The rest of the people on the canyon floor were running, some for the walls.

"We're losing some of them," Brown said with a worried look at Theo. "They're taking cover behind the rocks."

"Good," Theo said. "That will be our people."

"Mahania people, freeze," David said frantically into the microphone. "Don't move around anymore. I repeat, Mahania people, don't move!"

"There's one moving right up the middle of the canyon toward where two people disappeared behind the rocks," Brown reported breathlessly.

"Mahania people, stop! We're going to shoot anyone who's moving."

The figure kept running. Brown licked his lips and looked at David. "Tell 'em one more time."

"Halt! We're going to shoot the moving person."

But the figure in the scope didn't halt. Brown took careful aim and fired again. The figure went down.

"That was a woman," David said, almost whispering.

Theo nodded acknowledgement. "But not one of ours. Ours would have stayed put."

David wanted to agree, but he was too frightened for Sindon. How could he have thought for a minute that Sindon would obey his voice? Suddenly overwhelmed by fear, he put the microphone down and stared at the infrared scope.

There was no more movement in the canyon; the infrared images cooled and dimmed. In silence, they waited. Even when dawn broke over the strangely carved rocks, and the mists began to thin, nothing moved.

They left a crew with the infrared on the rim of the canyon to watch. David, Theo, Brown, and three guards went with Theresa in the shuttle. She pulled away, entered the canyon in

a wide area, then moved cautiously to where the bodies lay.
She set the ship down before a dead sticktail.

"What's on the scan?" Theo asked.

"Nothing," Theresa answered. "Just what you see in the
visuals." She looked up helplessly.

No one had said anything, but inwardly they had all been
hoping that the four women would make their presence known
the moment the shuttle set down. They watched a whirlwind
scatter bits of dried vegetation and dust over the rocks and
bodies on the canyon floor.

"They can't know their captors are gone," Theo suggested
reasonably.

"We can't be certain they're gone either," Brown said as he
got ready to leave the ship and look around. "Shut the hatch
behind us." He gestured for the three guards to follow him.

Breathless, David watched them run from piles of broken
red rock to piles of broken gray rock, darting around each as if
they expected to find someone alive.

They came to the first body, which the security chief rolled
over with his boot.

"It's a kid," came the husky sound of Brown's voice through
the comlink. He was looking around, less cautiously now. He
walked to the next body, and the next, and the next. At the last
one, he stood with his rifle hanging loosely from his hand.
"Two boys," he said softly. "Fully bearded, but just boys. An
old man, and a girl." He looked back at the shuttle. "There's
no one else here."

"What have we done?" Theresa said.

David moved to the hatch and jumped out. He stared up at
the canyon walls, strata of red and brown, blue and black,
green and gray, all nearly horizontal and void of soil or
vegetation. "Sindon," he shouted. "Sindon?" But he knew
there was no one there to answer. He watched Theo Tucker
climb out of the hatch, his white hair blending with the last of
the mist. He stood with his hands in his pockets, shaking his
head.

8.

IN THE DARK Canyon, where the ancient sandstone walls were black instead of yellow, they had waited a second day for Natarjan and the caravan. Then Rukmani Khan had sent ten of the vassal lords to look for them. When, on the morning of the third day, he heard paw-scraping echoing in the canyon, bannertails walking at a slow and deliberate pace, the Khan felt fear grip his heart.

"What's wrong?" Sindon asked, seeing his face.

Without answering, he got up from the little meal they were sharing and started walking up the canyon to meet the riders. He was vaguely aware of Sindon's following him. The other vassal lords and servants had stopped all activity and stood staring at the canyon mouth, listening in silence to the death knell in the pacing of the bannertails' steps.

In a minute, the first four solemn riders guided their mounts into view; they carried what could only be the dead behind their saddles, each body rolled in a fur rug.

"Who?" Rukmani Khan asked when Kangra halted Jabari before him.

"Natarjan, Hari, Moti, and Sundari," he said. Kangra's face was ashen, his voice unsteady. "Pellets like the ones the hunters from the shuttles used on waterfowl. They didn't even spare the beasts."

Bringing up the rear, Hazan could be seen guiding a few frightened servants. "But they spared the servants?" the Khan asked.

Kangra dismounted. "The servants said they came with voices like thunder. The servants ran away. Moti, Hari, and

73

Natarjan fell immediately. Sundari went to help them, then she fell."

Tenderly, Kangra loosened the straps from the hide in which he'd rolled Sundari's body. Rukmani Khan helped him, and together they took her body down and laid it on the canyon floor. The first cool breeze of autumn sent a chill up Rukmani Khan's spine.

"They covered them with rocks," Kangra said, anguished.

"But why?" Rukmani Khan said. He was shocked. Not even the hunters that came in shuttles had harmed any of the people before, and they had not left the bodies of their prey to rot.

"It's our custom," Sindon said, almost whispering.

"To kill children?" the Khan said, horrified.

"No," she said. "I meant covering them with rocks." She was staring wide-eyed at the body pack, tears starting to roll down her cheeks.

"She has no right to cry for our dead," Kangra said huskily.

"Why did they kill our people?" Rukmani Khan asked, looking at Sindon. "Did you know this would happen?"

"No!" she said, horrified, and Rukmani Khan believed her.

Hazan came forth and dismounted. "We should press on," he said nervously.

"Is their shuttle looking for us again?" Rukmani Khan asked him.

"We should take revenge," Kangra said firmly before Hazan could answer. He looked at Sindon, then across the camp to where the three other women stood. His eyes were filled with hate.

Hazan stepped between Kangra and Sindon. "You can't take revenge on these women," he said.

"Why not?" Kangra asked sharply. "Four for four."

"No," Hazan said. "You're distraught. These women are not the enemy. They're refugees from slavery."

Rukmani Khan put his hand on Kangra's shoulder. "We must return our dead to the Winter Palace for a proper funeral. Then we will speak of revenge."

Kangra looked at him with dull eyes, but he nodded agreement. "Bring fresh animals."

• • •

Any joy the residents of the Winter Palace might have felt at seeing the caravan come through the portals in the canyon walls was quickly stilled at the recognition of body packs. The crying started with Sundari's grandfather, then no one could greet them with anything but tearful questions. Rukmani Khan had no reasonable explanation to offer. The wails and miserable sounds of mourning echoed off the courtyard walls.

"They were murdered," Kangra said bitterly. "They were murdered and their bodies defiled by shuttle slavers."

Rukmani Khan looked up and saw Gulnar watching him from her balcony. She wore the same gray robe she always wore when working in the gardens, and it seemed as if she brought the smell of loam into the courtyard with her. She pushed hair too long and unruly to be attractive behind her ears. She gave no sign of recognition to Rukmani Khan, waiting instead for him to greet her first. He did not do so, and she frowned. Her gaze went from Rukmani Khan to the bodies being taken from the pack animals, then finally came to rest on Sindon, who was walking beside the Khan's mount.

Hazan kicked his tired bannertail into motion when he saw Gulnar, and hurried to Rukmani Khan's side. "Milord," he said. "I plan to shelter the three women in my chambers. I could just as easily shelter four."

"Don't start pitying me now, Hazan. I do this with perfectly clear vision," the Khan said. "Sindon stays with me, in my chambers."

"Yes, milord," he said. Reluctantly, it seemed, he turned his mount and started toward the three other women.

Sindon had been watching him, and when she saw him leave with the other women, she looked up at Rukmani Khan questioningly.

"No," he said. "You're staying with me."

She looked nervous, though it was probably just due to the somber crowd. She hadn't noticed Gulnar.

"Don't be frightened, Sindon." Rukmani Khan stepped down from his bannertail and handed the reins to a waiting groom. He reached for Sindon's hand, but she refused, clutching her translator to her breast. "Come with me," he said, gesturing for her to follow across the yellow sandstone floor.

Sindon smiled tentatively and nodded.

Rukmani Khan looked up at the balcony and saw Gulnar watching them. Impassively, she turned and stepped into her rooms, closing the carved door behind her.

9.

THE MORNINGS WERE cool now with crisp breezes flowing into the glacier valley from the mountains. The tall magtrees on the north lateral moraine were tinged with pink and yellow. David Quarrels dragged himself from his bubble office to Shuttle Two, where he found Brown and Theresa waiting for him. He had started to climb aboard when he noticed Shuttle One was still battened down, and there was no sign of the other search crew.

"Why aren't they ready?" David asked, gesturing toward Shuttle One.

"One's making a haul to *Pelican* later this morning," Brown told him.

"They've been pulled off the search?"

"Come on, David," Theresa Laurence said, her hand on his shoulder. "We've been looking for seven days and haven't turned up anything. You knew it couldn't go on forever."

"Who ordered them off?" David demanded, shrugging off her hand. Neither Theresa nor Brown answered. "Never mind," David said. He jumped off the ramp and started toward Theo Tucker's office dome. He knew who had ordered a cutback in the search parties.

At the CEO's office, he pulled open the door without knocking. Theo sat on the edge of his bunk, pulling his coveralls up over his underwear. He didn't seem surprised to see David.

"Why'd you pull Shuttle One off the search?" David demanded, arms akimbo.

Theo stood up and put his arms through the long sleeves. "We haven't found a sign of them. I'm going to give Shuttle

77

Two another week, then I want all of you back on the job. We have work to do."

"Look, you can't give up," David pleaded, trying to sound reasonable. "We haven't checked out a tenth of the canyons in Xanthippe's Chasm. They could be anywhere."

"That's just the point," Theo said. "They could be anywhere." He turned to comb his hair in front of a mirror. David saw him watching from the corner of his eye. "You can't even get into most of those canyons with anything as big as a shuttle, and you haven't found a trace of them in the ones you have been in. The mists are so persistent that even if they were there, you wouldn't know it. We don't even *know* they're in the Chasm somewhere. We've given this search more than reasonable attention. Much more would be stupid."

"We can't stop looking," David insisted.

Theo put down the comb and turned around. He looked fresh after a night's sleep. "Quarrels, I'm as sorry as hell, but the search can't go on indefinitely. We have work that's being neglected, and I wouldn't hesitate to continue neglecting it if we'd found some clue as to what happened to them. But we don't have *anything* to go on. I've talked it over with Brown. . . ."

"Brown? Why not me? Have you found out how the other managers feel about this? Maybe the concessionaire has an opinion or two to give. He's lost *three* people."

"Brown's responsible for security. But actually I did discuss it with almost everyone on a one-to-one basis. People are coming to the conclusion that those women left voluntarily, that they don't want to be found."

Exasperated, David shook his head. "I've heard that, too. They're basing it on the concessioner women's complaints about the low pay and Hazan's telling them the Winter Palace was paved with gold. Concessioners jump like fleas from a dog when they smell more money, but that doesn't explain Sindon's disappearance. Being cheap is not one of Mahania's faults. Sindon was pretty well paid."

"There's more to it than that," Theo said.

"Damn right there is," David retorted angrily. "You know as well as I do their lives are in danger. We *know* what they can do."

"That's not what I meant." Theo tried to explain. "There's

all this talk about the sexual prowess of the Persuaders. Added to the women's reputations, I can't help speculating that they might have gone voluntarily. It would explain how they knew about the locater-bracelets, and why we weren't aware of any struggle taking place in the palace that night."

"Sexual prowess," David threw back scathingly. "That's about the dumbest thing you could have said."

Theo shrugged. "Even your reports from the abos mention it. There must be something to it. People are people, and they've been known to do strange things when sex is involved. The concessioners were professionals; they'd know if they found something special."

"Jesus Christ!" David said. "Do you hear what you're saying? That these women would give up everything they know for a good lay?"

"And gold," Theo reminded him. "Look, I don't like how it sounds either, but if you had been listening to the grapevine like I have this past week, you'd be considering it seriously, too. Rumors usually have some basis in fact, and the fact is the women in this outfit know something we men don't want to hear."

"You've actually heard Mahania women say these Persuaders are such fantastic lovers that four of our women couldn't live without them?"

Theo looked at him and nodded. "I had Chloe make some inquiries. It wasn't easy; they were afraid they'd get in trouble, especially after the women turned up missing. But two finally told me about it on the condition that I wouldn't reveal their names or put them on report. I won't say I understand it—they said they were persuaded to climax. . . ." He shook his head. "But I believed them when they said it was the most perfect . . ." He looked at David with troubled eyes.

"But they didn't run away with them just because of it," David said.

"No one asked them to. It seems our friend Hazan did ask the concessioners. Looking at their personnel files, it's not hard to figure out they had little to lose."

"But Sindon wouldn't go," David said stubbornly.

"Yeah, she was a puzzle for a while," Theo said, going over to his desk. He picked up a dispatch from a stack there and stared at it. "She was a puzzle for a while because there was you. Most women who are romantically involved don't keep looking. Then, last night, Ivan gave me this." He handed the dispatch to David.

David looked at it. It was a transfer request from Sindon, dated the night of her abduction.

"I must have been wrong about you two," Theo said, rocking back on his heels.

For a second, David didn't know what to say. He and Theo were alone, so maybe he could safely admit his relationship with Sindon and make Theo understand why he couldn't give up the search. On the other hand, maybe Theo was looking for a foolproof way of forcing him off Cestry Prime so that he could abandon the search without interference from David. There was, after all, a forest of trees to fell, and the shuttles were needed to carry them to *Pelican*.

David handed the transfer request back to Theo. "Missed your big chance, didn't you?" he said.

Theo's face darkened. He put the dispatch back on his desk. "One more week, Quarrels. Then you get back to your job. I need those abos."

"I'm going back to it today," David said. "Brown and Theresa can handle the last week of searching by themselves. Maybe I'll get more information from the abos, be able to tell them where to look." He felt as desperate as he sounded.

Theo nodded curtly. "That sounds reasonable. And while you're about it, see if you can get the abos to work. We need help with the chute."

"Sure, Theo," David said. He stared at Theo a moment, wondering if the CEO believed any part of what he'd said today. David found it hard to reconcile this Theo Tucker with the one who'd taken responsibility for shooting three children and an old man only seven days ago.

"What?" Theo asked, seeing David standing hesitantly in the doorway.

"Nothing," David replied, and he stepped out into the morning sunlight. He had started back to his office when he heard Ivan Mendal call to him.

"Hey, Quarrels!"

"What?" he said irritably. He stopped and waited for Ivan, but Ivan just stood there, looking thoughtfully at David. "What?" David said again.

"Just was thinking of asking you to help me decide about that transfer request," he said, then added quickly, "Assuming they find her, of course. I could turn it down."

David shook his head. "Look, maybe we can talk again after we find Sindon. Right now, I don't care what you think of the transfer request. You can't act on it until we find her."

"You don't want me to turn it down?"

David shrugged. How stupid could the man be? What did it matter now?

"What's the matter, Quarrels? You worried she'll expect too much from you now?"

David stepped over to Ivan. "What do you mean?"

Ivan smiled and shrugged. "You've talked to Theo. You know."

"You want to say that a bit more plainly, Ivan?" David said.

"Say what, Quarrels? That maybe she's ready for a change?" He still wore a smug smile.

David hesitated, but the smile was too much for him. He clenched his fist and swung, landing a full blow on Ivan's chin. Ivan went down hard, and David threw himself down on top of him, ready to strike again, but someone caught his arm from behind. Strong arms dragged him to his feet.

Ivan got up, rubbing his jaw warily.

"Was my answer plain enough for you, Ivan?" David asked as he was being dragged away.

Ivan didn't reply.

10.

THEY HAD PLACED the biers amid blossoms and sparkling foliage that grew beneath the transluscent laminae that Rukmani Khan and his vassal lords had bound in place when they were not much more than boys. It was in this very segment of the enormous greencavern that Natarjan had first given thanks to the Almighty Persuader for sparing the young Persuaders from yet another holocaust. It was here the first crops flourished with gentle persuasion while white winter blanketed the canyon rims and the lava continued to flow through the once green pools of the side canyon that had been home for a generation.

Each morning Rukmani Khan had faced the rising sun to determine the orientation for the day's work. Then he and the others who could persuade the molecules of yellow sandstone to align in roughly crystalline fashion bound a new lamina to yesterday's lamina. Behind him, others had already persuaded patches of gray-green lichen onto the rubble, which would be persuaded to form an abundance of organic acid to decompose the rock, which detritus, in turn, provided enough roothold for seed. At sunset Rukmani Khan and Gulnar Khan had knelt with Natarjan in the poor soil of their own making, their bodies in perfect heliocentric orientation to the last rays of the sun, to receive Natarjan's blessings for the daily laminae.

Now it was sunrise, and Rukmani Khan stood in the greencavern where he had received thousands of Natarjan's blessings. While he listened to acolytes recite the service for the return of the dead, he lifted his eyes to the crude ribs of laminae. The words echoed in a familiar pattern off the transluscent crystal. He could see the flaws in his work, the grainy inclusions of sand and mica, cracks that glittered in the sunlight, imperfections that couldn't be found in the other end of the greencavern, many kilometers distant. Even during the fervor of those first years in the Winter Palace, Rukmani Khan and the other Persuaders had learned to make the crystal faultless. But not the very first year. That year they were desperate just to survive.

The sunlight brightened the greencavern; the mourners tensed. Nearly a thousand had gathered in honor of the old priest and the three children, ready to witness the return of the dead to the Almighty Persuader. The women wore pale-colored shawls over their gay pantaloons, and the men let their blouses hang inside-out from their waists, their chests bare. In the first few hours after Kangra had arrived at the Winter Palace with the bodies, the entire clan had heard the details of the senseless deaths at the hands of the New People. Some few, Natarjan's acolytes and members of the children's families, had then retired to prepare the bodies for return at sunrise. The rest of the clan had offered food to the most skilled Persuaders so that their work would go swiftly at sunrise. Rukmani Khan had eaten all that he was offered. He had done this service before, but in Gulnar's Winter Palace, where members of the elder generation who would be expected to die could be numbered on the fingers of one hand, death was always a shock. They could say of Natarjan that he had lived long and well, and some did say it. But he was the last priest among them. The children, Sundari, Hari, and Moti, had not lived long and well. Rukmani Khan would do the service required of him, but not without suffering.

The acolytes' recitations sounded muffled, and Rukmani Khan realized they'd knelt before the biers in final homage. The sounds of a thousand slowly going to their knees was surprisingly soft, more the rustling of foliage than the sounds of people. The Khan saw Sindon in the back of the mourners; she had the white shawl he'd given her for the occasion draped over her head. Only a few strands of her riotous red hair were visible around her face, but they caught the sunlight like filaments of gold and kept his gaze for a moment. She had chosen not to kneel but to step back from the clanspeople, as if to observe.

The bereaved families began to cry again, knowing this

moment of homage was the final signal. Rukmani Khan joined
the other Persuaders who were filing through the blossoms to
the biers. When dozens had gathered around the old priest's
bier, Rukmani Khan placed his hands on Natarjan's head, and
the other Persuaders followed suit until the old priest was
covered by a shroud of hands. Beneath his fingers, Rukmani
Khan could barely discern the skull through sheaves of herbs
and scented buds. He glanced around the bier to be certain the
other Persuaders were ready. Kangra was on his right, Hazan
at the priest's feet. The younger lord's teeth were firmly
clamped over his lower lip, his face tense and grave. Rukmani
Khan was certain this was the first return Hazan had participated in and that he was nervous, perhaps even frightened. It
was one thing to overstep and make a fool of himself in some
matter of protocol; it was quite another to worry that he
wouldn't perform perfectly when a dead man's family was
depending on perfection. There was probably no use in telling
Hazan that performing this service for the dead never got
easier; the fear was the only thing that kept any of them from
lifting their hands too soon, the fear that something grisly
would remain for the loved ones to see.

"Dust to dust, ashes to ashes," Rukmani Khan intoned, and
he closed his eyes. Beneath his hands, the herbs shriveled and
the old man's skull gave way. Vapors rose and stung his nose
for a moment; it was an odor no amount of sweet-smelling
herbs could disguise. Rukmani Khan strained to finish; the
acrid smell grew stronger and sweat poured from him until
finally there was only dust beneath his fingers. The first
morning breezes coming through the louvers in the ribs of
laminae lifted the sharp smells away. Rukmani Khan took the
cloth the acolyte offered him, wiped his hands, and gave it to
Kangra, who also wiped his hands and passed the cloth on to
the Persuader next to him. Another acolyte carefully swept the
dust from the bier into a vessel, then took the cloth from the
last Persuader who had participated in the return, and stuffed
the cloth into the vessel. The acolyte handed the container to
Natarjan's sister, who cradled it in her lap.

At a nod from Timon, the senior acolyte, Rukmani Khan
moved on to the next corpse—Sundari's. Ridpath, Sundari's
grandfather, was already standing in the place of honor at the
corpse's head. Rukmani looked at him, expecting him to give

way, for he was too old to persuade flesh and bone to disintegrate with the precision required. The old man's face was wet with tears, his hands trembling, but he did not step aside. Timon took Ridpath's arm, intending to lead him away, but the old man shook him off.

"No one asks *this* of you, Ridpath," Timon said gently. "The Khan himself stands ready. . . ."

"I took her from her dead mother's womb," Ridpath said firmly, "and I will help her return to the Almighty Persuader."

"But . . ."

Rukmani Khan silenced the acolyte with a shake of his head. Though clearly troubled, the acolyte withdrew. Now Ridpath looked at Rukmani Khan, who understood that the old man did not want him to stand by. Quietly the Khan stepped back a pace and put his hands behind his back.

"Ashes to ashes," Ridpath said. "Dust to dust."

Vapors rose from the shroud of hands, but flames leaped up between Ridpath's fingers. Rukmani Khan sucked in his breath as the old man cried out, but the Khan kept his hands firmly clenched behind his back, resisting the temptation to leap into the work. The flames leaped higher before the old man could dampen them, but at last they were gone and vapors rose from where the skull had been.

Ridpath took the cloth from the senior acolyte. Rukmani Khan could see that Ridpath's palms and fingers were blistered and raw. The acolyte was horrified. But the old man's eyes were at peace, and Rukmani Khan knew he had been right to let Ridpath participate in the return. Finally, the vessel holding Sundari's ashes was handed to her grandfather, and he stood by the clean bier, head bowed while the other Persuaders moved on to Hari's bier.

Rukmani Khan resumed his place at the corpse's head and formed the shroud of hands with his fellow Persuaders. There were thirty of them, men and women alike, some kneeling, some standing, some reaching around their comrades to touch the corpse. "Ashes to ashes, dust to dust," Rukmani Khan intoned. Again he did what was required. The smell burned his nose; he tried not to flinch. Finally he was reaching for the cloth.

As he stepped over to Moti's corpse, he saw Gulnar kneeling in the first ring of mourners, staring at him. This was her

Winter Palace, but in this she could not officiate, for her skills of persuasion were inadequate. Her gaze was not gentle or accepting.

"Ashes to ashes, dust to dust," Rukmani Khan intoned once more. He could not shut out what he was doing. He could only do it as well as he knew how, swiftly, thoroughly.

He wiped his hands and looked at Gulnar. She was no longer watching him. Her eyes were on Sindon, who but for Gulnar's gaze had attracted little attention in the back of the crowd of mourners.

When the senior acolyte handed Moti's parents the vessel of ashes, the service was over. The crowd began filing past the empty biers to a simple pathway through the plantings that wound its way the full length of the greencavern. Most would descend through stairwells to their chambers below; some would return to their work farther along in the greencavern. Rukmani Khan saw Sindon on the stepping stones at the back of the crowd and realized she was staying back to wait for the clanspeople to reach the path. He stepped aside to wait, too, and found Ridpath at his elbow.

"Revenge, milord," Ridpath said simply. "I demand revenge."

"It's a long way to the Summer Palace," Rukmani Khan said. "You haven't made the journey in years."

"You forget yourself, Ridpath, as do you, Rukmani," he heard Gulnar's voice saying.

Rukmani Khan turned; he had not noticed his wife step up behind him. She wore a long white shawl over the gray dress, and her hair was plaited into a thick braid. As was her custom, she was without adornment of any kind. He had not remembered her needing any as a young woman. But her face was more pinched now and would have benefited from bangles at the ears, or flowers in the braid, to soften the effect of her stern-looking mouth.

"This is the Winter Palace," Gulnar said, "and it is I who will decide how to avenge the deaths of our people."

"Forgive me, Gulnar Khan," Ridpath said. "I meant no disrespect. I just assumed . . ."

"That the Khan who has full powers of persuasion would be the one to take revenge?" she asked, a single brow raised in challenge.

"It is the custom, one that *you* cannot fulfill," Ridpath replied. His fingers tightened on the vessel, and tears sprang to his eyes.

"It is the custom in the Winter Palace to question the old ways," Gulnar said acidly.

"You would leave their deaths unavenged?" Ridpath asked disbelievingly, his eyes like lumps of lapis on old leather.

"Of course not," Gulnar said. "But I certainly question that it's necessary to send Persuaders on a hazardous mission to take revenge when we can ill afford to risk any more lives."

"But life without honor, Gulnar Khan, is no life at all," Ridpath said. He shifted the vessel that contained the ashes of his granddaughter Sundari so that he could bear its weight with his forearms instead of with his burned hands.

"Life with your precious honor could mean the end of us all," Gulnar said sharply. Gulnar looked from Ridpath's hands to Rukmani, her eyes filled with unspoken accusations. The Khan felt he could say nothing in front of the old man. He knew they needed the full service of every Persuader in the Winter Palace, even the enfeebled ones like Ridpath. Everyone had made sacrifices to ensure survival since the last holocaust, but Gulnar didn't seem to understand that some prices were too high. Rukmani Khan was certain he'd been right to let the old man participate in his granddaughter's return, even though it had caused him grave injuries.

Ridpath's physical strength had been failing for years, but his wisdom was well-honed with frequent use. He looked from Khan to Khana, apparently well aware that there was little more good he could accomplish at this moment. Still, his sense of honor must have compelled his parting comment. "It was my right, Gulnar Khan. Even if it meant burning my hands, it was my right." With that he turned to hobble past the empty biers.

"You do not have the right to behave foolishly," Gulnar called shrilly after him. "Look at what you've done to your hands. They must be tended by a healer, and we will miss the persuasive powers of that healer in the greencaverns every moment he is with you."

"It was my right," the old man said once again. He stepped into the space the people filing along the pathway had made for him. None looked at Gulnar Khan or Rukmani Khan, although the closest could not have failed to hear Gulnar's words.

Gulnar started to shout something after him, but Rukmani Khan grabbed her arm and pulled her to the farthest bier. "Gulnar," he said sternly.

"I don't care if they're *his* hands. *We* need their use!" she said. "You had no right to let him participate."

"If I had refused him, it would have been more than he could bear," Rukmani Khan said patiently. "He would have chosen returning for himself, and there would have been no use of those hands ever again."

"And that would have been the ultimate disrespect for everyone. A coward's choice," she said angrily.

Rukmani Khan shook his head. She refused to understand. There was no reasoning with her on matters of honor; she'd defined them in her own way and allowed no others.

"Why can't you see that performing the sacrifice of self for the good of the clan is the greater honor?" Gulnar Khan asked him.

The Khan could remind her that he'd forgone reigning in a Summer Palace for all the days of his youth to ensure that the Winter Palace was a secure refuge for all the people. He had not moved one molecule of Summer Palace stone until there were ten kilometers of greencavern atop the Winter Palace, enough space to allow some sections to lie fallow and still plant enough sections to meet their present needs for grain and root crops. He understood that she did not trust the whims of nature on the rim of the Chasm, and he'd been helpless to comfort her when his first crop of magnuts failed and she bemoaned the loss of fruitful labor from all the male Persuaders who had gone with him. She did not understand the right Rukmani Khan and his vassal lords had to be independent of the Winter Palace, especially not when they came back every year to partake in its bounty.

He watched Gulnar pull her shawl tight across her breasts, her fingers fidgeting at the fringe. She didn't know what to say when he wouldn't fight with her.

At last, she shook her head. "I will think on the matter of revenge, but you must not do anything until I have decided."

He nodded. "I will wait to hear from you," he agreed.

She started to step past the biers, then stopped and turned to face him. "There was someone with you when you arrived," she said.

Rukmani Khan nodded. "A woman of the New People."

"Why have you brought her to the Winter Palace?"

He shrugged. "She pleases me," he said, fully knowing how hurtful hearing that would be to Gulnar.

"You couldn't even wait until Sundari's return to find someone else, could you? Or are you just now willing to be so open about it because Natarjan is no longer here to impose penance?"

Rukmani Khan stared at her a moment, wondering if she would believe him if he told her again he had not broken his vows of fidelity to her with either Sundari or Sindon. Probably not. "Release me, Gulnar. I do not relish the thought of a life of sin, even when there's no priest to condemn me."

"You condemn yourself," she said scathingly. She turned on her heel and walked quickly away. The file of people on the pathway stepped aside to let her pass.

Hazan broke through from the other side of the path. "Milord," he said, sounding breathless. "Look who follows Gulnar."

Kangra was striding along the stepping stones on the far side of the path where he must have been standing with Hazan.

"You were watching Ridpath during Sundari's return. I was watching Kangra. I saw him make an oath."

"To take revenge?"

"He didn't speak it, but given the circumstances, I assumed that was what he meant. I waited to talk to him."

"And he said?"

"*I* said I too had made such an oath."

Rukmani Khan stared at Hazan.

"We need only four, milord, and now we have four. Ridpath, Kangra, you, and I. We should act quickly."

Rukmani Khan shook his head. "It must be sanctioned by Gulnar Khan."

"I would forgo the Khana's blessings willingly."

"And do whatever penance she imposes when she finds out?"

Hazan nodded. "Milord, if we don't, it's only a matter of time before the question of Sindon's life and the lives of the three other women from the New People are posed as fair vengeance. Remember what Kangra said when we brought in the bodies. Give me the word and I'll go after him right now, before he has a chance to speak with Gulnar Khan."

Rukmani Khan watched the last of the mourners passing from sight, almost a thousand having walked without endangering the delicate plant materials, their careful steps the result of years of practice. Gulnar and Kangra were nowhere to be seen. Rukmani Khan shook his head. "This is the Winter Palace," he said. "Gulnar Khan rules."

"Didn't you see how she looked at Sindon?" Hazan asked. "Hasn't it occurred to you that she would welcome any suggestions that would do away with Sindon?"

"Yes, it has occurred to me," Rukmani Khan said. "But I too have taken an oath. My life before Sindon's, and then we'll see if Gulnar finds taking revenge at hand so satisfying."

"Milord!" Hazan was shocked. "We must not let it go that far. If we were to leave now, before she could forbid . . ."

"She has already forbidden me to go," Rukmani Khan said. "Don't underestimate Gulnar Khan."

"But your life . . ."

"And don't underestimate me, Hazan," the Khan said. "Sindon and the others are not proper objects of vengeance. It would take a priest's counsel to permit such a deviation. And there is no priest."

Hazan started to smile at the thought, but he quickly frowned. "But Gulnar Khan can confer priesthood."

"She can, but that will take time and she would consult me first. Meanwhile, I will remain in an obedient state, and so will you."

"Yes, milord," Hazan said. He looked up. "Sindon is coming. Are you going to tell her of the danger she's in?"

"She's in no danger until there is a priest. I don't intend to trouble her with things that may not come to pass."

Hazan nodded. "I will tell the others nothing. But I will do as you do when you make your oath known. My life before Bonnie's, Heidi's, and Melissa's."

Rukmani Khan smiled. "It must have been an exciting night," he said.

Hazan's face was still red when Sindon arrived. Her interest, however, was on the biers.

"Rukmani," she said. "Where . . . ? How . . . ?" She

gestured to the empty biers. The shawl had slipped from her head and sunbeams radiated bright red and gold from her hair. "You did . . . what?" She spoke directly, her pronunciation poor but understandable. The translating box was safely stored in a trunk in Rukmani Khan's chambers. While she couldn't communicate well without it, she was learning, and she'd understood that its talking during the service might be offensive. "I have questions," she said seriously.

"I can imagine that you do," Rukmani Khan replied. He took her hand in his. For a second he felt Sindon's palm against his, and for a second he felt good. But then she pulled her hand away, pretending a need to readjust the shawl over her head, but he knew she was staring at his hands. Though she demurred like a shy and inexperienced maiden, Rukmani Khan did not believe she objected to his touch for quite that reason. Nonplused, he reached over and slipped the shawl down to the nape of her neck, delighting at the way the sun glinted in the luxuriant red tresses. "Does she not have beautiful hair?" the Khan said to Hazan.

"Yes, indeed she does, milord," Hazan said, staring openly at Sindon.

"Are you smitten, too, Hazan?"

"Yes . . . I mean, no. I mean . . . I'd better go. I left my three friends alone."

He watched Hazan leave, then turned to find Sindon waiting for his attention. Her light eyes were strange to him, like water in a pool, always changing color with the time of day. Just now they seemed more blue than green, more troubled than not.

"I have questions," she repeated. Her eyes darted to his hands and quickly away, as if she were drawn to look at them.

"You always have questions, Sindon. But so far they're not the ones I want to hear."

11.

WHEN RUKMANI KHAN had been a youth, he fractured rock late into the night to make way for the greencavern, flashes of light illuminating his fingertips as he worked. These days, with so many practiced hands, the persuasion of the daily laminae was generally finished before the sun reached its zenith. They had added thirty-five laminae since the day of the funerals, leaving two hundred and fifty more to do until it was time to leave once again for the Summer Palace. The older men watched Hazan set the last crystal hexagon in place, melding it with his fingertips before climbing down the scaffolding. He stood back to admire his work. The Khana scorned adornment in the Winter Palace, but seemed content enough when something so practical as the panes in the laminae managed also to please the eye. Rukmani Khan squeezed the younger lord's bare shoulder to let him know he liked the crystal.

The wind outside in the Chasm was fierce today. It screamed through the louvers and billowed the tarpaulin that covered the end of the greencavern.

"Snow up on the rim, I'll vow," Kangra said to Rukmani Khan as he brushed grit from his arms.

The Khan nodded. It rarely snowed down in the Chasm, but a big storm on the rim kept the depths misty and cold. The greencavern, however, was always warm. Whatever sunlight penetrated the crystalline ribs was trapped, and the plantings thrived.

The tarpaulin reversed its billow with a resounding smack. Kangra frowned.

"We'd better put up the stays before we leave," he said. "If the wind gets worse, we could lose the tarpaulin before dawn."

Kangra had worked hard and faithfully at Rukmani Khan's side on the laminae, as was his duty. But they no longer spoke unless the work required it, more Kangra's choice than the Khan's. Sundari's death seemed to have embittered Kangra, and the Khan knew that only proper revenge would begin to soften the loss. It had done little good to tell Kangra he shared his grief, and that he, too, would not be satisfied without revenge, for then Kangra had asked his support to have a new priest named. Rukmani Khan had refused; Gulnar might name one without his consent, but he had no trouble foreseeing that the first matter the new priest would deal with was the question of the four women as suitable objects of revenge. Rukmani Khan knew the longer the question was delayed, the more time Kangra and the other Persuaders would have to get to know Sindon, Bonnie, Heidi, and Melissa as individuals, and once that happened, they were all less likely to want to see the women dead. He refused his support in naming a new priest by simply not going to Moon Council meetings, and could only be grateful that for some thus far unfathomable reason, Gulnar had not taken that step on her own. Kangra had said nothing when Rukmani Khan refused, but the Khan knew his old friend too well to believe he might desist in deference to his rank. Kangra would do what he believed he must do. And Rukmani Khan would keep his vows, too, though deep down he knew it might mean facing Kangra one day in mortal combat.

Hazan appeared from the shadows with three coils of rope draped over his bare chest. He handed one each to Rukmani Khan and Kangra, then slipped outside through a slit in the tarpaulin. Rukmani Khan and Kangra followed.

For a moment, the three stood looking out at the high-walled corridor rising above their own parapet. The walls of the Chasm were dark and dense, making Rukmani Khan feel trapped. He shuddered and turned away. He put his hands on a buttress of sandstone to persuade tiny, controlled fractures in the rock, a crazing pattern that followed his own handprint, deeper on the outside edge of his palm where he willed it to be so. Light emanated from around his fingers as fractures penetrated the rock, and he felt the rock crumble until there was a sturdy nub left in his palm to hold the bight of rope. Quickly he knotted the twine and walked to the other side of the rib to make another nub. In a moment, Hazan and Kangra came to help with the work.

They were not half-finished when Rukmani Khan noticed Sindon slip out of a slit in the tarp. She watched the three men work for a moment, then walked along the parapet, away from the greencavern entrance. The wind whipped the ends of her shawl. Rukmani Khan watched her for a moment, his eyes transfixed as the wind plastered the thin pantaloons against her thighs. She climbed up the rocks to the center of the parapet, being careful enough about where she placed her feet that the Khan was not unduly alarmed for her safety. Then he turned back to the work, wanting to finish it now and to be with Sindon.

When the work was finished, he looked around for Sindon. She was nowhere to be seen. He looked at Hazan and Kangra; Hazan shook his head to indicate he had not seen where she had gone. Kangra stared at him, his eyes dark, angry, and defiant.

"I will not tolerate even unspoken insolence where there is so much as one person to see it," Rukmani Khan said, feeling especially angry that Kangra had chosen a moment like this to display his anger.

"That's not what the people say," Kangra replied coldly. "They say you deliberately look away so that you do not have to see their disgust."

"And you have just tested me and found it was not so," Rukmani Khan returned.

Kangra shrugged slightly. "Not this time," he said.

Rukmani Khan frowned. "Kangra, you are trying my patience. Stop it at once."

Kangra stiffened, and for just a second the Khan thought he might challenge him here and now. Hazan must have thought so too, for he saw the younger lord wipe his hands on his dirty trousers, his body tense, like a coil ready to spring to the Khan's aid. If attacking Rukmani Khan had been Kangra's intention, it passed now. He clasped his hands behind him in a gesture of obedience, and looked at the Khan.

The Khan nodded slightly, then turned to go after Sindon again, but Kangra called out to him. He looked back.

"Rukmani Khan, I need your help," he said. "The Khana . . . hesitates to name a priest without your support."

"Gulnar sent you to tell me that?" Rukmani Khan asked.

"No. She will not say why she waits. But I have known both of you all your lives, and I know she hesitates because of you. She fears your reaction to her once she does it, that you would be lost to her forever."

"That has already happened," Rukmani Khan said, and he turned to leave again.

"Milord!"

Again the Khan stopped and turned back to look at Kangra.

"Milord, have you told that to Gulnar?"

Kangra stood with arms akimbo now, his face carefully devoid of expression, the passivity there worse than any accusation. Rukmani Khan stared at him a moment. "She could not help but know," he said finally.

But Kangra shook his head. "Milord, you have willingly served penance for your transgressions in the past. How could she know this might be different?"

Rukmani Khan deliberated a moment. "You are not here as Gulnar's agent, so you don't deserve an answer. But I will tell you that I believe my wife knows it is done between us. This is the Winter Palace, and I have enough presence of mind to know it is her choice on how to deal with that. Her silence is clear enough for me, and you will have to accept it, too, though I realize it does not suit your purpose to do so. You never would have asked a second time what I've already refused if her silence were not so meaningful. But be warned, Kangra. I'll brook no interference from you."

"I believe you're speaking sincerely, Rukmani," Kangra said softly. "You'll just have to believe that I am, too. You're wrong, Rukmani Khan." With his hands still on his hips, Kangra turned and walked back to the greencavern.

Rukmani Khan exchanged a troubled glance with Hazan. Then he turned yet again to find Sindon.

He started walking along the parapet. The wind was not so strong as to make someone lose purchase on the slabs of flat rock, but he knew Sindon was adventurous. She might have climbed down to a ledge, attracted by a bit of green or an odd-colored rock. A gust of wind could have a disastrous effect on someone clinging precariously to vertical rock.

But she had not gone over the side this time. She was sitting on a boulder, staring up at the ribbon of white clouds.

"Sindon," he said. "We're finished. We should go back inside."

Sindon looked up at him and smiled. "I heard them say there's a snowstorm up on the rim," she said.

Rukmani nodded. "It will be as high as a man's knees by tomorrow."

"But nothing down here? Not even a little snow?"

"None. It's a lot warmer down here in the Chasm. We'll feel fortunate if we get some rain."

Sindon looked disappointed. "I've never seen snow. I was rather looking forward to it."

For a second, he considered offering to take her to the rim to see the snow. But as quickly as the thought crossed his mind, he banished it in fear. She might not want to return with him if she went to the rim.

"Perhaps you would enjoy an outing to the river," he said instead. "Below, in the inner chasm."

"We'd go alone, I suppose," she said suspiciously.

Rukmani Khan shrugged. "We could go with Hazan to the side canyon where the bannertails winter. Today, if you like."

She nodded absently, her gaze on the brooding chasm that spread out before her.

"Ho, there you are," Hazan said, dropping lightly from the rock above.

There was no trace of the trouble with Kangra on his face. False cheer, perhaps, but Rukmani Khan appreciated it.

"Taking more . . . what do you call it? Careful recordings?"

"*Notes*, Hazan. The word is *notes*," she corrected.

Rukmani Khan had observed with some discomfort that Hazan enjoyed an easy rapport with Sindon. Hazan teased her about the "work" she said she was doing, would become involved in discussions with her, and when Rukmani Khan asked what it was all about, she would tell him that talking with Hazan *was* the "work" she was doing. Rukmani Khan found it all very mystifying, and her attention to Hazan somewhat disconcerting. He did not, however, attempt to put a stop to it, for she was usually in a lighthearted mood after talking with Hazan. And certainly Rukmani Khan had done nothing to cheer her.

"I'm glad you found the right word," Hazan said. "Now if you would just teach a few to Bonnie, Heidi, and Melissa."

"They have no incentive to learn, Hazan," she told him. "You give them what they want, and they have each other to talk to."

"You want me to withhold my body from them until they learn to speak properly?" Hazan asked, feigning shock.

"Don't be stupid. That isn't what they want from you," she replied.

"It isn't?" Hazan wondered, suddenly genuinely puzzled. He sat down beside her. "What else could they possibly want? I have one bannertail, but they've shown no interest in livestock. And I have a few good rugs. Beyond that, I have nothing."

"So it must be your good looks?" Sindon laughed. "The diamonds, Hazan. That's what they want."

"Those little crystals?" Hazan shook his head. "I'm not even very good at it. But it amuses them when I persuade the lumps of coal to crystallize."

"Diamonds are very valuable."

"You can't eat them," Hazan said.

"They're difficult to obtain where we come from, and they're beautiful to look at, and for some people, that makes them valuable."

Hazan nodded thoughtfully. "We've put them in floors sometimes, just for the sparkle. They do look nice."

"You put them in floors?"

"I can't imagine what else to do with them," Hazan said. "I can't persuade anything big enough to be of practical use, say as crystal for the laminae."

"You'd probably kill yourself if you did," she said, half-laughing. When Hazan seemed puzzled, she added, "When you fracture the coal, the methane dissociates and leaves pockets of hydrogen gas that could explode. There's a lot of energy around when you persuade things. One stray spark, and *poof*!"

"There are many things we do not let children persuade, but in these hands," Hazan said, holding his up in a gesture, "nothing explodes unless I want it to."

Sindon was staring at Hazan's hands, big hands that were rough and dirty, fingernails crusted with grit. Rukmani Khan had seen her stare at the Persuaders' hands many times, especially his own. She never ceased to be amazed that they were merely rough, not blistered and burned by the energy let loose in their work. She still could not quite comprehend that the hands were merely a catalyst for what was in the brain.

"If I made you some diamonds," Hazan ventured, lowering his hands to his lap, "what would you do with them?"

"I'd make a necklace," she said.

Hazan frowned. "It's almost impossible to string them. At least I can't make a hole in them without shattering the crystal. Can you, Rukmani Khan?"

Rukmani Khan's skills were greater than Hazan's, but he did not think he could make a hole in a diamond. He shook his head, ignoring a look from Hazan that he took to mean the younger man was trying to turn the conversation over to him. Hazan seemed to sense that all was not going as the Khan desired with Sindon, and although it was evident he wanted to help, Rukmani Khan desired no assistance.

"We don't string diamonds," Sindon explained. "First they're faceted to reflect the light, then they're set in tiny clamps. When they're clustered, perhaps into the shape of a flower and worn at the nape of the neck, even tiny ones are very eye-catching."

"It's easier to make a necklace of soapstone," Hazan offered. "And more colorful, too."

"Trust me, Hazan. They want the diamonds. If you keep giving them diamonds, they'll have enough in a year to buy out their promises and keep them comfortable for the rest of their lives."

"I had better slow down," Hazan said, smiling easily. "A year isn't very long."

"What do you mean, buy their promises?" Rukmani Khan asked her. He always listened carefully when Sindon talked about the New People's ways. Asking questions, however, sometimes silenced her easy talk, and she seemed to answer guardedly. When she hesitated now, he thought this was going to be one of those times. But finally she shrugged.

"*Promises* is probably the wrong word, but it's about as close as I can come. They promised their boss to provide certain services. They're not supposed to break their promise. They left before providing all the service they agreed to do."

"A vow," Rukmani Khan said. He put his foot on the slab of sandstone where she and Hazan were sitting, and he leaned on his knee. Her strange light eyes were thoughtful, her cheeks pink from the bite of wind.

"Not exactly a vow," Sindon said. "In exchange for services, their boss gives them, well, gold. But he had to give Mahania Corporation gold to bring them to Cestry Prime before they ever began performing the services. So, in a way they're both in his debt and they've broken their promises. They could restore their good favor with almost everyone if they had enough diamonds."

"I don't think I understand," Rukmani Khan said. "How can gold, or diamonds for that matter, make breaking a vow all right with anyone?"

It was very complicated. Sindon explained a system of councils, a big one and many smaller ones, with agreements among them that weighed deeds against gold, silver, diamonds, and other pretty things. These things in turn were weighed against things they could eat or use for shelter. It seemed that in Sindon's world they lacked the ability to understand simple trade. Rukmani Khan didn't pretend to understand it all, but one thing he was certain of when she finished her explanation: The three women had not been slaves at all. They were servants, bound in some manner that was difficult to analyze, and they were errant for having left before finishing whatever it was they'd vowed to do.

"Then they're in a state of sin," Rukmani Khan said, unable to keep from frowning. "And so are you."

"Well, yes and no. They're in debt, but they'd be allowed to repay the debt with something of value. As for me, I'm still fulfilling my agreement . . . sort of."

"With your notes?" Hazan asked uncertainly. Frequently Hazan humored Sindon about her "work," but just now Rukmani Khan was sure he was making a genuine effort to understand. Hazan knew the implications of his three female companions not being slaves, even if Sindon did not.

"Yes, with my notes."

"And I have not rescued slaves," Rukmani Khan said, "I've spirited away some disgruntled servants and left a hole in your hopeless system of promises and agreements." He sat down on the rock next to Sindon. "Hazan, what have you gotten me into?"

"Debt," the young man promptly replied. "But it sounds like one easily repaid. Sindon, how much gold would it take to satisfy the agreements?"

Sindon thought a moment, then gestured with her hands an amount that would fill a drinking gourd.

"I can persuade that much gold from the quartz in the White Canyon," Hazan said, flashing a reassuring smile at Rukmani Khan.

"I'd like to watch," Sindon said, quickly, eagerly.

"It's more my responsibility than yours," Rukmani Khan said to Hazan. And when the younger man just smiled and shrugged, Rukmani Khan looked at Sindon. Her eagerness was gone.

She shivered and pulled the shawl down around her knees. "Why aren't you two cold?" she asked.

"I'm too well fed," Hazan said easily. "I can keep myself warm easily in weather like this. It would take a really bad storm and maybe a bit of starvation not to be able to keep up. A good Persuader can even keep another person warm, very easily on a day like this." He stood up, stretching his arms above his head, flexing his body in the cool air. "I'm going back inside," he said, which Sindon took as a signal to get up. Gently Hazan pushed her back down. "Stay. Let Rukmani Khan show you how a Persuader can keep a second person warm. Take notes, Sindon." He laughed and jumped up to the rocks above.

Sindon, still shivering but amused by Hazan's departure, had shaken her head and started to stand up again. This time Rukmani Khan pulled her back. "Stay, Sindon," he said. "Take notes if you must, but stay."

"It's too cold," she protested.

He reached over, picked her up, and put her on his lap, cradling her against his chest. He put his hand on her cheek to warm her, and after a moment she rested her head against him, nestling into his warmth. It was, he knew, but a brief respite. She could not truly get warm if they continued to sit in the wind on this rock. He looked around, saw a good niche in the rock on the leeward side, and carried her there. He put her down, pinioning her with his weight and warmth. While she squirmed, he began to warm the rock beneath her with his forearms and hands. It took her a moment to realize he was busy with something other than her, but at last she began to feel the warmth radiating form the rock, and she stopped struggling. He reached under her buttocks and warmed the rock, then he sat up and warmed the rock under her legs.

"Better?" he asked.

And when she nodded, he lay down next to her to block most of the cool air, and to radiate some heat as well. She would be warmed now from both sides, comfortable. For a while they lay there, Sindon tightly clutching the ends of her shawl to her breasts, staring out past him at the sky. He looked at her face, her smooth skin, her silken hair lying in tangles around her head. At last she met his eyes, smiled, and reached up to touch his cheek.

"I've never had a cold-weather survival lesson quite like this," she said. "The technique is almost the same; we snuggle up somewhere to conserve body heat. But it never really got warm like this. Does it take much effort? How much will you have to eat to make up for what you've done for me?"

Rukmani Khan sighed. Her interminable questions. "It's easy to do," he said. "Exciting the molecules in the rock so that they give off heat is the most basic kind of persuasion. And I will have, perhaps, an extra bowl of broth if we stay out here very long."

"We can leave now," she offered.

"No," he said. He put his arms around her, and she tensed. "Just this once, don't be afraid of me."

"I can't help it," she said. "I know what you can do."

"How can you know?" he asked. "You've hardly let me touch you since the night we met."

"I remember," she said.

"I do too," he said. "I think you liked being touched." When she didn't reply, he leaned over to kiss her. She didn't respond, but neither did she resist. He slid his hands down her back to her buttocks, touching her quickly in a way most women liked. She started to squirm again, and he slipped his hand between her legs, forcing a few pleasant contractions before she could move away. It had the desired effect. She moaned, and he began kissing her deeply. Now she responded, her tongue probing his mouth, her pelvis thrust up against him.

Ordinarily he could not be ready so soon himself, but the unexpected delight of her beginning to climax against him made him throb with desire. He lifted her skirts and parted the fabric of his pants, thrust himself easily into her and let the pulsations of her muscles start his own rhythmic ecstasy.

Afterwards she lay with her cheek against his chest, silent but for trying to catch her breath. Her heart was still beating wildly, as was his own. Too soon, she sat up, backing away from him.

"Please don't do that," he said.

"Do what?"

"Move away like that. It was too brief as it was, but at least we should stay close and enjoy the sense of relaxation."

But she wouldn't come back. She crouched in the niche of rock, hugging her shawl, until Rukmani Khan finally was certain she would not come close to him again. He got up and held out his hand to her. She got up on her own, brushing past him to walk back toward the greencavern. She slipped through the slit in the tarpaulin ahead of him, and was gone from view by the time he followed her inside.

Disgruntled and sad, he went below to the pool to bathe. He soaked away the grime of his labors, but even the warmth of the water could not ease his tense muscles. She was an enigma. Sindon had slept on a pallet in the corner of his own private chambers, refusing his large and comfortable sleeping mat from the first night. She allowed him to provide her with food, and she talked endlessly, through the translator at first, and more recently without it. She was an exciting companion, curious and very intelligent, and she was even pleasant and friendly—unless he tried to touch her. Then her glance could be as frigid as Gulnar's. Unlike Gulnar's, it passed quickly.

Rukmani Khan had made Sindon clothes with his own hands. He had persuaded fibers of silk into seamless skirts and pantaloons, bound fibers of wool into squares of cloth, using craftsmanship he thought he had forgotten, and she had seemed both grateful and pleased. She came daily to see his work in the greencavern, obviously fascinated by the persuasive arts, yet she was not interested enough to touch him or to allow him to touch her long enough to learn the real meaning of persuasion. And while her behavior was similar to that of a coy woman, he was certain she was not a virginal woman nor was she attempting to portray one. He believed her aloofness had to do with her work, the work that was not work at all, but just some peculiar state of being. Were all these New People required to suspend all sense of self while they worked? He was trying to understand, but it made no sense to him.

He washed his clothes and started back to his chamber, then realized as he entered that Sindon was there and that his nakedness would offend her. He hurried past her and saw her glance around with a bewildered look on her face. But she could not really see him, just a blur of distorted light. She looked up, startled.

"I wish you wouldn't do that," she said. She was sitting on the servant's pallet she had taken over as her bed.

Rukmani Khan started to explain why he'd slipped in so quietly, then saw that she was crying. Somehow he knew her crying had nothing to do with the surprise of finding him there when she thought she was alone. It was because they had made love, and seeing her cry about it made him feel worse than he'd felt before. He sat down on the edge of his sleeping mat and put his head in his hands.

"Maybe it was wrong," he said quietly. He looked at her, and saw that her face was very pale. "Certainly it was too fast, but I know if I'd given you time to think about what I was doing, you would have stopped me. I thought you would be pleased when . . ."

"I *was* pleased," she admitted, suddenly. "And I am very frightened."

"I can see that," he said. "But I don't know why. It's not some sexual taboos you're breaking, unless you've some different ones from those three Hazan's been romping with every night."

She shook her head and used the corner of the bedcovers to wipe her face. "It was so *good*," she said. "I knew it would be, and it was."

"And that makes you afraid?"

She nodded. "Rukmani, I don't love you."

"And it's not supposed to be good with someone you don't love?"

She nodded solemnly.

"Then, perhaps you do love me. At least, more than you're willing to admit, and that's why you let me make love to you."

"I don't think so," she said.

"You didn't resist," he said.

"No. I wanted to make love. I've been thinking about it, about what you Persuaders can do. I thought about asking Hazan to show me."

"Hazan!"

"For my . . . notes," she said. "Rukmani Khan, I don't want to dictate notes about what we did today, but I must. I can't have stayed here with you all these days without coming to know you and to like you, at least a little. With Hazan, I could have made notes."

"Sindon, what are you saying? That you prefer Hazan?"

"No, I'm saying Hazan doesn't care for me the way you do, and I could have been more objective afterwards if I had done it with him."

He stared at her, amazed. "I don't think I like this work you say you are doing. I don't understand it, I don't want to be a part of it."

"I know you don't. But it's important to me, and I must do it."

"With Hazan?"

Sindon shook her head. She got up, went to the basin, and splashed some water on her face. She took his brush and started running it through her hair. "Rukmani Khan, I'm pregnant."

"You can tell so soon?" he said, wondering what else he did not know about women of the New People.

She smiled and shook her head. "It's someone else's child. I suspected I was pregnant before I came here."

"Is that why you resisted me? Did you think I might hurt the child while we were having sex?" He shook his head. "It takes a very skilled healer to make *that* kind of contraction. The babies cling like . . ." He stopped and stared at her. "There's someone else," he said at last. "A man of your own kind."

She stopped brushing her hair. For a moment she looked sad, but then she smiled and shook her head. "Obviously once there was someone else. No longer."

He wasn't certain she was telling the truth. "If you're not trying to tell me you're afraid of me for your unborn child's sake, and that there is not someone else you love so much that it would make our loving a travesty of some kind, what are you trying to say?"

"Just that you have to understand that I'm going to leave you some day. I have work to do here, but when it's done, I'm going to leave."

Rukmani Khan pondered for a moment. "You have explained your work to me before, and I find it very mysterious. Work should be something that makes you sweat, something difficult. But your work consists of nothing more difficult than learning how to speak our language, which you do very well. Yet I know you're bound to do this work, and bound in some unfathomable way by a pot of gold to do it. What I still don't understand is, is having sex a part of your work? Are you some kind of whore?"

Sindon laughed. "I think I found out for sure this afternoon that I am not. No, Rukmani Khan. Having sex is not a part of my work."

"Oh," he said.

"Don't look so disappointed."

Rukmani shrugged. "I was hoping that if sex was a part of your work, I could help you. I am, after all, far more experienced than Hazan."

She came over to sit beside him on the bed. "I don't want Hazan," she said. "I want you."

In all his days, he had never had a woman approach him so oddly. He had very little idea of why she'd been so hesitant before, or how she could go from crying only moments ago to touching his inner thigh now. But he decided it wouldn't be wise to ask. He turned to kiss her and found her lifting her lips to him, putting her arms around him, and touching him until he could feel himself throbbing. This time he moved slowly with her, letting her sense every delicious tremor, and for a change, he knew the joy of having a woman beneath him who was not blocking. He felt himself floating, almost as strongly as if she, too, were persuading his body to ecstasy. Whatever had made her hesitate before, it wasn't holding her back now. He couldn't help but wonder how free she would feel when he paid the gold for her and broke the final bond to her people.

12.

DAVID AWOKE BECAUSE the yurt was chilly and the coals under his hammock had died. For a moment he lay shivering. His muscles were stiff with cold and his head ached. He could hear the soft flapping of one of the scaled skins that had broken loose from its tether, but the wind died even as he came awake, and then he could hear only the soft snores of Enam and her extended family. He glanced at his watch and saw that it was nearly dawn. In moments, the camp whistle would sound to awaken the abos, after which there would be no peace. He decided to get up now while he could savor a few moments of quiet, and take a few breaths of fresh air to clear the pain in his head. After carefully shaking out his boots, he put them on and stole outside.

Snow had fallen again last night, covering the muddy scar on the northern slope of magtrees, at least for a while. Most of Mahania's people would be in the concessionaire's two-decker eating breakfast, but in a few hours when they started bringing logs down the chute, the scar on the mountainside would look like giants had spilled and spattered blue ink. In just two months, the Mahania settlement had begun moving logs down from the slopes by using the irrigation canals as a log chute. They selected trees of the proper diameter, felled and limbed them, then buck-sawed them into logs, which were dragged to the chute for a serpentine ride to the little mill in the valley below. The logs were stored in the lake until needed, then hoisted into the mill. From the mill, boards were conveyed over a trestle to a kiln or into the yards for stacking and seasoning, and from there the boards were loaded into shipping containers, which were in turn shuttled to *Pelican.* The hold would be full in just a few more weeks, and *Pelican* would leave, and David could breathe easily again for a while. There would be no other transportation available until *Pelican* returned, no means for Theo Tucker to send him off-world. Until then, he intended to be a model employee. Hitting Ivan Mendal had put him on probation. It wouldn't take much of a transgression to earn a swift dismissal, with return to corporate headquarters on the first available transportation.

He walked down to the lake, following the path the abos used. The lake was frozen along the banks; he lifted a big rock and threw it through the ice. He could see mounds of white on the ice around his hole, snow-covered rocks the abos had thrown that didn't go through. The abos were too impatient to melt ice or snow over a fire, and he knew his next task was to get them a reliable source of water before the lake ice was so thick they couldn't possibly break it. The activity of getting the pipes laid was sure to amuse the abos, which might help keep them from thinking of leaving for a while. He leaned over to fill his canteen.

He had been living with the aborigines since the first snowfall almost a month ago when he realized they were packing their belongings and preparing to depart for warmer climates farther south in the lower altitudes. Company-issue boots and warm coveralls had been lure enough for the thirty men who had started working on the chutes, "being with the foreigners," as they called it. The men were delighted with their new clothes, eager to preen and to talk about the pockets they were finding, and at first they found the women and children eager audiences. But the cold weather continued for several days, and those without boots began preparing to leave again, and when the boot-owning abos discovered that, they too began to prepare to leave. He'd prevented their departure once again with issues of boots for everyone, and then by moving in with them. David and his belongings were *the* topic of conversation among the women and old men, giving them something of equal value to talk about when the men came home from the mill. He had come to understand that conversation was the abos' favorite form of entertainment, second only to story-chants and doing-songs, both of which had been enriched by the foreigners. It was challenging to find something each day for them to sing about; living with them made it easier. More importantly, it was easier to stay out of trouble than it had been in the compound, where he was certain he'd been under constant scrutiny.

The whistle blew, and David stood up to look across the meadow where the morning browsers were grazing under the trestlework that would support the new flume by next summer. Most just picked up their heads when the whistle sounded, but the grassbears roared their discontent and reared up on their hind legs. With the snow as background, they looked like trees in the distance, their red-brown coats rough as splitting bark. A few of the tiny flying mammals that had taken flight began settling again to work the droppings of the larger beasts. The number of animals that came into the glacier meadow was quite small now compared to the first few weeks. David wasn't certain if they'd left because of the season change, or if the growing community in the meadow was disturbing them.

He heard someone humming the Getting Water song on the rocks behind him, and turned to see the boy Akili coming down the path, making a great to-do of scuffling along in his new boots. He walked past David to the water hole in the ice, and began to fill his crockery. Since no greeting was customary among the abos, David capped his canteen and was about to start back to the yurts when Akili stopped his song and pulled on David's pants leg.

"This crockery is not persuaded. This crockery is persuaded. But Persuaders did not persuade this crockery," Akili said, pointing to David's canteen. Akili wanted to know who made the canteen.

The abos had asked this question before. The capping mechanism fascinated them, apparently because it fit over the neck of the canteen instead of into it and also had a cup over the cap. "Making it was made, making it was not made," David replied using the abo words for "I don't know." The lingochine was back in the yurt, and he continued to use it most of the time. But he was picking up the abo language, and could say many simple phrases now without bringing gales of laughter from the abos.

"Persuaders not give. Akili not give." The boy was puzzled. He had a difficult time understanding how one could come to have possessions not made by one's own hands, or the hands of a friend. Even the Persuaders knew who made something, though it was evident the Persuaders' methods baffled them, too. His crockery filled, Akili stood up to follow David.

"Giving, he did not give. We two *traded*," David said, using the standard word because there was no concept for trading or buying in the Aboriginese language.

The boy looked at him, his protruding eyes especially wide. "You two *traded*," Akili repeated, the bewilderment still in his voice.

As his elders had done, Akili parroted the word, and David followed through one more time in hopes of achieving with Akili what he had failed to achieve with his parents. He held out the canteen to Akili, and reached for the crockery under the boy's arm. "Trade," David said. "We two trade crockery."

The blue-skinned fingers of Akili's hand wrapped themselves around the grip of the canteen but he did not loosen his hold on the crockery. David, having lost three canteens to unsuccessful trades before, knew he needed to keep his hands on the canteen until he had possession of the crude crockery. At least that was to be the first step. Akili tried to wrest the canteen away, but couldn't. Anger flashed in his eyes.

"We two *trade*," David said firmly. "David gives Akili this crockery. Akili gives David that crockery."

"Will you give me the crockery?" Akili said, eyes wild with anger now. Since there wasn't any true interrogative form in Aboriginese, he could just as easily been saying, "You will give me the crockery!"

David had tried saying *yes* on previous occasions, which had resulted in the loss of the canteens and getting nothing in return, no matter how much explanation he added after saying *yes*. Saying *no*, especially now after having lost a few to the abos, brought sulking and retaliation in the form of teasing. "*Trade*," he said again, this time pulling the crockery from Akili's grasp. When it was securely in his hands, he let go of the canteen.

Akili was pleased to find the canteen in his hands; he popped the outer cap and pried up the inner one, and even took a quick drink. Then he carefully replaced the caps, obviously demonstrating to David that he understood the mechanisms. "We two can drink from this crockery," he said smugly, which statement David knew had nothing to do with sharing the contents but referred to Akili's knowing how to open and close the canteen, just like David.

"We two can drink," David agreed with a smile.

Akili, his lips still curled back over his snout in a smile, reached for the crockery in David's hands. When David didn't let go, Akili pulled, and when he still didn't let go, Akili hit him with his fist and started shouting. The words were coming too quickly for David to understand, but in moments there was a ring of children around him, most of them barefoot in the snow. Plainly Akili wanted his crockery back, and had called the other children for help.

"We traded," David said, trying to fend off another barrage of blows from Akili. The boy was too small to injure David, but the pinches and kicks hurt. Still, he didn't want to give back the crockery to Akili; somehow he had to communicate the concept of trade, and after so many failures with the adults, his last resort was to try with the children. He felt the same frustration he'd known with the parents. When David realized the children were picking up rocks, he knew exactly what they intended to do with them. Gritting his teeth, he smacked Akili across the snout with the back of his hand. The boy fell back, and the other children squealed and ran, certain they'd be next to be hit. Akili scrambled to his feet and ran after his friends. David felt only small satisfaction in realizing that Akili took the canteen, and he still had the boy's crockery.

Warily, David glanced across the meadow at the compound. There was no way of knowing where Brown had his telescopic recording equipment pointed. He could only hope it was not here, on him. He didn't think Theo Tucker would appreciate how desperate David was to succeed in his assigned task of keeping the abos working in the lumber camp.

Back in the yurt, there was an unusual silence when he stepped in. The men sat or lay in their hammocks, glowering at him. Only Enam seemed to be behaving normally, sitting cross-legged in her hammock, chanting a two-toned wordless chant as she pushed some twigs into her coals with a long stick.

David was putting the crockery under his hammock with his other things when his comm-unit tickled his hip. He reached back and unhooked the device.

"Quarrels, here," he said into the comm.

"Come to the observation tower, David," Brown's voice

said. "There's some image recordings I'd like to review with you and Theo."

"Shit!"

"What?"

"I'll be right there," David said. He snapped off the communicator and placed it back on his belt hook. Across the yurt, he saw that Akili had joined his mother by her fire. The boy was poking at the squirrel-bellies, which the abos cooked, stomach contents and all, in the coals. When he saw David looking at him, he made a rude noise. David felt an incredible urge to hit him again, but he just shook his head and said, "We two *traded* crockery." He draped his scarf over the crockery Akili had given him, in hopes that it would demonstrate even more positive ownership. Then he pulled on his coat and left the yurt. He threaded his way through the rocks, past the huge concrete foundation that would eventually be the floor of the big mill. He wondered if the builders would have the framework up before the weather really got bad.

Once across the meadow and inside the main compound, he walked past a cluster of kiosks and two-deckers that housed the pump house, foundry, cookhouse, and common house. There were skeletons of frames intended for cabins that would house the workers' families that would arrive next summer and a big structure that would be the main house and store. They wouldn't be finished until *Pelican*'s holds were filled and then a second shipload of lumber was packed and ready. If the families arrived before they were completed, they'd camp in kiosks, just as the workers had at first.

At the watchtower, David climbed the ladder to the deck from which Brown's security people had an excellent view of the entire compound. He opened the door and went inside. The heat from an open fire blasted him. They were burning sawdust, a convenient and very hot fuel.

David took off his coat. "What do you want?" he asked Brown.

"We'll wait till Theo gets here to look at the imagery," Brown responded easily.

David could almost feel the shuttle taking off under him, even though he was sitting in Brown's observation tower.

"I know what you're going to show us," David said, feeling very uncomfortable.

"Thought you might," Brown said, his tone still even.

"Adults hit the children all the time," David tried to explain. "It's part of the communication system. How hard they hit tells the kid if the adult is merely annoyed, or really angry. In this instance, my hitting Akili was no different than talking to him."

Brown swung around in his chair, his hands folded neatly across his lap. "You hit the abo boy? Are you mad?"

"You don't understand," David protested. "I was trying to do my job. I figured if I couldn't communicate the idea of trade with the adults, maybe I could get through to the kids who aren't so set in their ways. Hitting Akili was the only way left to convince him that he couldn't have the crockery back once he traded it for the canteen."

Brown frowned and shook his head. "At least you had enough sense to report it right away, but I'm . . ."

"Me report it? You mean . . ." David had enough presence of mind to stop talking. He leaned back on the foam stool, feeling momentarily dumbstruck. What rotten luck he hadn't been struck that way when he stepped through the door. Finally he sighed, and said with as much calm as he could manage, "You called this meeting; guess I should let you tell me what it's all about."

"Time enough for that when Theo gets here. Meanwhile, I'm hard pressed to understand why a grown man feels justified in hitting a small boy."

"Akili is not a small boy. I mean, let's make it clear that he's an adolescent, not a toddler. And in hitting him, I really was only doing my job," David said, and when Brown raised his eyebrows doubtfully, David resigned himself to explaining the circumstances fully. He could tell he had Brown Robert's complete attention, but it was very difficult to tell from the passive face what Brown's reaction was to the story.

"So what happened after you went back to the yurt?"

"I put the crockery with my things so everyone would clearly understand I considered it mine."

"You think the kid told them what happened?"

"I'm sure he did. The adults always chatter when they're awake, but this morning they were quiet. The men frowned at me and sucked their teeth, but none challenged me or tried to take the crockery back."

"From your reports, that's how they treat their own people when they're angry at them. You think it was smart to make them angry?"

"Maybe not, but I had to try something different."

Brown shrugged. "I guess if we require you to live with them to find out everything we need to know to keep them working, you're going to have to understand and participate in their customs and language, too."

David sighed in relief.

"You were wise to report the incident. If one of the abos had talked about it, people would assume you'd lost your temper again."

"Come on, Brown. Ivan had it coming. This was nothing like when I hit Ivan."

"When violence always involves the same person, it begins to become apparent, whether that person just attracts it or starts it. Frankly, either pattern is fatal to a bright career. If I were you, I would avoid *any* situations where you have to explain your actions, even among the abos."

He hated Brown when he patronized him with advice that the stupidest person would know without being told. And he hated Brown for focusing on one tiny part of the picture, as if the rest didn't exist. Usually such feelings frustrated him to silence, but this time he nodded dispiritedly. "I know that would be the wisest, considering my probation, but is it really the best for Mahania Corp.?" And when Brown gave him a puzzled look, he went on. "Theo needs those abos to get the work done. They may not be the greatest workers in the world, but aside from our people, they're the only ones. I can't figure out how to make them want to stay in the valley. So far the only thing keeping them here is my providing them with one form of entertainment after the other. Really! That's what the new clothes are—entertainment. Something they can talk about. Their whole culture seems based on nothing more than obsessions with meddling in each other's affairs, and more currently in ours. When they have nothing to do, they go watch the foreigners—us. They find everything from the way we dress to our incomprehensible preoccupation with cutting down the magtrees very entertaining. But now that the hides on the yurts have to stay down, it cuts off the flow of easy conversation, and I can tell they're getting bored with the whole thing. I have to find some way to make them want to stay."

"I heard Chloe say you haven't provided them with many of the gadgets we brought. You know, to tempt them."

"They're more interested in meat than gadgets," David said. "I tried showing them holostories, but of course the stories were incomprehensible to them, even when I tried playing them through the lingochine. Most of them left before it was finished, said they had headaches. Playing back their own voices amused them for a while, but they weren't dumbfounded or anything. I just can't get through to them."

"You have to keep trying, David," Brown said sincerely. "You'll find it, whatever it is."

Theo Tucker opened the door and let in a blast of icy air. "Damn, it's cold out there," he said, tossing his gloves onto the desk. He sat down on the chair next to Brown. "Now, what's this about our having a night visitor?"

Brown nodded and turned to flip the image screen behind him; it glowed and revealed the panorama as seen from the tower in infrared. "This is from last night," he said, watching the screen. At first there was nothing unusual, just the ordinary line of trees, wavy warmth from some burrowing animals, and a carnivore slinking along the edge of the hoist by the lake. Then Brown pointed with a finger to a warm speck at the corner of the image, a speck that grew larger as it approached the compound. It took a minute before it became large enough for them to make out the form of a man mounted on a sticktail.

"I'm going to speed this up," Brown said, flipping a switch on the control pod with his thumb. "He walked around the entire compound, followed the log chute for a little ways, then turned to the abo village. He got off the sticktail, walked over to the yurt, and . . ."

"Jesus," David said, feeling the hair on the back of his head prickle. "He went inside Enam's yurt."

"Exactly," Brown said. "We don't know precisely when he came out, for the scan passes the yurt pan only five minutes later. In another hour, we pick him up again, heading around the lake to the Winter Palace. If his pace was steady, and we think it was because the sticktail seemed tired compared to the recording we have of the sticktail Kangra raced around the compound that time, we estimate he was in the yurt at least an hour."

Now both Theo and Brown were looking at David expectantly. David shrugged.

"I never saw him," David said. "I slept through until dawn." He remembered how cold he'd been when he'd awakened, and shivered.

"Here's the best enhancement we could get of his face," Brown said. "Do either of you recognize him?"

The resolution was terrible, but the features seemed familiar.

"Hazan," Theo said with certainty.

"We've got to follow him," David said, leaping to his feet. "He'll have left tracks in the snow. We can follow him to Sindon."

"Sit down, David," Brown snapped. "I have two foot patrols trying to follow what little trace there is of his passing after the snow."

"The shuttle! We might still pick him up from the air; he'd be easy to spot against the snow."

"He's down in the Chasm by now," Brown said, "and there isn't any snow there. But it sure is misty. Even so, Theresa's been up in One since before dawn. She's doing what she can, even in the mist."

Frowning, David sat down. He hadn't heard the shuttle take off, though he usually did, even in the yurt.

"What do you suppose Hazan wanted?" Theo asked.

"Seemed to be reconnoitering," Brown replied. "But I was hoping David could tell us more about his visit in the yurt."

David shook his head. "All I can tell you is that I usually wake up during the night to bank the coals under my hammock, but not last night. When I woke this morning, I had one hell of a headache."

"Guess we both know why," Theo said, actually sounding almost sympathetic. "I think you'd better move back to the compound, Quarrels."

"I would, but I really can't be as effective with the abos from here," he said. "And Hazan didn't kill me, so I think I'll stay in the yurt. Maybe I should take a gun with me."

The security chief blanched. "No guns. Only the security force can carry them. If you were to make a mistake . . ."

"What kind of mistake?" David asked belligerently.

Theo half-grinned, but it was pained. "I'm not going to arm a man with your reputation, Quarrels. Move back to the compound if you're afraid."

"I'll think about it."

Theo gave a curt nod, picked up his gloves, and got to his feet. "Keep me posted," he advised Brown. "If your patrols find the girl or the Winter Palace, I want to be the first to know." As he reached for the door, he hesitated. "One more thing, Quarrels. Can you do something about getting the abos to work on time? I mean, I had good engineers spend hours putting up a whistle, and the problem still isn't solved."

"It's all I can do to get them there at all," David said.

"Yeah, well, work on it, would you please?"

"Yessir," he replied, though he hadn't any notion of what he would do. If he didn't get through to the abos soon, the novelty of the equipment in the mill was going to wear off and there would be no stopping them when they wanted to leave. He wondered if any of them had gone to work at all this morning, for he hadn't been there to cajole them into playing at the mill. And of course, there was the matter of their sullen looks this morning.

"Don't worry. If the patrols find anything, I'll call you, too," Brown assured him now that Theo was gone.

David heard him, but he was troubled, and didn't answer.

"Now, don't do anything you're going to regret, David," Brown cautioned in a patronizing voice.

"What? Oh, no. I'm fine. I was just thinking about the abo men being so silent when I came back in. Maybe it had nothing to do with Akili's crockery. Maybe they had headaches, too."

"You think this Hazan did . . . *it* to them, too?" He frowned. "There are a dozen adults besides you in Enam's yurt. He would have had to go from person to person, touching each, and being silent enough while walking about in the darkness not to waken anyone. Then he stays for an hour. Why? Not a bad way to have a leisurely look around."

"Enam didn't look like she had a headache," David said. "In fact, I'd say she was pretty chipper by comparison. I think I'm

going to go talk to Enam about how well she slept last night.
You'll call if there's any news?"

"Right away," Brown assured him. "And David . . ."

He paused with his hand on the door latch.

"Let me know how the crockery turns out, too."

13.

IN THE CANYONS of Blue-green Waters, Rukmani Khan stopped his work and looked up expectantly when the bannertail Jabari, who was tethered to a stunted tree below the Khan, woofed and rose to tripod stance on his hind legs and tail. For a moment Rukmani Khan saw nothing that might have caught the bannertail's attention, but from habit he continued scanning the escarpment. Then he heard the whistling of a bannertail at the neck of the canyon, and a pack of the animals scurried into view, the front-runners pausing to rise in tripod stance to sniff the cool breeze. As Jabari smelled the bannertails of his pack, he fell into a frenzy of scent-marking, backing his hindquarters against rocks and shrubs, dragging his anal pouch along the grass. Other bannertails from Jabari's little band raced out of the shadows to hug their tethered comrade while a few young males took up the scent-marking. While the tethered bannertail returned the hugs and fell into grooming rituals, Rukmani Khan turned back to pulling threads and scales of gold out of the quartz vein he had exposed in the canyon wall.

It was tedious work. The quartz vein ran so high in the wall that he had to carve niches in the granite for his feet. He plucked the threads and scales of gold until he had a handful, then fisted his hand to make a lump of gold, which he would drop into a fold of his belt before repeating the process.

One bannertail, a grizzled matriarch, finished at last with the ritual greeting, edged her way up from the grassy canyon floor to the rocks along the canyon wall and lifted herself to full height to sniff at Rukmani Khan's hands. The matriarch's muzzle was pockmarked with scars that exposed black skin. Finding nothing of interest, she dropped to all fours and ambled over to the tethered bannertail, where most of the band had piled up to doze in the afternoon sun with their friend. The gray matriarch had just started to settle her sleep-heavy chin on a shoulder, arms embracing a little female, when her black-ringed eyes flew open. In an instant, the entire band of jittery bannertails was in tripod stance, ears perked, and noses wiggling.

Rukmani Khan paused again, watching the neck of the canyon with the bannertails. Soon Hazan and his mount scrambled up the rock, and Jabari and the other bannertails stood like sentinels awaiting further developments. Under Hazan's practiced hands, his mount moved up over the dry yellow grass with perfect decorum, barely taking notice of the band, which stood like pillars in their tripod stances.

But the moment Hazan dismounted and pulled the saddle and bridle from his bannertail, the lanky beasts lurched forward to greet the freed bannertail. The biggest males began scent-marking, and smaller males flung themselves on their returned friend and parried with their heads thrown back and jaws wide to expose sharp teeth.

Hazan stood watching the jumble of beasts for a moment, grinning at them. A bannertail raced up to Hazan, barely skidding to a halt in time to avoid knocking him over, then hugged him before bounding away again. Slightly embarrassed now, Hazan stepped up the rocks to where Rukmani Khan was waiting. Bannertails generally invited only children to play with them, learning in time that most adults would not return hugs with more than ritual gratitude.

"Welcome, Hazan," Rukmani Khan said.

"You're alone, milord?" Hazan asked, the smile fading a bit as he looked around worriedly.

"Your women friends are fine, Hazan. They were bored with the outing within hours of your departure, so I've kept them sleeping in the grotto."

Hazan glanced at the grotto entrance, almost as if he were checking to be certain Rukmani Khan could see it from here. Then, apparently satisfied, he looked up at the Khan, squinting his eyes against the overhead sun, and said, "But Sindon's not sleeping, is she?"

Rukmani Khan shook his head. "She's somewhere up the canyon, picking up twigs and dried leaves."

"Alone?" Hazan was surprised. "Are you sure she's safe?" He turned to scan the higher reaches of the canyon walls, the places where there were no easy trails but where there were thousands of places for a determined man to conceal himself.

"The other half of the bannertail pack is with her," Rukmani Khan said. He climbed down the toeholds to the rock where Hazan was standing. "They've adopted her as thoroughly as if she were a child."

"But Kangra is a bannerman, and . . ."

"Kangra would not foul the Canyons of Blue-green Waters with human blood," Rukmani Khan assured him, moving out of the shadows to sit in the sun. "In any case, I tethered Jabari here with me so I wouldn't get fooled."

Hazan put his saddle down and leaned back on it like a pillow, sighing.

"You may not sleep until you tell me if the New People are still on the rim," Rukmani Khan said, his voice revealing just a trace of irritation so that Hazan would know he was overstepping. He saw the young vassal tense a moment as if to sit up, but he didn't.

"You would give a vassal lord of Kangra's stature leave to rest a while," Hazan said, frowning slightly.

"A vassal of Kangra's stature would not ask to rest first, nor even take a rest if I offered."

Hazan pushed himself up, leaning on his forearms, his easy grin a trifle insolent. "Have patience with me, my Khan. I'm more accustomed to ignoring the examples of my elders these days, else I wouldn't have defied Gulnar Khan by going up to the rim of the canyon to spy on the New People for you."

"Are you going to tell me what I want to know, Hazan?" Rukmani Khan asked tiredly. "Or are you going to continue reminding me of my debt to you?"

"The New People are still there," Hazan replied, his voice not at all repentant. "They number about five hundred. They go by daylight to the magtree stand to fell them and send them crashing down the mountainside in a chute to a great tent they have erected. I couldn't see what they did inside the tent, but the abos were in there with them. I waited until nightfall and went to the yurts."

"I would have expected the abos to be gone by now," the Khan remarked. "Hasn't snow fallen up there?"

"The snow is as deep as my bannertail's belly," Hazan told him. "But the abos are clothed now in the New People's garb. They didn't seem cold. The men had spent the day in the New People's big tent, and to judge by the stories they told when they came back to the yurts, they're in no hurry to go to the lowlands, despite winter being on them. They have many new experiences to spin into stories, lots more than they'd have from a trek to the lowlands. It sounds like they're learning some of the New People's language, too, and some of the words are giving them thorough belly laughs. The most recent topic was a man whose name was Scat."

Rukmani Khan smiled in spite of himself. Even Natarjan had found it was more profitable to untangle the syntax and meaning of the abos' language than to let the abos attempt the reverse. The abos were fascinated by puns and nuances they found in Persuader words, most of which completely bewildered every Persuader who tried to comprehend the joke. Although, the Khan admitted to himself, a man calling himself Scat would be funny to Persuaders, too.

"I waited until they were asleep, then persuaded all but the female, Enam, to sleep soundly," Hazan continued.

"Did you ask Enam what the New People were doing with the magtrees in the tent?"

"Eventually, yes," Hazan said, smiling easily. "She thought I was a dream lover. . . ."

Rukmani Khan said nothing, but secretly he wondered how Hazan could tolerate the smell of an abo woman long enough until, eventually, he got around to talking to her. "What about the trees, Hazan?"

"Enam said they cut the trees into slabs, which the abo men stack and bind."

"They cut the trees?" Rukmani Khan echoed, stunned. "How?"

Hazan shrugged. "With knives, if I'm to believe Enam. But then she also believes the New People have birds trapped in their shuttle to make it fly."

"I must ask Sindon," Rukmani Khan said, for he could neither imagine knives strong enough to cut magtrees nor the New People being strong enough to wield them if they did.

"Speaking of whom," Hazan said, getting to his feet to look up the canyon.

Sindon was riding bareback on a dun-colored bannertail that was carefully picking his way down the rocks next to the waterfalls. Above them the other bannertails were scurrying, leaping carelessly, no doubt having caught wind of the rest of their band with the tethered Jabari. The dun's ears pricked as his packmates bounded past, but he continued moving carefully, wary of upsetting his rider. The front-runners of the pack were already at the bottom of the falls, running along the edge of the blue-green pool toward Jabari and the others.

"Before she comes tell me if you saw a good way to take revenge from the New People," Rukmani Khan said.

"It will be easy, milord," Hazan replied, his eyes bright with anticipation. "They walk freely through the meadow, unarmed. Their sentinels are so few that the camp would be easy to penetrate." He shrugged. "Many, many opportunities."

"Opportunities that we can also walk away from unscathed ourselves? Remember their weapons, Hazan."

Hazan frowned. "I don't fear their weapons," he said, obviously lying.

"I do," Rukmani Khan said. "I saw the holes in Natarjan and Sundari."

At last Hazan nodded thoughtfully. He looked up to watch the approaching bannertails.

"You must make the plan for taking our revenge, Hazan," the Khan said, putting his hand on the younger man's shoulder. Hazan met his eyes with a look of amazement. "You have been there and seen what there is to see. You must have a plan ready when it's time. It must be a good plan, one that leaves no doubt in the New People's minds who did the deeds, but one that provides ample opportunity for our escape."

"When?" Hazan asked, looking eager.

"You'll know when the time comes. The plan must be ready. It would not be safe to speak of it in the Winter Palace, so you alone must make the plan."

Eyes bright with pride, Hazan nodded just as the first bannertail reached him and bowled him over with a hug. A few scarred matriarchs hopped friskily over Hazan and glanced at Rukmani Khan quizzically. The Khan ignored the bannertails, arms folded across his chest while he watched Sindon atop the dun bring up the stragglers of the band. Her hair streamed out behind her in the wind like red ribbons, her face was flushed and happy. The bannertail came to a mincing halt, eyeing its cavorting companions, trembling with anticipation. Sindon was staring at the heap of bannertails, as if disbelieving that Hazan was tangled in their midst.

"Come down," Rukmani Khan said, stepping forward to offer her a hand. "Your mount wants to play."

Sindon threw her head back and laughed. "Me too," she said, then flung her arms around her trembling bannertail's neck. The dun froze a second, then tentatively rose up to tripod stance and reached around with his arms to clasp Sindon. Sindon giggled, and the bannertail hooted and flung himself into the writhing pack, landing atop Sindon.

Though he knew the bannertail meant no harm, Rukmani Khan was alarmed for Sindon. It was a long way from the top of an upright bannertail's shoulders to the ground, even when the fall was padded by a layer of squirming packmates. He leaped forward to help her, and found arms—Sindon's and furred ones—pulling him into the pack. Furry arms encircled him and squeezed him lovingly, bannertails squirming and wriggling under him and over him, and Rukmani Khan let himself be drawn into their ranks. Some of the little females broke rank in pursuit of imaginary quarry that led them in short strikes back and forth across the cavorting bannertails, which they bounded over gracefully. He heard Sindon squealing happily, and Hazan laughing out loud, and Rukmani Khan knew the bannertails were tickling. The scarred old matriarch reached around the Khan, locked his head under her arm, and started tickling his ribs. He laughed until he was ready to cry, and he kept on laughing when the tickling stopped, lying amid the heap of bodies, one arm flung over Hazan, another over a furred chest, Sindon somewhere underneath.

They lay too tired and too contented from laughing and skirmishing to move. The bannertails, equally contented, began purring, vibrations alternating between larynxes and diaphragms until the whole pile seemed to be vibrating.

"Rukmani, what are you doing to these animals?" he heard Sindon ask.

Until Hazan burst out laughing again, Rukmani Khan had no idea what she meant. Then he chuckled, and turned over to haul Sindon out of the pack. Bannertail limbs and bodies moved accommodatingly to let her up. Her hair was tangled, and she had a few scratches on her smiling face.

"I love them," she said happily. "I love them and they love me."

Rukmani Khan hugged her tenderly, sharing the lingering feeling of complete abandon that was but one of the bannertails' gifts to the Persuaders. "I haven't cavorted with bannertails in years," he whispered.

"Why not?" she whispered back, almost fiercely.

"The musk," Hazan said, slipping down from the heap of bannertails to the ground and offering his hands to Sindon and Rukmani Khan. "The musk isn't bad at a distance, but after a session like that, it gets too strong." He helped them to their feet and took a quick sniff of each. "If I smell as strong as you two, I need a bath." Putting his arms around his Khan's and Sindon's necks in the same fashion a loving bannertail might do, Hazan guided them down toward the footbridge spanning a blue-green pool.

"That water's too cold," Sindon protested, trying to hang back.

Hazan winked at Rukmani Khan, who kept his peace and even broke out of Hazan's hold on him to go around to Sindon's other side as they stepped on the bridge.

"Oh, no!" she squealed, trying to break through the two of them. "I've been in that water. It's like ice!" She couldn't get loose of Hazan's grip on her neck, and now Rukmani Khan had his arm around her waist. "No, please," she implored them, giggling but also struggling valiantly. Then she changed her stance and grabbed Rukmani Khan's arm. "If I go in, you do, too," she warned.

"We're all going in," Hazan said, reaching over to scoop her up.

"No, please! I can't do what you can do. I'll freeze," she pleaded.

Rukmani Khan grabbed her feet and helped Hazan heave her into the deepest part of the pool. Then he stripped off his belt, which was bulging with lumps of gold, and dived into a cloud of bubbles. Hazan followed. The icy water engulfed Rukmani Khan with shocking numbness, but he stroked steadily for the far side of the pool until he felt a stream of warmth. He followed the warmth to its source and burst to the surface in a pocket of heat. Hazan was already there, laughing at Sindon, who was sputtering in the center of the icy pool.

"Over here, Sindon, where it's warm," Rukmani Khan directed, backing up to the fissure in the rock that was the hot spring's source.

"I know how you'll make me warm," Sindon said, teeth chattering. She started stroking for the other side of the pool.

Leaving Hazan laughing at Sindon's indignation, Rukmani Khan swam out after her, the icy water rippling over his shoulders. He caught her before she could get her feet under her; she was already too cold to struggle. Sindon flung her arms around his neck and pressed her cheek against him, expecting him, he suddenly realized, to take her out of the water and warm her in an intimate fashion. Her legs clamped around him in anticipation. But for Hazan's laughter reminding him that they were not alone, he would have climbed out of the blue-green pool and done what she wanted. He couldn't remember not responding to the slightest indication that she was willing since the day he started taking her. Now, for the first time, he wondered if it was willingness he was responding to or her resignation. Rukmani Khan sighed as he stepped back into the deeper water.

"It hurts," she said. "The cold hurts. Make me feel good, Rukmani Khan."

"Not *now*, Sindon," he said, at once amused and distressed at the shivering, cuddly woman in his arms. "I'm taking you to the hot spring."

He found the warm current and started toward the source. Sindon moaned and opened her eyes. "How can you . . . ?" She looked over at Hazan, who was sculling in the warm current. "It's just a hot spring," she said, squirming out of the Khan's arms to where she felt hotter water surging from the rock. She clung to the rock until she stopped shivering, and then she turned around to face them. "Brats!" she said, her mood returning to playfulness. "I should have realized running water carrying away body heat would make even a Persuader cold."

Hazan threw his head back and laughed again. "Did you like her better before she knew you had limitations?" he asked Rukmani Khan good-naturedly.

"What limitations? I wasn't cold," Rukmani Khan said. "Were you?"

Hazan opened his mouth to laugh again, and Rukmani Khan pushed his head beneath the water. Hazan came up sputtering, so surprised that his Khan had initiated some kind of frolicking, he wasn't prepared to defend himself right away. Rukmani Khan heaved Hazan out of the warm pocket into the icy depths of the pool, then turned to Sindon, who was laughing helplessly at Hazan. He splashed her, and she splashed him back. Then Hazan dived between them and unsettled both of them, sending them tumbling to the bottom. Rukmani Khan grabbed blindly, and felt something hard. Realizing he had Hazan's leg, he pulled the young man's feet out from under him. When the three of them came up for air, the Khan locked his elbows around Sindon's and Hazan's necks. Sindon had no more strength to fight, and again Hazan seemed startled. The Khan might have let go but for the strange feeling of peace that infused him from having these two people in his arms. He had shared Sindon's passion, which he thought was unmatched by any woman. Just as she did not block those pleasures from him, now the two of them, Sindon and Hazan, emanated a comfortable camaraderie. It was like being with the bannertails, and almost as addictive. He knew that like the bannertails, Sindon could not help sharing her joy. He could feel her blood coursing in the bend of his elbow, sending his own blood racing, and the even better feeling of boundless joy working its way from his elbow to his mind. The surprise was in feeling the same from the elbow on Hazan's neck.

"I can't remember when a Persuader has let me do that," Rukmani Khan said softly.

Sindon just looked puzzled, but Hazan understood what he meant. "When was the last time you tried, milord?" he asked, his voice equally soft.

Rukmani Khan sighed and lay back in the warm water to stare up at the canyon walls. They were hung with tattered curtains of stone, thin layers of travertine, deposits of minerals contained in the mists and spray from the falls. The walls glistened where sunlight shined, but the shadows were lengthening, and the day was nearing its end. At last the Khan let his arms slip from Sindon's and Hazan's shoulders. For a while they sculled in the warm water, basking silently in the comfort it brought them.

"You were going to ask Sindon how they cut the magtrees into slabs," Hazan said at last.

"With a . . . a big-toothed blade," she said.

"A saw?" Rukmani Khan asked.

"If that's what you call a toothed blade," she said, nodding. "The ones they use are disk-shaped."

"That must be the wrong word," Hazan said. "A saw can't be round."

"Round," Sindon said firmly, "with teeth all around the blade. It spins and bites with the teeth."

"How can they make a round saw spin?" the Khan asked, trying to envision how people who could not persuade would make the blade spin fast enough to cut the dense magtree.

"With a power source that you can't understand," she replied.

"Like the shuttles' power source?" When Sindon nodded, Rukmani Khan shook his head. She was wrong. He understood the source; it was fire or lightning, molecules set in motion in the most vigorous fashion imaginable. But how these New People harnessed that energy to make round saw blades spin or shuttles fly without immolating themselves was something he could not understand and Sindon could not thoroughly explain.

"When they're finished making slabs out of the trees, they haul the stack out the other end of the tent, put them in the shuttle, and fly 'into the blue,' as the abos put it," Hazan continued.

"Far away," Rukmani Khan remarked thoughtfully. "Too far for the abos to see where."

"Up to the orbiter," Sindon explained. "When the orbiter is full, they'll take it away to the Homeworlds."

"Why?" Rukmani Khan asked her.

"How far?" Hazan asked.

"What use are slabs of dead trees?"

Sindon spoke to them about cities above the ground, talking until her skin started shriveling and looking moribund. Rukmani Khan believed what she told him, but he could not understand why people would go through the trouble she'd described to make these cities stand when they could have removed rock beneath their feet to make dwellings.

"From what you've said, Hazan, my people must be in full production. Are they still looking for me?" Sindon asked. "For us, I mean. Do they send the shuttles into the canyons?"

"No, the shuttles only went up, into the blue," Hazan said. "I think they've stopped looking for you."

"Oh," she said, quietly.

"There was one surprise, my Khan," Hazan said, speaking quickly, probably hoping that the Khan would not notice that Sindon seemed disappointed. "When I persuaded the abos to sleep, I found that one hammock contained one of the New People, not an abo. It was one of the men you and I disabled the night we brought Sindon and the others away. It was the curly-haired man who called himself David Quarrels."

"David!" Sindon cried out. "What do you mean, disabled? What did you do to him?"

"Nothing," Hazan said, startled by her vehemence. "I simply put him to sleep rather abruptly while he was still on his feet. It does no lasting harm. He's fine."

Sindon's lips thinned and she nodded. "Let's go," she said when she saw Rukmani Khan staring at her. "I have more wrinkles than old Ridpath."

Rukmani Khan blocked her retreat from the pool with his arm. "Who is this man, this David Quarrels?"

"He's the one who studies the abos," she said, pushing his arm firmly out of her way. She climbed over the rocks with their gossamer travertine, to get out of the pool.

"Like you study us?" Hazan called after her. But Sindon raced back across the bridge in her dripping clothes without answering. Hazan turned back to Rukmani Khan.

"David Quarrels had the same kind of translator device under his hammock that Sindon uses. He was living with them, like Sindon lives with us. I think, milord, this work that Sindon does, David Quarrels also does. Notes and words." Hazan shrugged.

Rukmani Khan stared after Sindon, but not because he couldn't comprehend her work, though he couldn't, and not because he was surprised to find yet another of the New People engaged in similar work with the abos. He stared because he had seen the expression on her face when Hazan had talked about David Quarrels. Sindon had looked as if she'd been slapped and that the sting was still fresh. Her eyes had flashed at the mention of his name, and her lips had trembled when she'd uttered it herself. "He's the one," Rukmani Khan said, slowly hauling himself out of the pool.

"Who's the one *what*?" Hazan asked, following him.

"David Quarrels. The father of her child. The man she loves."

"Oh," Hazan said. "Sindon's pregnant? What are you going to do?" he asked, staring stupidly after the Khan.

"Kill him," Rukmani Khan said.

"No, I mean about her being pregnant. Gulnar Khan will think it's your child. She'll name a priest when she realizes Sindon's pregnant."

"Then that will be our signal to take our revenge on the New People. We'll leave the Winter Palace the moment the new priest is named."

Rukmani Khan went to pick up the gold where he had left it in his belt on the bridge. He hefted it and smiled. There was enough to fill one pot. "We should go back to the white wall. With both of us working, we could have enough gold for all four women by tomorrow."

"No need, milord," Hazan said. "I came out here the night after Sindon told us, and I took enough gold from the vein to fill three pots."

"In one night?" Rukmani Khan asked, surprised.

Hazan shrugged modestly. "It was a very long night."

But he had produced three times more gold than Rukmani Khan. No wonder all three women remained content with Hazan. His persuasive skills were enormous.

14 .

THE SNOW IN the glacier valley was deep enough now to insulate living things beneath it; snowflakes trapped air and slowed the transfer of heat and cold, and kept tiny animals and dormant plants safe from lashing winds. Layers of snow accented gnarled limbs spreading at abrupt angles and curves from branching trunks in a small grove of trees at the southern end of the frozen lake. Snow covered the grime of Camptown. The flume that carried lumber from the makeshift mill to the drying yards spilled water until lumber and tools were covered with ice. Builders and flume tenders worked with numbed fingers. David edged his way along the catwalk on a flume switch in the drying yard. The flume boxes were too low to use as a railing, but the flume tenders had cleared the catwalks of snow, making it easier to walk up there than to break through waist-high drifts below. A crew was pulling clamped bundles of lumber from the flume and stacking them to dry. The crew's boots were caked with ice. They stopped their rhythmic hauling to greet David and to let him pass on the narrow platform.

Ahead, the slender wooden trough snaked through the drying yard to the mill at the edge of the lake. Between the drying yard and the lake were the little geodesic domes they'd used the first months on Cestry Prime and the recently completed two-deckers, square buildings sided with slab-sawn lumber that were the cookhouse, dormitory, and offices. Behind the two-deckers was the boiler house, which was a squat building also sided with slab-sawn lumber and with great chimneys protruding through the roof. One chimney carried dark smoke that stained the snow gray, and the other carried steam. When the flume trough and catwalk curved up to the mill, David climbed down the trestlework and started to walk the path of tamped snow that led to the boiler house, where he had a crew of abos working unsupervised. Since steam and smoke poured copiously from the stacks, he believed all was going well. But then the door to the boiler house opened and Theo Tucker stepped outside, his comm-unit in one hand and a sheaf of printouts in the other. When he saw David he cut short whatever it was he was saying into the comm. He put the unit back on his belt and tucked his hands out of the wind, crushing the printouts in his armpit, waiting for David.

David tried not to let the hesitation he felt show in his steps. He had made a point of not being alone with the CEO since the search for Sindon had been abandoned, and he had made a point of being a model of perfect behavior for a Mahania Corporation employee. David believed he had succeeded despite the close call with Brown when he had struck Akili. He had most of the abos reporting to work regularly now, and in just a few more days, *Pelican*'s holds would be filled with prime magtree lumber, ready to return to the Hub. When the transport ship was gone, deportation would be impossible, at least for a while. But *Pelican* wasn't gone yet, and David felt nervous. When he was close enough to see the frown on Theo's face, he broke out in an icy sweat.

"I just took this away from your abo buddies in the boiler house," Theo said, removing the printouts from under his arm and slapping them against his thigh. "What the hell are your abos doing with a copy of my project status report?"

"Oh, well, they're probably sounding out words," David said awkwardly. He was wishing he had given Theo a report on his latest project with the abos, but it had progressed more quickly than he had expected and with greater success than he'd dreamed was possible. He had thought to give it another week before he described it in any detail. "I didn't realize they'd be so resourceful in supplementing the reading material I've been supplying. They probably filched that from the trash."

"You're teaching the abos to read?" Theo asked, looking doubtfully at the printouts. "I thought they didn't even speak our language."

"They don't," David said. "They're reading it, and in so

doing are learning to speak it, too. They wouldn't bother trying to learn it until they wanted to read."

"Seems backwards to me," Theo said.

"It explains some of the puzzles I've had about their association with the Persuaders, though," David said.

Theo's brow shot up. "Have you got another theory about these so-called powers of persuasion?" he asked wearily.

"I don't think they're theories anymore," David said evenly. "They're speculative, it's true, but they're based on empirical evidence I've found in this valley and in the Summer Palace. However," he added hastily when he saw Theo's patience waning, "it also reveals a lot about the abos' disinterest in learning other languages. I've determined that the abos know less than a dozen of the words the lingochine has on file from the Persuaders' language. They conversed regularly with the Persuaders but apparently only in Aboriginese."

"I'd like to see that in a report," Theo said. "If the abo language is dominant, it lends some support to the Persuaders being interlopers."

"I'll be sure to mention it, but I think all it supports is the abos' being very provincial about language. Their point of view seems to be that if we want to communicate with them, we must do it in their language, because they don't want to be bothered with learning ours. At least, they didn't until they started to understand what they call 'word tracks' on the printouts. I don't think the Persuaders had anything similar to catch their interest."

"That's not good," Theo said. "Persuaders not having a written language is a point in common with the abos, which could mean the Persuaders are native to Cestry Prime . . . but, maybe less advanced than they seem?" he added hopefully.

"A lack of abstract representations of language isn't unprecedented in higher civilizations, but it's useful to know the Persuaders probably don't have one. We can stop trying to decipher etch-lines in their murals on the Summer Palace walls; they're probably no more than etch-lines that convey the shadows they seem to be. If there had been some coding, the abos would have known about it. They're so fascinated with our writing that I'm sure they haven't been exposed to anything similar by the Persuaders."

"Is this a conclusion you can support from studies that will be acceptable to the Council of Worlds?"

"I wish I could say I learned of it during a formal experiment, but it was accidental. Once the abos realized I wasn't going into some kind of fugue state when I sat down to read, they became very curious about how the printouts could keep my attention for so long. Akili, one of the adolescent boys, likened the written words on the page to animal spoor on the ground. It only took a few evenings of working with him and some of the men before they knew all the possible phonic combinations of the alphabet. Sounding out words has kept their interest. They've stopped grumbling about going back to the lowlands for the winter. It's as simple as that."

"Another form of entertainment for them, eh?"

David shrugged. "This one has lasted longer than anything else."

"But why? Why would writing interest them when they don't even speak the language? They don't speak it, do they?" Theo asked.

"No, and that's slowed them down a bit. They usually have a word or two per person each night for me to define. I should have guessed they were stealing reports and notices out of the trash, because the words have been ones like *sharpening, winch, burls, angle*." David shrugged. "I thought they were words they overheard during the day while at work. The translations are difficult, even with the lingochine. The frame of reference is so different, and they have nothing like homonyms or synonyms in their own language."

"But why would they want to read a language they don't even speak, at least, not speak yet? I mean, what good is a printed word here and there, especially if they don't understand what it means?"

"They do come to understand, sort of. They tell me it's more like reading tracks in the snow than speaking, as if a set of grassbear prints were alongside an abo's. If both sets of prints are reasonably fresh, you couldn't know for certain if the grassbear were stalking the abo or the abo were stalking the grassbear."

Theo looked at him blankly.

David smiled and shrugged. "Yeah, I know. But their fascination is related to the unfolding mystery of the language and the contradictions." When Theo still seemed unconvinced, David shrugged again. "All I know is it's working. Come inside and I'll show you what I mean."

David stepped past Theo to open the door. The heat in the boiler house was stifling and the abo men working inside had stripped down to their polka-dot loincloths. Their blue skin shone with sweat and silvery sawdust so that those who were shoveling the sawdust into the furnaces sparkled almost as much as the tongues of flame engulfing the magnesium-rich fuel. They saw David and Theo and they stopped, leaning on their shovels.

"I'm never sure if I should wave or smile," Theo said, a half-smile aimed at the abos.

"It doesn't matter," David said, starting to pull his parka off. "They don't greet the way we do."

"Why'd they stop working?"

"Because we're more entertaining than shoveling sawdust into the fire. Don't worry, though. They understand that if they let that fire go out I won't bring them a story tonight." David tossed his parka on the floor.

"You've been printing stories out of the *Pelican*'s . . ." Theo suddenly looked at David, sniffing the air with a look of disgust and amazement on his face. "Good God, Quarrels. You smell like an abo!"

"Sorry, sir. I eat and sleep with them. It's hard to avoid."

"Maybe you better start taking some meals in the cook-house," Theo suggested, pulling his own parka off. "It will give you an excuse for a shower. And tell Chloe I authorized a second wardrobe for you, one you can keep in the dorm."

"Yes, sir," David said, feeling thoroughly chastised. He was inured to the smell himself, but he remembered how overpowering it had seemed when he and Sindon had first contacted the abos. For a moment he and Theo stood looking at each other, David certain the CEO was wondering if the abo smell on him was indicative of some significant aberrant behavior, like having sex with the abos or a deep-rooted depression over Sindon's loss. "I'm fine," David said suddenly, sharply. "Now, let me have that report, and I'll show you what the abos do with the words."

Theo handed over the sheaf of printouts, still scrutinizing David. "You're defensive. I guess I might be, too, if our circumstances were reversed. Just make sure you start showing up for meals at least once a day. I don't want you going native on me and forgetting who you are."

"I won't forget who I am," David retorted, "nor who you are, nor who I lost." He ripped two sheets off the bottom of the report and handed the rest back to Theo. "Akili," he called out loudly so that all the abos would hear. "Akili, word tracks for you."

The boy appeared almost instantly, silvery sawdust clinging to his snout like a mustache. Akili snatched the printouts from David's hand and stared, and as he stared he squatted until his buttocks touched the floor planking. The other abos started gathering around Akili, whose lips were moving silently as his stubby fingers tracked the words. "Blue clothes!" Akili suddenly shouted with glee, and the other abos started snorting. They squatted around Akili, their eyes squeezed shut in mirth, the snorting puffing out their snouts.

"Blue clothes," one of the adults repeated, and added through spasms of snorting, "are hard to wear." Which comment brought such explosive gales of snorting from the others that their eyes disappeared under the inflated snouts.

"Hard clothes make me blue," said Akili, obviously proud when the adults giggled over his cleverness. He put one hand on his snout to flatten the air pockets so that he could see.

"What's the joke?" Theo asked, intrigued by the abos' reaction but obviously mystified, too.

"Well, in their language, something very far away is said to be 'in the blue,' which refers I think to the blueness of the horizon and even the sky, both of which are distant. They keep some of that literal translation when reading in our language, yet they know blue is the color blue, and even that it can mean feeling sad. They seem to go through the various translations or implications of blue clothes . . . sad clothes is a silly personification, and distant clothes is almost like a contradiction of terms, which seems to delight them. We had a blue lover in a fairy tale I read them last night, which they converted to a distant lover and made them laugh. Then someone layered the blue-distant concept into 'unseen,' which I guess something very distant can be. That, in some peculiar way, translated into a Persuader lover, at which Enam and the other women laughed very hard but which the men didn't find enjoyable at all. They're especially fond of a cruel bent if they can find one." The CEO was staring expectantly at David. David gestured with upturned palms. "That's it. There's no punch line."

Theo shook his head incredulously. "Did it occur to you that these language jokes might be at our expense?"

"I'm sure a lot of them are," David agreed. "But they turn them on themselves just as readily. A lot of our words are creeping into their vocabulary. They can barely put on their boots without also trying to give the first passerby *the* boot."

Theo groaned. "A race of punsters?"

David grinned sheepishly and shrugged.

Theo watched the abos for a moment longer, then reached for his parka. "Whatever works, I guess," he said. "The number of them coming to the mill keeps growing, and they're even starting to come on time."

"Oh, yes," David said. "They get a special delight out of the morning bell *ringing*, although I confess I haven't even a clue on that one."

Theo hesitated. "Sound going round? Wearing sound on your finger?" He frowned and shook his head. "Keep up the good work, I guess," Theo said, shoving his hands in his pockets.

David picked up his own parka. He was pleased that he'd succeeded in keeping the abos at work but he felt foolish knowing it was just blind luck that he'd stumbled on reading as a key. Even worse, he didn't have a clue as to how that key worked.

"Have you ever been to Clemson's Planet?" Theo asked as David was reaching for the door. David shook his head. "There's a subspecies on Clemson's Planet, not human, but fairly intelligent. We called them Clemintines and they packed ore out of tunnels when we had power failures, which was pretty frequent in the early days. Clemintines were easy going, obedient, never questioned any command they understood. They never caused a bit of trouble, unless you blew your nose or sneezed. Then they went for the throat, usually got the jugular on the first bite, and they didn't even have teeth, just a ridge of bony surface they used to grind their food. We learned to blow out our eardrums before letting a sneeze loose if a

Clemintine was around." Theo shrugged. "That's it. No punch line. Now open the door and let me out of his hot box."

David pulled the door open, and Theo stepped out and started off on the path of tamped snow toward the two-deckers. David glanced back at the abos. A few had gone back to shoveling sawdust into the furnace, tossing comments to their companions as easily as sawdust into the fire. Akili was still squatting on the floor in reading position, one hand over his snout so that he could see, the other touching the word tracks.

"Blue trees," one said.

"Blue from the boot," Akili shouted.

David closed the door on their laughter.

Across the frozen lake he could just make out the lights of the guards' stations at the top of the Summer Palace's steps. Like Theo Tucker, David didn't care if he ever knew why abos liked to work at the mill as long as there were fairy tales and words to play with when they got home or why Clemintines became vicious killers when someone sneezed. But he wanted very much to know where the Persuaders had taken Sindon, and now, at last, he believed he could pursue that matter without being afraid Theo Tucker would boot him off the planet. He headed toward the two-deckers, already looking forward to a shower.

15.

SINDON WAS GONE.

Rukmani Khan had known the moment he entered the bedchamber that she was not there. Her breakfast food lay soggy in a crystal bowl near the flat-topped rocks he heated for her each morning so that she could soften foodstuff fibers on her own. In the center of the polished calcite floor lay the woolen shawl that she used to ward off the caverns' chilly breath. It lay crumpled, as if it had slipped from her shoulders unnoticed. As he looked about the empty bedchamber, Rukmani's heart suddenly began to pound. He knew she would have noticed the shawl slipping away. He knew that if she had chosen not to wear the shawl, she would have folded it neatly and placed it in the dolomite box he had made for storage of her things.

Behind him, in the corridor, he heard someone running. As he turned, Hazan skittered to a breathless halt under the stone arch.

"My friends are gone," he gasped, not waiting for Rukmani Khan to give him leave to speak. His face was ashen, eyes wide with fear.

"Gone where?"

"Below, to the Lower Deeps."

"What kind of foolishness . . ."

But Hazan cut him off. "Taken. Sindon, too."

"Taken by whom? Where in the Lower Deeps?"

Hazan gulped some air. "By the acolytes. To their new priest for sacrifice on the Altar of Justice."

"Which one did Gulnar name priest?" Rukmani Khan asked,

138

stepping over the fallen shawl to the niche where he kept his ceremonial knives.

"Timon," Hazan said, the flat of his hand touching his hip to indicate he had no knife.

Rukmani Khan tossed him a sheathed knife, then buckled another to his own waist before racing past Hazan into the stone corridor that led to the other end of the Winter Palace and the stairs to the Lower Deeps. Abruptly he stopped. Using the stairs would take too long. He turned back and ducked down a side corridor to the closest shaft that led down to the Lower Deeps where the religious community dwelled.

The shaft was a steam chimney used to convey hot water vapors to the upper chambers in the Winter Palace. It was crudely chipped through layers of dark rock, the hole plumb for a hundred body-lengths and wide enough to accommodate a man's shoulders. There were niches in the sides, put there by the Persuaders who had fashioned it so they could climb back to their work.

Rukmani Khan hesitated, wondering if Hazan had sufficient control to deal with the scalding hot steam for as long as it would take to climb to the bottom. For himself, the steam was a negligible hazard when his heart was beating furiously with fear for Sindon; justice could come with terrifying swiftness when there was a priest willing to wield a knife, and Timon, he was sure, would be willing. Rukmani Khan grabbed two icy crystal condensing spines and lifted his feet over the lip of the shaft into the hot steam. Hazan would have to make his own decision.

Almost instinctively, the Khan calmed the excited molecules that came in contact with his skin. Water sheeted from him like fountains of sweat. His feet found purchase on tiny protrusions. They were slick with minerals deposited over years of steam. The deeper he went, the more he needed to concentrate on the mounting vector of steam lest the Persuaded water molecules scald him. The volume of water pouring off him increased, not just because he was getting closer to the source but also, he realized, because Hazan was above him and water was streaming from him, too. The water was warmer now; it felt like blood, Sindon's blood.

Rukmani Khan kept pushing down with his hands, and stuffing his feet into slippery, wet cracks. An image of Sindon lying on the altar flashed in his mind, her eyes closed as if in sleep, the altar rock hot and slippery with her blood. Determinedly, he moved more quickly. But moving with pure counterforce tired him; persuading the scalding water molecules to a calmer state tired him. Just as he was beginning to wonder if he'd have the strength to finish, he heard the sound of boiling water below him. He let go of his holds and plunged the last few lengths into the bubbling caldron, the water breaking his fall, the hot and cold of it closing over him. He grabbed the rim of the stone caldron and felt it break away in shocked response to his icy touch. Water gushed through the crack and steamed away into the darkness. He climbed out, took one look back to see that the waterfall descending into the frothy caldron also contained Hazan, then started running down the hot corridor toward the fissure in the kneaded rock that would take him into the natural caverns, the Lower Deeps.

The altar chamber had clear selenite crystals protruding from the sides like great beams, though only one extended entirely across. At the high point in the floor, crystal sword-like blades formed a path to a slab coated with blood-red mineral deposits. Sindon lay on the altar, her hands clasped over her breasts. She looked asleep, as did the three other women. They were pale in the glimmering light, as pale as death. Two acolytes kept watch over the sacrifices, their hands in ritual placement, palms down, on the altar, which was proper posture for the beginning of the ceremony. And the end. Behind him, Rukmani Khan heard Hazan gasp.

Then a light in the far corner of the cavern caught the Khan's eye and he saw Timon, the newly named priest, step out of a grotto formed by two white limestone blocks. He was dressed in Natarjan's chasuble and carried four luminescent crystal vases that would dim and blacken when filled with blood. It was not too late, but while Sindon still lay on the altar, the Khan's fear for her life would not diminish.

He stepped into the chamber, reached overhead at the same time to excite the chain of luminescent torches around the cavern, and realized the acolytes and the priest were not alone. Gulnar Khan sat in a grotto with Moti's and Hari's mothers, and Kangra sat with them. All were attired in ritual finery, even Gulnar, who so rarely wore any adornment. When Kangra saw

Rukmani Khan, he started to his feet, but Gulnar Khan stayed him with a hand.

"You may sit here," she said evenly to Rukmani Khan, "with me."

Rukmani Khan stared at her, incredulous. But there was not a trace of mockery in her voice, and her eyes looked almost soft, perhaps hopeful. "You insult me with the suggestion," he said, and he could see that his words stung her. Insulting him had obviously not been her intent; he was amazed.

Rukmani Khan looked at Kangra. His vassal lord's hand was on his knife hilt, his face sad but calm. The Khan realized Kangra was resigned to opposing him. "You have not attended Gulnar Khan's Councils," Kangra said quietly. "Your absence was taken to mean you did not wish to influence Gulnar Khan's decision to name a new priest."

"You misunderstood," Rukmani Khan said. Now he looked back at Gulnar, who seemed to be controlling herself with effort. She made a gesture with her hands, to reach for the shawl that was not there. Instead she smoothed lace on her unwrinkled sleeves. "I did not believe you would name a priest without consulting me."

Her eyes flashed with sudden anger. "I rule the Winter Palace. And if you chose not to come to Council to give me the benefit of your opinion, then you must have been confident I would choose correctly for both of us. I believe I have done that. I was mindful of the old ways that demand vengeance for the murders the New People committed. I listened to each acolyte who aspired to priesthood and conferred the status on the one whose plan for vengeance seemed to satisfy everyone's needs."

"Everyone's?" Rukmani Khan shook his head. "I see Hari's and Moti's mothers, but not their fathers. And Ridpath is not here."

"I will perform Sundari's revenge," Kangra said with sudden fervor.

"On a woman who has been persuaded to sleep?" the Khan retorted with deliberate scorn. "Who will learn not to harm our people if you kill four sleeping women? Where are the horrified witnesses?"

"We will deliver their bodies to the New People," Kangra

said, but Rukmani Khan could hear the doubt in his vassal lord's voice.

The Khan walked across a crystal slab to the grotto where Timon, the priest, still stood with his four vases. Timon was trembling with fear at being approached by an armed and angry Persuader. Stepping purposefully between the priest and the altar, Rukmani Khan fastened his gaze on the man's face. There was a peculiar, vacant look in Timon's eyes, and the Khan wondered if he was participating in this gruesome ceremony only to please Gulnar Khan. Angrily, Rukmani Khan took the vases and smashed them against a limestone block. "This killing would satisfy only one need. Gulnar Khan's need to have Sindon out of her way." Rukmani Khan turned to look at his wife again. "You can't straddle a fissure, Gulnar. In the end, the rock falls away to one side or to the other. There is no way to please everyone. You misunderstood the message I intended when I did not come to Council. I believed by staying away, no priest would be named. I thought I had prevented . . . this."

"And that you'd never do penance for having that woman in your chambers?" she asked sharply. "Because there was no priest to call you out?"

Frustrated, Rukmani Khan shook his head. "You could have called me out yourself, though I admit I know you are too proud to do that. My bitterest disappointment is your thinking I would not interfere in this travesty. Did you also believe that once it was done, I would come back to your chambers?"

Gulnar Khan said nothing, but he could see the burning hope in her eyes, and it sickened him. He turned away, staring dumbly at the scintillant shards of crystal at his feet. He could persuade bits to cling and cleave until the vases were whole again. But if he had all eternity to restore what had fallen apart between him and Gulnar, he knew he could not do it. It frightened him to realize that Gulnar believed otherwise.

"Well," Rukmani Khan said, breathing hard now, trembling and unnerved by Gulnar's passion, which he badly underestimated. "Let there be no mistake in my intentions this time. You cannot have the life of that woman up there on the altar without first taking mine."

"And mine before my three friends," Hazan said.

Rukmani Khan drew his knife and walked up the aisle of

swords to the altar, Hazan directly behind him. The two acolytes withdrew their hands and started backing away.

At last Kangra stood up, knife in hand. "Say the word, Gulnar Khan." He glanced over at the new priest, who gulped but who also drew his knife. The acolytes, few of them older than boys, followed their priest's example and pulled obsidian blades from beneath the metallic luster of their robes.

Gulnar Khan was on her feet, hands wringing the ends of the long, lace sleeves as she stared first at Rukmani Khan and then at Kangra. There was no mistaking the vassal lord's murderous intent, and there was no question that with the support of the priest and the acolytes Kangra had the advantage in numbers, if not in fighting skills.

"Gulnar, you must decide," Kangra said, but the Khana seemed paralyzed, staring only at Rukmani Khan in anguished disbelief.

For a moment Rukmani Khan stared back at her, feeling wholly penetrated by the blackness of her eyes. At first he didn't understand her hesitation. But then he thought he did. Suddenly dropping from the altar to the floor, he walked steadily to Gulnar and Kangra. Standing before them with his hands open and weaponless, he said clearly to Gulnar: "I will die defending Sindon."

"No," Gulnar screamed, putting fisted hands against her cheeks. She glanced at Kangra, who had positioned himself so that a single, quick thrust would deliver a fatal wound to Rukmani Khan's breast. "No," she said again, and they could hear a sob catch in her voice. Then she gave a shriek of frustration, and she turned and fled.

While they listened to the dimming echo of Gulnar's footsteps, Kangra remained in his threatening stance. The anger in Kangra's eyes was so great, Rukmani Khan believed he had misjudged his vassal lord's control. But then Kangra stepped back, saying, "I have no wish to kill you, milord, but I cannot live with a heart turned to stone."

The fire in Kangra's eyes burned ruby red and for a moment Rukmani Khan thought his vassal lord intended to turn the knife on himself. But before Rukmani Khan could reach for it, Kangra averted his eyes and slipped the knife into the sheath at his waist. Kangra hung his head, hands clasped behind him in complete humility.

The Khan felt no joy in Kangra's submission. It was made all the worse with Hari's and Moti's mothers looking on.

"Go now," he said gently to the two women. Then he turned to the priest. "You leave us, too. Take your acolytes with you."

The new priest nearly dived into the grotto, not even glancing at the acolytes who, but for one, had begun scrambling for exits the second Rukmani Khan gave leave to their priest. The composed one, however, stepped carefully past Hazan and walked slowly down the path of blades. When he stopped, the Khan recognized Amar, a lad Natarjan had called to the Lower Deeps only last spring. Amar stood as if planted in stone, his troubled gaze on Rukmani Khan.

"Speak, if you wish," the Khan said, feeling a touch of admiration for the least and youngest of the acolytes.

"I don't have words to describe the shame that I feel," the boy said, his jaw trembling.

"The Almighty Persuader cannot be pleased with the priesthood this day," Rukmani Khan agreed.

"Nor with his Khans, who seem to have forgotten what place honor has in Persuader life," Amar said, his voice cracking despite the softness of the words. He backed a few steps away, then turned to walk into the shadows.

Rukmani Khan watched the boy until he disappeared into the grotto.

Kangra was staring after the boy, too. "His eyes were bulging like a squashed toad," Kangra said, "but he had enough courage to speak the truth. Four lives gone without revenge, my Khan living in dishonor and without doing penance, my Khana so blind she does not even realize she named a priest more to serve her wishes than the Almighty Persuader's, and myself numbed to silence as shameful as yours, all because we carry the laws of the Summer Palace in our hearts while trying to abide by the laws of the Winter Palace."

Rukmani Khan nodded. As a very young man, the Khan had tried to be a living example of how to live in the Winter Palace where the Khana, who could barely persuade a leaf to turn brown, ruled. She had never asked the vassal lords nor even the few women who could persuade not to use their abilities, not even when Natarjan himself had abstained for so many years after the holocaust. Indeed, she had seemed gifted in directing Persuaders in how to use their considerable talents for all, so that the Winter Palace had grown large, comfortable, and self-sufficient.

But while Rukmani Khan had never admitted it aloud, he had finally realized she would never understand his dissatisfaction with rough-cut passages and chambers that were less appealing to the eye than the crystal of the natural caves in the Lower Deeps. He had had no desire to hurt her by telling her how much he longed for the time to smooth a wall or to release the fascinating symmetry of crystals grown into a cavity lined with ordinary quartz and feldspar. When the time had come, he had simply gone to establish his Summer Palace, just as his forefathers had done before him, although there was no longer a need to take the bannertails to summer pastures.

Rukmani Khan sighed. "How do you feel about hurrying summer?" he said to Kangra.

Kangra frowned. "You have not openly opposed Gulnar. If you mean to take vengeance on the New People, I don't believe she will overlook that."

"No, I'm sure she won't," Rukmani Khan said. "And there will be hell to pay for having done it."

"Not if you don't come back to face her," Hazan said.

Startled, Rukmani Khan looked at the altar where Hazan was sitting with Sindon and the three other women. For a moment, the Khan contemplated Hazan's suggestion, envisioning living in the Summer Palace with Sindon at his side, never having to return to the Winter Palace with its endless greencaverns. But, grimly, he shook his head. "I could not live in peace knowing the boy Amar and other of his ilk would be left alone to deal with that priest and Gulnar."

Hazan took a deep breath. "Then, we'll pay whatever hell demands," he said resignedly. "But if you don't mind, I will also take my pots of gold when we go to the rim to make right their staying here with me." He gestured to his three friends.

"I'll do likewise with Sindon's gold," Rukmani Khan said thoughtfully.

Sindon was getting to her feet, moving gracefully even though she was so big with child. She heard her name and looked at Rukmani Khan. She didn't return his smile.

"They paralyzed me," she said. "I could hear them talk.

And I saw the crystal beams before they closed my eyes. I knew it was the Altar of Justice. Hazan told me. I knew it was, and it is. The crystal beam, the swords, it's the Altar of Justice. Isn't it? He told me they bring the damned here."

"You are safe now," the Khan said, reaching for her.

She jerked away from him. "They were going to kill me, weren't they? I heard you talking, Rukmani Khan. Why the hell was I lying on the Altar of Justice? Who is the woman I heard scream? Why did she want to kill me? If you hadn't come . . ." Anger abruptly gave way to sobs, and Rukmani Khan realized how frightened she was, and that for all her angry bravado, she had enough knowledge to realize she had been in danger, and understood, too, how helpless she'd been to prevent it. He took her in his arms and held her sobbing against his chest.

"It may be that Gulnar's hell isn't the only one to pay," Kangra said quietly, and gestured to Hazan that they should leave. But the younger lord shook his head.

"I will join you at dusk," Rukmani Khan said.

"Dusk?" Kangra queried. "We should leave at dusk. We need to begin to make plans now."

"The plan is made. Hazan will tell it to you."

Kangra raised his brows at Hazan's obvious pleasure. "And who will be the fourth avenger in this well-planned venture?"

"Fourth . . . what?" Sindon asked, rubbing her eyes with her fist.

"Ridpath," Rukmani Khan said to Kangra.

Kangra nodded curtly. "I'll get him," he said, then turned and disappeared into the black depths behind the altar.

"Are you going to tell me what's going on?" Sindon demanded, her voice more angry than frightened.

"Yes," Rukmani Khan said, and he took her hand and led her to the blood-red altar stone. They sat side by side while he explained everything that had happened, and the longer he talked, the more he could sense a distance growing between them. When she crossed her arms as if to warm herself, he tried to draw her close to him.

"Don't touch me," she said.

"You're cold," he urged, his arms open to her.

"Don't touch me," she repeated. "Not to warm me, not for . . . anything. Not ever again."

"Sindon, you can't mean that," he said. He reached to pull her close to him, but she slipped away.

"I want to leave," she said, staring evenly at him now. "I want to go back to my own people."

"No, Sindon. You're just frightened because of what happened."

"Of course I'm frightened," she said, almost shouting. "You have a wife, and she wants to kill me."

"She will do nothing as long as she knows I would die before letting anything happen to you," he said stonily.

"That's not any comfort, Rukmani Khan. You have a wife! I want to leave. If you won't help me . . ." She got up. "Hazan, will you take me back?" Her voice was pleading.

"I . . ."

"What do you think you're going back to?" Rukmani Khan asked her before Hazan could answer. "Do you think you'll want to be with him after having been with me?"

"Don't," she said, her hands clutching her belly. "You wouldn't be able to understand."

"And what if he's not there?" Rukmani Khan asked. "Would you still wish to leave me if he were dead?"

"David—dead? He's not . . ." Her face turned pale. "The vengeance. You'll . . . oh, God, no! Don't kill David." He thought she was about to cry again when she suddenly caught a deep breath. She straightened to her full height. "Did you think that I would trade my freedom for his life?" she asked. When he didn't answer, she gave him a haughty look. "Did you think that I could live with you all this time and not learn anything about Persuader pride? I will not trade my freedom for David Quarrels' life. I will go, and if I have to go alone, so be it. But you will not kill David Quarrels. You deceived me, Rukmani Khan, and you owe me much for that deception. I want your promise never to kill David Quarrels."

"Do you still love him?"

"You have no right to ask, Rukmani Khan. You have a wife!"

He winced. "She'll extract punishment enough without your adding to it," he said. "I will take you back to the rim, if that is your wish. I would not have bartered your staying with me for his life. There's already one woman chained to me by duty;

I don't want another chained with fear. I'll spare David Quarrels' life, but . . ."

"But what?" she asked, her back still straight, her shoulders squared.

"You must take the means for returning to me—freely."

"What means?" she said suspiciously.

"Bannertails," he said. "Beasts born and bred in our stables. They'll carry you back to me whenever you choose to come."

"They could also lead strangers to the Winter Palace," Hazan pointed out with alarm.

"Only if Sindon allowed them to be used for that purpose, but she won't," Rukmani Khan said. "Will you, Sindon?"

"And give someone else a chance to take another set of notes?" She shook her head. "The location of the Winter Palace is safe with me."

"Then it's settled," Rukmani Khan said, getting to his feet at last. "Hazan, you should find Kangra and Ridpath. I will help Sindon put her belongings together."

"Just show me the stairs," Sindon said. "I can pack by myself."

16 .

DAVID QUARRELS WALKED around a cornice of new snow that the wind had plastered against the sentinel post during the night, to find Brown Roberts standing in his shirt-sleeves on the other side. Brown was staring at a trail of broken snow on the impossibly steep, glacier-carved steps leading up to the guard shack atop the rock island.

"Did some grassbears pay you a visit last night?" David asked good-naturedly after a quick glance at the spoor. The grassbears had grown bolder since the first snowfall and, with their white winter coats, much more difficult to see. Occasionally they strayed through the perimeter electronics, too, and Brown and his people had to track them down and chase them away with prods they'd jerry-rigged from tinglers and pipes.

"Not just grassbears," Brown said, rubbing the back of his neck. His face looked pained. "Sticktails, too. And they were probably carrying riders."

David looked more closely at the spoor in the snow and realized the big spoor of the grassbear had crossed the deep clawprints of sticktails. The prints were deep and splayed, a sure indication of riders.

"The grassbears came through the perimeter like falling trees through cobwebs, just like they always do. Don't know how the sticktails got through," Brown said unhappily.

"Perhaps with the grassbears?" David asked. "By letting the grassbears absorb the tinglers?"

Brown considered for a moment, then shook his head. "I think when we look at the scanner memories, we'll find the timing's wrong. The sticktails and their riders were inside the perimeter before the grassbears." Brown shivered and started

149

to rub his arms to ward off the cold. "Come on up to the shack. There's something I want you to see."

Hugging himself for warmth, Brown led the way around another snow cornice to the gentle slope on the up-valley side of the rock island. The normal walkway, lined and planked with rough-hewn timber, had been cleared of snow. Brown took the man-made stairs two at a time.

Inside the guard shack, medics were attending to two of Brown's people who sat on the floor, heads in their hands. A third guard sat at the console. His forehead was furrowed as if in pain, but he was less groggy-looking than the two guards on the floor.

"They'll be all right," the senior medic said when she saw Brown. "At least, we can't find anything wrong. I'd like to check you, too."

"I just have a headache," he said, waving her away. Brown looked at David. "I figure they did to us whatever it was they did to you and T.T. last summer. We saw the perimeter break, figured it was grassbears, got to staring at the scanners. The next thing we knew, it was dawn and we were waking up with headaches. Never heard them come in, didn't see anything."

"No one saw them the night they came into the yurts, either," David said. He rubbed the back of his neck, remembering how badly his head had hurt.

"Too long ago for them still to be around, but I sure wish the shuttles were here. They've got enough of a start on us that I don't think we can catch up with them on sleds before they get to the rim."

"I'd like to try," David said, speaking carefully, trying to sound calm. "This time we might at least be able to follow their trail through the snow to the rim and find out how they get down into Xanthippe's Chasm. If we knew that much, it would narrow down the possibilities of where the Winter Palace might be in that maze."

Brown shot David a disapproving frown. "I have two crews getting ready right now, one to backtrack, and one to follow the new spoor, in case they go back a different route."

David nodded, not trusting himself to speak. He wanted to join the search, but he knew Brown would never agree to it. He hoped that by not protesting he could escape special scrutiny, and perhaps slip away from camp later to search on his own.

Officially the search for Sindon was over, but David would never accept that as final.

"Look over there on the table," Brown said, and David turned. On the table were four clay pots brimming with what looked like lumps of gold. David went over and picked up a lump; it was cool and heavy, and fit neatly in his clenched hand. He opened his hand to look more closely at the gold. Its shape was unlike any natural nugget he could imagine, and a quick glance told him the others in the clay pots were similar.

"They left that stuff on the table, I assume so that we'd be sure to find it. As far as we can tell they didn't take anything or damage anything. They just came in and knocked us out so they could leave the pots."

"But why?" David asked.

"You're the alien culture expert, not me," Brown said. When David did not offer any explanation, Brown continued: "Four pots of gold can't be coincidental. I figure it's some kind of appeasement for our four women, maybe even payment. Maybe they've been watching us all winter and figure we're pretty tough, so they decided to try paying us off."

"And maybe it's their custom to put four pots of gold on this particular rock island every winter," David retorted brusquely. "Maybe this rock is the altar for their gods, and this gold is an offering to keep the spring melt from flooding the Summer Palace, and you and your guards were in the way."

"Maybe you don't want to consider what appeasement might mean," Brown said.

"Maybe I don't want anyone assuming Sindon or any of those women are dead or beyond recovery until we know a hell of a lot more than we do now," David said, Brown's innate calm infuriating him.

"I've assumed nothing, David," Brown returned softly. "But I do insist on caution now more than ever. We don't have any shuttles just now, and no orbiter to retreat to if we did. Now, tell me if it makes sense to believe these four pots of gold have something to do with the missing women?"

Reluctantly, David nodded. "In terms of what we know from the pictorial mosaics and even what the abos have told us, it's not appeasement."

"Payment, then?"

David shrugged. "The nuggets aren't natural. They're all

shaped like slips of clay that have been squeezed in a potter's hand, then discarded and left to dry." He tested the lump in his fist.

"Do you think it's real?" Brown asked.

"Looks real. Won't be hard to find out for sure." David tossed the nugget to the senior medic, who caught it handily.

"I'll check it right away," she said, turning it over and rubbing her thumb along a ridge, getting the feel of it.

"Did you tell Theo?" David asked.

Brown shook his head. "He's up on the ridge with the sprinkler crew, checking their repairs on the ice chute. I don't want this on the airwaves; we'd just alarm the whole camp. I'll go up in person to talk to him. You might as well come along."

"Let's take some of these to show him," David said, reaching into the pot again. He pulled out two nuggets, gave one to Brown and pocketed the other.

Brown turned to pull his coat from a hook. "Check the scanner memories," he said to his people, "and get someone up here to inventory that stuff in the pots. Sign one nugget out to the clinic for analysis, and one each to David and me." He started to pull the bright blue coat on, hesitated with one arm in the sleeve, then shook his head and pulled the sleeve through to reveal the white winter camouflage lining. "They're gone by now if they have any sense, but I'll wear my whites anyhow. You, too, David."

David turned his coat inside out, though he couldn't believe a white coat would fool people who could creep through electronic perimeters and enter guard shacks undetected. They seemed to know more about camouflage and stealth than Brown or David or even the abos, and he wondered now what they knew of electronics, especially about laser fences and tinglers. He wondered what Sindon had told them, and he wondered why she had told them anything. The answer his mind conjured up frightened him.

The sleds were fully charged and moved efficiently along the packed path the loggers used to get to the higher ridge. David and Brown passed an unused flume-tender cabin, left vacant since the night of the Persuader's visit to the abo yurts. All the loggers returned each night to the security of the camp, although now, David realized, that security was questionable.

Brown would want to confer with Theo before taking precautions against more unwanted night visitors; anxiety among the camp's inhabitants ran especially high during those cycles when the shuttles were gone with the *Pelican*. There was no retreating to orbit if things went badly planetside, no backup medical facilities if injuries were more severe than the clinic could handle, no backup anything. They feared the unimaginable. Grassbears were almost humorous, despite their potential to cause damage simply with their bulk; it was amusing to watch Brown's people chase them away with the prods, and as long as everyone stayed indoors until they were gone, the possibility of getting hurt was remote. But anything that could get through their camp perimeter's electronics both unharmed and undetected was unimaginable and therefore feared.

The magtrees on the lower slopes had been cleared, but higher up the loggers were selecting and felling only mature trees. The silvery limbs took on a deep gray cast without sunlight to brighten them, and looked like etchings against the snow. Clouds grazed along the ridge, threatening thick fog. Brown stopped his sled to look beyond the frozen flume for signs of the crew, then pointed north. Among the trees, David could see the bright blue coats of the company people and a party of orange-clad abos with them. With the wind so still he could hear almost all the notes of the song the abos were singing, and he thought he could detect the less melodious voices of loggers, too. The crew was slightly below them, and they had started to turn their sleds when David saw four sticktails bound from a thicket near the loggers, leaping so high despite the weight of their riders that they seemed to hang in the air for a moment. As the sticktails landed, David realized their leaps had been controlled, for each beast landed with its front paws on a logger's shoulder, felling him like a stick. The four riders slid to the ground, and on their knees straddled the fallen loggers under the sticktails' bellies.

"Come on," Brown shouted, his sled already moving off the path and through soft snow toward the logging crew. But David hung back a moment.

The riders were already ducking out from beneath the sticktails and starting to remount when the abos saw them. Abruptly the abos stopped singing and let go of their hold on the sprinkling hose to stare at the Persuaders. The rest of the logging crew struggled with the squirming hose for a few seconds before they saw what the abos had seen. Then they too dropped the hose and started shouting and running toward their fallen comrades. It took no more than a dozen steps to reach them, but by the time they did, the sticktails and their riders were well up the slope, the sticktails looking like waves washing through the trees and their riders like bobbing corks.

From the corner of his eye, David could see that the four loggers were still down, sprawled in the snow, but he could not take his eyes off the Persuaders. They were stripped to the waist, and red cloths were tied around their heads and wrists, streaming behind them like bloody banners. They passed close enough for him to recognize Rukmani Khan, Kangra, and Hazan. A gray-haired man he'd never seen trailed the three, but not by much. When the last Persuader topped the ridge and was out of sight, David started the sled. He wanted to follow the Persuaders, but he wondered about the four fallen loggers. He couldn't believe the Persuaders had leaped so dramatically into action merely to put four more people to sleep. Indeed, the number—four—couldn't help but remind him of the four stone graves left in the chasm bottomlands. He raced toward the blue-clad loggers, the sled virtually flying past the thicket from which the Persuaders had come. The abos had moved off to the side, muttering among themselves, snouts pointing at David as he stopped the sled.

"Get the life-keep kit from your sled, David," the security chief ordered, his own kit already in his hands. "We don't have enough."

"The life-keeps aren't working," the crew chief said. He was kneeling beside one of the fallen loggers, the mask already over the man's face and the probe stuck into his chest. "Get the medics up here." The crew chief sounded desperate.

"I've already called for the medics," Theo Tucker said. He was on his knees next to the crew chief. He reached over the fallen logger and reinserted the probe in his chest. From the shake of his head, David guessed it still wasn't working.

David took the kit from his sled and knelt beside the only logger who didn't have a life-keep over her. Her eyes were wide open, already looking frozen and lifeless; her face was a grimace of pain. Someone pushed David aside and slipped the mask over the woman's face. Other hands pulled open the bright-blue coat so they could slip the probe into her chest. David was sure it wouldn't do her any good. He glanced at the three other fallen loggers and realized two of them were men. Only one woman. David felt his scalp tightening as he turned to go back to his sled.

"Where the hell do you think you're going," Theo snapped.

"To follow them."

"We have injured people; we need your sled to transport them."

"You have dead people. They won't mind waiting for transport. I'm going after those killers."

Theo stepped in front of him, blocking his way. "Only the medics can decide if . . ."

David darted around him, but Theo caught his coattail. "I said . . ."

David whirled with his hands clenched. His left fist caught Theo in the stomach, and the CEO doubled over, letting go of David. David ran for the sled, not heeding Brown's shouts, Theo's curses, or the abos' roars of laughter.

The sled was capable of great speed on level ground in good snow, but in the forest of magtrees David had to travel slowly, turning the short steering skis around trunks and thickets, following the path of broken snow left by the sticktails. Halfway up the ridge, David's shoulders ached from all the sharp turns and from holding the nose of the sled steady as it dipped and climbed over the uneven terrain. The Persuaders, David was sure, were having a much easier time of it on the agile sticktails.

When David topped the ridge he saw that the trail turned north, which surprised him, for Xanthippe's Chasm and the safety of the Winter Palace lay to the west. He turned north, leaving the silvery magtrees behind. Dense fog enveloped him, cutting off the view of the glacier valley below, but the spoor left by the sticktails was clear, so David kept going.

Vegetation changed from magtrees to grumetrees with thick brown-purple crowns. Pendulous gobs of sap, stiffened by the cold weather, hung from drooping branches while the brown, deeply corrugated bark on the trunks flaked off in velvety chunks. The bark flakes littered the forest floor like leaves in autumn, and smelled just as musty. The grumetrees, David knew, stood by the millions along the high ridges from Xanthippe's Chasm to the edge of the glacier, disdaining only ravines and valleys, and the slopes on which the magtrees grew.

The radio on David's sled whistled. Instinctively he reached for the receiver, then caught himself. He left the receiver in its cradle and snapped off the audio. The message light on the instrument panel flashed anyhow, but he hardly noticed because his attention was on the spoor in the snow. In only a few minutes, his personal comm-unit tickled his hip. There wasn't any way to turn it off. He ignored it.

As the wind picked up, fog clotted on the edges of the grumetree bark and along the knuckles of David's gloves. Then he realized it was not fog, but snow, and he cursed and kicked the sled to a higher speed. The spoor was still plainly visible in the snow, and now he was fairly sure it was leading him straight to the glacier. He had no idea of why the Persuaders had not turned for the Chasm, but he was grateful they hadn't, for he wouldn't have been able to follow them past the rim in the sled. Here in the high-country snow, he guessed they were not very far ahead of him, that he might even be gaining on them. Surely the sticktails were tiring now.

The snow thickened, his comm-unit kept vibrating, and soon it beeped, as well. David was stiff from tension and cold when he broke from the grumetrees into a snow field. He'd reached the edge of the glacier. The snowy slope was deceptively gentle. Its broad expanse was an inviting relief to muscles that were aching from the heavy steering demands of the forest. The falling snow was growing thicker. David knew he should not take the sled onto the glacier, especially not after last night's fresh snowfall, which might have hidden crevasses. He could still see the tracks of the sticktails, and as perishable as they were in the falling snow, he knew he must follow them now before they were gone forever, along with any hope of finding Sindon. Very carefully he nosed the sled out onto the snow field, keeping the sled exactly on top of the spoor, trusting that the sticktails' safe passage was sufficient proof that the sled would pass safely, too.

He followed the trail around an icefall and saw a sag in the underlying pattern of suncups formed by solar radiation, but covered now with snow. He shivered, though not from cold. The area could be honeycombed with hidden crevasses, especially near the edge of the glacier where the underlying ice was stressed as icefalls broke off. The spoor left by the sticktails was beginning to fill in with snow, and David had to slow even more to see it well enough to stay on top. The sled's compass suggested the course he was following might lead over the hip of the glacier, but he couldn't be certain; magnetic compasses were not completely reliable on Cestry Prime, and he was already beyond the range to make instrument corrections with the beacon back in camp.

Soon the tracks were almost impossible to see, and he might have missed yet another turn if a bit of dung hadn't caught his eye. When he stopped to check it out, he realized it was visible only because its warmth was still melting the blowing snow. Back on the sled, he forged ahead eagerly.

Through the swirling snow, David saw something dark ahead, perhaps massive rocks or the crowns of grumetrees at the edge of the glacier. He followed a faint trail that seemed to parallel the edge of the glacier, then turned abruptly into a gut in the ice, which was nearly filled with snow debris. The rubble of snow made it possible to pass through the crevasse to the lower end, which opened against a steep slope of windswept rock. The angle was too steep for the sled, and David stopped. He would have to abandon the sled to continue following the Persuaders. His comm-unit had not stopped beeping. Certain that the Persuaders could not be far ahead, he took the communicator off his belt and left it on the sled.

He powered down the sled and stepped up to the slab of rock; it had been scoured clean, even of small niches and knobs, by the glacier. Using the full flat soles of his boots for support and his hands for stability, he climbed up the slab to the top. There was more rock and scrawny bits of vegetation. He climbed on, following what he thought was the route the sticktails had taken. By the time he found fairly level ground again, he realized he had made a mistake. He could no longer see any signs of the sticktails passing, and the wind had whipped the snowfall into a full blizzard. He tried to turn back, trusting that as long as he was going downhill he would have to intersect the glacier again. If he could find the abandoned sled, he could use its emergency equipment and bivouac safely until the storm ended. It was just possible that the storm had forced the Persuaders to seek shelter, too. When the storm was over, he might pick up their trail again. The sled couldn't be

very far, and the glacier was a feature he couldn't fail to
recognize even in a blizzard.

An hour later, David still had not found the glacier. His
hands and feet were cold, each step becoming more difficult.
He realized he must have climbed out of the glacier valley.
His downhill trek must have taken him into some other
valley. He tried backtracking, but his footprints were gone, and
all he could see was a bewildering world of white snow. He
struggled on, forcing himself to keep moving against the
wind.

He fell, but he picked himself up and walked on feet that felt
like lumps of ice. When he fell again, he rested a moment
before getting up. At least he thought it was only a moment. Or
maybe he had fallen, rested, and gotten up, and this was
another fall. He knew he had to get up; if he lay here for very
long, he'd fall asleep and freeze to death, and then who would
there be to look for Sindon?

"You need help," he heard someone say. "Don't try to
move." The voice was vaguely familiar, yet utterly alien;
David's foggy brain couldn't think why. "I said don't try to
move."

David tried to open his eyes, but they were frozen shut. The
blizzard still raged and he realized he'd just been awakened
from what would have been a fatal sleep. He had no idea of
when he'd fallen again.

"Just a moment," the voice said again. The words were
heavily accented.

David felt something warm on his forehead; then he could
blink his eyes. He opened them to see Rukmani Khan staring
at him. The Khan's bare hand was on his head, its warmth like
fire. Snow frosted the hairs on the Khan's forearm. Instinctively, David tried to grab the Khan, but his arms wouldn't
move. They were frozen, and so were his legs. He flopped
back helplessly in the snow.

"I'm going to persuade your legs to thaw," Rukmani Khan
said, brushing new-fallen snow off David's face. "It will hurt,
but we don't have time to do it any other way. There's a cave
where we can take shelter, but I can't carry you that far. You'll
have to walk."

He put his hands on David's left calf. The Khan's touch
burned like fire, even through David's leggings. He groaned as

the pain spread down to his foot. Then the other leg came to life, aching and throbbing. David screamed until the Khan touched his head again, and then the pain went away. David stared at him, amazed.

"That won't last long," the Khan said apologetically. "It's not something I do well. But it will have to do. Come on. On your feet."

The pain returned before they'd gone only a few steps, but by then the Khan had a good enough hold on him to keep the forward motion going. David groaned with every step, but he didn't stop.

His eyes froze shut again; he stepped where the Khan led him. His feet and legs throbbed, his arms hung like useless sausages in his sleeves.

Finally the wind stopped and he felt rock and dirt under his feet instead of snow. He sensed the Khan's warm touch across his forehead again, thawing the ice on his eyes. When he opened his eyes, his vision was clear. The Khan was still holding him up, vapors issuing from his bare forearms and hands, his torso now covered with fine split-skin robes, too thin-looking to keep out the biting wind. The bright red banners were gone.

"Just a few more steps," the Khan said.

The Khan had brought David into a little cave. David forced himself to take two more steps, then gasped for air, his breath coming in shallow but frosty streams.

Then the Khan touched David's head, and David felt himself sinking to his knees, collapsing, unable to help himself, strangely willing to succumb.

Succumb to what? Sleep? Unconsciousness? Not death, or he wouldn't be able to wonder what the Khan had done to him. He realized whatever it was was over now, for he was aware of his supine position, his tingling feet, and still-frozen hands.

He opened his eyes again just in time to see the Khan coming back in through the cave entrance, carrying some frozen logs under his arms. The Khan put them down in front of David, arranging them just so before placing his bare hands on the bottom two logs. Steam and smoke rose from between the Khan's fingers, then flames burst through. The Khan jerked his hands away from the fire.

"Jesus!" David breathed.

"You're awake," the Khan said, looking at David. He was a big man, his hair brown and curly. Even his beard was curly, and very thick. "We can get started. Your hands won't be as painful as the legs; we have time now." The Khan gestured to the fire. "It's easier than persuading the rock."

"To do what?" David asked, but he thought he knew. The warmth of the Summer Palace walls had lasted months after the Khan was gone, and they'd used the time to arrange the heating coils the crew had brought inside.

The Khan knelt and took David's hand in his. David couldn't feel anything, not for a long time. But finally he felt a tingling in his fingers, and then some aching. But it was not so painful as when his legs had thawed.

"What are you doing to me?" David asked. "I mean, how?"

The Khan's smile was surprisingly pleasant. "Persuading the molecules in your hand to behave as they did before they were frozen. Exciting them, but carefully, to minimize damage." His purple eyes met David's for a moment. "I wasn't as careful with your feet, but it was haste or your life."

The Khan examined David's tingling red hand and nodded. He fumbled with the closure strip on David's coat, got it parted, then placed David's hand under the flap next to his breast. David gasped, but the Khan was only seeking the greatest warmth for the injured hand. Then he took David's other still-frozen hand and cupped it in his own. The Khan's fingers moved slowly over David, causing dead white flesh to slowly turn pink, and finally scarlet. Satisfied, he opened David's coat again, and David crossed both hands over his chest. The Khan fastened the garment above and below David's wrists.

"Flex them gently," the Khan instructed him. "Stop if it hurts too much. No need to rush now. How are your feet?"

"Cold," David said. Icy cold, but he could move them.

The Khan nodded, unconcerned, and he sat back by the fire, looking easily at David. "Even the abos know better than to stay out in weather like this," he said. "We thought you New People were smarter. What kept you from seeking shelter?"

"I'd have lost your trail in the storm."

"It was our intention that the storm discourage you. The people behind you turned back at the edge of the glacier. Why didn't you?"

At first David shrugged, but the Khan's eyes were so penetrating that David felt defiance rising despite knowing it might be wiser to keep silent. "You killed four people today. We don't let violence like that go unpunished."

"Nor do we," the Khan said, the stare unflinching.

"If you thought we could sanction your taking revenge, you thought wrong. And you are still holding four of our people captive. Until they are free, we'll come after you every chance we get."

"We have no captives," the Khan said.

"You're lying!" David was breathing hard, trembling, unnerved.

"No captives," the Khan repeated. "Sindon and the others came willingly. We left gold in your camp in respect for your custom of contracts. If you're as smart as we think, you'll have similar respect for our customs, too. You should not have followed us."

"Sindon is all right?" David asked shakily, and he could tell the Khan had heard the fear in his voice.

For a moment, the Khan studied him with intense and suspicious eyes. "You're David Quarrels," he said, finally. "I remember you. I hadn't realized you were the one."

"The one?"

"The one . . . Sindon left. Not surprising now that I realize who you are. You ignored Sindon. You were the one who preferred chipping pieces of the palace and putting them in your pockets to wine, music, and some camaraderie. And now you've become lost in the snow. It's not hard to believe Sindon would prefer a stronger man."

"I don't know what you mean," David said, taking his hands out from underneath his coat.

Rukmani Khan fixed him with a long, hard look. David knew when he was on the receiving end of an appraising stare. He sat up and glared back. "You do not misunderstand me," the Khan said at last. "I've learned your language from Sindon and I've used the expression with as much precision as is possible. Do you really need me to be more blunt?"

"I don't believe . . ."

"Lovers," The Khan said. "But really lovers. Nothing like the pitiful spasms you gave her."

"If you hurt her . . ."

"I don't think it was pain she writhed in when she sat atop my member. She took all that I could give her, and she asked me for . . ."

And David leaped on the Khan, pulling his knife out in midair, fully intending to kill him. But the Khan's hand closed around his wrist, and involuntarily David's hand opened and he dropped the knife. With his other fist, he landed a hard blow on the side of the Khan's face before the Khan reached around to touch his spine, and David felt himself fall against the big man like jelly. David couldn't move, not a single muscle.

The Khan pulled himself free as if David were no more than a grain sack. Then he stood for a moment with his hand on his jaw, moving his fingers as he had when he'd warmed David. David was certain he'd broken the man's jaw, but it gave him little satisfaction. He was lying helpless before the Khan, unable to move, angry, and terrified.

"Frightening, isn't it?" the Khan said, stepping more fully into David's view. "I could just reach out and stop your heart, and you know it, don't you? You watched what happened in the orchard. Oh, yes. I remember you. I was looking for you because I'd promised Sindon you would not be one of the four. And I'm sure if I'd broken my word, I'd have lost her forever. Even now, you have Sindon to thank for your life. I could throw you back out into the storm and leave you to freeze to death, and maybe she'd forget you soon and come back to me. But then I'd have to live with knowing she never had an opportunity to choose between us. Watching her choose me is a pleasure I will not miss, not even for the satisfaction of having your life."

The Khan pushed him over onto his stomach, and David sprawled helplessly.

"She's mine, David Quarrels. You may sleep alongside her and think she's yours, but it's nothing more than borrowed time. She'll never be able to forget what she had with me. She's mine, and I'll claim her again, and when I do, she will come willingly, just as she did the last time."

The Khan sat down beside him. "She may try to forget, but every time you touch her, she'll be longing for more than you can give. Let me tell you about the many ways I pleased Sindon . . ."

By the time David could move again, the little fire had almost died out, and he was cold. The Khan, of course, was gone.

17.

HANDCUFFED AND FETTERED with makeshift chains and wire, David looked on as a security technician installed perimeter lasers and tinglers over the door and window of an upper-floor room in the two-decker that had served as dormitory and central living area since winter began. The technician had just finished anchoring tingler sockets in the metallic foam under the window sash when Brown Roberts returned with Theo Tucker.

"How high should I set the tinglers?" the technician asked.

"All the way up," Theo replied before Brown could.

"Jesus! Do you want to kill me?" David said, aghast. "You don't set them that high for grassbears."

He'd been manhandled from the moment Security found him walking home in the snow, then interrogated as if he had stolen the power sled, even though David knew they had recovered the sled before finally finding him through his locater bracelet. His explanation of the signal's being cut off while he was in the cave with the Khan didn't seem to satisfy the interrogators at first.

"Just want to discourage you from leaving," Theo told him.

"This is rather extreme," David said, straining his wrists against the wires that cuffed him to the barrel-like metallic-foam chair.

"You should have thought of that before. Theft and assault are serious offenses," Theo retorted. "Either one can get you fired."

"I'll bet Chloe is celebrating," David said sarcastically. Then he shrugged. "Tell her I said fire me and get it over with. There's still four months until *Pelican* returns, four months to look for the Winter Palace." He looked pointedly at Theo, but the CEO merely shook his head and sat down on one of the other chairs.

"You talk to him, Brown," Theo said.

"Theft and assault are also criminal offenses," Brown said bluntly. "We'll have to keep you confined until *Pelican* returns, if we decide to press criminal charges."

Stunned, David stared at the security chief. "You can't mean it," he said at last. "You found the sled, so it isn't as if I'd lost completely unreplaceable equipment. And I didn't hit Theo any harder than I needed to keep him from stopping me."

"There's also your failure to give assistance to injured workers . . ."

"They were dead!"

". . . failure to obey return summonses, failure to notify Security of your whereabouts and condition, not to mention endangering your own life by following suspected felons or what may turn out to be enemies of state, such endangerment being a policy violation, and doing it during a storm, which is further endangerment and further violation."

"How long did it take you to comb Company Policy and Criminal Statutes to come up with all these charges?" David asked angrily.

"Now that I have your attention, maybe we can talk," Brown said, his voice quiet. He took the tingler control box from the technician and gestured for him to leave. When the door closed, he reset the tingler and turned back to David. "You haven't been charged . . . yet. A lot depends on how you conduct yourself in the next few hours."

David looked at Brown quizzically.

"Sindon's back," he said, pulling up a stool to sit facing David.

"Sindon! Is she all right? Where is she? Let me see her," David demanded, pulling against the restraints so hard that the wire started to cut through his flesh.

"Sindon is fine. The medic said she's more fit than most of us. She's still in the clinic, but only because we didn't have a bunk assignment for her right away." Brown took a laser wire-clipper out of his pocket. "Now, if you'll stop pulling, I'll cut you loose."

David gripped the arms of the chair to control his impatience. As Brown started to clip the wires on his wrists, he asked, "When did she get back?"

"She came in when the storm broke, riding on one of their sticktails. She claims she spent the storm in the stable in the Summer Palace, sleeping. We followed her footprints back, and found no prints leading up to the Summer Palace, so it appears she was telling the truth. There'll be an inquiry into why she didn't try to warn us, since she tells us she knew of the Khan's intention to kill four people."

"She couldn't if she was persuaded to sleep," David argued, working the kinks out of his hands now that they were free.

Brown shrugged as he leaned over to clip the wires on David's ankles. "We still don't have any real knowledge of what it means to be persuaded to sleep. There'll be questions about whether she could have resisted."

"Yes," David said, not wondering at all about her resisting sleep. Would the Khan have delighted in telling David otherwise?

"You think she could have resisted?" Brown asked, sounding surprised.

"No. I was saying *yes* to there being questions," David said, recovering. "I've been through it three times now; I know there's no way to resist." He looked at Theo, expecting a confirming nod. The CEO sat impassively.

"David, have you given any thought to how much credence will be given to a man who is already on probation for violating his model behavior clause, and who, while on probation, further violated policy and may even have criminal charges pending?"

"Why do you doubt her?" David asked, his anger mounting. "She's a victim, not a perpetrator. Or is this your way of getting back at me?"

Brown exchanged a worried glance with Theo.

"Brown's trying to let you know how serious this situation is, for both of you," Theo said, leaning too close, gazing fiercely into David's eyes. "You see, Sindon wasn't kidnapped. She went with the Khan voluntarily."

David almost snapped. That was the last thing he had expected to hear, and irrationally, it made him angry and ashamed. The Khan had told him the truth; he'd kept no captives. Suddenly every word of love David had spoken to

Sindon seemed spoiled, because they couldn't have meant much to her if she had gone with the Khan.

Theo was still talking. "She lived with him in the Winter Palace, and those are her words, David, not mine . . . that she lived with him."

"I know," David said tonelessly.

"When she decided to return, he personally escorted her back. She, too, is in violation of policy, and because of the deaths of the four lumberjacks the day before yesterday, she may also face charges for criminal negligence."

David shook his head. "She wouldn't . . . she couldn't . . ." He looked from Theo to Brown; their faces were grave. "Let me see her."

"Soon," Theo said. "If I'm assured of your cooperation."

"Cooperation for what?" David asked.

"She was with them for more than what? eight months?"

"Almost nine standard," David said. Every day of which had been a nightmare for him, and every night of which he'd spent sweating in terror for her life. Had she thought of him at all during that time? Or had she forgotten him the moment the Khan touched her?

"A long time no matter how you measure. She says she recorded everything. If she did a good enough job on language studies, it could prove the Persuaders are interlopers."

"Now I understand," David said, almost allowing himself to smile. "You need me to certify the report; after all, Sindon's only a tech."

"That would help," Theo admitted. "But first we need you to get the data from her. She says she made the study on your instructions, and that chain-of-command policy requires that you see it first."

"Really?" David said with a casual shrug. He remembered how upset Sindon had been when David had scolded her for filing the report on meeting the old Persuader without letting him see it first. It was just like her to cling to the letter of his mandate even though the circumstances were not even vaguely similar. It also made him worry about what instructions he had given her to make a report. He didn't remember doing it.

"I want that data," Theo said.

"I'll bet you do," David said. They stared at each other, David realizing that Theo did not fully trust him to do his duty and hand the data over. "I want to see Sindon. I'll do whatever you ask."

"Then you'll get the report and turn it over to us?" Brown said, looking greatly relieved.

David nodded.

"Well that's clear enough, isn't it, T.T.?" Brown asked.

But Theo was frowning, his arms folded across his chest. "What about certification?"

David shrugged. "I won't know until I see the data, will I? Or are you asking me to certify it sight unseen? Is that what this is all about? All these charges of policy violation and possible criminal charges . . . do they evaporate if I agree to certify the data?"

"Of course not," Brown said quickly.

But of course the charges would be dropped, David believed now. He should have guessed the moment Brown started talking about how much trouble he was in. Theo had come along to make sure Brown did the job right.

"My investigative reports of your conduct and Sindon's will only have the facts," Brown said a little too indignantly. "Besides," he added, somewhat sadly David thought, "the decision won't be mine."

"It's mine," Theo said ominously. "And no, I don't want you to certify the data without seeing it. But I don't plan to evaluate Brown's reports . . . for a while. You might want to think of it as my wanting to see if you can behave in a professional manner now that the strain of your . . . tech . . . having been gone is relieved."

"You'd never make a charge of theft of the sled stick in a court of law," David said. "Not under the circumstances. What possible profit could I make? Who was I going to sell it to? The abos?"

"Don't antagonize him, David," Brown said under his breath. "That assault charge could keep you off the payroll of every major company in the Hub, and whether or not to press it becomes a personal matter for T.T."

David glanced up at Theo. "It all rests with you, doesn't it? Assault charges for me, and corroborating or not corroborating that persuaded sleep can be resisted." David detected a troubled shadow in the deep-set eyes, but then Theo got up and turned his back on David.

"Let's go see Sindon," Theo said.

Silently, David got to his feet.

They went to the far side of the two-decker and downstairs to the area that was used as a clinic. The first room served as a lab and examination room, and the one behind it was a three-bed infirmary. David was relieved not to see perimeter tinglers installed here, which he hoped meant that Brown believed Sindon's claim of being persuaded to sleep so that she couldn't warn the lumberjacks—even though Theo might choose to cast doubt on the notion that such sleep was irresistible. It seemed faintly ludicrous; surely Theo knew that empirical evidence would prove him wrong. Brown himself, along with several supposedly stalwart security officers, had been persuaded to sleep. Still, David supposed, the CEO's decision could carry the decision on Cestry Prime, that in the end every one else had only opinions.

As soon as Brown opened the infirmary door, David could see Sindon lying on the closest bed. Her back was to them, her red hair cascading over the edge of the bed, halfway to the floor.

"Sindon?"

"David!" She turned quickly, as if she meant to leap out of the bed and into his arms. But she saw Theo and Brown standing there with him, and maybe she saw the horror on David's face when he saw her bulging stomach. She hesitated, then snatched up the bedcovers and drew them up to her chin.

"Whose child?" David asked her, trying to remain calm.

"Um, I'm back," Sindon said, ignoring his question. Her face was a mask of business-as-usual. "I have a lot to tell you. Or you can read it in my report."

"Whose child?" David persisted. "Whose?" he shouted.

The mask broke, and she frowned and shook her head slightly.

"Mine?" David asked, shaking off Brown's quick restraining hand. He forced himself to be calm, to keep the accusations inside.

She seemed rooted to the bed, frozen. He didn't know if she was angry or frightened. Her face was impassive now, and pale.

"The Khan said . . . things I didn't want to believe." Minutes ticked by while he waited for her to deny it. The silence grew until David could not live in it any longer. "But you did sleep with him, didn't you? All this time I've been worried sick wondering if you were even alive, you've been fucking a goddamned . . ."

"Read my report," she said furiously, cutting him off. "It was research!"

"Resear . . ." He choked, felt every bit as helpless as when the Khan had rendered his limbs useless and told him how he had made love to Sindon.

"Yes, research," she repeated. She dropped the covers and pulled down the front of her gown, briefly exposing her swollen breasts. She pulled a locket from around her neck, fumbled with it to get it open, and dumped out some memory capsules. "It's all in these," she said, offering the memory capsules with an open hand. "The language data, observations I made of the Winter Palace, their food, habits, everything."

When David didn't step forward, Theo did. He took the capsules from Sindon.

"How did you obtain this data?" Theo asked.

"With the lingochine," Sindon replied, obviously relieved to face someone besides David. She sounded proud, not defensive. "It's a fairly decent scribe when you know how to use it."

"Tell me he forced you," David said, not caring about anything except the raging jealousy he was feeling.

"You'd know when you checked the report that it was a lie," she said, crisply, angrily, as if she felt David were somehow at fault for wanting to hear her denial.

Anguished, David slapped her hard across the face, and raised his other hand to hit her again. Brown grabbed him and pulled him back through the door. "I could kill you," David screamed. Then Brown slammed the door.

Brown left him alone in the room upstairs, the room that was a cell, the room that was a torture chamber. Twice, in the days that followed, David started to look at the data in the capsules Sindon had carried back with her from the Winter Palace. Her entries were dated, and each observation carefully cross-referenced with at least four similar ones before stating as fact that Persuaders could turn water into steam or ice, fracture rock or melt it, stimulate plants to grow or wilt, turn sandstone into crystal and coal into diamonds. A touch from a skilled healer could mend abrasions or broken bones; a mother's touch quieted wailing babies immediately. A lover's fleeting touch brought instant ecstasy. Twice he stumbled on entries that described in meticulous detail her unabashed pleasure in being touched by the Khan, and twice he smashed the screen, first with his hands and then with his feet, until the instrument was as lifeless as he wished the Khan were, and maybe Sindon, too.

"I didn't know quite what to expect," Theo Tucker said when he brought in the third screen, "but I'd say your deliberately smashing company property is unprofessional. I'm sorry about what happened, but I need your certification on this data."

"Get someone else to do it," David said, "and let me out of here. Fire me and get it over with."

"There isn't anyone else who's qualified to certify this data. I've gone through it myself, and to me it looks good. She flagged every word she thought might have Indo-European origins, but her flags aren't enough. You've got to corroborate her methods in gathering the data, too."

"I can't do it. Not until I've killed the bastard."

"If I thought you might succeed where I could get at the body, I might be tempted to let you."

David looked at him strangely.

"Genetic comparisons," he said simply. "I've been searching the computer memory for a way of not using this report. A strand of DNA would do it. I wish I had known when we buried those people in the Chasm. Too bad we were so determined to treat the bodies with complete respect."

"And ended up insulting them anyhow," David pointed out, remembering what he'd read in Sindon's report of the Persuaders' horror at finding their dead buried. Only cremation was acceptable to them.

"I even asked Sindon for a tissue sample from the child when it's born," he said. "She turned me down."

"Why?"

"To protect the child's rights. The DNA might not be human, and then there'd be some legal questions about the child's right to inherit, if anything happened to Sindon."

David shrugged. It hadn't occurred to him that Rukmani Khan might be *that* different.

"David, I need you to certify that report. I've tried to spare you, but I can't. People's livelihoods are at stake. Your own is."

"I don't care if you fire me," David said.

The CEO sighed and sat down in the only other chair in the room. "Listen to me, David. I've tried to tell you before that I know you were in love with Sindon, and I've tried to make it clear that I didn't want to have to put that in your records. But you're acting like you want me to throw the book at you, now, when it's all over. What good is that going to do?"

David shrugged. "I don't know, but I don't care, either."

"You say that now, but a year from now you'll feel differently."

David shook his head.

Again Theo sighed. "Sindon has asked to be released from her contract with the Company."

"She wants to go back to the Hub?" David asked, feeling a twinge of fear he didn't know was there. If she left, all hope would be gone.

"No. She wants to stay. She wants to be the first home-steader on Cestry Prime. She can get out of the contract because of the pregnancy. She'd be on maternity leave when the renewal comes up, so she can negotiate it now. I can accept her resignation and deed over a section of land to her in lieu of her reenlistment bonus."

David looked at him expectantly. "Or?" he prodded.

"Or I can charge her with neglecting her job for eight months."

"If this report turns out to be any good, she could sue you."

"I can charge her with sleeping with her supervisor."

"You'd need proof, and I don't believe you have any."

"Your word would be sufficient. Then I can send her back to the Hub, and she'd be discharged there."

"Why are you telling me?"

"Because I want you to tell me what to do. Tell me what would inspire you to work on this data."

"Let me see if I've got this right. If I do the report, I get to decide if Sindon stays or goes?"

"Let's just say I'll give careful consideration to your recommendation."

David laughed in spite of himself. "Sindon would take your eyes out if she suspected."

Theo nodded. "She has a lot of . . . spunk."

David closed his eyes and tried to think. The CEO was offering him a bit of revenge, if he wanted it. And why not take it? Sindon betrayed him, ruined every dream he ever had of making her his wife some day, if not here on Cestry Prime then on some other planet where he could be his own boss on his own piece of land, with no company to tell either of them they weren't meeting expectations or that they were off the plan. Even if there were some way for him to finally bring himself to forgive her, and if she even wanted forgiveness—which he didn't think she did. Not Sindon!—he doubted that he could ever forget. And if he tried, wouldn't seeing the child every day remind him of the Khan's words? (*Lovers*, he had said, *really lovers*.) David shuddered and shook his head.

"What would she do as a settler?" David asked, opening his eyes and looking at the CEO. "Has she said?"

He nodded. "The sticktail she rode in on is male, but there are two others in the stable in the Winter Palace which are in foal. She says they will both bear female sticktails, something the Khan told her. She considers them the start of a herd. The land's abundant; she might make it."

"Payment for services rendered?" David asked, feeling hot and angry.

Theo shrugged. "She's quite specific about their being a loan, not a gift. Probably a ruse so that the Company doesn't try to take title. But she needn't fear. We don't have any interest in sticktails."

"What if she doesn't make it?" David asked. "Homesteading is hard. And what if the Company fails and withdraws?"

"We're not going to let her starve, if that's what you're worried about. She has some benefits coming, you know. And the Company is not going to fail."

"You going to get rid of me?"

"Why would I do that?" Theo asked irritably. "The Company has a lot invested in . . . in your learning curve."

"You mean you already own me," David said resignedly. "At least you will when I ask you to let her stay."

"Then you'll do the report?"

There was only a faint tremor in his voice as he said, "Yes, I'll do the report."

18.

Servants had cleared away Sindon's uneaten meal, laid out an abundance of fresh food for Rukmani Khan, knowing he would be starved on his return. They'd even put new wool in his cushions and beaten the carpets and swept the floors, but they had failed to notice the few petals that had fallen from Sindon's hair. He sat staring at them, ignoring the food even though he was famished. He had not believed she would leave him, still could not believe it would be forever. She had been angry with him for deceiving her into believing she was welcome and safe in the Winter Palace, and she had been frightened at finding herself on the Altar of Justice. And he knew he had to let her go, if only to find out for herself that no man of her own kind could touch her body or her heart like Rukmani Khan. Yet when he remembered David Quarrels' reaction to Sindon's name, he shivered and wished Sindon had not made him promise not to kill him. David Quarrels, Rukmani Khan knew, did not believe Sindon was out of reach to him.

He realized he was still staring at the flower petals. He picked them up carefully, fingertips freshening the flaccid edges until he caught a trace of the scent molecules in his nostrils. He put the petals in a clear jar near his bed cushions where he would remember to tend them so that he could smell their fragrance every night and while he dreamed.

He looked again at the table, sighed because despite his hunger and even beginning to feel chilled from the need for food, he didn't want to perform this duty alone. But he did; he couldn't help doing it any more than he could help breathing. And he did feel better when it was done.

174

The chemlamps were dwindling of their own accord, and he sank back in the cushions to sit in the darkness. Then Rukmani Khan heard Gulnar's footsteps on the walkway outside his chamber. He'd half expected her, and completely dreaded her arrival. He reached up and persuaded the lamp to glow as Gulnar threw open the door. She stood in the doorway, her shoulders thrown back and her eyes piercing, staring at him. Her garment, he noticed, was new, though she wore the same pitiful shawl over her thin shoulders that she always wore. As tired as he was from the long journey back from the rim, he sat up, leaning against the gritty sandstone wall to face her. It was inevitable, and better done sooner than later.

"I did not give you leave to take vengeance from the New People," she said, standing stiffly in the doorway.

"Nonetheless, I did," he said. He thought he heard someone whispering in the hall.

"You deliberately defied me."

He nodded. "Deliberately."

"Why?" she asked, her voice shrill and pained. Then someone whispered again, and she stiffened. "Such behavior cannot go unpunished."

"I know," he said, feeling sad. Gulnar didn't want to talk about punishment, but the presence of whoever was in the hallway—the new priest, no doubt—was preventing her from talking about anything else. And him, too. "Gulnar," he said gently, "why don't you come in and close the door?"

She didn't answer.

"Witnesses!" he said bitterly. "Is that your idea, or the priest's?"

"I could have summoned you," she said, a tinge of indignation in her voice, as if saving him a summons were a grand concession.

"If you believed you needed witnesses to coerce me into submitting to whatever punishment you deal, then you should have summoned me," he said, even more indignant than she.

She took one step inside, glanced hesitantly at the empty cushions Sindon had used, then closed the door.

Rukmani Khan waited patiently while his wife stared at him. He could tell she was near tears, struggling inside, and he could not help feeling moved, even if only a little.

"They say you sent her away," she said, her voice barely a whisper.

He could have left it at that, spared himself and her any further pain, but he knew how deeply Gulnar plumbed for any glimmer of hope. "No," he said. "I did not send her away."

"Kangra said she was gone!" Gulnar said, tears springing to her eyes.

"Kangra spoke the truth. Sindon is gone," he said, full knowing it was easier not to mention that Sindon's leaving wasn't of his choosing. Even now he wouldn't say it, but from the look on Gulnar's face, she understood completely.

He might just as well have slapped Gulnar. She turned her back to him, and he knew she was crying. "If only *I* could have given you a child," she said between quiet sobs.

"You'll never understand will you?" In disgust, Rukmani Khan pushed the cushions aside and got up. "Our not having a child had nothing to do with it."

Gulnar stopped mid-sob. "But I thought . . ."

"Thought what?" he said when her voice trailed off. "That I stopped loving you because you couldn't conceive?" When she nodded, he shook his head. "Gulnar, we knew when we married that you would be unlikely ever to conceive. You cannot persuade an egg to cling."

"But even Natarjan said I should not stop trying," she said, "and his being one of your confidants, I was sure that meant having a child was important to you."

Rukmani Khan sighed. "Natarjan meant well. He was trying to tell you to let me help you."

She paled visibly, the muscles in her face becoming taut. "That's disgusting," she said. "I couldn't allow that any more than . . . than the other."

It was Rukmani Khan's turn to feel struck, and he turned away. There was a silence; then he spoke over his shoulder. "Would it have been so bad to allow your body to succumb to the pleasures I could have persuaded? How could it have been bad for you to feel good for a while in my arms?"

"It would have been humiliating," she said, nearly spitting the words at him. "Lying there like an abo with you rutting like an animal!"

"So you blocked," he said, finally accusing her. "You used

what little persuasion you have to feel nothing. Nothing at all! Did you never give some thought to how I must feel?"

"You didn't need me for your pleasures," she said archly.

She was referring, he was sure, to dalliances with sporting women, and girls who came to the Summer Palace, and to Sundari who was innocent, and to Sindon, who was not. "I used to feel guilty for my amorous playing," Rukmani Khan said to her. "But that was not as bad as the other feeling. You had it right when you said I was like a rutting animal; that's what it felt like with you." Rukmani Khan turned to find her staring at him. Her purple eyes were pools of anger.

"You obviously liked it well enough to take up with another woman who could not persuade her body to do what you wanted it to do," she said sharply.

"The difference is that she was content to let me persuade her to heights you refuse even to imagine, and it was easy to do when I didn't encounter blocks," he said. "And I know you think less of her for not being determined to do it on her own, but I, for one, was grateful."

"It has always been that, hasn't it? You never could forgive my not being as persuasive as you. You used to tell me it didn't matter, but it did. I could not give you the kind of sex you wanted."

Rukmani Khan shook his head. "You refuse to understand. Even when we were young, I knew you were bitter over not being able to persuade as well as I. But I believed a time would come when you would realize it did not matter."

"Perhaps you think Natarjan should have set me aside," she said, "that we should not have married, that he should have chosen some other woman to be Khana."

"It never occurred to him or to me," Rukmani Khan said, though he wondered now why it had not. And then he remembered why, and knew that given the same circumstances, it had been right to marry her. "A khana who could not persuade would not be tempted to venture into forbidden realms like our fathers were. A khana who could not persuade would be able to lead us in new directions; I followed faithfully."

"And we are nearly free of relying on persuasion for our very lives," she said. "We couldn't go on the way we were, living from season to season, thriving or failing at the whim of the rain. I thought you understood."

Her eyes were red, brimming with tears. It wasn't easy to remember how lovely those eyes had been when he'd married her, hard to recall how fine he'd felt when he'd looked into them. He remembered the vows he'd made to her, though—and knew he had lived by them all these years, except for one. Breaking that one made him feel ashamed sometimes, but he couldn't help himself. And he couldn't forgive her for not releasing him from it. "I built your greencaverns. You have redroots, dewberry, and graincrops ripening summer and winter. What more can you want from me?"

"It's true. The crops in the greencaverns are thriving. But how much better would we be doing now if you and your vassal lords did not waste yourselves on the Summer Palace?"

"The waste is here, Gulnar. A waste of talent that could have been used for more than persuading greencaverns out of stone."

"Oh, yes, your art. How could I have forgotten?" she said. "And what do you think Hari, Moti, and Natarjan would say now about this incredible compulsion you and your vassal lords have to build magnificent chambers? Do you think they would agree with you now, that it's just as important as grain in the cellars?"

"You forgot Sundari," he said.

"I've forgotten nothing," she snapped.

Nor forgiven the girl, Rukmani Khan thought, even though she'd done nothing to earn Gulnar's enmity. He wondered if her spies ever told her that nothing much had come of his notice of the girl, that Sundari had chosen Kangra. Probably not. And she'd probably never even wondered why Kangra had provided so much support to Gulnar in getting the new priest named and in arranging to take vengeance on four innocent women. "You may choose to think lightly of what we do in the Summer Palace, and you may choose to believe that the lives of innocent women taken without risk would have been satisfaction enough for honor. But I choose to believe in the old ways, and you cannot stop me."

"I don't want to stop you," she said carefully. "I merely wish to restore balance between the old ways and the new. I want our people safe from the horrors of unbridled persuasion, and you must admit that we are, at last, on the brink of finding that."

"Yes, but you never really understood that the greencaverns themselves would never have been if I and my vassals could not have persuaded them out of the stone. I will always wonder, Gulnar, what natural inclination you might have had if you weren't so preoccupied with what you didn't have."

"I don't see that leading our people in new ways has anything to do with sex, except that I know it keeps us apart." She bit her lip. "I miss you at my side, Rukmani Khan," she said, her words sounding a bit too soft, as if they had been carefully rehearsed. "Perhaps I too have been negligent of duty. I will"—she took a deep breath—"let you do what you want."

"Timon doesn't mince words the way Natarjan did, does he?" Rukmani Khan said, quite surprised the new priest had guessed the truth. Or maybe he hadn't guessed. Perhaps Natarjan had told a great deal to his acolytes over the years, though obviously not everything. "It's too late, Gulnar. I no longer desire doing *anything* to you."

He thought she might cry again, but she merely nodded. "We expected a reply like this," she said. "I will not beg you to do what's needed to make an heir, but I will not stop hoping that you'll change your mind. I am forced to remind you of your vows: to obey the laws I have imposed in the Winter Palace, to provide the sweat of your brow for the Winter Palace, your sword and life in defense of the Winter Palace, your honor, your fidelity."

"Release me, Gulnar. I cannot be faithful to you, and in not being faithful, I've lost some measure of my honor as well."

"Is that why you defied me, in some mistaken attempt to restore your honor?"

"Obeying the laws of the Summer Palace for revenge was not a breach of honor," he said. "I vowed to keep them, too, remember?"

"And we knew the laws for summer and winter might be in conflict from time to time, and we agreed to settle such conflicts in council chambers."

"Not with only one of us present," he reminded her sharply.

"Then why weren't you there?" she asked.

"I made a mistake," he said gloomily. "But I won't make it again."

"I take that as a good sign," she said. "A gesture of your willingness to restore the balance. I look forward to having you at my side again in the Moon Council."

"Gulnar?"

"Yes?"

"Release me."

Tears sprang to her eyes.

"Let me go!"

"I won't," she cried.

Nearly as anguished as she, Rukmani Khan just shook his head. He realized that she couldn't let go, and he wondered if there were anything he would ever be able to say or do to change that. Probably not, he decided. The shame of his infidelity had not done it, not even when he had ceased being discreet by keeping Sindon in his chambers. "Take what satisfaction you can in knowing that I will always find it difficult to live with any measure of dishonor," he said. "But if you cannot bring yourself to release me from my vow of fidelity, then I will learn to bear it."

"I have offered to humiliate myself under your hands and you dare talk to me about dishonor?" she cried out, grief suddenly turning to rage.

"That much dishonor I cannot bring myself to do," he said, equally angry.

"You leave me no choice," she said. "I will not overlook your indiscretions any longer. You will do penance."

"As you see fit," he said, clasping his hands behind him in formal submission.

"For each month you spent with her, you will spend two years in the Winter Palace," Gulnar said coldly.

He stared at her, almost not believing. It meant not going to the Summer Palace for sixteen years. "You are cruel beyond belief," he said. "It's a wonder you wanted witnesses. What will my vassal lords think of you when there is no one to lead them to the Summer Palace for sixteen years?"

"They will resign themselves to the laws of the Winter Palace," she said.

He nodded, realizing she had thought this punishment over very carefully, probably discussed it at great length with the priest, as well. "But they will not have forgotten the ways of the Summer Palace, not even after sixteen years. And, Gulnar, nor will I," he said.

"Sixteen years is a long time. Anything can happen."

"The glacier might grow to cover the Summer Palace, or the abos or even the New People might decide to live in it, for you're right. Sixteen years is a long time. But, Gulnar, I will never touch you again, not in sixteen years and not in eternity. Not quite *anything* can happen."

"I will not hold you to that," she said, turning at last to open the door.

"How bitter must my words be to make you understand? It's no longer in your power. I won't ever touch you again," he said softly.

Gulnar shook her head with a hint of nonchalance, and Rukmani Khan knew there was nothing he could say to dissuade her. He watched her open the door and pass into the hall, listening to her footsteps until he could no longer hear the faintest echo. Then he realized the priest, Timon, had stepped into the chamber and was waiting to be recognized.

"What do you want?" Rukmani Khan asked, tired now and depressed, as much over the discussion with Gulnar as the unexpectedly severe penance she had imposed.

"Some penitents find it easier to endure if the penance is well known. It would save you the embarrassment of telling your vassal lords why they must cease making plans to return to the Summer Palace."

"You dare suggest I cannot face my own vassal lords and tell them myself?" he said, astounded at the priest's open lack of trust.

The priest blinked nervously. "They will be disappointed. Sixteen years will seem like forever, and they will hold you responsible."

He stared at the priest, disbelieving. "How much more do you know?" he said. "Is it you she turns to for advice now that Natarjan is gone?"

"Since she cannot go to her own husband, where else would she go?"

"I don't know. *But I don't trust you the way I trusted Natarjan*, he thought unhappily. He hadn't always liked Natarjan, but he did trust him. If he had been inclined to excuse this new priest for the travesty at the Altar of Justice because of exuberance due to the newness of his office (or even to blame himself for being so ignorant of what was going on), Rukmani Khan no longer felt even the slightest charity now. "But I know this," he said solemnly. "A priest who would even hint that I would not step up to the responsibility of doing my penance without his help is neither true priest nor worthy of my notice."

"But I *am* the true priest," Timon said with an unpleasant smile, "and not even you can change that."

"Dead priests can't give advice, not even poor advice," Rukmani Khan responded.

Timon paled. "You wouldn't risk the Altar of Justice," he said finally.

"You aren't certain though, are you?" Rukmani Khan gave a false laugh. "You see the problem more clearly now, don't you? You don't know what I'm capable of doing. Keep that in mind from now on, Timon. And don't ever make the mistake of impugning my honor again."

"I never meant any offense," the priest said.

"I know," the Khan returned. "But you gave it by not knowing what it means to be the Khan of the Persuaders. Now get out of my sight before I change my mind about this not being the moment to risk the Altar of Justice."

The priest didn't wait to be asked again to leave, but Rukmani Khan knew it was not the end of dealing with Timon.

PART
II.

19.

THE KHAN'S SUMMER Palace evoked awful memories in David Quarrels. They had paved the gardens to make landing pads for windshots and installed poles higher than the tallest turret from which flew flags of half the known worlds, with corporate banners beneath every one. But that did not keep fine-grained limestone walls from glowing like gold ore in sunshine, and it didn't change what the Khan had done. David had looked at the Summer Palace every day for sixteen years, and he still shuddered when he had to go inside.

Chloe Brass had summoned David, and he couldn't think of why. They rarely saw each other, for she had ridden the swell of a growing corporation until she was Theo Tucker's second in command, but David's status had, if anything, dwindled. The abos had been absorbed into the community, and there was little in the way of challenges for change-engineering anymore. He taught at the Company school now, and this year he'd moved into the dormitory that housed boarders from the outlying ranches and mines. Tara, Sindon's daughter, was no longer the oldest child on Cestry Prime; homesteaders had arrived with children of all ages.

"Why has Brass Woman called for you?" the abo fisher asked him. Like most abos, the fisher was short and wiry, his pale blue skin sunburned purple after the first warm days of spring. His light hair was curly, evidence of his ability to buy curling lotions at the company store.

David was in the bow of the skimmer, staring at the Summer Palace. The sun was to his back, projecting a long shadow boat before them. He just shook his head. He hadn't a clue as to why she would want to see him now.

"Not for funandgames," the fisher said. "Windships been going in and out of the blue ditch all day."

"To the Chasm," David said, startled. The Khan's Range was off-limits to company craft. Not that they respected the Khan's wishes, but the natural navigational hazards of fog and winds were real enough for the company not to take chances with expensive windshots.

"Brown's Fleet," the fisher said. "I know what I see, that the airships are not brown but Brown's." For a moment, the abo chuckled; they still found the language of the Company people amusing, especially when personal names were the same as ordinary nouns. Brown, David knew, translated as shit in Aboriginese. Few poked fun at David Quarrels, for disagreement and murder were synonyms in Aboriginese, and some of them remembered how he had struck the CEO and that he had been brave enough to follow the Khan into a blizzard. The abo started to trim the sail, for they were coming up on the stone wharf. "And I know something else, too," the abo fisher said, his voice singing and tantalizing.

David turned to look at the fisher, squinting because the sun was in his eyes. The fisher grinned, apparently glad to have David's attention at last.

"Brass Woman lost a shuttle and inside was a vip." He pronounced VIP as it was spelled, another testament to bootleg literature among the aborigines. They loved reading to each other during the long winter months; few had failed to acquire the ability. The Company censored their literature, but the abos stole books, papers, and printouts with remarkable ease.

"Lost?" David asked. "Lost in the Chasm?"

The little man shrugged. "You'd know more about that than me, Company Man," he said. "I know only what I hear on the radio. It's big enough to hear across my whole lagoon," he said proudly. "But it said no words about a vip."

"Then how do you know?"

The abo smiled. "I have been persuaded to know that it has happened."

David frowned. "Persuaded? You know they don't come into the valley anymore."

The abo laughed gaily. "You don't see them; who can see how something has been persuaded?" He laughed again.

David shook his head. He'd heard nothing about a lost

shuttle, nor even that a VIP was expected. That wasn't surprising, for the school attracted little attention from visitors. If a shuttle was missing, there should have been a security alert. None had been issued. Still, his feeling of foreboding intensified.

The fisher had the sail down and expertly brought the skimmer alongside the wharf. Two security guards caught the lines and held them fast while David stepped out. The wharf was slimy from little use. The guards argued with the fisher about his fee, which was set by the Company and not to the fisher's satisfaction. He kept them standing there until one of the guards dug into his own pocket and added another coin to the fisher's outstretched hand.

After the fisher pushed off, the guards led David down a staircase to a channel cut in the stone where a hovercraft waited. They boarded for the short ride through the channel into the bowels of the palace and into what had once been the Khan's private pool. Theo had had it converted into moorings for the company hovercraft. A dozen were settled placidly in the clear water, separated by buoys anchored in the mosaic. Pleasure islands were connected now by utilitarian bridges of planking, most of the tall greenery hacked away, the singing fountains clogged with algae and discordant. There was a repair bay, with an overhead crane, bulky-looking and crude against artful clouds carved from the tuffaceous limestone ceiling. The Company had put the Khan's pool to good use, and had room to install more moorings if they ever wished. Theo's reports to company headquarters only mentioned the conversions as being practical, but David had always believed it was inspired by the CEO's contempt for Rukmani Khan.

He followed the guards off the hovercraft. David's footfalls echoed as leather-clad feet never had. The palace brought back memories that try as he might he'd never forget.

Chloe Brass and Brown Roberts were waiting for him in Theo's office, once the Khan's bedroom. The furnishings were the CEO's, of course, but the setting and ambiance were indelibly the Khan's. Here the blood-red walls soaked light like sponges soaked water, and the desk wasn't big enough to cover the stylized flower glazed into the floor where soft petals had formed his bed.

"We have a message from the Khan," Chloe said without

preamble or introduction. She handed over a memory capsule encased in a crystal box. The crystal was persuaded to be hollow and to part with a twist, the workmanship a striking signature. "They forced the shuttle down in the Chasm, then sent the pilot out with this."

"You need me to translate?" David asked, feeling the crystal with his fingertips. It was smooth and phallic.

"Of course not," Chloe snapped. "I've got the translation from the lingochine: 'Return what's mine, for the years are sixteen.' I know what it says, but I don't know what it means. What does he want? The palace? More women? The whole valley? What?"

David shook his head, really looking at Chloe Brass for the first time in years. She was staring through him, or trying to. David decided she was still pretty, or would have been but for the froth of spittle in the corners of her mouth and the intensity in her expression.

"Can't you tell me anything?" she asked.

David hesitated. "It has been sixteen years since Sindon came back. Also sixteen years since Theo took over the palace and we've expanded through the valley. I guess it could mean anything."

"He doesn't know either," she said, angrily snatching the crystal from David's hands. She glared at Brown. "Get me someone who understands what Rukmani Khan wants."

"Now just a minute, C.B.," Brown Roberts said, his tone as calm and quiet as hers was excited and shrill. "We've talked to everyone who was there sixteen years ago, except David here and . . ."

"You haven't brought in that Sindon woman, and she's the one we need."

"We don't know that, C.B. It was David here who finally caught up with the Khan himself, and he's had conversation with the man face to face."

"He didn't sleep with him for eight months," Chloe said flatly. "Get me Sindon Liang."

"Now, you know I would if I could, but . . ."

"Oh, shut up," she snapped. What small patience she possessed had already gone. "You, too, David, unless you know where the hell that Sindon woman is. Or maybe her kid?" Chloe Brass put the tablet on her desk and looked up at him, her expression a trifle more mellow than seconds before. "Is the girl in the school?"

"Tara wasn't even born," he started to say.

"She's in the school? Get her," she ordered, addressing the security chief. And to David: "Do you know where the mother is?"

"I can find her," David said quietly.

Brown Roberts looked surprised, but he said nothing. He didn't have time.

"Get moving. Get her and bring her here. I want to know what the hell the Khan wants in exchange for Les Landers and Theo."

"Rukmani Khan has Theo? And the corporation's auditor?" David asked. So the abo fisher had been right.

"L.L. and T.T. had a meeting with C.B. here at three," the security chief said conspiratorially. "They missed it."

"Brown will get the girl," Chloe said decisively. "Quarrels, you bring the mother to me. She couldn't have slept with him for months without learning something about him. And probably couldn't resist telling the girl something about her father. It just . . ." Chloe stopped and slammed her fist on the tablet. "He wants the kid! She's sixteen now, been in our schools for ten years already, learned almost anything he'd want to know about us. He wants the little bastard."

David shook his head. "No. Not Tara." Chloe looked at him hard. "I think it's Sindon he wants."

"The tech? Why'd he let her go if he wanted her? He didn't let the others go. But of course, you were sleeping with her too. I always suspected it, and now I know it was true." She stepped back to her desk to look at some papers there. She nodded. "Theo's notes say you must have had 'a close physical and emotional relationship with her' to go off your rocker like that. I don't understand why he didn't fire you." She looked at him. "I'd have fired you. I *will* fire you if you don't bring Sindon Liang to me before sunset."

David nodded. He knew that she didn't always carry out her threats but did so enough of the time for people to take her seriously. "Sindon's not an employee. She doesn't have to come here if she chooses not to."

"Better see to it that she does," Chloe said. "Now get out of here, and be quick about it. You, too, Brown."

She sat down at the desk, picked up a stack of printouts and started flipping through them. David headed for the door. Brown Roberts followed, and David waited for him to close the heavy door.

"If she gets any ideas about trading Tara for Les and Theo, you better change her mind," David told him. "It's illegal, dead wrong, and I'll hold you personally responsible if she does."

"I know the regs," Brown said. "Khan's child or not, Tara's surely Sindon's, so she has full citizen's rights. No call to threaten me, David. I know my job."

"If you'd done it sixteen years ago, we wouldn't be having this conversation."

"You still hold the Company responsible, don't you? Can't let bygones be bygones."

"Bygones? Eight slaughtered people are nothing but bygones to you?"

"Didn't mean it like that," Brown said. "You know I didn't."

David felt his fists clenching almost involuntarily. Brown Roberts was pathetically sincere, and it was galling to him that the man could be astute enough to know David understood Brown had really done the best he could. Finally he nodded. "Just remember what I said. You let her bend the regs and I bend you. Keep Tara safe."

"It's my job," the security chief said, shoving his hands in his pockets, as if deliberately ignoring the repeated threat. "Old C.B. talks kinda tough, especially when she has to take over for Theo, but she wouldn't risk her job by breaking rules. She'd know I'd have to report her."

"Yeah, but from what I've seen, if she knows she can get away with it, she does it every time. So you need to remind her . . ."

"I know my job, David." He rocked back on his heels. "The Company likes my work. And if I were you, I wouldn't be standing here talking about . . . things I can't control. I'd be thinking about the task C.B. gave me, see if maybe I couldn't do it to perfection." He shook his head. "I couldn't find Sindon today. Think you can?"

David shrugged. "Where'd you look?"

Brown smiled now. "Out to her place. She wasn't there. Just her abo housekeeper."

They started walking toward the staircase to the Khan's pool. Underfoot were patterns resembling mosaic geometrics, but which on close examination were seamless and smooth. David had spent too much time that first night in the Khan's Palace, on his hands and knees, running his hands over the floors in disbelief. He should have been with Sindon.

"The abo said she didn't know where Sindon was. You know how Sindon is. Disappears for weeks at a time."

"Did you leave a message?"

"Sure thing."

"Just to call? Or did you explain what's going on?"

"Wrote enough to let her know how serious the situation was. Wrote the Khan's message, too, so she could be thinking about it on her way here. She hasn't been home yet to get it, though; know that for a fact because I checked with her abo on the landline just before you came."

"Don't count on it," David said. "Sindon may not have gone home, but I'd be willing to bet she got your message. The abo grapevine works faster than the landlines."

"Then why didn't she come here?" he said, looking puzzled.

"Because if I know Sindon, she's on her way to the gold."

Brown Roberts frowned, a rare expression for the security chief. But the furrows between his eyes were well established from bewilderment, so it was a very deep frown. "The Khan's gold?"

David nodded. The last pot of gold was still atop the rock island at the mouth of the hanging valley above the glacier valley. Theo had ordered that the four pots of gold be left on the rock island when they moved the guard tower into a permanent installation. It was a gesture of contempt, but it backfired. The abos called three clay pots full of gold the Company's gold, for they understood why the Khan placed them there. The pots sat on the rock island, waiting for the taking, and the abos had taken every lump. The Company might be stupid enough to disdain the gold the Persuaders had paid, but this was the Company's gold so the abos hadn't waited long before stealing it. The fourth potful of gold they called the Khan's gold. That they wouldn't touch. The company people left it alone for the same reason. But Sindon might take the gold if the stakes were high enough.

20.

ENTERING HANGING VALLEY on foot entailed a tedious climb over an alluvial fan, then a cold wet traverse through the cascading waterfall. The traverse was the worst part, for there was no way to avoid the almost frozen spray, and David was soaked to the skin when he reached the massive boulder where the Khan's gold had lain. The pot was empty, as he'd known it would be, and he found Sindon's discarded bedroll and supplies. It looked as if she'd left everything behind but the gold, the quantity of which he guessed was more weight than she'd ordinarily carry. With luck, it would slow her down enough for him to catch up to her, maybe even before sundown. He started walking, and though the sun was strong on his back and drying his clothes, his wet socks were chafing in his shoes. He wasn't dressed for trekking in the wilderness, but he hadn't dared take the time to prepare. If she got out of Hanging Valley before he found her, he might not ever find her, for the ways to the Khan's Winter Palace were many, the legends said.

David walked quickly, head up and watching for signs of Sindon. There were enough broken shrubs and bent ferny new growth for him to be sure she'd passed this way before him. She wasn't trying to hide her passing, at least not yet. He was certain she didn't expect him or anyone to be following her.

He caught up with her in the narrows, caught a glimpse of her resting on a boulder, her hands trapped under her pack-straps as she tried to ease the bite into her flesh. If she'd seen him first, and not been postured just so and overloaded, she might have dropped to the ground behind the boulder, and he might have walked on by. Instead, she stood up and said, "What the hell are you doing here?"

"Looking for you," he said. "I've come to stop you from taking the gold back to the Khan. That's not what he wants, Sindon. But you'll be playing right into his hands if you take it to him."

She frowned. "Go away, David. It doesn't concern you anymore."

"But it does," he said.

She continued frowning, and started shaking her head. He knew why. It *was* between her and the Khan. Both had made that plain years ago. But he couldn't stay out of it now any more than he could then. But now he was trying to convince himself as much as her as to why. "I'm still a Company employee, and so are the hostages he's holding. I'm here on Company business. Chloe Brass wants to see you."

"Tell Chloe I'm busy saving her hide, and probably Theo's and the VIP's, as well. She can thank me later."

Sindon started to get up, but David easily pushed her off balance just by touching her shoulders. The packful of gold pulled her back to her seat. The second time she came up swinging, but she was too clumsy with the weight on her back to land a blow. He dodged, and dodged again, but missing him only infuriated her. She picked up a rock, threatening to smack him alongside the head. He grabbed her hand and held on. "Stop it, Sindon," he said angrily. "You've got to go back to talk to Chloe. I'm afraid she might use Tara if you don't."

"Tara?" she said, her eyes growing wide. "How?"

The force had gone out of her arm, and David let go. She let her arm fall to her side, but she didn't drop the rock.

"As a trade for the VIP; she knows Tara is the Khan's daughter," he said, watching Sindon stand there dumbly shaking her head. "She believes it's either Tara or you the Khan is demanding. She wouldn't let Brown Roberts put out a general security alert, which I figure can only mean she doesn't want too many people knowing the details. It's always better that way if you're going to do something illegal."

"Damn," Sindon said. "And you want me to walk back into that?"

David nodded. "You, me, and anyone else we can tell about

before we go back to the Summer Palace. She won't like it, but she'll not be free to decide on her own."

"Do the civil authorities know?"

"I doubt it. Only Company people so far, Chloe and Brown."

"And you," Sindon said pointedly.

David shrugged. Technically that was true, though he hadn't felt like a Company man for many years. He wasn't the settler type though, so the only way to stay on Cestry Prime was to keep on working for the Company.

"All right," she finally said. "Let's go back. I'm not going to let her use Tara. It's me he wants, but it's the gold he's going to get, shoved down his throat nugget by nugget, if necessary." She turned and started walking uptrail.

"Sindon?"

She paused and looked back, the last rays of sunlight glowing in her red hair like a flaming frame around her face.

"What if he means he wants both you and Tara?"

Sindon stared at him, thinking. Then she shook her head and turned, saying, "He didn't claim your child then, he wouldn't do it now."

Slowly her words penetrated his brain. He felt his knees buckling and tears springing to his eyes. Tara was his after all, yet Sindon had denied it to him, to Brown Roberts, and even to Theo Tucker. Sindon's hatred of him was stronger than he'd ever imagined, or she wouldn't have deceived him all these years. But why? What had he ever done to make her hate him so? He wanted to run after her and shake her by the shoulders until she told the truth. He wanted to smash her face with his fist, and he wanted to hold her tenderly while she cried, and love her. But he stayed where he was, his knees like jelly and his heart pounding wildly, knowing that if he touched her in any of the ways he wanted to, Sindon would resist to her last breath.

Finally he could breathe almost normally, and he started walking after her. She was already out of sight, and he had to hurry.

They had come as far as the base of the falls when they spotted the lights of a windshot coming up the glacial valley.

"It may be Brown Roberts," David said. "He knew where I

was going to look for you. I was due back at sunset. If Chloe Brass got impatient, she may have sent him to find us."

"He can't land here," Sindon said. "Let's walk down to the meadow."

The windshot searchlight encircled them before they got that far. David gestured, but the windshot wouldn't move off. They walked the rest of the way to the meadow bathed in bright light. Finally the aircraft settled on the tundra, and Brown Roberts stepped out. Usually Brown went unarmed, but he was carrying a sidearm now. He stood by the open hatch, waiting for Sindon and David.

"I've news you're not going to like, David," the security chief started to say. David tensed, and Brown put up a staying hand. "Now, it's not what you think, but it's just as bad, or maybe worse."

"Tara?" he said, feeling panicky.

"Yes, but . . ."

"I'll kill you," he said, swinging for Brown's jaw at the same time.

Brown ducked and leaped away, coming up with his sidearm in his hand. "Hold it right there," he said. But David had stopped before Brown spoke. The barrel of the gun had a surprisingly sobering effect, especially extended from Brown's hand. "I was hoping I wouldn't have to do this, but you know I'll use it if you try to hit me again."

"You smarmy useless piece of shit," David said. "You let her do it. You let Chloe Brass send Tara to the Khan."

"No I didn't," Brown said. "I said I wouldn't and I didn't, but I sure knew you were going to go off your rocker on me again, so this time I brought some help. So just lie down on the ground, face down, and put your hands behind your neck. Go on, now. Do it, and then I'll tell you what happened."

Brown was tense and sweating almost as much as David. David was certain he was not going to be mollified by anything Brown had to say to him lying down, because that could only mean he expected David to react violently. David went down to his knees, wondering if he'd ever get to see his daughter's face while knowing she was *his*.

"All the way, David. Spread out."

Already in tears he lay face down, pounding the dewy turf with his fist.

"Is Tara all right?" Sindon asked.

"I don't know."

"You don't know? You're supposed to know," Sindon said angrily.

"Lie down right next to him, Sindon. Right now," he heard Brown say.

David watched her kneel next to him, her eyes on Brown.

"All the way. That's fine. I'm going to tell you everything."

David squeezed his eyes shut.

"I brought Tara to the Summer Palace so C.B. and I could talk to her. It was pretty obvious she didn't know what the message meant when she got there, but by the time she left I think she was convinced she was what the Khan wanted. You know, that she was his daughter and all. You know how C.B. talks. . . . Then she heard me telling C.B. I couldn't allow her even to offer to trade Tara for L.L. and T.T., and I thought that was that. I took Tara back to the dormitory.

"Couple hours later I saw a routine absence notice from the school dining room about Tara, and decided to check. She's gone, and so's her cold weather gear. The abos say she's going to the Khan. I figure, Tara being the nice girl she is and all, maybe she felt responsible for the Company men and decided to go to the Khan on her own. Maybe she did, and maybe she didn't. I decided not to take a chance. I have searchers out looking for her, and I came to get you. I brought the gun because I was afraid you'd jump me before I got a chance to explain."

"Tara wouldn't do that, would she?" David asked Sindon, his throat so tight and dry he could hardly get the words out. "Jesus, I don't even know what kind of person she is. She wouldn't try, would she?"

"I would. You would. Why wouldn't she?"

"You can get up now," Brown said.

David turned over and sat up. Brown's gun was already holstered. He looked miserable.

Sindon rolled over onto the pack of gold and looked back toward the falls, which were hidden by darkness. "I'm going back to the Winter Palace. You can tell Chloe Brass I'll do what I can to save her VIP and Theo, but my primary concern is Tara."

"I'm going with you," David said.

"Figured you might say that," Brown Roberts said, scratching his head. "And I can't let you go. Neither of you. Leastways, I can't let you go alone. The man's a killer, and your safety is my responsibility."

"So is Tara's safety!"

"We're going, Brown," David said. "You may stop us for a few hours by forcing us to go back with you at gunpoint, but you can't hold us long."

Brown was shaking his head. "You didn't understand me. You never do, David. I said you can't go alone. I'm going with you." The security chief smiled slightly. "We'll make better time in the windshot." He patted the hull lightly.

David didn't know what to say to that. Sindon did.

"Why would you do that for us? It's against regulations to take a windshot into the Chasm. You could lose your job."

"Well, first of all, maybe we won't even have to go," Brown said. "Maybe the searchers will find her soon. We'll know if they do." He paused as if just remembering something, then reached inside the windshot and flipped a switch. "We can monitor the whole search right from here, even participate if you want. And maybe we'll hear soon about how someone's spotted her."

"You won't find her," Sindon said. "If Tara doesn't want to be found, she won't be."

"I was afraid you'd say that." Brown crossed his arms over his chest. "All those abo stories about not seeing Persuaders when they don't want to be seen. They're true, aren't they? They've been coming into the settlement whenever they want, haven't they?"

David stood up. "Yes, but . . ." Sindon grabbed his hand to stop him from talking.

"It's true. They can change skin color like a chameleon. It's a simple adjustment of how they reflect light," she said. "I mentioned that in my first report when I got back."

"T.T. labeled it confidential," Brown said, "but I always wondered if it was true. I got to read it for the first time this afternoon. Still didn't believe it."

"It's true. But I still don't understand why you want to come with us if we have to go all the way to the Khan's Winter Palace to find Tara."

"You mean, me of all people?" Brown asked.

Sindon nodded.

"You probably will never understand what it's like to have the blood of all those innocent people on your hands. I can tell you about the dreams, but I still don't think you'd understand."

"Try me," she urged him. "I have to understand to let you come along."

Brown nodded slowly, then shrugged. "It's just the same two dreams, real as life and taken right from it. First we find the kidnappers in a mountain pass. The rock is all black, the clip-clopping of the beasts' hooves echoing like heartbeats. They have you, Sindon, and the other three women, in cabs on the big beasts, and they're carrying rifles and trying to make the beasts go faster. When we're certain it's only the four of them, we get excited because not only can we surprise them, we outnumber them three to one. We make our preparations. Carefully place all our sharpshooters so there's no chance we're going to miss. We're going to get you out, Sindon, and we know about not getting close enough for them to touch us. The ruthless bastards aren't going to get close enough to stop our hearts. I give the signal, and twelve shots fire like a single round, and they drop dead." Brown's jaw was quivering, and for a moment he sobbed silently. "But when we went to let you out, Sindon. When we uncovered those cabs . . ."

They were filled with pots, pans, and nuts, and the dead were carrying no weapons. It was a dizzying mixture of fantasy and reality. David turned away as Brown began sobbing openly.

"And the bodies," he said still crying, "dear God, the bodies were . . ." He turned away to hide his face in the crook of his arm, stood leaning on the windshot, sobbing.

Sindon was biting her lip. "They were children no older than Tara," she said to David. "Hari, Moti, and Sundari, and an old priest named Natarjan. We four women were in a different caravan, nowhere near them." She glanced over at Brown Roberts and shook her head. "I can imagine the second dream. The Khan and the other three just stepping up to four people in the magtree grove and stopping their hearts."

"No one ever saw them come in," David said. "But everyone saw them leave."

"They wanted to make sure the entire settlement knew they'd taken their revenge," Sindon said. "It's their way."

Coolly, she slipped the pack of gold off and stood up, deliberately not looking at David. And she went to Brown

Roberts and put her hands on his shoulders. "Brown, what's coming with me going to do for you?"

Brown shook his head, face still buried in his arms. But finally he sighed and turned around to face her. "They say you can change your dreams," he said. "They say the dreams belong to you, so you can change them, imagine new alternatives even in your sleep, right at the critical moment. The problem with my dreams is when I wake up, the truth is still there. Eight people are still dead, and none of them deserved to die. I can't change what happened. I've lived all these years with it, and maybe I'll survive the rest of my life seeing those dead faces. But not one more. Not *even* one more. That I couldn't live with. Not one." Brown looked from Sindon to David. "We've got to find Tara. I don't care if it means losing my job. I've got to . . . to *save* her."

David nodded. All these years, he'd thought he understood Brown Roberts. And to some degree, he'd been right. Brown had served the Company in a capacity that was beyond his capability, and he was not an evil man. Hating him seemed pointless now, for Brown hated himself enough and probably had suffered more than David could wish on him.

"Sindon, what happens to Tara if she reaches the Winter Palace before we find her?" David asked now. "What will the Khan do to her?"

Sindon shook her head. "He won't want to hurt her. He didn't want . . ." Again she shook her head. "What you don't understand is that Rukmani Khan doesn't rule the Winter Palace. Gulnar Khan does. I don't know what *she* will do when she figures out Tara is my daughter. She's very jealous."

"Is that why you left him?"

It was probably the wrong thing to ask, for Sindon's lips went thin. "I'm going to listen to the searchers," she said, heading for the hatch of the windshot. "Come on, Brown. Let's see where they're looking. Once we know, we must go to my ranch for the bannertails. Can we get three of them into the windshot? We can save time if we can fly to the bottom of the Chasm."

"I don't know," Brown said. "They're so tall, and if they spooked . . ."

"I can keep them lying down, and I can keep them quiet."

"I guess we can try," Brown said, but clearly he was doubtful.

21.

Brown Roberts landed the windshot in a shadowy canyon, maybe the one in which the killings had taken place sixteen years ago. They hoped it would be a good starting point for the bannertails. They'd seen no sign of Tara, and heard only dispiriting reports of failure from the organized search still going on. David was tired, knew Sindon and Brown were tired, too, but he wanted to get started. There was no question in his mind Tara was on her way to the Khan, and he didn't want her to reach him.

"We *have* to eat," the security chief said patiently, "and take just a few hours of sleep, or we'll be too tired to spot her." He killed the coldjets with his palm, and waited for Quarrels to open the hatch.

David shook his head but Sindon reached past him and shoved the lever. The hatch fell open. The bannertails leaped out, obviously glad to be released from the confinement of the shuttle. "He's right, David," she said. "We have to take a break."

"I'll get the rations from the emergency stores," Brown said. "You build a fire."

"No fire," David objected.

"We know where the other searchers are," Brown said, "and that's nowhere near here."

"It isn't the searchers I'm worried about," David said. "This is the Khan's Range."

David stepped out of the windshot, his cramped leg muscles aching. Sindon stepped out, too, stretching. She bent over to touch her toes, a mass of red curls falling over her face. She still moved like a cat, and he still liked watching her. He forced

200

his eyes away, scanned the shrubs at the edge of the meadow and the scraggly windblown trees. He'd never even heard the Khan the last time, probably couldn't have done anything about it if he had with his limbs half-frozen.

Brown took another call on the windshot comm-unit. Chloe Brass ordered him to return, and Brown refused. She fired him on the spot and Brown shrugged. He snapped off the comm-unit and walked off into the brush.

The evening breeze blew through David's thin shirt and he shivered.

"Have another piece of cheese," Sindon offered, slicing off a chunk from a greasy-looking bar.

David realized he'd been chewing on some, and he swallowed. He took another piece. "Where's Brown?"

"Relieving himself in the bushes," she said. She sliced some cheese for herself.

"Do you think he's telling the truth?" David asked her. "Or is this just a setup he and Chloe thought up to get us to lead him to the Khan?"

Sindon frowned. "I believe him. He's too transparent for it to be anything but the truth."

David nodded, for he agreed. But he trusted Sindon's instincts, and wanted to hear her opinion. "The Khan said you'd come back to him of your own will," he said. "But even he couldn't have foreseen Tara being the reason. Could he?"

"He's not prescient, if that's what you mean," she said, taking another bite of cheese. Then, "What do you mean, he said I'd come back?"

"That's what he told me," David said. "I didn't know you were already back at the settlement when he saved me from the blizzard. When they found me the next day and told me you were back, I was so relieved. You really were there, pregnant, too. And you told me the baby wasn't mine."

"I lied."

"Why did you let me believe Tara was his child all these years?"

"I never said she was his," Sindon said.

"What the hell did you expect me to think?"

She shrugged and sliced off more cheese.

"Why?"

"Because you would have claimed her, and I didn't want that

happening to my child any more than I wanted it to happen to me."

"You make me sound like him," David said, "like the Khan."

"You are like him," she said. "Arrogant and possessive."

David just stood there watching her eat the cheese. They might have been talking about the weather to judge by the interest she showed. Finally he shook his head. "I can't even begin to imagine what I ever did to make you think I'm possessive or arrogant. Even if it was over between us, I just wanted to acknowledge my child, if she was mine."

"Did that give you the right to hit me? If Brown hadn't held you back that night, I think you would have killed me. You said you wanted to."

She'd stopped eating the cheese, and maybe that was a good sign. But David's shoulders sagged. He hadn't exactly forgotten hitting her, though he often wished he could.

"All you wanted to know was if I'd slept with him. You kept shouting, 'Did you?' and you were not listening to anything else I had to say. And when I answered you, you hit me. I figured right then and there you were no kind of father for my child."

"It was stupid of me, but that slap doesn't equate with what you did. You couldn't possibly have expected me to be pleased to hear you'd been sleeping with him, not when you knew how much I'd loved you. I had a right to the truth, a right to know Tara as my daughter." She was staring at him, shaking her head. "And a right," he added, though he knew it was probably stupid to say it to her now, "to want you to deny sleeping with him. That is, I did if you ever loved me."

"I brought you a damn good report about Persuader life in the Winter Palace. It covered eight months of study, and I expected a little more than a slap in the face for it."

"How could you expect me to appreciate a report at a moment like that?"

"Why wouldn't I?" she demanded, sounding exasperated. "You were my boss."

"Next you're going to be telling me you only went in the first place for the opportunity to study them."

"Yes," she snapped. "Exactly. I saw an opportunity of a lifetime, and I took it. I thought you'd be proud, but instead you hit me and let Theo Tucker mark that report confidential so it wouldn't get any attention. I got nothing from it except black marks in my personnel file for jumping my contract for months, which I didn't do, as my report plainly shows. You didn't defend me."

David stared at her a moment, astounded at the intensity of her outrage. "Sindon, in a million years I wouldn't have guessed you'd go with the Khan's people to study them. I thought you'd been kidnapped, and then, when I began to realize you'd gone of your own free will, I assumed it must be because you loved him and not me. That's what I acted on, that's why I hit you—because it hurt so much."

Sindon bit her lip and started slicing cheese again.

David shoved his hands in his pockets as a fresh gust of wind passed through the meadow. The windshot shuddered and bounced as the wings lifted slightly. "I let you down," he said. "I was a lousy boss and I let you down. You needed me, the boss, and there I was playing the outraged lover. But Sindon—don't you ever think about the trust you betrayed when you slept with him?"

"All the time," she said.

"Then, you must agree you share some blame in what happened."

"Not a bit," she said crisply. "I blame you, and I blame the Khan."

"He raped you?" David said, at once suspicious, for her willingness had always been an issue she'd never denied.

"No. He persuaded me." With that, Sindon offered him a slice of cheese. He grabbed cheese and knife from her hands, and she stepped back warily.

"Sindon?"

"Don't ask, David. Let's just find Brown and get the hell out of here." She whistled, and the bannertails came frolicking toward her. David had seen her play with bannertails, and he knew from their behavior these were ready to play. But when she didn't respond to their overtures, they calmed down, apparently ready for serious work. He turned to get the tack out of the windshot.

22.

RUKMANI KHAN SAW her first, a huddled form on the ledge outside the greencavern wall. The sandstone wall was thick and only translucent at that level, but he could tell it was a red-haired woman, and he knew only one red-haired woman who would come to the Winter Palace.

"Sindon," he said, and Gulnar heard him.

His wife got up from her knees where she'd been pinching buds on a tiny dewberry plant. She stared at the silhouette on the southern wall. Others, men and women of the clan working the hotbeds, began to notice and stood also, shielding their eyes from the glare of the hot afternoon sun streaming through what had once been ordinary sandstone.

"That's a dangerous place for her to be," Kangra said. He'd come to Rukmani's side quietly, Hazan and Amar following. "She must have climbed from below when she couldn't find the entrance."

"Open the ventilation slot," Rukmani Khan directed.

"Someone will have to go out to get her," Kangra said, glancing nervously at Gulnar, who was staring thin-lipped at Rukmani Khan. "The traverse isn't an easy one. She might fall."

"I'll go," Amar offered, not waiting for either Khan to answer.

They watched Amar open the ventilation slot and slide through, then move toward Sindon, bare arms and legs outstretched like a spider on the glass. Then there were two spiders crawling toward the slot, and Rukmani Khan watched as if transfixed. He wasn't completely engrossed, though; he simply didn't want to look at Gulnar, and he didn't really want Sindon to find him up to his ankles in dirt and soilage.

Kangra was whispering to him. "I didn't believe it would be this easy."

"It's only the beginning," Rukmani Khan said, but he knew what Kangra meant. The rest of what was his would not come to him as Sindon had.

Amar slipped back in through the slot, his hand carefully still holding Sindon's. He was frowning at Rukmani Khan.

"Is she all right?" the Khan asked, worried even though he'd seen her move with ease across the traverse with little more help from Amar than to show the way.

Amar nodded. "It isn't Sindon," he said, guiding the woman's legs onto the flatbed just below the open slot. She slipped her torso through the opening.

And now Rukmani Khan could see for himself. She stood with her hand still in Amar's, her eyes wide, as if amazed by the abundant flora in the cavern. She was a slip of a woman, a child really, breasts formed but not full, hips almost boyish. Her hair, though, was red as the trees in autumn, and her eyes were blue.

Gulnar composed herself more quickly than the others. "Who are you?" she demanded.

"I'm Tara Liang," the girl replied. "I'm the one you wanted. I'm the Khan's daughter."

Rukmani Khan's mouth dropped open as Gulnar whirled on him. "Your daughter has come home," she said angrily to him. "Was Sundari pregnant, too?" And then she turned to the clan, shouting, "Is this the kind of Khan you'd follow to the Summer Palace? One who cannot keep even a vow of fidelity? A Khan who makes bastards when he can't get a legitimate child from his wife?" Gulnar gasped for air, her rage sapping her strength. "He swore—" Her face was red, her breath quite gone. Then she must have seen their faces, collectively embarrassed, and realized it was as much for her losing control as for what she was saying. She straightened, scooped her shawl from where it was draped over a dewberry bush, and started walking through the rows of plants. "Just remember," she said, still sounding shrill. "He did this with some foreigner, not a Persuader. He isn't worthy of being Khan."

"I didn't," Rukmani Khan said, so quietly only the few

clansmen at his elbows could have heard. He looked up at the girl, taking in her fair skin and red hair. "She isn't my child. But she's unmistakably Sindon's."

Rukmani Khan held his hand up to Tara. She'd been frightened by Gulnar's display, her face pale and grave. But she took his hand and smiled bravely, looking very much the way Sindon had looked when he took her to his bed.

"I'll take her," Timon said. Gulnar's little priest appeared, his hand reaching out to Tara. "You must agree, Rukmani Khan, that she is rightfully a prisoner of the Winter Palace."

"A lone girl can hardly be considered an invader."

"Perhaps not," Timon said, "but her custody is still Gulnar's, not yours." Again he reached for Tara.

Rukmani Khan drew her back. "Lead the way, Timon," he said coldly. "I will escort her."

23.

THE WIND WAS rising, and probably made short work of the shrubs and branches they'd pulled over the windshot to keep it from being found easily. But that same wind would ground any searchers Chloe sent to find them, so they didn't complain too much about being cold.

"You're sure this is the right canyon?" Brown Roberts asked. The bannertails were walking easily, their footsteps echoing.

They had only starlight to show them the way between steep walls, black schist on one side, sandstone on the other. The ground was rubble and shrubs, no hint of a trail.

"I'm sure," Sindon said, shivering.

The wind was quieter now, less strong, but it was colder the higher they went, and the canyon floor definitely sloped upward.

"It's the right one," Sindon assured them again. "The bannertails know the way." She was carrying the gold again, and had refused to let either man bear part of the burden.

Sindon sat straight in the saddle despite the cold and the heavy pack. David's feet were chafed by stirrups he was unaccustomed to, but he said nothing. Something crashed off into the bushes on their right, and Brown held up his hand, stopping them.

"An animal," Sindon said, moving her bannertail past him, and the men followed.

Another hour passed before Sindon stopped. "This is it," she announced.

"This is what?" David asked. There still were only schist

walls to his left, sandstone to his right. The night was quiet now, no wind at all.

"Look up," she said. "You can see the glint of glass even in the starlight."

At first he stared without seeing what she meant. He could see the canyon walls, dark against the starry sky. Then he noticed a subtle difference in what should have been sandstone. Black, too smooth, almost like the schist wall behind them. It towered for fifty meters and went up the canyon, seemingly forever.

"It's the Winter Palace," Sindon said. "It looks like they've finished persuading the whole south-facing wall into glass. It's twice the length it was when I last saw it. It's crude in places, but it lets in the light all year long so Gulnar can grow her crops."

"But it's huge," Brown said, pointing out what even the darkness couldn't hide. "How could we have missed it in our aerial surveys?"

"What's to see?" Sindon said. "The glass looks almost like the schist, and it follows what's a completely natural line of the canyon. Only the greencaverns follow the sinesoidal pattern."

"So how do we get in?" David asked. "Climb up and knock on the window?"

"No," said a loud voice from the darkness behind them. "We have a perfectly fine door you can use."

They reined in the bannertails, peering into the darkness.

"Hazan?" Sindon said. "Hazan, is that you?"

"Dismount," the voice said.

Sindon dropped to the ground. "Get down," she said to the others sharply. "If they turn the bannertails on you, it will be worse."

David and Brown dismounted.

For a moment there was absolute silence, then David felt someone grab him, and he heard Sindon and Brown struggling, too. There were too many hands, too much strength, and in a second he was on his knees, held there by sheer force. Sharp stones bit into his flesh.

"I think you know what happens next if you resist," said Hazan's voice again, but not as distant as before.

Someone's hand was on David's chest, and his heart was beating wildly.

"It's the gun," Brown said. "I forgot to take off the gun."

"Dammit, Brown! Why did you bring . . ."

"You can take the gun, Hazan," Sindon said rapidly. "David and I aren't armed." She didn't sound alarmed, but David couldn't relax with a Persuader's hand on his chest.

They searched him thoroughly, and finally the hand came away from his chest, and other hands released him. Slowly David stood up. He recognized Hazan, even though he had not seen him since the murders in the magtree grove.

"The Khan's been expecting you, Sindon," Hazan said. He was wearing a garment girdled over his loins, and another over his shoulders that left his chest partially bared. He wasn't boyish-looking anymore.

"See what I mean about arrogance, David?" Sindon said. "Hazan, it isn't what he thinks. I'm just here to return his damn gold. He shouldn't have sent any for me. I wasn't jumping my contract. He *knew* that."

"You'd better talk to him," Hazan said easily.

"I'm planning on it," Sindon replied.

"He may want you to keep it . . . for your daughter."

"Tara . . ." David said, instantly frightened. But Sindon's hand closed over his, restraining him.

"She isn't for sale any more than I was," Sindon said.

"She seems to think of herself as trade goods. I don't know, Sindon," Hazan said, shaking his head. "You New People have very peculiar customs. Freedom of choice, but at the cost of a pot of gold, which only the Khan has in sufficient quantity. What kind of freedom is that?"

"Just let me talk to Rukmani Khan," Sindon said, sounding irritable now. "You're still doing imitations of him, and poor ones at that."

Her words obviously stung the Persuader, but when she brushed past him, heading blindly toward the sandstone wall, all he said was, "This way, Sindon," and started walking back down the canyon.

Sindon turned and followed, Brown behind her, and then David. He looked back to see how many men were behind him, and saw none. He knew he hadn't imagined the hands on him. Uneasily, he stared at every bush they passed.

The way into the palace was in a depression in the sandstone. First the way was chiseled stone, then natural caverns, and finally passageways of glazed sandstone at perfect right angles. The floor was absolutely level. It was like being in the Summer Palace: Mosaics without seams—blends of stone, metal, and wood—all looked as if they'd come together of their own accord in perfect geometric shapes. Carpeting underfoot showed no trace of weave or threads. And the passageways were warm, though there was no sign of a heating source, no warm breeze. David knew already the walls would be warm to the touch. They'd almost ceased to amaze him, these Persuaders, with what they could do. All he wanted to know now was at what expense.

"David," Sindon whispered. "It has changed. The Winter Palace didn't have the beauty of the Summer Palace, but now it does."

"They've had a lot of time to work on it," David said.

"Too much," Hazan added.

Hazan halted at an intersection.

"Rukmani Khan will want to see you alone, Sindon," he said. "I'll take you to him. Kangra will take the men." From the shadows, another Persuader appeared. He was older than Hazan, more fierce-looking.

"Now just a minute," David objected. "We came for Tara."

Sindon nodded. "I don't want to see the Khan until I know Tara's safe."

"She's quite well," Hazan assured her.

"Where?" Sindon asked.

"On a pleasure island in the Deeps."

"In Gulnar's custody?"

"Yes, but Rukmani Khan is presiding for her in this matter," Hazan said, folding his arms across his chest. The garment glittered when it creased under his arms. "Kangra, take these two to the same place; they'll be safe with Tara. But you, Sindon, *must* go see the Khan."

Sindon nodded, but David said, "No! Don't see him alone. Tara . . ."

"She's safe. Hazan wouldn't lie. I'll go see the Khan."

"I'm going with you," David said firmly.

"No you're not," Hazan said, moving his hands to his waist. "Don't make trouble in here. You're no match for us when you don't have your weapons."

"Do what he says," Sindon whispered, and she hurried away.

"There's two of us," David said to Brown, hoping he was ready.

"No," Brown said. "I told you I was going to do this peaceably. No more deaths, especially not yours. We'll do what he says until Sindon gets back."

Without Brown to help him, David had no confidence that he could stop the Persuader. He remembered only too well how easily the Khan had fended him off without killing, how easily he could have killed if he'd wished. Kangra gestured for him to walk down the hallway, opposite to the way Sindon and Hazan had gone. Unwillingly, he went where he was told. Then he remembered he'd soon be looking at his daughter, truly seeing her for the first time. His eagerness didn't outweigh his apprehensions for Sindon, but he did resolve not to let that dilute the experience.

For a moment he thought he was back at the Summer Palace in the Khan's private pool. Then he realized the differences: a single pleasure island, the water flowing with a swift current, cool and deep-looking.

Tara sat well back from the pool, her arms around her knees. She wore the same bored look he'd seen on her face many times when she sat in class. Still, she was pretty to look at, her complexion fair, and with Sindon's red hair. He looked more closely at her face this time, tried to see, perhaps, his nose, his mouth. He realized he'd done this hundreds of times before, and failed to see any resemblance to himself. Then Tara looked up and saw him. She scrambled to her feet.

"Am I in deep trouble?" she asked, looking from Brown to David. "Look, I thought I could help. I'll make up my classes, but I . . ."

"You're not in trouble," David told her.

"Then why are *you* here with Mr. Security?" she asked suspiciously. She cocked her head to the side, frowning.

"Because . . ." And then it hit him that of course she didn't know who he was. If she'd known, she'd never have felt compelled to come to the Khan's Winter Palace.

"I'll bet Mom's mad," she added.

"I'd say yes," David said. "But not at you."

"Not me?" She frowned. "Then, who? My father?"

David nodded. "But it really depends on who you think your father is."

"The Khan, of course," she said, looking at him as if he were stupid.

David shook his head. Did he have the right to tell her the truth? These were certainly not the circumstances he'd have chosen, with her glaring at him as if he were some ordinary school official.

"Come on, Mr. Quarrels. What makes you think I'm not the Khan's daughter?" And when he didn't answer, she looked at Brown. "Mr. Roberts? You heard what Ms. Brass said. Wasn't she right? Won't someone please tell me!"

"I'm your father," David blurted.

She looked disappointed, or maybe she was just stunned. She squinted and looked at him dumbly. "But, why . . ."

"Not because I didn't want you," he said, quickly guessing what she might be thinking. "I didn't know until yesterday."

"But why didn't she tell *me*?"

David shook his head. He could see Tara was on the verge of tears, but there had been unmistakable anger in her voice. "I don't know why, Tara. Not really." Tara's jaw was quivering, and her face was scrunched up in an angry and hateful expression. But David wasn't certain it was for him. "Do you want me to tell you what I know?"

She barely nodded.

David went over to the cushions; he would have liked to help her down onto them and hold her. But she crossed her arms over her chest and glared at him. He didn't touch her. She was her mother's daughter, too, and he knew that a wrong move, a premature gesture of love—and oh, how he loved her and wanted to hold his child in his arms—and she'd resist, stubborn, implacable, and with a child's complete lack of understanding, too.

"It's not everything, and I hope you're old enough to understand. . . ."

"I'm old enough. Bastards are born old," she said.

Don't cry! he told himself sternly. "I'll tell you what I know," he said. "It will have to do until your mother can fill in. . . ." But he couldn't stop himself, he was crying.

24.

RUKMANI KHAN DIDN'T like sharing his bedchamber with the two prisoners they had taken from the shuttle, but there was nowhere else in the Winter Palace the damned little priest, Timon, wouldn't go unbidden. Even so, the arrangement had had its rewards; Theo Tucker had spied Sindon's abandoned translator and had been willing to use it to make a recording of Rukmani Khan's message to send with the frightened pilot when they were ready to turn him loose. Occasionally Theo Tucker would ask what he had meant when he threatened to wash them from the valley, and of course Rukmani Khan would not tell him. Then Theo Tucker would speculate about how difficult it would be for Rukmani Khan and his vassal lords to undermine the dam at the lake. And little by little Rukmani Khan had learned more than he had known before about the defenses of the New People. He had just finished another of these conversations with Theo Tucker; the white-haired man had finally tired and settled back in the cushions, trying to get as comfortable as he could with his hands persuaded to clasp behind his back. Beside him the man called Les Landers had fallen asleep and was snoring gently when Rukmani Khan heard noises from the courtyard. He stepped out onto the balcony. Below him he saw Hazan arguing with Timon and Gulnar Khan. With them was a red-haried woman.

For a second he thought it was Sindon's daughter, that she'd somehow escaped the chamber in the Deeps where Timon had imprisoned her, but then he realized it was Sindon herself. She wore drab dun-colored pantaloons and shirt cut in the New People's style. Her beautiful red hair spilled over one shoulder in a thick plait that almost reached her waist; slung over the

213

other shoulder was a sack which, judging from the way she held the strap, was too heavy for her. Briefly her clear gaze met his, her green eyes as cold as glass.

Rukmani Khan stared. Then Sindon raised her arms to tuck a strand of hair into the braid and he remembered how she had looked when she came from the baths to his arms, smelling of soap, her damp shift dropping away at his touch. He remembered that he had made love to her as if they had waited a lifetime for the chance, some part of the two of them that had slumbered restlessly in separate lives wakening into a single existence. For hours each day they had been consumed by flames of passion that had insulated him from everything but her. Then late in the afternoon Sindon, still glowing and warm, would rise from their bed to dress. When she was finished, she would raise her arms to tuck a flower in her curls, an exquisite gesture that he loved to watch. Her fingers would guide the stem, weaving it and tugging it firmly in place. Then she would smooth her hair with the flat of her hands and smooth the drape of her shift along her hips so that the folds fell in front over the curve of her belly. None of the gestures had changed, but her belly was no longer big with child.

"I told you you would come back one day," Rukmani Khan whispered, but she couldn't hear him.

Hazan glanced up at the Khan, his shoulders slumped in defeat. Then he turned and led Sindon back across the courtyard through the archway that led to the Deeps. Gulnar Khan stared up at the balcony.

"Your whore is back," she said shrilly. "This time I will not turn my head."

"Nor will I," Rukmani Khan said. "I demand a Moon Council—tonight! You'll not decide her fate or her daughter's alone."

"She brought armed warriors with her," Timon said. "Invaders. She'll stand accused with them."

"Sindon is no invader," Rukmani Khan scoffed.

"And what of the prisoners you have secreted in your room?" Timon asked. "Will you decide their fate alone?"

Rukmani Khan nodded. "I brought them here. They did not come on their own."

"But they are in the Winter Palace and are therefore subject to its laws," Timon said. "Gulnar Khan demands that you produce them in Moon Council."

"They have nothing to do with . . ."

"Tonight," Timon added, as if to a recalcitrant child, mocking Rukmani Khan.

Gulnar nodded and pulled her shawl more tightly across her shoulders. Timon was smiling smugly now.

Angry with the priest's haughty manner and Gulnar's complicity, Rukmani Khan stepped back into his bedchamber and found Theo Tucker watching him. The white-haired man was frowning, but it was an expression of interest. Unable to get at the little priest, Rukmani Khan grabbed Theo by the neck. The man's eyes bulged with fear, then he sagged, unconscious.

25.

WHERE THERE HAD been the sound of David's voice, low and sometimes choking on the things he had to say, now there was only the sound of water trickling through the pools like tinkling bells. Tara had stood with her arms locked across her chest the whole time David had talked to her. The fluffy cushions lay unused at their feet. When David had been telling her about the morning Rukmani Khan and his avengers had left the gold nuggets in the guard shack, Tara had shifted restlessly from foot to foot. David had gestured again to the cushions, but Tara shook her head. He tried to tell her only what had happened, tried not to wallow in the pain and rejection he had felt when Sindon finally had come back. He knew he hadn't succeeded in making her understand. Tara had listened, he was sure, but her eyes had looked so distant.

He considered leaving her alone to think for a while. But if she were as much her mother's daughter as he believed she was, leaving her alone wouldn't be wise. Tara would brood. Once he had made up his mind to stay with her, he wasn't quite sure what to do or to say. Finally, uneasily, he asked: "I'm wondering what you think of what I just told you. I'm wondering what you think of your mother and me."

"That you were both pretty stupid and never gave any thought about how I might feel growing up with a bunch of lies."

"I never told you any lies, Tara," he said, reasonably, "I didn't know the truth myself until just yesterday."

"You should have known in your gut that I was your child. It shouldn't have taken you sixteen years to find out the truth," she said, her face flushed with anger. "I had a right to know that my father was just . . . an ordinary man."

"So you're angry because I'm not . . . like the Khan?"

"Well, I always thought that . . . well, that someday he would come for me and that I'd be like a real princess. But then he didn't *come* for me. He *sent* for me, at least I thought he did. Only it wasn't me he wanted. How do you think I feel now?" Tara asked, her locked arms flying open in a questioning gesture, and then not waiting for him to reply, rushed on to tell him. "Stupid! When my friends hear that I had to be rescued because I wasn't the Khan's daughter after all, they're going to laugh." Tara brushed away tears. Her fingers were dirty and smudged her cheeks. "All this time I thought I was Rukmani Khan's daughter."

"We all did," David reminded her.

"I thought I was someone special," she said, the bitterness unmistakable in her voice. "I was going to save the world and become famous. Now everyone will laugh at me, even Rukmani Khan."

David almost smiled, but he realized how deadly serious his daughter was. The man she had thought was her father was the central character in a story that was nearly legend on Cestry Prime. David was much too accessible to have become a romantic figure like Rukmani Khan. He didn't much blame her for feeling disappointed. He said: "You are special, Tara. It took a lot of courage for you to come here to the Winter Palace all alone, no matter what you believed. Your friends won't laugh. Not true friends. It was a brave gesture."

"Gesture," Tara scoffed.

"I think your coming here was one of the bravest things I've ever seen," he said gently.

"You really think so?" she said, looking a little bit pleased in spite of herself.

David smiled and nodded. "Really," he said.

Tara stared down at her toes, but not before David saw that the corners of her mouth had turned up and how pretty she was when she smiled. When she looked up again, her face was serious. "Now what?" she asked him.

"We figure out how to get us all out of here safely," he said.

"No, I mean you, me, and Mom."

"What about us?"

"Are we going to try to be a family?" she asked.

David was taken aback. He had given up hoping years ago, consciously wrestling himself away from any thoughts of Sindon and himself getting together, turning instead to the bitter and humiliating memory of Rukmani Khan tormenting him that night in the cave. He was not often a man who deliberately contemplated revenge, but he'd forced himself to think within the codes he believed Rukmani Khan conformed to, and convinced himself that forgiving or forgetting was meaningless. Rukmani Khan did not have the same kind of conscience as men of David's society. David had suffered for his determination to have revenge; his wounds had stayed fresh and were easily opened, like now. He still loved Sindon, but she had given not the smallest hint that she might still care for him. Indeed, her not telling him the truth about Tara was convincing evidence that she hated him. She'd kept his daughter from him all these years, and though he'd surprised himself by feeling drawn to Tara even when she was a tiny child, unable to feel any resentment toward her despite what he believed about her parentage, he wondered how he could presume to step into her life at this stage and be a father. Besides, what did he know about being a father? Nothing! "I don't know, Tara. There are so many unanswered questions."

"Like what?"

"Like what your mother feels about me, like how she feels about the Khan."

"Why doesn't anyone care about how I feel?"

"I do care, Tara. I care a lot. But . . ."

"But what?" she asked impatiently.

David shook his head. "You don't know . . . everything. You don't know what the Khan is really like and what he's done to . . . us."

"You think I don't know," she said, "but I do. I know what they say about the Khan, that women can't resist him. If it's true, why should my mother have been any different? Why wouldn't you forgive her?"

David sighed. "I don't know. I guess what hurt so much is that she didn't want my forgiveness. She wanted something else from me that I didn't understand then and I don't understand now. But whatever it was, I wasn't capable of giving it. I'm sorry."

Tara stared at him. "Why did you even bother to tell me? If you don't intend to change anything, why did you make me stand here and listen to you?"

"I thought you would want to know, that you deserved to know," he said, hurt that she might have preferred not to know.

"Why? So we could talk over the *good old days*?" she said. Then she crossed her arms again and screwed her face into the most contemptuous expression he'd ever seen, and added scathingly, "*Dad*."

"That might be a start," he said, giving in to irritation. "For having the most exasperating woman on Cestry Prime for a mother, I always thought you were a great little kid. You grew up full of spunk, but nice. People liked you, me among them. It's a whole lot better start than it might have been if you had always been a brat."

"Like my mother?" she said cryptically.

"You don't stop, do you?"

"Stop what?"

David shook his head. "She didn't either," he said softly. "She'd never just . . . stop . . . fighting with me. She always had to win."

"I'll bet it was easy for her, too."

David hesitated, unwilling to make the inflammatory comment that came to mind. Then he realized that the hesitation was an answer in itself. "I think it may be easy for you, too . . . if that's all you want from me."

He would have said more, but just then they heard footsteps, and they turned to see the door burst open. Sindon stepped in, Hazan behind her. Sindon was pale, obviously shaken, and she still carried the gold.

"Someone will come for you when it's time for the Moon Council meeting," Hazan said, speaking standard and talking as much to David, Brown, and Tara as to Sindon.

"Wait a minute," Sindon said, grabbing Hazan's arm when he turned to leave. The big Persuader could have brushed her off, but he allowed himself to be held back. "Whose prisoners are we?"

"Gulnar's," Hazan replied.

Sindon stood there until Hazan shook off her hand. Then he backed through the door, pulling it shut. "Damn," Sindon said, and she threw down the rucksack of gold. It split, and the nuggets scattered across the rose-colored floor. Sindon didn't seem to care. She looked at Brown. "I think the bitch still means to kill me," she said. Her eyes were wide with fear.

"Who?" Brown said. He had started picking up the nuggets.

But then Sindon saw Tara and held her arms out to her. The girl fled to her mother's arms. Sindon closed her eyes and held Tara tightly, her face momentarily at peace. Then she looked questioningly over her daughter's shoulder at David.

David nodded. "I told her what I knew."

Sindon whispered something in Tara's ear, and the girl nodded. She hung on to her mother for a while; it was obvious to David both of them enjoyed the prolonged hug. He felt a little envious.

Finally Tara dropped her arms and said something under her breath that he couldn't hear. Sindon glanced at David, more resigned than reproachful he thought, and then she put her arm around her daughter and led her off to the brightly lighted atrium, where they whispered intensely.

David couldn't help watching them, knew they were talking about him, but could not bring himself to intrude on their conversation—or believe that it was right to remain apart.

"I know she needs to be with the girl just now, but . . ." Brown had dumped the contents of his own rucksack and put Sindon's split one inside. Now he handed the gold to David. "Just who tried to kill her? Why? And why now?"

"She must mean Gulnar Khan," David said.

"Who's Gulnar Khan?" the security chief asked.

David looked at him in surprise. "You must not have read Sindon's report," he said.

"Not the original version," Brown told him. "As I recall, only T. T. and you read the original version."

"Gulnar Khan was in it when I was done with the report," David said.

"She wasn't in it when I read it, and I know that's a fact because I reread it when the Khan's message came, and so did Chloe." Brown was frowning. "There's no one named Gulnar Khan in that report."

"Then someone edited it after I was finished," David said, knowing that the someone had to be Theo Tucker. "Theo complained about . . . what he called sex fantasies." David shook his head. "I thought he was trying to make me feel better, but I guess he just didn't want to believe what Sindon said about this sexual prowess."

"I guess I'd know who Gulnar Khan was and why she wanted to kill Sindon if T. T. had left the report alone, and I do wish he had, because it seems like you're never going to tell me."

"Sorry, Brown," David said, and explained that Gulnar Khan was Rukmani Khan's wife and that Sindon had not known about her until the very end of her stay in the Winter Palace. "Sindon finally figured out that Rukmani Khan had deliberately kept her out of the mainstream at the Winter Palace, probably so that she wouldn't find out about Gulnar Khan." He didn't add that Sindon had not expressed any remorse over sleeping with Rukmani Khan, not even when she found out he had a wife. And her ire at the Khan for endangering her had been less obvious than her gratitude for saving her from certain death on the Altar of Justice.

"Maybe Rukmani Khan will still protect her, and us," Brown said, glancing over at Sindon and Tara. The two were still deeply engrossed in their private conversation. "What do you think, David?"

"I think we should ask Sindon what he said. Maybe we'll get some idea of what to expect." This time he didn't hesitate. He walked directly over to Sindon and Tara. "We need to talk," he said.

"I don't think—" Sindon started to say, her tone haughty.

"About what Rukmani Khan said to you just now," David said, cutting her off while making a mental note that it might not be going too well for him in their private mother-daughter conversation. "We'll talk about the other later," he added, to let both of them know he had some intentions.

"I didn't talk to Rukmani Khan. The little priest, Timon, I think his name is, stopped Hazan and made him take me to Gulnar Khan. She's Rukmani Khan's wife," Sindon explained as if David would not know. "She's the one who tried to have me killed. She failed, but just barely. I think she had forgotten that I understand their language. She asked Hazan where he was going with me, but he wouldn't tell. I think she knew he was taking me to Rukmani Khan, and she was angry when Hazan wouldn't admit it. Finally she ordered him to take me back here. And he did!"

"You seem surprised," David said.

"Hazan is Rukmani Khan's vassal lord. I didn't realize he would obey Gulnar. I mean, I know they appear to obey her, but I thought Rukmani Khan's orders were higher priority."

"What now?"

Sindon shrugged. "We wait for the Moon Council meeting."

"What happens there?"

"I don't know. I never knew Moon Councils existed until just before I left. I didn't know a lot of things until not knowing almost got me killed. There is probably a lot more I don't know. Even the palace looks different, almost as pretty as the Summer Palace. Something has changed. Something very basic has changed."

"You're not alone this time, Sindon," David said. He had hoped the thought would be some comfort to her, but then her eyes fell on Tara and he saw Sindon's shoulders shake.

"If any of them touches Tara, I'll . . ." She put her hands over her face, but not before David saw her terrified look. Her hands muffled the sound of gasping sobs.

"Mom, what's wrong?" Tara asked in alarm.

"Sindon, that's not going to help," David said sternly, even though he wished it were possible to take her into his arms and comfort her. "We need to know everything you know about Gulnar Khan and the Council."

"You would know everything I know if you'd read the damn report," she said, turning on him savagely. "It was a thorough report on everything: language including grammar and syntax; clothing, how they made it, which styles for what occasions; how they grew food and eating customs; how they persuaded and what they didn't—even persuasion applied to civil engineering and what I could extrapolate to the art I'd seen at the Summer Palace. I spent hours every day recording empirical data, corroborating every entry with at least four observations before drawing any conclusions about what I'd seen, and none of those conclusions was judgmental. I checked and rechecked, and I know there was not a single personal, unsubstantiated, or unprofessional statement in the entire report. It was disciplined, unemotional, and full of dull facts, and you wouldn't be asking me for more damn data, data, data, if you'd read it in the first place."

David stopped breathing as comprehension infused him like

ice water. Where he had expected Sindon's usual breezy, haphazard, and hasty conclusions, he had gotten instead her first attempt to keep her report on a business rather than personal level. "I . . . read . . . the . . . report," he finally managed to say.

Sindon pulled her shirttail up to blot the tears from her face. She looked bewildered.

"The report was good enough to support three separate appeals to have the Persuaders declared interlopers by the Council of Worlds. Even though the final appeal was turned down, it was based on Council's position that there was opportunity for the Persuaders to acquire Indo-European–based words from the hunting parties, not because the data wasn't gathered properly. The report was excellent. But," David added uneasily, "it didn't say anything to contradict Tara's being the Khan's child."

"Tara's parentage was unrelated to the subject of my report," she said dully.

"But you spent almost nine months here in the Winter Palace, and the only time you even mention being pregnant is when Rukmani Khan told you that you'd have a girl."

"That entry specifically stated that his ability to predict correctly would be further substantiated or absolutely discredited once the sex of the child was known. If he had been wrong, we would have known one more area in which persuasion is unreliable. I wouldn't have even made that entry about my being pregnant if it hadn't been pertinent. There was nothing, absolutely nothing, extraneous in that report."

"Sindon, I don't want to argue with you about the contents of the report. It was a good report, but . . ." He looked at Tara and fell silent.

"I'm not leaving," Tara said, apparently sensing what he hoped.

"Yes, you are," Brown said, leaning over to take her hand. "We both are." He pulled Tara to her feet, put his hands firmly on her shoulders and led her away.

David sat down on a cushion near Sindon, vaguely aware of a spicy aroma enveloping him. "Sindon, we have to talk, not argue. That child over there wants answers from us, and I'm not prepared to give them until I know where I really stand with you. And somewhere in this palace is a woman who wants to kill you, maybe all of us, and it might help to know how you really stand with the Khan. Will you let go of who's right and who's wrong and just talk to me?"

"I remember your little talks wherein *supposedly* no one's right or wrong, but it was always me who needed to do something different than what I had been doing as a result of those conversations. I never could do anything right for you. Something would always be wrong."

Inwardly, David sighed. Maybe there was nothing he could do or say so that she wouldn't be defensive, but maybe he could at least keep her on track and be very careful about being noncritical, which might minimize her defensiveness. "You did a lot of things that were right for me. Your enthusiasm for the work kept me excited about it, too"—*while your enthusiasm lasted*, he thought—"and I got to know a lot of good people really well that I probably wouldn't have but for your friendliness. I miss all of that."

Her expression softened almost immediately, and she sat down next to him. "Most people like you once they find out you aren't half as stuffy as they think you are."

"And they like you right away," David said, then added in a tone so even and calm he surprised himself: "Even the Khan."

"Yes."

"And you liked him, I assume, because you went away with him without telling me or anyone else. I think," he said, quickly so as to cut off a reply that was accompanied by an arched brow, "that you called it an *opportunity that couldn't be wasted* in your report, and some more words about all the Persuaders leaving before they had been studied properly and being offered a chance to make close-up observations instead of distant ones. All that seems very logical insofar as it goes, but when I read that part of the report, I also knew you were very angry with me, and I saw your leaving as an attempt to punish me."

"You hurt me," she said. "You just threw me aside when it got too tough for you." She shook her head. "I sure had no reason to want to stay."

"So you left on impulse."

"I wouldn't say that."

"I did. That's how I saw it. Pure impulse. Right or wrong, Sindon, that's how I felt."

Sindon shrugged.

David wanted to shake her and ask her if she wouldn't just once try to consider his feelings, but he knew that his feelings were secondary to hers, perhaps especially so after all these years. He could only hope that maybe a little of what he was trying to say might seep past that façade of indifference. At least he hoped it was a façade. "Your report contained a lot of good data. I'm sure I would have been far more impressed if I hadn't been feeling so much pain myself." David took a deep breath. "I hated reading about the Khan's sexual practices; you didn't try to hide that you'd gotten the information firsthand."

"I wouldn't have believed what he could do if someone had just *told* me about it. You have to experience it to understand that it's almost like being in . . ."

He thought she was going to say "heaven" and he knew his eyes were filling with tears.

". . . like being addicted," she said.

"No desire to resist," David couldn't help adding.

"None," Sindon said. She was looking at him, maybe for the first time with a trace of embarrassment. "David, you were a good lover, but what the Khan can do puts him in another class altogether. Don't even try to compare yourself to him."

David wanted to choke her, but was strangling himself on he knew not what. Was there no end to her desire to hurt him? He squeezed his eyes shut.

"David." He felt her hand on his knee and tried to open his eyes. "David, he was different, not better. I tried to explain. . . ."

"So did he," David said, "but he wasn't clinical in his choice of words. I could not read what you had written without hearing Rukmani Khan's words." It took all his strength not to let the threatening sobs take hold.

"What words?" Her grip on his knee tightened.

"When he saved me from the blizzard, after he realized who I was. He told me that you had made him promise not to kill me. . . ." David felt an ironic laugh come forth unbidden. "It would have been better if he had. I didn't believe anything he said, not deep down. I kept clinging to his telling me you wouldn't let him kill me, and I thought that must mean you still

loved me. Then I saw you, obviously pregnant and I went nuts
remembering what he had said. You wouldn't deny anything,
and then I read the report. You admitted everything."

"That sneaky bastard," she said. "He did it again to me.
David, listen to me. Rukmani Khan . . . sex with him *was*
addictive. But not so addictive that I couldn't stop when I had
good reason to, and I did when I found out he was using me to
try to force Gulnar Khan to release him from his vow of
fidelity. And worse, that he deliberately kept me from knowing
about her and how much power she had. She almost had me
killed!"

David nodded. "Your description of the ritual preparations
was very complete, down to symbolic restraints on every
finger, even though you and the others were not Persuaders."

"I was paralyzed during that entire time, and utterly terrified. Have you any idea of what it's like to hear everything, see
things that cross your field of vision, even to smell the scent in
the priest's robes, but not be able to so much as twitch an eye?"

"Yes," David said. "I do. Rukmani Khan immobilized me
in that cave, and he talked to me about you for what seemed an
eternity. He loved you, Sindon."

Sindon nodded. "I know."

"Did you love him?"

"I thought he was my friend," she said cautiously.

"And lover," David added.

"I explained that," she said impatiently. "You would have
done the same if you had had the opportunity."

"No, Sindon, I wouldn't have. Not in a million years. And
I'm trying to remember that your being so different from me is
what made me love you in the first place, and that I can't hold
that against you."

"But you do anyhow, don't you?" she demanded to know.
"Even though you told me we were finished and drove me
away. You expected me to turn into some kind of hermit just
because that's what you did? Rukmani Khan was good to me,
a whole lot more thoughtful than you ever were."

"I know, I know. And no, I don't hold your sleeping with
him against you." He paused, reflecting on what he had just
said. "Not now, I don't." He didn't offer anything more on
that, for he didn't think she would understand that only now, in
talking to her and seeing her talk about Rukmani Khan and

having sex with him, did he know the memory of it was not half as important to her as the thought of it was to him. "I have just one more question," he said.

"What is it?"

"Did you refuse to let us do the genetic screen on Tara because you knew it would reveal she was my child?"

Sindon pulled her hand away. "I promised you I'd never let upper management know about our . . . affair. They'd have had proof positive if they'd tested Tara."

"Oh, my God," David said, amazed that she had even thought of the promise under the circumstances, and astounded that she would keep it to such an extreme. "Sindon, they knew. They couldn't help but know. I was like a madman while you were gone."

Sindon shrugged. "They had no proof. I wasn't going to give it to them. Besides, if I had, they could have sent me back to the Hub—alone."

"Does that mean you loved me?"

"Did you love me?" she asked, looking somewhat defensive.

"What's the matter? Are you afraid to admit it before I do?" He hoped to tease her, but didn't push too far. "Yes," he said. "I loved you. I think I still love you." And finally he was rewarded with her smile, a beautiful one.

"Think? Do you want another sixteen years to make up your mind?" she asked, equally playful.

David laughed. "Touché, my love. I love you, Sindon. I have always loved you, I love you now, and I will love you forever. Thank you, too, for such a beautiful daughter." He held his arms out to her and he held his breath. When he felt her slip into his arms, he started breathing again, and he could feel the tension give way as her arms encircled him. It felt as if they had melted against each other, her breath like perfume against his cheek. "Say it to me, Sindon. Please say it."

"I love you, David."

26.

RUKMANI KHAN SAT at Gulnar's left hand, alone on the curved black shale bench that formed the eclipsed side of the Moon Council chamber in the Winter Palace. Gulnar sat at the tip of the longest white marble bench, her customary place in the Winter Palace. At Gulnar's right was Timon, the priest she alone had named, and behind him were Amar and one other priest Gulnar had not named alone, and Kangra, Hazan, and the other vassal lords and ladies who were of sufficient rank to sit on the shiny white curves. As was customary in the Moon Council, Gulnar Khan recognized one speaker and one questioner at a time, and the remaining priests, lords, and ladies listened attentively to the dialogues.

The prisoners were kept standing outside the circle near the base of the moon, the two men from the shuttle in the shadows on the dark side, Sindon and the other three bathed in light. Rukmani Khan had found it difficult to concentrate on the dialogue, difficult not to stare at Sindon and her daughter, their red hair washed gold in the harsh light, skin like fine porcelain. Though Tara was almost as tall as she, Sindon kept her arms around her daughter, an unmistakably protective gesture. The two men flanked Sindon and Tara closely, one whom Rukmani Khan only vaguely recognized, the other the man he would never forget: David Quarrels. Sindon did not look at Rukmani Khan with that clear-eyed gaze of hers except once when he had interjected a comment in the dialogue, and even then he thought she deliberately broke eye contact by turning to whisper to the other prisoners. David Quarrels' scrutiny seemed fixed on Rukmani Khan, which merely annoyed him until he began to sense the intensity of concentration. Could

David Quarrels possibly know how insolent his behavior was? The vassal lords had begun whispering among themselves, drawing each other's attention to the prisoner who glared so rudely, until even Gulnar took notice.

Gulnar held up her hand to silence the current questioner, the priest Timon, who was so intent upon the questions he was putting to Hazan that he did not notice Gulnar's signal immediately.

"How can a man sworn to defend the Winter Palace say these are not invaders when one carried a weapon of the kind that has already killed four of our people?" Timon was saying. "Would you also deny that you took enough missiles from them to kill every person in this chamber?"

Hazan looked grateful to have to defer to Gulnar Khan's raised hand, and probably enjoyed Timon's confusion when, instead of answering, Hazan looked expectantly at Gulnar Khan. Timon was bewildered when he realized it was the Khana who had cut off Hazan's reply. To Gulnar's credit, she paid no heed to the priest's stern look. When she stood to speak, Timon had no choice but to sit down.

"Who is that man?" Gulnar said, pointing at David Quarrels.

"Your prisoner, one of the New People," Hazan said. Hazan's gaze stayed directly on the Khana, but Rukmani Khan knew that the younger man was waiting for permission from himself to elaborate. When permission was not forthcoming and Gulnar Khan was not satisfied, she gestured for Hazan to sit.

Gulnar turned to Rukmani Khan. "Who is that man?" she said again.

"One I swore not to kill," Rukmani Khan replied, offering no further explanation in response to her puzzled frown. He was looking at Sindon, who had abruptly stopped her whispering to look at him. There was something desperate in her eyes; she must have already discerned how vulnerable their position was. But she could only surmise why he would tell Gulnar about the promise he had made so many years ago.

"That seems in conflict with your vow to defend the Winter Palace," Gulnar said.

Rukmani Khan stiffened with indignation. "I have broken but one vow, and for that I have done the penance you imposed. I resent your implication that I would not fulfill my vow to defend the Winter Palace. You can't seriously believe three people came to invade the Winter Palace with only one weapon among them against hundreds of Persuaders. They came to bargain for my prisoners, and no doubt for Sindon's child."

"I wouldn't consider bargaining with these invaders for your child," Gulnar said, her voice trembling almost as much as her fingers as they worried the edge of her shawl. "Though she is not the child of my body, she is the child of yours, and my duty is clear to me. I will nurture her and guide her as if she were my own."

Rukmani Khan was stunned. Even if Tara had been his offspring, he would not have expected Gulnar to make an offer like this. Then he realized that despite the generous sound of her words, Gulnar's face looked sick and stricken. It was not a choice she made freely, but one of duty. She was repulsed, but determined. He breathed uneasily. "Gulnar, Tara is not my child."

Gulnar's lips twitched, but she said nothing. Timon touched her sleeve, and she sat down.

"Being herself a woman of delicate persuasion, it is understandably difficult for the Khana to discuss the deeper lusts," Timon said, getting to his feet.

"Timon," Rukmani Khan said, struggling for patience. "The girl is not mine."

"Rukmani Khan, the mother lived with you for the entire cycle of embryonic development," Timon said, his voice infuriatingly paternalistic. "Do you think we did not count the number of moons?"

"The mother was not a Persuader," Rukmani Khan said.

"We took that into account," Timon said. "Abos' gestation takes eight moons, too."

Rukmani Khan stopped to consider. He knew Sindon's pregnancy was very long by Persuader standards. But Sindon had considered the length of time quite normal, and he could tell the infant was firmly planted in her and developing well, even if slowly. He realized now that he'd not only done Sindon a disservice by keeping her away from the midwives at the time, but also himself. There was no one who could attest to the differences of embryonic development, except Sindon herself. He did not think they would believe her. He looked at

Sindon. She looked frightened, but was wisely not speaking out. He marveled at her restraint. Sixteen years ago he did not believe she possessed the patience to be frightened and silent simultaneously. He also did not believe that Gulnar wanted Sindon's child to raise, not even if she thought the child was also his. Rukmani Khan stood up and put his hands behind his back, the gesture of restraint setting the lords and ladies to whispering behind their fingers. "Sindon's child took nine moons to develop. That is the truth of the matter, but I will allow you to pursue this accusation despite my denial if you will tell me now where it leads. What do you want of me?"

Timon was momentarily taken aback by the Khan's submission, even if it was not complete. He glanced at Gulnar, who nodded. "You brought two of the New People into the Winter Palace as prisoners, without consulting the Moon Council," Timon said. He pointed to the two men standing on the dark shale.

"My prisoners have nothing to do with the Winter Palace," Rukmani Khan said. "My penance is finished, and I wish to return to the Summer Palace. But I cannot, because in my absence the New People have expanded throughout the valley. They even live in my palace."

"We guessed that was your intent, Rukmani Khan, and we believe that your returning to the Summer Palace is not in the best interest of the Persuaders. We have lived in peace these sixteen years in but one palace; we had hoped you would come to recognize that the solidarity was healthy for everyone. Especially now, when New People who are not helpless against our persuasions have come to live in the Summer Palace, we believe the time has come to end the two reigns."

The Moon Council chamber filled with murmuring, and it did not sound much like dissent to Rukmani Khan. After sixteen years of complacency under Gulnar Khan's reign, he had expected only a small following to the Summer Palace. But he had also expected time and freedom for that following to grow in the years ahead. "So your plan must now be for not only me but Gulnar, too, to relinquish our rule to this foreign child?"

Timon nodded. "Your child came seeking her destiny. Gulnar Khan has acknowledged the hand of the Almighty Persuader guiding the child here."

Rukmani Khan was too angry to laugh at the absurdity. "She rode a bannertail born and bred in the Winter Palace stables. The beast came home; the child was clever enough to stay on its back." He took his hands out from behind his back. "I will not relinquish my right to rule, especially not to a child that isn't mine."

But Timon was not intimidated by Rukmani Khan's giving up the abject posture. "If you do not relinquish, you will be judged unfit. We will not be ruled by a Khan who cannot keep his vows."

"I have paid for that with sixteen years of total submission to the Winter Palace," Rukmani Khan said.

"You refer to your vow of fidelity, which you broke by rutting with the foreign woman," Timon said. "You may have made amends for the sake of your eternal soul, but in the eyes of your fellow mortals you will always be suspect. And when you break your vow to defend the Winter Palace, you will be judged unfit."

"I never asked to be released from my vow to protect the Winter Palace, and I never will."

Timon smiled. "Then will you accept the honor of wielding the ritual knife when we put Sindon and the other two invaders on the Altar of Justice? Or will you obey the conflicting vow to put your life before hers? And the man you vowed not to kill . . . Will you refuse to raise the knife to him, too?"

"First it must be decided whether or not they are invaders," Rukmani Khan said, trying to regain his composure. "Until then, I have no dilemma and you have no broken vows to flaunt."

"Then, let the lords and ladies tell us now if they believe these people are invaders," Timon said with great confidence.

"No," Rukmani Khan objected firmly.

"No?"

"No," he repeated. "I won't permit the vote."

"Rukmani Khan," Timon said, his voice chiding. "Is that an honorable position to take when your people are so full of doubt? Do you not owe them proof of your worthiness to rule?"

"My honor has less to do with worthiness to rule than my ability to see through such thinly veiled manipulations as yours. I owe it to my people not to allow myself to be forced into breaking my vow to defend the Winter Palace or my vow to put my life before Sindon's. I do not believe they would ask that of me but for your unconscionable manipulations. You may sit down now, Timon, for I have questions to ask so that this Council may decide for itself if a false priest such as you has place in this body."

"But . . ."

"Sit down!"

Timon looked furious, but he sat. He had to know he had sown terrible seeds of doubt in the rest of the Council, seeds Rukmani Khan could not ignore by simply refusing to let it come to a test. The Khan could see the consternation in all their faces. "Hazan," he said, and the vassal lord got to his feet. "Hazan, I wish to ask a deeply personal question of you, one that decency would normally preclude my asking. Will you agree to answer it frankly and truthfully?"

"Ycs," Hazan said without hesitation, though Rukmani Khan could tell he was puzzled. He probably could not imagine anything the Khan could ask that he would not want to answer, especially if it could help.

"It's common knowledge that you have lived with three of the foreign women without benefit of matrimony. It's possible that you live as brother and sisters, but I think not."

"You're correct, milord. We do not live as brother and sisters."

"Why have you never formalized your bond with any of them?"

Hazan flushed. "I . . ." Hazan swallowed hard. "They're foreign women."

"Acceptance does not seem to be a problem from what I've observed, Hazan," Rukmani Khan said gently. "And you are enough of an iconoclast not to care if it were. I believe that sixteen years says something about your devotion to them, too, so it's not a matter of not loving them either. It must be something else."

Hazan nodded. "I would like children some day, and I . . . If I marry one of them, I can't some day marry a Persuader woman who can give me children."

"Does that mean you have tried to make a baby with the three foreign women? Tried and failed?"

"Repeatedly," Hazan said, apparently understanding at last

that their inability to carry his seed might say something about Tara's parentage. "I even went to the midwives to learn how to tend a planted seed. There is one midwife in this Council who consented to help me with her own hands. But . . ." He shrugged and shook his head. "She said that despite their appearance being even closer to ours than the abos, she believed we could not successfully get them with child."

A lady seated behind Hazan nodded slightly, and set the other lords and ladies to whispering behind their hands again.

"Hazan, only Sindon understands our language, and any answer she might give is suspect. Since you speak the New People's language, will you ask David Quarrels to explain why he would glower at me so insolently, and why . . ."

"I understand the question," David Quarrels said. "I do not wish to add to your troubles, but it seems I can't help myself and the others unless I do."

Rukmani Khan was surprised. "I underestimated you," he said. "If you know our language well enough to speak it, you probably also know that to stare at me with hatred in your expression would have been adequate reason for me to punish you, or maybe even challenge you to combat."

"The latter is my fervent hope," David Quarrels said, his stare still unflinching.

"Then you're still a fool," Rukmani Khan said, realizing the full intent of David Quarrels' insult. "I won't excuse you now that I know you didn't insult me in ignorance. Submit now or take the consequence. I trust you know how it's done."

Sindon looked frightened and whispered something to David. He shook his head. "I don't believe you will kill me, Rukmani Khan, at least, not just now. And anything short of that I'll willingly endure, so that I know you're certain I am your sworn enemy, one who knows what it means to be a sworn enemy."

"Hazan," Rukmani Khan said, gesturing with disgust at David Quarrels. He needed to say no more. Hazan leaped over the bench and pulled David's arms around to his back until he winced with pain, forcing him to assume the posture of submission. Sindon kicked Hazan, and he said something sharp to her which, Rukmani Khan noted, didn't seem to deter her. But the other man pulled Sindon back and held her firmly.

Hazan stepped back, leaving David standing with his hands behind his back, his face grimacing with pain as he fought to gain control of arm and shoulder muscles that wouldn't obey.

"The people of this court think, especially my wife, that you hate me because I grew a baby in Sindon," Rukmani Khan said.

"Tara's mine," David Quarrels said, his face contorted with pain. "Tara's my child, not yours. I won't leave her here. She goes back with me. With Sindon and me."

Rukmani Khan didn't think anyone would doubt that David was telling the truth, except perhaps Gulnar, who might not want to believe. It was, after all, hard to be a martyr foster-mother if there were not a child of Rukmani Khan's to be a martyr about. "Then what's all your anger for, David Quarrels? It might have made sense if I'd planted my child in her womb. We have similar sensibilities here in the Winter Palace."

"You deceived her and kept her with you for your own amusement," David said.

"Amusement," Rukmani Khan repeated, mocking him with the word. "Do you think I would break my vow of fidelity for simple amusement? Amusement I can take in discretion with sporting women."

"Then it's worse," David said, looking now as if he had become accustomed to the pain he was feeling. "You loved her."

"Not loved, David Quarrels. *Love*. I love her, and I think she still loves me, too. That's what makes you so angry, isn't it?"

David Quarrels didn't answer, but he stared defiantly at Rukmani Khan.

The Khan turned to look at Gulnar, who was holding her head in her hands. "My wife won't release me from my vow of fidelity," he said to the Moon Council. "And she thinks and some of you think that because I broke that vow, all other vows are suspect. I won't apologize for what I did. I would have gone to the Summer Palace if Gulnar had released me, and half of every year I could have been with the woman I loved. But she would not release me, still will not release me, will you, Gulnar?"

Stoically, Gulnar raised her head. "No," she said. "I will not release you. You are the Khan! Ours is not some ordinary bond. Ours cannot fail."

"It failed more years ago than I care to remember," Rukmani Khan said. "But I no longer believe it's just your pride holding me to you. I think you want me to fail so that this court will judge me unfit as Timon said. You would not rule well alone, Gulnar Khan; you've always needed someone to depend on. When it couldn't be me anymore, you turned to this false priest, who would rule beside you in my stead. I can't let that happen, Gulnar. My people mean more to me than even my own happiness. I will lead my vassal lords back to the Summer Palace. I will have Sindon at my side, but I will keep my vow of fidelity to you until you choose to release me from it."

"The child . . ." Gulnar started to say.

"The child is not mine. And in keeping my vow, we both know there will never be one."

"But . . ."

"Never," Rukmani Khan said. "When you and I have returned to the Almighty Persuader, there will be a new Khan and Khana, and neither will be a child of mine or yours."

Gulnar looked at him, her eyes brimming with tears. But the eyes of the false priest glittered. "So be it," Timon said. "And let us see how long you can keep your vow with Sindon at your side."

"What do you mean, with me at your side?" Sindon asked, speaking up for the first time. "Don't I have anything to say about this?"

"No," Rukmani Khan said. "You do not. You may accompany me as honored guest, or as prisoner of my love, but this time you may not choose to leave."

"You'll have to deal with me first," David Quarrels said.

"I expected as much," Rukmani Khan conceded. "But that need not concern this Council." He looked at Hazan. "Take all six of the prisoners to the stable. Prepare mounts for them. We leave tonight for the Summer Palace."

Hazan got up to obey, and Kangra and two other vassal lords rose to help him. Rukmani Khan stayed on his feet until all six prisoners had passed through the moongate on the far side of the room. Then, satisfied that none would interfere, he followed them.

27.

WHEN THE PERSUADERS shoved them out of the Moon Council chamber, David's fingers were still laced in a convulsive grasp behind his back and the painful spasms in his shoulder muscles had spread to his neck and lower back. At least now while they were walking he could stretch against the involuntary contractions by turning his head and pulling his shoulders forward, which helped to alleviate the pain he'd tried not to show while in the Moon Council. Suddenly he felt a pair of hands on his shoulders, fingers massaging the aching tendons. He looked back to find Tara walking behind him.

"Does that help?" She looked pale and frightened, but very determined despite the frown her ministrations brought from Hazan.

"Yes, thanks," he said. Her fingers were not strong enough to knead the knots out of his muscles, but her touch was comforting.

"Dad?"

"What?"

"Nothing," Tara said. "I just wanted to call you that."

David wanted to put his arm around her and hug her, but of course he couldn't. "Thanks, sweetheart. I love you."

They went through a maze of corridors, most of which were straight and level, carved out of ocher-colored sandstone or green-black shale. They passed massive stone mushrooms that dripped water from radiating gills into white enameled troughs, which David realized were the distillation apparatus for recapturing the water brought up through steam shafts from below. Some of the water collected in pools that were brightly lighted with magnesium lamps and surrounded by crystal stools and polished stone benches. He saw fine mosaics in some of the larger chambers, one of which caused him to catch his breath and gave a start to Theo, Brown, and Sindon, too. A wintry scene of a magtree forest, covering an entire wall, it was immediately recognizable as Mahania's northern slope of magtrees by the bisecting scar of white quartz that represented the icy trough used to slide the logs into the valley below. The scene depicted the murder of the four loggers, bright blue eyes frozen in stone at the moment of death, the abos looking on in fear, and even the metallic glitter of two sleds far up the hill, their occupants clad in white coats. Hazan and the other guards allowed them to pause only briefly before jostling their elbows to move them into yet another corridor.

Somewhere in the maze, they started down a dimly lighted staircase. It seemed to go on forever, cutting through deep layers of ocher sandstone, red sandstone, white limestone, gray marine shale, and finally shiny black layers of unrecognizable rock that was streaked here and there with crystal. David knew they had to be near the floor of the canyon again.

When the staircase ended, they walked alongside a subterranean river for a while, then turned into what seemed to be a seminatural corridor where only the floor had been somewhat leveled. David stumbled more than once in the dimly lighted passageway.

"The stable," he heard Sindon say when they stepped into a vast chamber.

The stable was nothing more than a low-ceilinged natural chamber that opened onto the moonlit canyon floor. The chamber was humid and smelled of leather and dung. A trough carved out of the black-red rock caught trickles of water from natural seepage and spilled the excess into a crude gutter to a pool where enough collected for the animals to drink. Near the pool, an array of saddles, bridles, and other leatherwork David didn't recognize hung on a latticework of pegs and poles that were firmly anchored in the stone wall. Hazan pushed David into the maze of leatherworks and ran his hands along David's biceps and forearms, releasing the cramping convulsions. Before David could even think to offer a begrudging thanks, Hazan fixed the fingers of David's right hand around a pole and left him standing there, his fingers clenched around the pole. He couldn't let go, and he couldn't pry his fingers loose with his other hand. Frustrated, he watched as Sindon and the others were treated likewise. Then the Persuaders slipped out of the stable into the night, presumably to find their bannertails somewhere in the canyon.

"Is everyone all right?" Theo asked. He was still wearing his summer dress blues, short sleeves and short pants. His arms and legs were scraped and scratched from riding through the bush country.

"It's you we've been worried about, T.T.," Brown said. "You and L.L., of course. The pilot told us what happened, but it didn't make a lot of sense to me. How could he mistake Xanthippe's Chasm for the landing pad?"

Theo shook his head, perturbed. "The pilot couldn't see. He followed the beam in, but it was the wrong beam. It brought us down in the Chasm. What I want to know is how they got a beam." He was looking at David, expecting an answer.

"A shortwave beam wouldn't be too hard for them to manage," David said. "They've had sixteen years to find or make just the right quartz crystal to rectify the signal. Bring a beam-rider right in."

Theo raised his brows. "They didn't know anything about radio sixteen years ago." Now he was looking at Sindon. "I don't remember your report saying anything about radio transmission or reception."

Sindon frowned. "I had some discussions with Hazan about frequency modulation and crystals. It wasn't in the report because discussions like that were superfluous to understanding their culture. I didn't tell him very much."

"Apparently enough," Theo commented.

"We've lost a lot of equipment over the years," Brown interjected. "You've seen the reports, T.T. We attributed the thefts to the Abos, since the Persuaders supposedly weren't around. It makes me wonder now." He looked at David. "Makes me sorry I didn't listen to some of the things you tried to tell me."

David shrugged. There was no sense in berating Brown now for not having believed David's theory that the Persuaders were responsible for many thefts. Books, bright clothing, and gadgets like watches and radios attracted the abos. But power packs, altimeters, and temperature gauges did not, and although many of these items had been stolen over the years, too, David had rarely seen any of them in the yurts.

"What will happen to us?" asked Les Landers. The corporate auditor looked exhausted and very frightened.

Everyone looked at Sindon. "You know as much as I do," she said, her voice irritable.

"He doesn't know anything, Sindon," David said, hoping he was saying the right thing to put Sindon at ease. Her defensive reactions were so automatic, so strong. "He doesn't understand the Persuaders' language. Neither do Theo or Brown."

"You certainly understood," she said, her tone accusing but her expression one of surprise.

"It's my job," David said. "I had a long time to study."

"My report?"

David nodded. "No one's blaming you, Sindon. We know you couldn't possibly put every detail in your report. But you know them better than we do. It's important that you share some of that knowledge with us now."

Sindon pushed her hair back from her face with her free hand and, with what David thought was little embellishment for her, she explained what had transpired in the Moon Council, her voice trembling through the part where Gulnar Khan had tried to claim Tara. "We're better off than we were an hour ago," she said in conclusion. "We're all Rukmani Khan's prisoners now, and that's safer than being Gulnar's."

"I'm not sure I see the difference," Theo said. "Especially in view of what he said to me earlier about not being willing to negotiate. He sounded downright hostile. And I don't think it was very smart to antagonize him like you did, David."

"If David hadn't stared him down, the whole Moon Council would have thought we were a bunch of cowards," Sindon replied hotly. "They have no respect for anyone who shows fear or lack of resolution. Especially not Rukmani Khan. David did the right thing."

"Easy, Sindon," David said, wanting to calm her and get her back on track, despite being pleased that she had jumped to his defense. "I knew it was a point of honor; Theo didn't. What we need to know now is: Is there even any point in trying to talk to Rukmani Khan?"

"From his viewpoint, it's you who are being unreasonable," Sindon said. "You stole his palace, his lands, everything."

"Yes," Theo put in, "but this guy has to be made to understand that we operate under World Council laws, not his."

"You explain that to him, Theo," Sindon said with a sardonic smile.

Theo didn't begin to see any humor. His frown deepened. "I'm asking you how to do that. What can I say that will make him understand that not even I have the authority to evacuate the entire community?"

"I already understand," said Rukmani Khan in standard. He stepped out of the shadows. There were a dozen vassal lords with him and a young priest, yet none of the prisoners had heard them come in. Even now they moved silently, some stepping into the light with Rukmani Khan, others melting back into the shadows.

"I'm not sure you do," Theo said, turning as best he could to face the Khan. "The World Council governs thousands of worlds and has vast resources, military resources, for dealing with rebellions. You don't want to get into a contest with them, Rukmani Khan. You can't even imagine the forces they can bring against you, not in quantity nor in capability. Believe me, I'm telling you the truth."

"It takes you months to get word to your World Council," Rukmani Khan said contemptuously. "It will take them more months to decide what to do. In the meantime, I will have already settled the matter."

"What are you going to do?"

But Rukmani Khan merely smiled. "Whatever it is, I wouldn't be foolish enough to tell you."

"I don't want any more . . . incidents between your people and mine," Theo said. "We—" He seemed to catch himself. "I made a terrible mistake years ago in killing some of your people. Under our laws you were wrong to retaliate even though I committed the first wrong. I don't think either of us wants any more of our people to die because of our mistakes."

"There is only one way to prevent war," Rukmani Khan said. "You must take your people out of the valley. Return what is mine."

"There are other fine valleys," Theo said. "I'll see that you get title from the World Council itself to any one you select.

We'll build you a good road, dig wells or build dams, anything you want."

"But any other valley wouldn't have the Summer Palace," Rukmani Khan said, "so no other will do."

"We'll build you another palace, a better one."

"If you would do all this to appease me, why not just move your people elsewhere?" Rukmani Khan asked.

Theo hesitated a moment, then said: "Because the World Council supports my position, not yours."

The Khan shrugged. "Then defend it as I will defend mine, with my life."

Theo's lips thinned. "You don't understand what you're facing. You can't win."

But Rukmani Khan had already stopped listening, his attention turning to Hazan and the three other Persuaders who were herding a pack of bannertails into the stable. The Khan spoke rapidly to the vassal lords who had come in with him, and within moments the stable echoed with the stamping and whistling of the bannertails as the men reached for their tack.

David watched Rukmani Khan walk over to Sindon and whisper something to her as he put his hands over her clenched fingers. She snatched her hand away from the pole and out from under his touch. She shook her head, and David could hear her say, "No!" very sharply. She rubbed her hand as Rukmani Khan continued whispering to her. She shook her head again and looked at David with frightened eyes. David tried to pull his own pole free with his frozen fingers, but it would not budge. The effort, however, caught the Khan's attention. He looked at David sourly, then came over to him.

"Behave yourself," he said crisply when he saw David's fist. Unhesitatingly, he stepped up close and put his hand over David's fingers—and David felt his fingers relax their unshakable hold on the pole. Free now to take a swing at the Khan's jaw, David resisted the impulse, knowing it was pointless with so many other Persuaders nearby. His tone still crisp, Rukmani Khan now said, "I want to talk with Sindon, but she is afraid to be alone with me. You will come with us, and you will remember to keep your hands behind your back or I'll put them there for you."

David nodded and clasped his hands behind him, rubbing his

tingling fingers. Rukmani Khan gestured toward the canyon, then trusting him and Sindon to follow, he led the way.

A gathering mist was softening the moonlight, turning clumps of bushes into wraithlike shapes. David and Sindon followed Rukmani Khan down a narrow path to a still pool that looked like molten silver in the velvety darkness. The Khan stopped at the water's edge, and David and Sindon stopped, too, staying a few meters away from him.

"I think you know what is expected of you, Sindon," Rukmani Khan said, his dark eyes glistening like the pool. "You must be at my side, constantly at my side, except at night when I retire to my bed."

"I won't do it," Sindon said, shaking her head. "I don't want to be some kind of symbol for you or for your people. And I don't want to come anywhere near you."

"Why is that, Sindon? Is it because you know you would not be able to resist my touch?"

David saw Sindon wince before turning her head away. He almost reached out to take her in his arms, the abortive gesture bringing Rukmani Khan's full attention to him. Resignedly he clasped his hands behind his back again. "Maybe," he said sharply to the Khan, "it's because she doesn't believe you have sufficient honor and willpower not to touch her."

"I probably don't," Rukmani Khan said. "But it's only necessary that I not have sex with her. Indeed, I could entice her with my touch and have her begging for culmination, and there are those who would admire me for doing it."

"As long as you left her begging, right?" David said, disgusted with the man's arrogance.

"You understand, David. The question is, does Sindon?" The Persuader moved toward Sindon, who was crying softly into her hands.

"Don't touch her!" David shouted, and stepped between them. He kept his hands behind his back, hoping the combination of submission and verbal defiance was sufficient to deter the Khan.

Rukmani Khan reached behind David, and David fully expected to go down in a powerless slump. But the Khan just smiled, and gently pulled Sindon around until the two of them were standing in front of David. Rukmani Khan looked at Sindon, but said to David: "Don't do anything stupid." He was so close, David could smell him and hear him breathe. "You aren't quick enough, and if you were, it would only mean a moment's delay before I put you down like a sack of dirt." He lifted Sindon's chin, his fingers so gentle along her skin that even David could not deny the tenderness in the gesture. "When you wanted to leave, I let you go. You know what I could have done and that you wouldn't have left if I had. Why do you fear me now?"

Sindon squeezed her eyes shut against tears she couldn't hold back. "Because you had to *let* me go or I couldn't have left. No one should have that kind of power over another person, not even you, Rukmani Khan." Her voice caught on sobs. "I don't ever want to feel so powerless again," she said. "And I'm afraid because so much time has gone by and so much is at stake now, maybe you won't care enough to restrain yourself. You've lost everything that had meaning to you."

"Yes," he said as he brushed her tears with his fingertips. "I've lost everything."

"I didn't know what I was costing you," Sindon said, and she opened her eyes and met his gaze. David held his breath. Their faces were so close, he thought the Khan was going to kiss her and that Sindon was going to let him. But Rukmani Khan only pushed a strand of hair from her damp cheek.

"Do you believe I'm so desperate I can't be trusted?" he asked.

"I don't want to do what you're asking of me. I don't want to be at your side. Whether you touch me or not, it would be repugnant to me, humiliating."

The disappointment on the Khan's face was immediate and profound.

"Let me go, Rukmani Khan. Let me take Tara and leave. In the name of whatever it was we once had, please let me take my child away from here."

The Khan's face hardened. "You heard the priest. It is a challenge, a test." He dropped his hands to her shoulders, his fingers sliding down her arms. "Sindon, I can't let you go this time. You must stay with me."

Sindon moaned and crossed her arms in front of her chest. "Oh, please, don't . . ." She closed her eyes, her face contorted with pain and ecstasy.

David knew that if he lashed out against Rukmani Khan,

Sindon would have to face him again—alone, and that David might have to watch what he once thought he would die from hearing. Slowly he moved one hand out from behind his back and slipped his arm around Sindon's waist. "Sindon," he whispered. "Sindon, it's me, David."

Sindon gasped and, wrenching herself away from Rukmani Khan, she threw herself against David's chest. He put his arms around her, half crying himself while trying to stare defiantly at the Khan. "Why don't you ask her again?" he said to the Persuader. "Why don't you ask her now while she's in my arms? Ask her without touching her?"

"Because it doesn't matter what she answers," Rukmani Khan said bitterly. "She will do it." He looked at David. "The only question is, do I go through you to convince her? Or through Tara?"

Sindon gasped and turned. "Tara? What do you mean?" David held her tightly, though he knew she wanted to be loose of him now. "You're not going to claim her after all, are you?"

"As my child?" Rukmani Khan shook his head. "But I need a beautiful red-haired woman at my side who will be the symbol of my strength. If you won't do it, perhaps I can convince Tara that . . ."

"All right," Sindon said, breaking free of David's grasp with frightening strength. "I'll do it if you'll swear that you won't ever touch Tara."

"Sindon, he's bluffing," David said.

"I'm not going to take a chance on that," she said. "You don't know . . ." She turned back to Rukmani Khan. "Swear," she demanded.

"He *is* desperate, Sindon. You can't believe anything he says."

Rukmani Khan held out his hand to her and said, very gently: "I swear."

Sindon stepped forward, but she did not take his hand. "All right," she said. "What do I have to do?"

"It's as I said," the Khan replied. "You must ride at my side, you must eat what I have prepared for you, and you must suffer my touch when it is right and good for a lord to touch his lady. But you will sleep alone, and so will I."

"It would be humiliating for you to touch me inside," she said, her eyes downcast. "I can't bear the thought of Tara seeing me like that. She's just a child; she knows so little of life."

Again, with that tender gesture, Rukmani Khan lifted her chin. "Trust me, Sindon," he said, promising nothing. At last he bent over and kissed her chastely on the forehead. Then he reached into his robe and withdrew a bundle, which he handed over to Sindon. "Wear these," he said. "It's clothing more suited to a symbolic person than the dowdy garb you're wearing."

She hesitated a moment, then took the clothes from him and walked around to the other side of the pool, behind some rocks. Rukmani Khan simply walked the other way around the pool. When David realized the Persuader's intentions, he followed him.

"If you want to share the view, you'd better put your hands behind your back again," Rukmani Khan said curtly. "And if you had a mind to prevent me from this, step up so I can be done with you quickly."

David took a deep breath and put his hands behind his back again. "I wonder how honorable you can be feeling right now," he said, stepping up beside the Khan, but turning his back to Sindon.

"Not very," the Khan said. "But I felt a flicker of hope three times, David Quarrels. She never mentioned the one thing that might have stopped me from doing what I did. She never said she didn't love me, or that she did love you." He glanced briefly at David to take in his expression, then turned back to watch Sindon.

In his mind's eye, David could see Sindon pulling off her shirt. Moonlight gleamed on her breasts, her flesh like white marble. She sat down to pull off her boots, and then she wriggled out of her pants. She sat there in the nude, sorting out an array of filmy things until she decided which to put on first. She slipped an almost transparent tunic over her shoulders. It hung to her knees but hid nothing in the moonlight. He heard Rukmani Khan draw in his breath, and he saw the reflection of Sindon in the deep purple eyes.

"She doesn't love you," David said, blinking frantically and looking away. "At least when *I* touch her, I know it isn't because her body can't resist even when her mind believes otherwise. She's there because she wants to be."

"Ask her some day, David. Ask her whose arms she'd rather be in."

"Have you already forgotten it was mine she came to?" David said. "Even when you were trying to persuade her otherwise?"

Rukmani Khan looked at him, and David glanced up quickly to meet his gaze. "You think you won something here tonight, don't you? You think I'm just a little bit afraid of you because she wanted you with her, and because you were there for her when she wanted to tear herself away from me. But you know why I didn't put you out of the way, too, don't you?" Rukmani Khan smiled and crossed his arms in front of his chest. David could see Sindon reflected in the Khan's eyes again. She was lifting pantaloons over her hips, tucking the tunic inside. Again David turned away. "She'll put you aside herself, and I want you alive and well until she has the opportunity to do it. She denied you three times tonight, David. She asked to leave with her daughter, not with you. I think you're clinging to an imaginary bond, or at least to one that doesn't exist for her."

"It's not imaginary for me," David said.

"Then why do you not meet my eyes?"

David jerked his head up.

Sindon drew another tunic over her head and tied a sash around her waist. Then she lifted her arms to tuck the flower Rukmani Khan had given her behind his ear. David turned and stared. It seemed to him the most heartstopping and alluring thing she could do before his eyes and it left him breathless. "I love Sindon with all my heart, and I'm not going to let you hurt her."

"And I shall not let you have her. She is mine, and one day I will have her again."

"Your words amaze me, Rukmani Khan," David said. "I heard you repeat your vow of fidelity to your wife. How does an honorable man do that, yet say to me what you have just said?"

"Hope, David Quarrels. It's something Sindon brought into my life that no one can take from me, not even Sindon's resistance, not even you. It's mine."

28.

BACK IN THE stable, Rukmani Khan saw that the servants had arrived with traveling gear and staples, which they were busily dividing among the waiting bannertails. They lifted wine casks and tent rolls, sacks of rootstock and grain, utensils and clothing. Sindon's reappearance in silky tunic and pantaloons persuaded to shimmer like gold leaves in the wind created a murmuring among the servants and vassal lords alike. Even the other prisoners seemed awed by her beauty, the men almost unable to wrest their eyes from her. They watched as Rukmani Khan's servants, pretty young girls and handsome boys, shyly approached Sindon, offering a selection of shawls, cloaks, and footgear. Sindon seemed to understand her role in the pageantry, allowing the youngsters to slip each shawl over her shoulders, then giving a nod or a shake of her head.

The daughter, a beauty in her own right, had watched her mother preening in a fine woolen shawl for a moment, but then her attention had been drawn back to the young priest Amar, who was, Rukmani Khan realized, ministering excessively to Tara's hand. He had released her from the pole and was now persuading the accumulated acids in her muscles to be absorbed and neutralized. Amar, he knew, was especially skilled in the arts of persuasion as they related to the body, and this was a task he could have finished in seconds. The girl was fascinated, long red hair cascading from her bent head nearly veiling their cupped hands. The young priest would ride with them, and Rukmani Khan would be glad of his company; there were still only twenty vassal lords in the stable, only twenty to reclaim the Summer Palace. He hoped it would be enough.

The servants were slipping gold split-leather boots onto

Sindon's feet. David was nowhere to be seen. Rukmani Khan cursed himself and almost shouted an alarm. He should have taken David into close custody again immediately upon returning to the stable. But then he saw him huddled with the white-haired prisoner, who was still firmly persuaded to hold onto the saddle rack. In retrospect, he supposed he needn't have worried. He didn't think David would leave Sindon behind. He let David be.

In the long row where the bannertails were tethered, Kangra had finished saddling Jabari. He persuaded the tether to release and led the big black to Rukmani Khan, offering the reins to him. Jabari's muzzle had become grizzled, but he remained the strongest and most beautiful of the bannertails. Even here in the stable Jabari arched his tail and carried his head high. His prominent black eyes glistened without any trace of the milky haze that often seemed to accompany the grizzled muzzles; his nuzzling Rukmani Khan's arm seemed a personal invitation to take the reins. But Rukmani Khan declined. "You and Jabari have waited patiently these many years. Now you deserve to be together for this campaign. I'll take the chestnut pair for Sindon and me."

"As you wish," Kangra said, but Rukmani Khan could tell his old friend was pleased. Then the look of gratitude changed to one of concern. Kangra spoke softly, conspiratorially: "We number only twenty and the priest, and though there are twice that many servants coming, there are but a few untried Persuaders hoping to prove themselves among them. I had hoped we Persuaders would number sixty."

"I did not realize I had lost all but these few. Our task will be difficult without the others."

Kangra nodded. "But not impossible," he added. "However, I think we should unburden ourselves of the prisoners. It will take too many of us to guard them properly, leave too few for the task."

"Are you suggesting that I leave them here, to Gulnar's discretion?" Rukmani Khan was shaking his head even as he said the words. "Look at that child holding hands with Amar," he said. The young priest had obviously run out of excuses to be touching Tara's hands, but neither seemed to have noticed. "Do you believe Timon and Gulnar wouldn't seize an opportunity to use her in my absence?"

"That girl is almost as much a threat as her mother," Kangra said bitterly.

"I have the threat from Sindon under control," Rukmani Khan assured him.

Kangra looked dubious. "I mean no offense, milord, but when you find me constantly at your elbow, remember that I am witness to your strength, and friend to lean on in weakness."

The denial of weakness died in Rukmani Khan's throat when Sindon stepped into view with her head held high and wearing an enigmatic smile. If she were still frightened of her role, it did not show now. She approached him alone, a servant, leading the pair of chestnuts, following at a respectful distance.

"Rukmani Khan," she said, as usual not waiting for leave to speak, "I am ready." She had the woolen shawl pulled over the glittering pantaloons and tunic, to ward off the chill in the night air. Her hair looked like tongues of flame against the green wool.

Kangra frowned. He had never liked Sindon's bold manner, and the years had done nothing to change his disapproval. But he held his tongue, recalling that she did not respond well to rebukes under any circumstances. "I'll tend the prisoners," he said to Rukmani Khan. Kangra gave Sindon a formal bow, and he led Jabari away.

"I will help you mount," Rukmani Khan said, signaling the servant to bring the bannertails closer.

"I am quite capable of mounting a bannertail on my own," she said, turning to take the reins of the closer beast.

Rukmani Khan closed his hand over hers and squeezed it, whispering: "Nonetheless, I will help you mount."

She let go of the reins and he put his hands around her waist to lift her. "A leg up will do just fine," she said sharply, hooking her thumbs against his palms to push his hands away.

But he shook his head and, signaling the bannertail to kneel, he lifted her into the saddle. Upon feeling her weight, the bannertail rose to all fours. Rukmani Khan adjusted the stirrups and handed the reins up to her, but he took a braid of silver from under his tunic, and fastened the tether to her mount's bridle. "The tether is symbolic," he said to her as he mounted his own bannertail.

"And I suppose we'll leave through the courtyard, and not

through the stable canyon," Sindon said, "so that everyone who isn't coming can see how fine I look in my new clothes?"

"Of course," Rukmani Khan said with a smile. The vassal lords had the prisoners mounted, and they and the servants were mounting their own bannertails. The beasts sensed the excitement, and some had begun squealing.

"And shall I smile at Gulnar Khan?" Sindon asked, sarcastically as he expected.

"That would be unnecessarily rude," Rukmani Khan said, signaling his mount to move off toward the corridor.

But she stared at Gulnar Khan when she saw the Khana on one of the balconies above the courtyard. Rukmani Khan was surprised to find he felt a twinge of fear when Gulnar stared back and whispered to Timon, who was, of course, at her side. He could not help but regret sometimes that he had deliberately ignored his duties in the Winter Palace and allowed himself to become preoccupied with Sindon for those eight months. The effect had been the opposite of what he had expected. Instead of wearing Gulnar's patience with him into releasing him at last, Timon had wormed his way into her confidence and given her strength to put Rukmani Khan in bondage for sixteen years. Only now could he begin to end it; this time he would not underestimate Gulnar or Timon.

They rode the surefooted bannertails through the night, past dawn and well into the afternoon, Rukmani Khan and Sindon leading the entourage the entire way. He wanted to be very far from the Winter Palace when they camped, as if distance would diminish those Winter Palace laws he so abhorred. And besides, their pressing on would make it more difficult for Gulnar's minions, who would secretly be following and watching their every move. There were not many strong Persuaders among them; the lack of persuasion was, he had belatedly realized, Gulnar and Timon's greatest appeal. The rhetoric of the strong serving the weak was attractive, unless you were the strong and believed your strength was being abused as Rukmani Khan believed. He hoped the camp followers were tired by now, and that when night fell again they would get very cold and stiff. He would sleep warm, the very earth beneath him persuaded to keep him that way.

When Rukmani Khan called a halt for the day, he helped

Sindon down from there banntertail and sat her conspicuously on a rock in the center of the camp. Hazan persuaded the other prisoners to sit at her feet, where they were held fast to some bushes that they might have pulled up if they tried, but which effort would do them no good with the activity of setting up camp surrounding them. The prisoners talked among themselves and with Sindon, which Kangra disapproved of but which Hazan insisted served to keep their spirits up.

The Khan's servants had spread a fine carpet of woolly skins for the vassal lords to sit upon while they ate their evening meal. When all was ready, he went to Sindon and offered his hand to bring her down from the rock. She glanced at David before accepting, as if seeking his permission or perhaps to reassure him. David started to get to his feet, but the branch in his hands was too low, and he settled for glaring at Rukmani Khan from his cross-legged position.

There was little talk at the ceremony of the meal; Rukmani Khan had expected that. Only Hazan would feel at ease with Sindon in their midst, and even he would not trust her enough to discuss their plans in front of her. No one would want to mention their disappointment in how few they numbered, and everyone was being offered his capacity in food, which took time to consume.

When the first of the Khan's vassal lords was finished eating, Sindon's plate was also empty. It was dark, so he let Sindon return to the prisoners. She sat down between David and the white-haired leader, talking quietly to them.

"I'll see to the prisoners' food, if you wish," Amar said, pushing his empty bowl away.

Hazan looked up in surprise, for the prisoners were his responsibility, but he nodded agreeably. "They will prefer to tenderize foodstuff on a hot rock," he said. "If you persuade it for them, they may refuse. They know we do it only for children and lovers."

The priest reflected a moment, then smiled and left. Hazan watched him duck into the tent where the foodstuff was stored. Rukmani Khan guessed he would find only four rocks that were just right for heating food, and one of the prisoners would have to suffer being aided by Amar. He didn't blame the young priest; Tara was almost as beautiful as her mother, and the youthful impulsiveness that had brought her to the Winter

Palace had considerable appeal, even among Persuaders. Maybe especially among strong Persuaders, whose abilities were rarely challenged properly in the Winter Palace. More than one vassal lord envied Hazan his three foreign women, and some even attributed his considerable persuasive abilities to there being three. It was silly, of course, for it was the other way around. It took three women to match a Persuader who needed to consume more food now than Rukmani Khan himself. In olden times, Hazan might have challenged Rukmani Khan's leadership. But some of the ways of the Summer Palace had fallen away forever, and Hazan remained a loyal vassal, not even so insolent as he had been when he'd come to such strength so early in life. Rukmani Khan questioned in his own mind whether Hazan would have remained loyal were it not for Gulnar's influence, and he decided he would not. But it was good that one Persuader did not have to die defending his right to lead, for the loss of such strength was always devastating to the entire community. In some things, he admitted, the ways of the Winter Palace were good.

Rukmani Khan had been right. Amar lingered among the prisoners as they prepared their food. Tara hardly seemed to notice that her meal was being treated differently; she ate what Amar offered, not directly from his hand to her mouth, but still accepting each morsel from him. The older prisoners were too deeply engrossed in conversation to notice at first, but when they did, Amar had the good sense to withdraw before they could object. Rukmani Khan watched Amar go to his tent.

"The servants have Sindon's tent ready, milord," Hazan said. "You can escort her to it any time you're ready."

"Now, I think," Rukmani Khan said getting to his feet. "I'm ready to sleep. She must be exhausted."

But he had to admit that Sindon did not seem particularly tired, and she certainly wasn't pleased at the prospect of sleeping alone in a tent.

"I'd rather stay out here," she said when he offered his hand.

"It wouldn't be fitting for the object of my affections to spend the night out in the bush," Rukmani Khan said. "You'll be warm and comfortable in the tent."

"If I can't stay, at least let them come with me," Sindon said. Her gesture lingered on Tara, but Rukmani Khan shook his head.

"You must sleep alone," he said. "Gulnar's minions will be watching."

"So will I," David said.

Rukmani Khan shrugged. "You may spend the night as you wish, David Quarrels, but do not slow us down tomorrow, or you'll regret it."

"They'll be cold," Sindon said, quickly taking Rukmani Khan's hand.

"Hazan will see to it that they have enough bedding," he assured her. His fingers closed over hers, and she allowed him to lead her to the little tent the servants had set up behind his.

"I feel stupid," Sindon said when Rukmani Khan bowed ceremoniously to her.

"You look beautiful," he said.

Sindon glanced around, as if trying to search out the unseen watchers.

"We won't see them," Rukmani Khan said. "But they are there. They're watching everyone, but especially you and me."

"Don't you have to kiss me or anything?" she asked. "To show how irresistible I am? Wouldn't that make them admire your ability to stay in your own bed tonight?"

"Do you want me to kiss you?"

Sindon frowned, and turned abruptly. She slipped through the flap of the tent without answering him.

In the morning, they ate lightly, sitting quietly again on the skins. Sindon was wearing fresh clothing, dusty ocher-colored veils with a matching woolen shawl. Once her hunger was satisfied, she was plainly bored. She watched the servants take the tents down and pack them, and she brushed imaginary dust from her boots. Finally the servants brought the bannertails.

"If I have to ride next to you all day again, I'd at least like to say good morning to my daughter before we leave." Sindon said, glowering at the waiting bannertails.

"Do so," Rukmani Khan said. She nodded, and started toward the bushes where Hazan was releasing the prisoners so they could get ready to ride. He watched her hug Tara, and for a moment he thought she was going to hug David, too. But though David only looked at her, Rukmani Khan wished he had not let her go to the prisoners; his sense of foreboding was strong.

While Rukmani Khan watched, David plucked some blossoms from the bush, tiny pink blossoms that had more greenery to them than bloom. But Sindon accepted them with a shy smile, and lifted her arms to tuck them behind her ear. David's arms were crossed over his chest, and there was a smile on his face that infuriated Rukmani Khan and made him want to tear the flowers from Sindon's hair. But she seemed completely unaware of their effect on either man.

Rukmani Khan grabbed the reins of the chestnut bannertails from the waiting servant and hurried toward Sindon.

"I'll help you mount," he said gruffly.

"Stay with David," he heard Sindon whisper to Tara, and then she turned to Rukmani Khan. "I'm ready," she said, her hand checking to see that the flowers were firmly entwined in her hair.

Rukmani Khan lifted her into the saddle and clipped the silver tether to the bannertail's bridle. He mounted the other chestnut bannertail, then guided both beasts to the head of a line of riders and their mounts. David and the other prisoners would be behind him, in the center of the line, surrounded by the Khan's lords and servants. He imagined David looked smug at knowing Sindon was wearing his flowers in her hair while riding next to Rukmani Khan.

The Khan set a fast pace for his entourage that day. They ate their midday meal in the saddle, and pressed on until long shadows led the way. When finally he called a halt, it was in a canyon with scrubby bushes that had already spent their blooms. While the servants set up camp, Sindon waited with the prisoners. By the time he fetched her to the woolly carpets, she had removed the bedraggled flowers and brushed her hair smooth. She ate well, and then sat cross-legged for a while, seemingly bored with the silence and the monotony of watching the Persuaders eat.

"Sindon," Rukmani Khan said. She turned, boredom still fixed in her eyes. But they lighted wonderfully when he offered her a yellow star flower, the blossom as big as her fist. She took it and smelled it, breathing deeply. Then she lifted her arms to tuck it behind her ear.

"Flowers become you," Hazan said, his tone admiring and polite.

Sindon smiled, momentarily happy. Rukmani Khan stared out into the darkness, but he could not see David Quarrels' face. Likely David could not see the diners well either. A pity.

"I'll feed the prisoners," Amar said, swallowing his last gulp of food. Now that the silence had been broken, Amar was not going to chance that another might overtake the group. Hazan nodded.

"I'll help you," Sindon said, getting to her feet. She should have asked permission, but Rukmani Khan let her go without comment; he wanted David Quarrels to see Sindon with the Khan's flowers in her hair.

At last, only Hazan and Kangra remained with Rukmani Khan on the thick carpeting. Kangra finished the last of his food, and waited patiently for Rukmani Khan and Hazan to do likewise.

The Khan pushed the last empty bowl away, and looked expectantly at Kangra. "There's something troubling you," he said.

"I think you should keep Sindon away from the other prisoners," he cautioned. "You have among them a rival who is so insolent, it's all I can do to keep from slitting his throat. The white-haired one is their leader, another the master of their guard. These are not opponents to be taken lightly."

"But her daughter's there, too," Hazan commented. "Sindon would not tolerate being away from her very well. This way we're assured of her cooperation."

"You're both right," Rukmani Khan said, getting to his feet. "I will keep her contact with them to a minimum."

"I think we should be rid of them," Kangra continued. "They'll draw on too many resources, especially when we get to the glacier."

Hazan shoveled the last of his food into his mouth and looked at the Khan.

"I'll think on what you've said, Kangra," Rukmani Khan replied. "For now, I'll take her away from them."

He went directly to where the prisoners were sitting and held his hand out to Sindon. He had expected her to complain, but instead she greeted him with a smile, and took his hand. When he helped her to her feet, she left her hand in his.

"Can we walk down to the river so that I can bathe?" she asked. "I'm covered with dust from the the ride."

"The servants will bring you bath water."

"I'd rather swim," she said, tugging him just a little in the direction of the river.

Rukmani Khan relented. He liked the feel of her hand holding his, the sight of her hair, and the scent of the star flower tucked behind her ear. They walked silently, picking their way carefully through clumps of grass and rocks until they were at the river's edge. He expected her to let go of his hand then; he was almost positive she did not realize her hand was still in his. But she took the lead now, walking along the river bank, not letting go of his hand. He felt her fingers ripple in his, electrifying him. "What can this mean?" he said, pulling her to a stop.

Sindon had never been coy with him, not once they knew each other well. She slipped her hands under his tunic onto his bare chest, and he could feel himself swelling in response. "You said it was permitted for you to touch me," she whispered.

"Yes, but not . . ."

She kissed him, her tongue parting his lips to find his, and he could not resist giving her what she sought. His arms encircled her, his fingertips on the soft mounds of her breasts, her pelvis thrusting at him in rhythm with his tongue in her mouth. Hungrily she sucked at him, and he gave her more, remembering how much she loved his setting her body into rhythmic spasms, which he could help her sustain while his own desire mounted to incredible intensity. He groaned when he felt the first contractions swell her breasts to hard hot things under his hands, and the urge in him became overwhelming. "Sindon, I can't . . ."

"Touch me," she said. "Touch me the way only you can. Touch me."

He refused to let abandon overtake him, though he loved that it had overtaken her. He helped her to the ground, or had she helped him? She pushed herself against him with an intensity he remembered from her most passionate moments with him, and he knew that her greatest satisfaction would come when the skin of his penis touched the walls of her vagina and caused it to close over him like a glove. But that most wonderful of moments was no longer permitted to them, so when he slipped his hand inside her pantaloons, he did not pull them off. He touched her from the outside with his fingertip, her own natural responses almost enough to bring her to climax.

"Inside," she said, her voice dreamy, enticing. "Touch me inside."

He was drawing back, almost frightened by her intensity, which he knew he was helping along, but which he also knew he had not brought on.

"Inside," she said again, her legs trembling against him. "I want you inside."

Hearing her again cleared his brain, though his body ached to do her bidding. "Sindon, you delightful whore," he whispered. He pressed his fingers against the tiny mound and forced from the outside what she wanted to come from within. She convulsed helplessly and with great abandonment under his hand, and she begged him to go inside, until she could barely breathe, and all she could do then was to convulse with the pleasure. He loved seeing her like this, wanting what he could do to her. At last he could see her pleasure becoming too intense. She writhed helplessly as the pleasure turned to pain. He stopped when he saw tears in the corners of her eyes, and she looked at him in panic. "Do not tempt me again like that," he said, almost breathless with the pain in his groin. "Not even you can make me break my vow."

"You hurt me," she gasped, looking as much amazed as distressed.

"Not as much as you hurt me," he said, getting up and away from her.

She held her hand up to him. Rukmani Khan hesitated, then pulled her to her feet. He wanted to kiss her; even though he was angry, he wanted to kiss her. Even with her looking at him like a petulant child, even knowing she had tried to make him betray himself with her, he wanted to take her back in his arms and put himself in her and love her like he knew only he could love her. He shoved her toward the river. "Take your swim," he said hoarsely. "Now!" he added sharply when she hesitated.

Sindon turned and fled into the river, not bothering to take off her clothes. Rukmani Khan watched her, then sat down and put his hands to his groin and urged the blood flow away from his genitals. His heart raced in response, and soon he felt better. He'd barely taken his first even breath before he heard someone stumble. He looked up to see Kangra. He was walking too quickly to be on a casual stroll.

"You could be more attentive to my elbow," Rukmani Khan muttered.

"You didn't . . ."

"No, I didn't."

"I came as soon as I realized David was snarling over his food and that you were too long alone with her," Kangra said. He was looking around, trying to see, no doubt, some sign of Gulnar's spies.

"I just hope they were close enough to see the truth," Rukmani Khan said, feeling dejected now as he thought of what merely the sounds of what he had done would seem like from the bushes.

"I need only your word to swear otherwise, and that you've given," Kangra said solemnly.

Rukmani Khan sighed, and checked to see where Sindon was swimming. She'd paddled far out; she must be freezing. "She didn't do this on her own," he said, suddenly thoughtful.

"The white-haired one," Kangra said. "He and David exchanged sharp words. Hazan wasn't around to translate."

"I think you're right, Kangra. They're too much a burden, and too strong an influence on Sindon. When we get to the rim, I'll deal with them."

"How?" Kangra asked pointedly. "If we kill them, Sindon won't cooperate. And we can't send them back to Gulnar. She would love to get control over that girl."

"I'll let them go," Rukmani Khan said.

"I'm not sure I like that idea either," Kangra said, shaking his head. "They'll warn the others, have time to plan."

"There's nothing they can do to stop us, as long as they don't find us before our plan is set in motion."

Kangra thought a moment, then nodded. "They won't find us," he said. He sat down by Rukmani Khan, and they watched the river a few moments in silence. Sindon was slowly paddling back. "I will take her back if you want to leave now," Kangra finally said.

"She'll be cold," Rukmani Khan said.

"I have a cloak to give her," Kangra replied.

Rukmani Khan nodded, and he got up to walk back to the camp alone.

29.

DAVID HAD FLATLY refused to leave Sindon alone with Rukmani Khan and his party of warriors, although Sindon had begged him to take Tara to safety when the Persuaders offered them the chance at the rim of Xanthippe's Chasm. He understood that she wanted Tara away from the Persuaders, especially away from the young priest who always seemed to be on hand to thaw Tara's fingers or even to heal a scratch on her leg. Though he didn't believe the circumstances would allow the priest an opportunity to take advantage of Tara, David found himself bristling when the young Persuader was around—but not as much as when Rukmani Khan took Sindon away from him each morning. Not even Sindon's reminding him of Gulnar's threat could convince him his place was with Tara and not with Sindon. He had turned, stupidly believing he'd have his way if he just stayed firm, and he crashed to his knees, feeling the pain of impact before passing into unconsciousness. He awoke with a headache and found Theo, Brown, and the corporate auditor had been similarly dispatched. Tara had been spared the headache, having been induced merely into deep slumber, from which she awakened with revolting freshness. So in the end, he had led Tara, Theo, Brown, and the exhausted corporate auditor, on foot to Camptown. Brown's people backtracked and searched, but they found no sign of the Persuaders and Sindon.

David slept in his daughter's room at the school dormitory, and he was glad when she could laugh at his determination that Gulnar Khan not steal her away from him. But even in Camptown, with all Brown's security, he could not believe his daughter was safe from the Khana. He knew only too well how easy it was for determined Persuaders to sneak past the perimeter when they wanted to.

David was there with Tara when she cried with worry over her mother, and he tried to comfort her when she blamed herself for Sindon's absence. When she attended class, surrounded by young friends who now thought Tara to be the most notorious person on Cestry Prime, he left her safety to Brown's people and counseled daily with Theo Tucker, Ivan Mendal, Chloe Brass, and, much to Chloe's chagrin, Brown.

The perimeter power had been intensified, the guards tripled, and within a month of their return, the population was restless from the constant wariness. Then the abos left. All of them gone this morning, whatever they could carry gone with them. Not everyone had fully comprehended their absence, but those who had were even more worried. Except Chloe Brass.

"Maybe he changed his mind," Choloe offered after having to carry another set of complaints about restricted privileges to Theo Tucker. She'd been the first to give him a verbal report about the abos, too, but since none were on her staff she hadn't attached much significance to it.

"And he left and took the abos with him I suppose," David said, not trying to hide his sarcasm. Sometimes he believed Chloe Brass was just plain stupid.

"It's creepy without the abos," Ivan said. "Never thought I'd say that, but it's too quiet without them."

"Do we know that all of them are gone?" Theo asked.

"We're checking that now. We don't know for sure yet, T. T.," Brown replied, "but it looks as if not a one stayed."

"I'm going to have trouble meeting shipping quotas without them," Ivan commented, no doubt to forewarn Theo.

"My people are already working on recruiting replacements from among the settlers," Chloe said brightly.

But if she had been attempting to impress Theo with her efficiency, it didn't seem to be working, for all he did was raise his eyebrows a bit and ask, "Where could they have gone?"

"With the Khan," Chloe said. "He may have seen just how strong our defenses were, and turned around and gone home."

"This is home," Theo said dryly. They were sitting in Theo's office, a room in the Summer Palace that David believed was once the Khan's own room. It was the largest, had the finest mosaics on its walls, and carpeting so thick the cold from the rock below never seeped through. "I just hope Sindon followed my advice and let him know that my offer of another palace still stands."

"That better be the only advice you gave her," David said, not for the first time. He had let Theo Tucker be until he had Tara safely tucked away in the school dining room with two hundred friends and a dozen of Brown's people around her. Then he had found Theo and let him know exactly what he thought of his suggesting to Sindon that if Rukmani Khan could be enticed into breaking his vow, there'd be no followers, no point in continuing the campaign. David had broken Theo's nose, blackened both his eyes, and was working on doing real damage to his bones and guts when people outside the office had burst in and pulled him off the CEO. Nobody asked why Theo didn't press charges against David, or why he endured David's presence at the daily meetings he called to discuss the Persuaders. The Persuaders had at last earned great respect from the Mahania CEO, and he was, even if belatedly, not going to fail to make use of the only Persuader expert left to him on Cestry Prime. Theo had an incredible knack for drawing out the smallest details from his people, and an amazing array of plans and ideas. Unfortunately, for all the action he proposed to deal with the problem of the Persuaders, there had been no results. Still, even David admired Theo's determination not to give up, and he was grateful to him for it, too.

"If that little seduction scene had worked, you'd have been just as angry," Theo said philosophically. It was the first time he'd acknowledged his complicity, and it made David angry all over again to think of Sindon alone and unprotected with Rukmani Khan. Of course, it hurt almost as much to realize that she might reach a point where she no longer wanted protection. Eventually, she might come to desire the Khan. But he tried not to dwell on that, especially now while Theo was talking. "I don't know how to fight a Persuader, but it was you who gave me a clue that this honor thing might be a weapon. I tried to turn it against him; it didn't work, but it might have. We're not going to beat him if we can't figure out how to use his strengths against him."

"The guy sounds superhuman," Ivan said. "Strong, smart, and hung well enough to delight women." He expected a chuckle, but got none, not even from Chloe. Ivan shrugged.

"But he doesn't sound like anything a bullet can't take care of."

"That would be murder," Brown said, looking tired at having to repeat himself.

"But he's a killer," Ivan argued.

"Killer or not, you can't just shoot him without provocation," Theo said, "or David, here, will send a report to the World Council that will leave a vapor trail from Cestry Prime to the Hub."

"So, are we going to continue sitting around and wait for him to provoke us?" Ivan asked.

"No. We find a way to provoke him," David said. "Theo's right. If we shoot him on sight, which I think he's too smart to give us the opportunity to do, we'll have to answer to World. But it could be over in minutes if one of us—me, for instance—could meet him one on one."

Theo shook his head. There were still deep purple streaks under the CEO's eyes, which had the startling effect of making him look wise. "If you're close enough to touch him, you're as good as dead. If you're far enough away to shoot him, you close down Mahania on Cestry Prime, at least for the duration of a thorough investigation, and that could take years."

"I think I can turn his persuasion against him," David said. "But I have to find a way to be right in his face with a gun."

"I already said no shooting without provocation," Brown said, sounding stern and angry for Brown Roberts. "And I don't mean just any kind of provocation. I mean deadly force."

"When he reached around to put me down, I'd say that's sufficient provocation," David said. "I've seen that man kill with that touch, and so have you."

"And if he succeeds, you're dead," Brown reminded him.

"He won't kill me; it would be a violation of his honor."

"That doesn't seem to stop him from tormenting the hell out of you," Theo said. "Even if we could find him and you could get close enough with a gun, I wouldn't put odds on your succeeding. And if you kill him, I'm not sure a jury back in the Hub wouldn't find his promise not to kill you a real knot in a hangman's noose for you."

"I'll take that risk," David said. "He's not ever going to subject me to what he did again. Never!"

"Sweet Jesus, I'm sitting here while you plot a murder," the security chief said, shaking his head. "I can't listen to this. I won't."

"Then get the hell out, Brown," David said vehemently. "The bastard masterminded the murder of four of ours, and he's planning to kill the rest of us."

"He never said he would kill us," Brown said sullenly.

"My God, Brown. What does it take to convince you? He said he would wipe us from the valley down to the last child."

"*Wash* is the way you translated the word."

David threw up his hands. "Wipe, wash. They translate identically. You'll be just as dead if he wipes you or washes you."

"I know. But talk is easy from a desperate man. What can he do against our guns? There are only twenty-one of them, sixty-three if I count the servants. I have twice that many guards guarding the lake and dam. They can't all slip through my perimeters by just absorbing the energy like they used to. It does burn them. The power is all the way up now."

They all sat in silence for a while. Theo chewed on his thumbnail, agitated by Brown but obviously not convinced that he was right. "You're right about one thing, Brown," he said at last. "Rukmani Khan is a desperate man. I don't underestimate desperate men, but I count on them to make mistakes. Can I count on you to know it when you see it, and then to do something with it to put an end to this damn mess?"

"You can," Brown said resolutely.

With so little to offer themselves in the way of solutions, everyone in the room wanted to believe Brown. David couldn't.

30.

RUKMANI KHAN HAD come out of the tunnel under the glacier and started up the hill back to the camp when he realized Sindon was standing on the trail before him, watching him approach. Two frightened servants were with her, clearly expecting him to reprimand them for allowing her so close to the work. He didn't disappoint the servants. Then he turned to face Sindon. He had known it was only a matter of time before Sindon discovered what he and the other Persuaders were doing.

"What will happen when you're finished?" she asked, turning to look out over the valley. They could just make out the flags, which marked the palace courtyard in what little natural contour there was left in the valley. The rest of the valley looked like a mosaic to Rukmani Khan, one made of pieces that broke only at right angles, incredible stacks of lumber waiting to be bundled and loaded onto the next shuttle. The lake he had made with the earthen dam was clogged with silver-colored logs that glittered in the sunlight.

"I think you know what will happen," he told her.

Sindon glanced up the vast expanse of the glacier, its still-frozen flow unbelievably massive. "The palace will survive," she said slowly. She shuddered and turned to look at him. Her face was pale.

"It may survive, so much of it being underground. If it does not, I will begin another where it stood."

"Rukmani Khan," she said, starting bravely. "Tara is . . ." And then she cried, "Oh, please don't kill Tara."

Did she say nothing about David because she had forgotten him? Or was it only because she knew that mentioning David's

266

name would anger him? He doubted she would tell him the truth, not while she was frantic over the safety of the child. "I'll bring Tara out," he said.

"When?" she asked, trying to compose herself.

"Tonight," he said.

"Would you have done that if I hadn't found out?" she asked.

He nodded.

"But the others," she said. "Won't you give them a chance, too?"

"Who do you mean?" he asked sternly. "David Quarrels? Theo Tucker? Didn't I give them ample warning to return what was mine?"

"I mean the children, the others beside Tara. And all the innocent lives that will be lost if you let that glacier go."

Rukmani Khan shrugged. "It comes from following the wrong leader."

"But . . ." She put her hand on her forehead, as if she were experiencing great pain. Rukmani Khan reached out to soothe her, but she shook off his hand. "Our leaders are not like you, Rukmani Khan," she said. "Theo Tucker is an important man, but he's not like you. He can't command his people's lives beyond what their contracts allow. Someone like me he can't command at all."

"They allow him to lead, just as my people allow me to lead. And they abide by his decisions just as my people abide by mine."

"Oh, but it's just not the same. You can't do this, Rukmani Khan. They wouldn't do it to you."

"They cannot take what is mine," he said. "They cannot."

"What about the abos?" she asked, her voice desperate. "You have an obligation to them, don't you?"

"They're already gone," Rukmani Khan told her. "They left when they were told to go, days ago."

"If you warned them, why won't you warn my people?" she asked.

"I didn't warn the abos," Rukmani Khan said. "I told them to go, and they left. I told your people to go, and they did not."

"Is there nothing I can say to dissuade you?" she asked.

"Nothing," he replied. "And if you pursue it much longer, I may change my mind about Tara."

"I think you should change your mind about me," she said, her voice brutal. "Let me go die with my daughter."

"That's not a choice I will give you," he said gravely.

"Then stop threatening me," she said fiercely. "You know the one hold you have over me is Tara. I don't think well of you for using it."

Her words stung, and he could do nothing but watch her walk back to the camp. His heart ached to have her, his arms ached to hold her, and not even her anger could stop his longing. But for all of this, he felt frightened, too, as if the hope that had strengthened him for so many years was flagging at last.

"I should go," Hazan said when Rukmani told him and Kangra of his intent to remove Tara from the valley. "I'm stronger and can get past their perimeter with less damage to my flesh."

"I need you here, Hazan," the Khan said. "You must feed thoroughly, and be fresh. You will need all your strength tomorrow. Even Persuaders who are not here will be depending on you. Their future will be in your hands."

The younger man twitched. He looked about to say something, but in the end he was silent.

"Sindon approaches," Kangra said, a warning in his voice.

"You'll need a map," she said, kneeling before Rukmani Khan. "Our buildings are not like yours. I've marked Tara's room"—she pointed to the scratches she had made on the back of a scrap of leather—"and this is where the guard stands, and there will be others here, and here."

Rukmani Khan stared at the lines she had drawn, crosshatches, squares, and secants, and eventually he began to see their resemblance to the mosaic pattern in the valley. "Tara's room," he said, pointing to the place she had shown them. "Guards, here, here, and here." He frowned. "What is this?" he asked, pointing to a series of squiggles.

"The rim of the canyon," she replied. "So you'll know which way her room faces. They may be guarding her," she said. Then she took a deep breath and added, "David may be guarding her."

"Your representation of the rim is very poor," Rukmani Khan commented. He was almost eager to encounter David Quarrels again, but he didn't think Sindon needed to know. She would fuss and find some way to remind him of his promise.

"The sketch is from memory. I know the town fairly well, but the rim is just a guess."

The Khan nodded, but he was surprised to see how pale her face had become. He thought for a moment that she might ask him to take David away with him, too, and he did not like the thought of trying to explain to her how he could keep his vow not to kill David while leaving him behind. But she did not ask, and he began to feel just a little hope again. Gulnar was still likely to precede him in death. If David were also gone, he and Sindon might know some peace with each other, him without guilt and her without an unsettled love. He took Sindon's hand and kissed the tips of her fingers. Then he took her poor map and put it inside his tunic, and he left them to get Tara.

31.

DAVID HAD EXPECTED Gulnar's minions to try kidnapping Tara, not a lone Persuader, and certainly not Rukmani Khan. David was asleep on his bedroll under Tara's desk when a peculiar smell awakened him. Opening his eyes, he looked up to see Rukmani Khan climbing in the window. Swiftly he reached behind him, groping for the gun he'd been sleeping with for a month. He felt only the barrel of the rifle. Damn; he'd never be able to maneuver the rifle. Where was the gun? He couldn't find it. Panicked, he looked back at Rukmani Khan, and again he smelled the odor that had awakened him. He could place it now; it was the smell of burnt meat.

The alarm should have sounded in the guard shack by now. David knew he needed only stay silent enough to keep the Khan from realizing he was in the room, too, and in moments a dozen of Brown's security guards would arrive. David didn't think even Rukmani Khan could immobilize a dozen fully prepared guards.

He watched the Persuader bend over the sleeping girl to reach under the covers. When his hand came out, the locater bracelet Tara had been wearing this past month was in it. The Khan laid it out on her pillow next to her cheek, then leaned over again, to smooth Tara's hair away before resting his fingertips on her forehead. Unlike the unconsciousness produced by touching the back of the victim's neck, this touch to the forehead, David knew, resulted in a sleep that was very deep, but more natural and without the painful aftereffects—no doubt a special consideration for Sindon's child. Awkwardly Rukmani Khan wrapped Tara in a blanket and picked her up, one-handed. Now David could see that the Khan's left arm hung useless. David was sweating. He had hoped Brown's guards would arrive before the Khan touched the child. Now he prayed the security chief had instilled in his people the same restraint Brown himself used in firing weapons, for the Persuader was clutching Tara to his breast. He hesitated a moment, and David thought he was sniffing the air. Sindon's report had not mentioned an especially acute sense of smell in the Persuaders, but with so much sweat pouring off David's forehead, he was beginning to think that even a man with ordinary powers could smell him from across the room. Warily, David started groping for the gun again. But then he realized the reason for Rukmani Khan's hesitation. The Persuader had dropped something, and with the use of only one hand, he would have had to put Tara down to pick it up. The Persuader stepped back through the window and into the shadows, leaving what he had dropped behind. David's hand finally closed over the gun. It had been under his pillow.

Where were the guards? David reached around for the rifle, and scrambled out from under the desk. He hurried to the window and poked his head out just in time to see Rukmani Khan dart around the corner of the building. David ducked back to pick up the object the Khan had dropped, a scrap of leather. It was partially charred, but enough remained for him to tell it was a map with a note in Sindon's hand at the place where the rim of Xanthippe's Chasm should be. He read the few words that were still legible. Only one word made any sense to him: *Evacuate*. But he knew Theo had already eliminated evacuation from consideration. He pulled his comm-unit from his belt and started climbing through the window. Almost as an afterthought, he tossed the charred scrap back in Tara's room.

"Brown, he's gone around the corner of the dorm, heading north up the street toward the drying yards," David whispered into the comm-unit.

"Who is this?" came a sharp reply.

"It's David Quarrels. I'm on the scene of your alarm," he said.

"What alarm?" asked the voice.

"Shit!" David said. He jammed the comm-unit back on his belt and started running in pursuit of the Khan.

It was a quarter of a mile to the perimeter, up a straight and narrow street. Ahead he could see the Khan, already mounted on a bannertail that was moving at top speed past the newest kiln, then between man-high stacks of drying lumber, then under the spidery trestlework of the big flume. As they approached the perimeter, which was marked with nothing the human eye could see, the bannertail launched itself into the air like an ascending rocket, up and over the laser detection beams and the energy fence that had so much power in it these days that it could char the beast, rider, and Tara in a flash. David held his breath. He heard the *whumph* of the landing on the other side, a sound of impact on the earth and the air blowing from the bannertail's lungs like a punched balloon. A hard landing, but a safe one. Already the bannertail was racing away. David ran for the groundcar lot behind the dormitory and jumped into the first car he came to. His company code worked on the energy source, and he raced the small bubble-tired unit out of the lot past the kiln.

"Turn off the power on the north perimeter behind the dorm," he shouted into the radio. Stacks of lumber checkerboarded his peripheral vision. "Rukmani Khan has Tara. Turn off the power."

"David?" He recognized Brown's voice at last. "David, the breach in the north perimeter is just a bird."

"Goddamn you, Brown. It was Rukmani Khan. He's already got Tara."

"Just the top beam broken, David. It's only a bird. We're backing up the recording now to double check, but . . . Oh, my god," he heard Brown say. "Turn off the power in section three. . . . Now! Wait! David, we have Tara located in her room."

"He took the damn bracelet off and left it there," David said. He was past the trestlework and facing the invisible perimeter with a second to decide if Brown's command to wait was because the power in the fence had not yet been turned off or because he wanted David to listen to him. And then the moment of decision had passed and David was through the perimeter at full speed—safely.

Rukmani Khan had left the road immediately, the bannertail galloping past the log hoist nestled on the rocks at the end of the lake toward the neck of the hanging canyon. David knew the groundcar wouldn't make it through the rocks, so he followed on a parallel course, staying on the graded road as long as he could. Finally he had to cut across the meadow. The groundcar lurched and bounced, but the bubble tires moved well over the turf. He had one more glimpse of Rukmani Khan before he ducked under the decrepit trestle of the abandoned flume and the density of the canyon underbrush closed in on him. The bannertail was limping badly. What Brown had thought was a night bird must have been the bannertail's paw.

He drove the little car up the trail, heedless of scrapes from rocks and trees. The path was serpentine, not much needed since this flume spur had been abandoned when the timber on the high ridges had been spent. New undergrowth forced bends occasionally too sharp for the vehicle, and he had to stop and back up to make the turn. It was taking him forever to navigate the narrow trail in the groundcar, and so much time had passed now that he was sure he had lost Rukmani Khan in the underbrush. He drove on through the darkness, knowing the lights on the groundcar were like a beacon pinpointing his exact location for the Khan. But he had no choice; he couldn't drive without lights. He was on a short straightway when he heard Brown on the radio again.

"We're following your locater bracelet."

"I think I've lost him," David said.

"I'll have air cover there in a few minutes. We'll light up the canyon. He won't get away."

Brown's habitual calm infuriated David. He knew Rukmani Khan might already be out of the canyon, straight up the rock walls where David could not go in the groundcar.

"Put your flights above the canyon," David shouted. "Search the ridges."

"Will do," Brown said. "We found something in Tara's room. Did you see this thing? Is it Sindon's handwriting?"

David swerved around the bole of a grumetree. "Yes. It's a map and a note, but I couldn't understand it."

"Looks like he may have tried to burn it," Brown said. "Don't know how he could have shorted the alarm like he did unless . . ."

David turned again, and the headlights caught the flash of the bannertail's haunches as it leaped to a rock and stumbled, nearly upsetting the Khan with his precious cargo.

David slammed on the brakes, but by the time he pointed the headlights where he had seen the bannertail, it was gone. The falls were just ahead, and he knew that the bannertail could climb the steep rocks, but he'd have to leave the groundcar. Then his headlights caught the bannertail again and he stopped in time to keep the beast in view. It screamed at him, riderless but defiant, its left hind leg dragging uselessly. The beast reared up, balancing itself on its stiff tail and one good leg, and its forefeet came down through the windshield as David grabbed the weapons off the seat next to him and rolled out. The handgun slipped from his fingers and discharged. The bannertail screamed again, this time in pain, but David knew the shot had gone wild. He reached for the gun. The bannertail's hindquarters flopped over the front of the groundcar, the tail pounding like a club only inches from the gun. It heaved its forequarters as it tried to extricate itself from the shattered plastic. David didn't wait to see if it was successful; he abandoned the handgun and ran toward the falls. He still had the rifle in his hands.

Somewhere distant, perhaps on the other side of the canyon he heard the *wuup wuup* of the windshots. Behind him the bannertail still screamed, and there was a distant thumping of muscle and bone against crumpling plastic. Either the beast was trapped by its own flesh or it had stayed around to beat the groundcar to death. In either case, David could only be grateful the living war machine hadn't come after him.

Then there was only the sound of his own footfalls; not even the night insects chirped. He slowed down, walking more carefully, much more quietly. He felt the cool night air brushing his sweaty bare chest, the hairs prickling his skin as they dried and curled.

"David!"

The voice startled him so badly, he dove instinctively for a nearby thicket. He was still airborne when he realized it was Brown's voice on the comm-unit, not Rukmani Khan's.

"David, I'm recalling some of that air support," Brown said. "We deciphered the charred part of the note. They're going to wipe us out with the glacier, not the lake. I need those windshots for the evacuation. David. David? Can you hear me? There's enough mass in that glacier to scour the valley clean."

David looked around, despairingly. Whatever secrecy he'd managed with his quiet approach was now lost if the Khan was within earshot. He put his back against the bole of a tree, leaned the rifle stock against his knees and pulled the comm-unit out.

"Don't reply."

David froze. This time it was Rukmani Khan's voice. He felt the comm-unit being ripped from his hands. He let it go, rolled, and came up with his rifle aimed at the tree. Rukmani Khan stepped out and stared into David's eyes, ignoring the rifle barrel that was only inches from his chest. He held up the crushed comm-unit and let it drop to the ground.

"Don't move," David said. "Don't move or I'll blow your damn head off."

"Even one-handed I can take your weapon before you can use it," Rukmani Khan said. "I can take it and put you down faster than your eyes can blink."

David realized that the Khan's left arm was burned halfway up the sleeve, his fingers barely stumps, the flesh oozing through cracks in the char.

"Your perimeter," the Khan said, glancing down at the hand. "I tested it with my hand." David's eyes did not move from the Khan's face, and when the Khan looked up, he smiled. "Last time it only took a few days to heal the burns. Nothing will heal this," he said, gesturing to the charred hand. "But I still have this one." He raised his right hand and David realized he was going to grab the rifle stock. David squeezed, but only his fingernail clipped along the edge of the trigger, and that was not enough. The rifle was in Rukmani Khan's good hand, his fingers gripping the breech and magazine. David stood empty-handed, feeling utterly vulnerable with nothing more effective than a glare to use as a weapon. Rukmani Khan's face contorted. He clenched his teeth and held the rifle out in a gesture of suppressed anger, grunting as he tightened his fist around the breech.

"Don't," David said as the receiver caved in. "Don't, you'll . . . "

As the breech exploded in Rukmani Khan's hand with a sound like stacked thunder, the force of the blast hurled him against the tree. The look on his face was one of total surprise. He slumped to the ground, blood pumping from the stump of his hand. Wide-eyed, he stared at the flow, but even as he stared, the flow stopped. With a start, David realized that the Khan had stanched the flow of blood himself, somehow willed the blood elsewhere or pinched it off from inside. His chest was bloodied, too, no doubt from pieces of the barrel that had blown apart.

David's ears were ringing and he was so stunned that he almost didn't understand what had happened, but he was unscathed otherwise.

"One hand I could do without," Rukmani Khan said, staring at the charred remains of the one and the bloodied stump of the other. "Two I cannot abide."

David moved his own hand and felt dirt and twigs between his fingers. He realized he was sitting on the ground, but he was fairly sure it was only because his knees had collapsed or perhaps the blast had knocked him over. He didn't think any of the rifle pieces had hit him. He started to get to his feet. "You'll probably live, you bastard," he said to Rukmani Khan.

But Rukmani Khan shook his head.

David stood where he was, afraid to go near the Persuader even though he had no hands. "Are you hurt somewhere else?" David asked. There was a lot of blood on the Khan's chest. His garment was ripped enough for David to see there was only one other wound. It was well below his heart, and almost clean of blood. The rest of the blood on his shirt must have come from his hand.

Again Rukmani Khan shook his head.

"Dad?"

Tara's voice, somewhere close by, muffled, frightened.

"Are you all right," he heard her say, and he breathed deeply, gratefully. "Where am I?" she wailed.

"She's wedged under a rock," Rukmani Khan said to him. "Her arms are tight in the bedclothes. She won't get loose easily. Go to her."

David shook his head, his eyes on the Khan. He knew that most ordinary men could not move with wounds as grave as Rukmani Khan's, not even if the wounds were confined to their hands. But Rukmani Khan did not seem troubled by pain, and David knew that the lack of it was not the only thing that made him extraordinary. "Stay where you are, Tara," David called, picking up a rock, determined to hit Rukmani Khan in the head if he tried to get to his feet and leave.

"Do not return to the valley if you wish to live, David Quarrels," the Khan said tiredly. "Do not take Tara back there.

My vassal lords will scour everything from the valley before the sun sets again."

"Where's Sindon?"

"Safe," he said. He shifted his shoulders so that he leaned more fully against the tree, and sighed. "Just remember when you touch her that but for this"—Rukmani Khan held up his grisly stumps—"it would have been me." He lowered his arms to his lap, and sighed again. He closed his eyes. "Give her a flower for me, David Quarrels, a scented one to wear in her hair." David saw him grimace a moment, then Rukmani Khan was completely still.

David stood there, rock in hand, suspecting a trick. Rukmani Khan did not move. He did not breathe.

"Daddy?"

He saw Tara from the corner of his eye, still wearing her nightclothes, the blanket that was supposed to have kept her bound wrapped around her shoulders. "Stay back, Tara," he called out, still not believing Rukmani Khan could be dead.

But Tara stepped around to see what he was looking at, and she gasped. "Did you kill him?"

David shook his head. "No," he said. And finally he stepped over to Rukmani Khan. Carefully, still not trusting, he put his fingers on the Persuader's neck, feeling for a pulse. Though his skin was still warm, nothing flowed beneath it. "I think he killed himself," he said. He turned to Tara and was startled to see Hazan and Kangra behind her. They were staring at Rukmani Khan, the older man with tears in his eyes.

"My dad didn't kill him," Tara said defiantly.

"I can see that," Hazan said sadly.

David pulled Tara to him, watching the two Persuaders. For a long time, they just stared at the Khan's body. Then Hazan looked up, suddenly alert. A few seconds later David heard the *wuup wuup* of a windshot and he could see the glare of the searchlight coming over the ridge. Hazan looked at Kangra, and the older man nodded.

"Come with us," Hazan said, raising his hands in a threatening gesture toward David. Hazan tapped his wrist, and David finally understood he wanted the locater bracelet. David took it off and handed it to him. The Persuader hurled it deep into the night. "Walk ahead of me, right now, and very quickly, or I'll put you down and take Tara without you."

"Let's go, honey," David said, pushing Tara ahead of him. He saw Kangra pick up Rukmani Khan's body and follow.

Above the falls it was easy to elude the windshot, and Hazan and Kangra had bannertails waiting there. Kangra put the body on the saddle of the big black bannertail, then climbed up behind to ride on the beast's haunches. David and Tara squeezed into the saddle of the other bannertail, and Hazan rode on the haunches. The load slowed the bannertails down a bit, but David knew it was not enough for the single windshot to have time to give up its search in the lower canyon area and come scanning for them high above.

It was nearly dawn when they reached the edge of the glacier. Above and to the right under a dense stand of grumetrees, David saw the Persuaders' camp, a virtual town of tents shrouded in mist that swirled around icicles of sap. The forest floor was like winter without snow, the grume sap congealed in stalactites and stalagmites, pools of it in solid slabs. He understood now how they had escaped detection, both from the air and from the ground.

The young priest was with Sindon, and he held her back and gave a shout to the others when they saw what was approaching. Persuaders and servants swarmed from the tents, dozens of hands helping Kangra lift his burden from Jabari's back, angry hands jabbing at David and Tara until Hazan spoke sharply to them.

Sindon lifted her arms to Tara, her face streaked with tears. Was it joy at seeing her daughter safe? Or was it sorrow in knowing Rukmani Khan was dead? David couldn't tell. He just knew that she let him put his arms around her and Tara, and no Persuader stopped him.

"You didn't kill him," Sindon said, half question, half statement.

"He killed himself," David said, finally certain that was what had happened.

Sindon bit her lip, shocked. "He killed himself? But why?"

"He lost both his hands," David said.

Horrified, Sindon buried her face in Tara's hair and sobbed.

The Persuaders huddled, talking softly among themselves, glancing at David from time to time, murmuring. The servants had taken the body and rolled it in a carpet, and now were gathering flowers and fresh leaves, burying the carpet with greens and blossoms.

"David, come here," Hazan called, looking up from the assembled Persuaders.

David kept his arms around the two women, taking them with him as he stepped onto the thick-piled carpet, the very one Rukmani Khan and Sindon had sat upon while David had watched him feed her with his fingers.

"What did Rukmani Khan say before he died?" Hazan asked.

David struggled to remember. "Something about his hands," David finally said. "That he couldn't . . . abide not having any."

"What else?" Hazan asked.

David remembered, and shook his head. "It was for my ears only," he said.

He thought Hazan smiled a little, but then he looked stern again. "What else?"

"Nothing else," David said, looking straight into Hazan's purple eyes, praying there was nothing in his own to betray the lie.

"It's our decision, then," Hazan said, turning back to the other Persuaders.

"Yours, Hazan," the young priest said. "Your decision, Hazan Khan."

David heard Sindon's breath catch in her throat. "Hazan, is it . . . ? Oh, please don't go through with it. What point is there to killing them now? He can't ever live in the Summer Palace again. Hazan, please?"

Hazan seemed irritated by Sindon's outburst. He shook his head sharply. "It's not mine to decide, for I cannot be Khan."

"You must," Amar said. "You're the strongest, and without an heir of Rukmani Khan's to rule in the new tradition of the Winter Palace, we must obey the laws of the Summer Palace."

"But I can't," Hazan protested. "The right thing to do is to go away from here and for the new Khan to build a Summer Palace of his own. But I cannot. I must return to the Winter Palace. I cannot leave my foreign women."

"Almighty Persuader, save me from these foreign women," Kangra muttered. Then he looked at Hazan. "Hazan Khan,"

Kangra said solemnly, "I will return with you to the Winter Palace."

"I will accompany you, as well," said Amar.

"And I," said another Persuader, and there followed a chorus of assent.

Hazan seemed stunned, but he shook himself. "So be it," he said, raising his hands and looking at them. Then he looked past the boles of trees to the distant valley below where the lake gleamed golden in the first rays of sunlight. Even at this distance they could see red dust clouds rising from the roads. "I have no stomach for crushing fleeing ants," he said to the Persuaders, and they nodded. He lowered his hands and looked at Sindon, David, and Tara.

Sindon burst out from under David's arm and stood on tiptoes to kiss Hazan's cheek. Her own cheeks were wet with tears. "Thank you, Hazan," she said. David knew the kiss was not the custom among the Persuaders, but Hazan seemed to like it.

"You may stay for the return, if you wish," Hazan said kindly.

"And then?"

"You and Tara are free to leave whenever you wish," he said. "And as for you, David . . ."

David steeled himself. Did a newly appointed Khan assume the enemies of the old? Did Hazan hold him somehow responsible for his friend's death? Did he know David had lied to him about what Rukmani Khan had said before he died?

"I charge you to take Rukmani Khan's ashes to the Summer Palace. You must place them in the niche near the staircase," Hazan Khan said.

"It's not fitting . . ." Kangra started to say.

"David Quarrels was a worthy opponent," the new Khan said, cutting off the older man. "It was Rukmani Khan who chose to die without finishing what was between them. David can do this much for his old enemy."

David nodded, trying not to look as relieved as he felt. He could hardly believe that the danger was over, simply because he'd not disclosed Rukmani Khan's warning to keep Tara away from Camptown. He tried to look into Hazan's suspicious eyes again, and wondered then if the Persuader had really believed him or if he had simply chosen to believe him. Whichever it was, he wasn't going to disappoint the new Khan now. "I can take the ashes," he said. "I will place them where you wish."

"The vessel must not be disturbed once it is placed in the niche," Hazan Khan said. "I will come from time to time to see that it is so."

"The ashes will not be violated, Hazan Khan. But do not come into our valley. Even Rukmani Khan found it was not so easy to do. We know now that you cannot pass through our defenses unscathed," David said. "You, Hazan Khan, are a marked man among us. You and Kangra, and another man I do not see here."

"Ridpath," Hazan Khan said. "We who took revenge."

David nodded. "I cannot guarantee your safety, even if you come openly in peace, let alone by stealth. You would surely be suspect."

Hazan frowned. Clearly this was not acceptable to him.

"A different emissary, milord?" Amar suggested.

Hazan brightened. "The priest?" he asked David.

David nodded.

Hazan nodded, too, more curtly and not without a frown. "Wait over there for us," he said, pointing to Sindon's tent. "Leave us alone while we prepare for the ceremony of Rukmani Khan's return."

Sindon tugged on David's sleeve, took his hand and Tara's and led them away.

32.

FROM SINDON'S TENT, they had watched at a distance as the Persuaders ate mounds of food. The meal seemed to take half the morning. Finally the Persuaders had pulled their shirts off, leaving them hanging inside out from the sashes at their waists. Then David had watched Rukmani Khan's flesh consumed by fire under the Persuaders' hands, steam and smoke floating up into the grumetrees to mingle with the vapors that already lingered there. He had been grateful they were not using their hands on the glacier, for he sensed there was less energy spent in controlling the funeral pyre than could have been unleashed wantonly. Sindon had cried and he tried not to be angry with her for that, and he tried to forget Rukmani Khan's words when he put his arms around her to comfort her. He had felt no remorse himself, only a profound relief that Sindon would never again suffer—*enjoy*—Rukmani Khan's touch. He had believed there might be some hope for himself and Sindon and Tara becoming a family in the fashion he knew he wanted and Tara wanted—and some of the hope had been that Sindon would want it, too. From a begrudging respect for the ceremony of the cremation and for Sindon's tears, he had said nothing about the future to her while they were with the Persuaders. But later, with Rukmani Khan's ashes in a vessel that was tied to his back, walking shoulder to shoulder with Sindon and Tara down the slope, with the Persuaders breaking camp behind him, he said to Sindon:

"I want us to get on with our lives now. I want us to put all this behind us. I want us to be together."

"I know," she said, but she wouldn't look at him. Finally she looked up, her chin trembling, her eyes blurring again with

282

tears. "I love you, David Quarrels. I never stopped loving you, not even when you hurt me."

"I never meant to hurt you," he said, wondering if he should go down the list that started with not reading one report and ended with reading another. He decided not to; he was sure to leave out some hurts that fit in between. "Please forgive me," he added, turning to hold out his arms to her. She nodded slightly, and he took her into his arms right there on the trail, with the grumetrees above them and the white glacier below. She felt so good in his arms, her hair smelling like flowers.

"What's wrong?" she asked.

"Nothing," he said, trying to loosen the muscles she'd felt tense up. But he knew he would never see her with a flower in her hair without thinking of the blossoms Rukmani Khan had given her.

"Were you very angry with me?" she asked him.

He was surprised by her question, but he didn't let her know. "Very angry," he said. "Very hurt. Devastated from losing you."

"There was nothing I could do to prevent it," she said, and he smiled to himself because for all the years of agony, Sindon had not changed. This was the real Sindon in his arms, and he loved her, and he had stopped caring that she would never take her share of the blame for anything. He had shoulders large enough for the two of them.

His shoulders itched, the straps of the makeshift pack biting into his flesh. He ignored the pain, determined to enjoy having Sindon in his arms, even if it meant carrying Rukmani Khan on his back forever. Sindon, of course, didn't notice his discomfort as she pressed herself against his chest. He didn't care about that, either.

"You lovebirds done yet?" he heard Tara ask. He opened his eyes to see her sitting on a rock alongside the path, her chin in her hands as she looked up at them. She smiled shyly; she was happy to see them this way.

"Maybe for now," he said, good-naturedly. With a smile for his daughter and a reassuring squeeze for Sindon, he stepped down the trail, walking with his arms around Sindon.

It was going to be all right, he decided. The CEO would see putting the ashes in the niche as a small price to pay for Hazan's good will. The priest would turn up at Sindon's ranch on some high holiday, and David would be there, David with Sindon and Tara—and if not on the ranch, then somewhere in Camptown, but it would be David with Sindon and Tara. David would escort the priest to the Summer Palace, and between the priest's visits David would not think about the Persuaders.

Sindon stopped on the trail, almost tripping him. "Tara?" she said.

They both turned around to see Tara standing on the rock where she had been sitting, her back to them as she waved to someone high above. In the mists, David could see the priest's robes flutter as he waved back.

"Tara, come on," Sindon said.

David watched his daughter turn, her face flushed with excitement. She bounced happily down the trail toward them, catching David's hand to slow her momentum, nearly wrenching his arm. He tried to return her happy smile. The crude pack bit into his back. Rukmani Khan's ashes felt heavier with every step he took.